THE BABY
CONTRACT

BY
BARBARA DUNLOP

MILLS
BOON

Published in Great Britain 2015
by Mills & Boon, an imprint of Harlequin (UK) Limited,
Eton House, 18-24 Paradise Road, Richmond, Surrey, TW9 1SR

© 2015 Barbara Dunlop

ISBN: 978-0-263-25277-4

51-0915

Harlequin (UK) Limited's policy is to use papers that are natural, renewable and recyclable products and made from wood grown in sustainable forests. The logging and manufacturing processes conform to the legal environmental regulations of the country of origin.

Printed and bound in Spain
by CPI, Barcelona

Barbara Dunlop writes romantic stories while curled up in a log cabin in Canada's far north, where bears outnumber people and it snows six months of the year. Fortunately she has a brawny husband and two teenage children to haul firewood and clear the driveway while she sips cocoa and muses about her upcoming chapters. Barbara loves to hear from readers. You can contact her through her website, www.barbaradunlop.com.

For my daughter

One

Troy Keiser halted his razor midstroke, glancing to the phone on the bathroom counter.

"Say again?" he asked his business partner, Hugh "Vegas" Fielding, sure he must have misheard.

"Your sister," Vegas repeated.

Troy digested the statement, bringing the cell to his ear, avoiding the remnants of his shaving cream. Sandalwood-scented steam hung in the air, blurring the edges of the mirror.

"Kassidy is *here*?"

His nineteen-year-old half sister, Kassidy Keiser, lived two hundred miles from DC, in Jersey City. She was a free spirit, a struggling nightclub singer, and it had been more than a year since Troy had seen her.

"She's standing in reception," said Vegas. "Seems a little twitchy."

Last time Troy had seen Kassidy in person, he was in Greenwich Village. A security job with the UN had brought him to New York City, and the meeting was purely by chance. Kassidy had been playing at a small club, and the diplomat he'd been protecting wanted an after-hours drink.

Now, he glanced at his watch, noting it was seven forty-five and mentally calculating the drive time to his morning meeting at the Bulgarian embassy. He hoped her problem was straightforward. He needed to solve it and get on with his day.

"You'd better send her up."

He dried his face, put his razor and shaving cream in the cabinet, rinsed the sink, and pulled a white T-shirt over his freshly washed hair, topping a pair of black cargo pants. Then he went directly to the kitchen and poured himself a cup of coffee, downing it to bring his brain cells back to life.

His and Vegas's side-by-side apartments took up the top floor of the Pinion Security Company building in northeast

DC. The first two floors housed the company's reception and meeting areas. Floors three to seven were offices and electronic equipment storage. The computer control center was highly secured, directly below the apartments. The basement and subbasement were used for parking, target practice and storage for a vault of weapons.

The building was state-of-the-art, built after Troy sold his interest in some innovative security software and Vegas hit it big at a casino on the strip. After that, their company had grown exponentially, and they'd never looked back.

The buzzer sounded, and he crossed the living room, opening the apartment door to find the six-feet-four, barrel-chested Vegas standing behind his sister, Kassidy, who, even in four-inch heels, seemed barely half the man's size. Her blond hair was streaked purple, and she wore three earrings in each ear. A colorful tunic-style top flowed to a ragged hem at midthigh over a pair of skintight black pants.

"Hello, Kassidy." Troy kept his voice neutral, waiting to ascertain her mood. He couldn't imagine it was good news that brought her here.

"Hi, Troy." She slanted a gaze at Vegas, clearly hinting that he should leave.

"I'll be downstairs," said Vegas.

Troy gave his partner a short nod of appreciation.

"Is everything okay?" he asked as Kassidy breezed her way into the penthouse foyer.

"Not exactly," she said, hiking up her oversize shoulder bag. "I have a problem. At least I think it's a problem. I don't know how big of a problem."

Troy curbed his impatience with her roundabout speaking style. He wanted to tell her to spit it out already. But he knew from experience that rushing her only slowed things down.

"You got any coffee?" she asked.

"I do." He cut through the vaulted-ceilinged living room, heading for the kitchen, assuming she'd follow and hoping she'd compose her thoughts along the way.

Her heels clicked on the parquet floor. "I've thought about it and talked about it and I'm really sorry to bother you with it. But it's kind of getting away from me, you know?"

No, he didn't know. "Does 'it' have a name?"

"It's not a person."

He tried and failed to keep the exasperation from his voice. "Kassidy."

"What?"

He rounded the island in the center of the expansive kitchen. "You've got to give me something here, maybe a proper noun."

She pursed her lips tight together.

"What happened?" he asked. "What did you do?"

"I didn't *do* anything. See, I told my manager this would happen."

"You have a manager?"

"A business manager."

"For your singing career?"

"Yes."

The revelation took Troy by surprise.

Sure, Kassidy was a sweet singer, but she was really small-time. Who would take her on? Why would they take her on? His mind immediately went to the kinds of scams that exploited starry-eyed young women.

"What's the guy's name?" he asked suspiciously.

"Don't be such a chauvinist. Her name is Eileen Renard."

Troy found himself feeling slightly relieved. Statistically speaking, females were less likely than males to exploit vulnerable young women in the entertainment business, turning them into strippers, getting them addicted to drugs.

He gave her face a critical once-over. She looked healthy, if a bit tired. He doubted she was doing any kind of recreational drugs. Thank goodness.

He retrieved a second white stoneware mug from the orderly row on the first shelf of a cupboard. "Why did you think you needed a manager?"

"She approached me," said Kassidy, slipping up onto a maple wood stool at the kitchen island and dropping her bag to the floor with a clunk.

"Is she asking for money?"

"No, she's not asking for money. She likes my singing. She thinks I have potential. Which I do. It was after a show in Miami Beach, and she came backstage. She represents lots of great acts."

"What were you doing in Miami Beach?" Last Troy had heard Kassidy could barely afford the subway.

"I was singing in a club."

"How did you get there?"

"On an airplane, just like everybody else."

"That's a long way from New Jersey."

"I'm nineteen years old, Troy."

He set a cup of black coffee in front of her. "Last time we talked, you didn't have any money."

"Things have changed since the last time we talked."

He searched her expression for signs of remorse. He hoped she hadn't done anything questionably moral or legal.

"I'm doing better," she said.

He waited for her to elaborate, taking a sip of his coffee.

"Financially," she said. "Good, in fact. Great, really."

"You don't need money?" He'd assumed money would be at least part of the solution to her current problem.

"I don't need money."

That was surprising, but good, though it didn't explain her presence.

"Can you tell me the problem?" he asked.

"I'm *trying* to tell you the problem. But you're giving me the third degree."

"I'm sorry." He forced himself to stay quiet.

She was silent for so long that he almost asked another question. But he told himself to pretend this was a stakeout. He had infinite patience on a stakeout.

"It's a few guys," she said. She reached down for her

shoulder bag and dug into it. "At least I assume they're guys—from what they say, it sounds like they're guys." She extracted a handful of papers. "They call themselves fans, but they're kind of scary."

Troy reached for the wrinkled email printouts, noting the trace of anxiety that had come into her expression.

"What do they say?"

While waiting for her answer, he began reading the emails.

They were from six unique email addresses, each with a different nickname and a different writing style. For the most part, they were full of praise, laced with offers of sex and overtones of possessiveness. Nothing was overtly threatening, but any one of them could be the start of something sinister.

"Do you recognize any of the addresses?" he asked. "Do you know any of the nicknames?"

She shook her purple hair. "If I've met them, I don't remember. But I meet a lot of people, a *lot* of people. And hundreds more see me onstage and you know…" She gave her slim shoulders a shrug. "They read my blog, and they think we're friends."

"You write a blog?"

"All singers write blogs."

"They shouldn't."

"Yeah, well, we're not as paranoid as you."

"I'm not paranoid."

"You don't trust people, Troy."

"Only because most of them can't be trusted. I'm going to hand these over to our threat expert and see if there's anything to worry about." Troy remembered to glance at his watch. If he wasn't done soon, Vegas would have to take the Bulgarian meeting.

He polished off his coffee, hoping Kassidy would do the same.

She didn't.

"It's not just the emails," she said.

"Oh?"

"People have started hanging around the stage door after my show, looking for autographs and selfies."

"How many people?"

"Fifty, maybe more."

"*Fifty* people wait around to get your autograph?"

"You know, your confidence in me is inspiring."

"It's not that."

Actually, it was that. He was surprised she had anywhere near that kind of a following.

"Things are moving fast," she said. "Downloads of my songs, ticket sales, offers for gigs. A guy on a motorcycle followed me back to my hotel in Chicago last week. It was creepy."

Talk about burying the lead. *That* could be truly dangerous.

"Were you alone?" Troy asked.

"I was with a backup band."

He was relieved to hear it.

"I was wondering. You know, thinking." Her blue eyes were big, and her face looked pale and delicate. "Do you think I could stay with you? Just for a little while? It's really safe here, and I'm having a hard time sleeping in my apartment."

"*Here?*" Troy's sense of duty went to war with his desire for privacy.

"Just for a little while," she repeated, looking hopeful.

Troy desperately wanted to say no. He searched his mind for a way he could do that.

The two of them shared a father, but he had died several years ago. And Kassidy's mother was a certified flake. Last Troy heard she was living with some kind of hippie junk sculptor in the mountains of Oregon.

For all intents and purposes, Troy was Kassidy's only relative. He was definitely her only stable relative. How could he turn her down?

"How long?" he asked.

Her face burst into a brilliant smile, and she hopped down from the stool, hurrying around the island. "You're the best."

He wasn't the best. In fact, he hadn't even agreed to let her stay yet.

But she surprised him by wrapping her arms around him and squeezing tight. "Thank you, big brother."

Something tugged at his heart. "You're welcome," he told her.

She drew back. "You're going to love Drake."

Wait a minute. "You want to bring a *boyfriend* here?"

That put an entirely different spin on the situation. No way, no how, was some random guy going to stay in Troy's apartment.

"Drake's not my boyfriend," she said, her eyes still bright with joy. "He's my son."

Mila Stern was on a mission.

At times it seemed doomed, but she wasn't giving up, because Sterns never gave up. She had three siblings and two parents who proved that to her every single day.

Coming up on noon, she approached the front door of the Pinion Security building, squaring her shoulders, drawing a bracing breath and mentally rehearsing her opening lines.

Five minutes, she'd tell Troy Keiser. He only needed to listen to her pitch for five short minutes. That was barely any time at all, and it had the potential to increase his business by 10 percent.

Did 10 percent sound like enough? she wondered. Maybe she should claim 15 percent. Or was fifteen too much of a stretch?

No. It wasn't a stretch. The number of women in need of some form of personal protection was growing by the month. In fact, it was growing by the week. Maybe even by the day. Should she say day?

Yes. By the day. That was a perfectly fair claim to make— 15 percent and growing by the day.

Dressed in pale gray cargo pants, a blue sweater and sturdy leather boots, she pulled open the stenciled glass entry door. The Pinion reception area was compact, decorated in gray tones, with a sleek steel-and-smoked-glass counter curving around the back wall. A man stood behind it dressed in black. His hair was cropped short, his chin square and strong, and his arms and shoulders all but bulging from the three-quarter sleeves of his T-shirt.

"Can I help you?" he asked in a deep voice.

She smiled, trying to look friendly and innocuous, like the kind of person a man would want to help. "I hope so," she said, striding forward to the countertop. "I'm looking for Troy Keiser."

The man hit a couple of keys on a computer terminal recessed into the desk in front of him. "You have an appointment?"

"Not for today," she answered. "We've been corresponding for a few weeks, and my plans were fluid." She stopped talking, hoping he'd draw the conclusion that Troy Keiser was willing, even intending to make an appointment with her.

"Your name?" he asked.

She wished he hadn't asked that, but she couldn't see a way around giving it to him. "Mila Stern."

Troy Keiser—and, she had to assume, the entire human resources unit of Pinion Security—would recognize her name as the woman whose job application they'd rejected three times over.

The man pressed a button on his compact headset.

Mila continued to smile even as tension built within her. She was fully qualified to become a security agent at Pinion, even if Troy Keiser wouldn't admit it. She had a degree in criminology and a black belt in Krav Maga, along with significant technical surveillance and tactical weapons training.

The man waited, and Mila waited. She knew if he talked to Troy Keiser, it would be game over before she made it past the lobby.

Her gaze flicked to the elevator doors behind him. No doubt they were controlled by a passkey. If she was lucky, there was also a staircase from the lobby. She drew his attention by smoothing back her brown hair, pretending to check the French braid that held it in place. At the same time, she surreptitiously scanned the room.

There it was. A stairway door. She let her gaze slide right past it without pausing. If Troy refused to see her, she'd make a break for the stairway. Reception man would have to circle the end of the counter to come after her, giving her a head start of two, maybe three seconds.

He might call for backup on the second floor, but that would take five to seven seconds. She could run a flight of stairs in three, and this was only a nine-story building. She'd duck out at the fourth floor and try to lose them. Assuming the stairwell doors weren't locked. They could easily be locked.

The man ended the phone call without speaking and pressed another number.

Mila waited, hoping a new call might work in her favor.

"Vegas?" the man said into the phone. "There's a woman here for Troy. No, no appointment. Mila Stern."

He paused, his eyes narrowing on Mila.

She shifted her weight to the ball of her left foot, getting ready to sprint.

"Will do," he said. The suspicion seemed to go out of his eyes.

She took a chance and waited a moment longer.

He ended the call. "You can meet Hugh Fielding on the second floor."

Yes. At least she'd make it out of the lobby.

"Is Troy here?" she dared ask.

"He's busy at the moment. But Vegas should be able to help you."

She wanted to ask what Troy was doing, or more importantly *where* Troy was doing it. Was he on the second floor or somewhere else?

The man pressed a button, and a light on the elevator behind him turned from red to green.

"Thank you," said Mila, heading for the elevator.

She knew that Hugh Fielding, nicknamed Vegas, was Troy's business partner. He might not have recognized her name. Then again, he might be planning to run interference, to keep her away from Troy, maybe even to escort her directly out of the building.

During her research of the company, she'd learned Troy Keiser undertook most management functions, including making the hiring decisions. It seemed Vegas Fielding was the technical expert.

She stepped inside the elevator. The two was already lighted on the panel. Taking a chance, she reached out and pressed nine—might as well get as far away from Vegas as possible to start her search. The white circle lit up.

The doors closed, and she moved to a front corner, flush against the wall beside the door. If she was very lucky, Hugh Fielding would think the car was empty and assume she was catching the next elevator.

It stopped on two, and the doors whooshed open.

Mila held her breath, hearing phone chimes and several voices outside. No footfalls approached the elevator, and none of the voices seemed raised in alarm.

The doors closed again, and she let out her breath, easing out of the corner as the numbers counted to nine.

When the doors opened on the ninth floor, Troy himself stood outside. His arms were folded over his chest, and his feet were braced apart. It was obvious he was expecting her.

"Seriously?" he asked with an arched brow.

"Hello, Mr. Keiser." She quickly exited the elevator.

If it descended without her, she'd have at least a few moments with him.

"You just broke into my building."

"No," she disagreed. "Mr. Fielding invited me in. I'm sure nobody could break into the Pinion Security building."

A flare came into his blue eyes. She could only hope it was amusement and not anger.

"Vegas invited you to the *second* floor."

"But the person I really want to see is you."

"So you hijacked the elevator to the private floor?"

Mila glanced along the short hallway that ended in two doors. "I didn't realize it was a private floor." She wasn't about to admit she'd planned to search the building from the top down in order to find him.

"How can I help you, Ms. Stern? And no, you can't have a job. Sweet-talking your way past reception does not prove your superior tradecraft skills."

"That wasn't my intent."

"What was your intent?"

"To talk to you in person."

"Let's get this over with."

Mila's brain immediately leaped to her rehearsed points. "I don't know if you're aware, but the number of high-profile businesswomen, female politicians and celebrities in need of some form of personal protection is rising every year. Estimates show that companies focusing on that fast-growing demographic can see an increase in business of up to 15 percent per year. And offering services that cater specifically to—"

"You're making that up."

She didn't let the interruption rattle her. "I'm not. Any number of public sources can point to the rise in female political figures, industrialists, high-powered rock stars."

"The 15 percent. You made up the 15 percent."

He had to be guessing. Mila was a very good liar.

"It's more anecdotal than scientific," she allowed. "But the fundamental point—"

"We already cater to women," said Troy. "We protect hundreds of women, with better than a 99-percent success rate."

There was something slightly off in his expression. He

was lying right back at her. But why would he lie? And then she got it. He was making up the 99 percent to mock her.

"You're making that up," she said softly.

"Any number of sources will verify that we have a robust female clientele."

She struggled not to smile. "You're making up the 99 percent."

"It's my company."

"You've got a tell."

"I do not."

She lifted her chin. "Right there. Next to your left ear. There's a muscle that twitches when you're lying."

"That's preposterous."

"Tell me another lie."

"I'll tell you the truth," he said. "I'm not hiring you, not now, not ever."

"Because I'm a woman."

"Because you're a woman."

"And you think that means I can't fight hand to hand."

"I don't just think that. It's a fact."

"I'm pretty good," she said, putting a challenge into her tone. "You want to spar?"

He gave a chopped laugh. "You're weak *and* delusional."

"I don't expect to beat you."

Her statement seemed to puzzle him. "Then why the challenge?"

"I expect to do well, surprise you, exceed your expectations."

"You'll get hurt."

She gave a shrug. "Probably a little."

"Probably a lot."

"I really want this job."

"No kidding. But I'm not going to give you a job because you're foolish enough to challenge me in hand-to-hand combat."

"Try me."

His phone rang in his pocket.

"No," he said to her before answering it. Then he made a half turn away from her. "Yeah?"

Mila regrouped. She knew she could hold her own against him, and she knew she would surprise him with her skills. She also knew one of his major objections to hiring women security agents was the fear they couldn't handle themselves in a fistfight.

She considered simply up and attacking him. He'd have to defend himself. Then at least he'd see what she could do.

"That was fast," he said into the phone. "I'm already up on the ninth."

He was distracted at the moment, half turned away from her. It would give her an advantage in the first few seconds. His ribs were exposed, and his stance was slightly off balance.

He glanced at her and instantly drew back, an expression of surprise on his face.

"Gotta go," he said into the phone. "Don't even *think* about it," he said to Mila.

So much for her advantage of surprise. Still, the tactic had a reasonable chance of success.

The elevator pinged behind her.

It was enough of a distraction that Troy was able to grab her left wrist. He tried for the right, obviously intending to manacle her hands behind her back. But she was too quick for him.

She was about to catch him in the solar plexus when a baby's cries came through the elevator doors. She reflexively looked toward the sound.

Troy snagged her other wrist, disabling her.

"That wasn't fair," she grumbled over her shoulder.

"Nothing in this business is fair." He let her go.

The elevator opened to reveal an attractive young woman with purple hair, a colorful bag dangling over her shoulder and a squalling baby in a stroller out front.

"He's hungry," the woman said to Troy as she moved forward.

Troy looked quite horrified by the sight.

Mila knew he didn't have a wife. Maybe this was a girl-friend.

"Then feed him," said Troy, sounding impatient.

"I *will*." The woman bumped the stroller wheels over the lip of the door.

Mila could see her conversation with Troy coming to an abrupt and final end as the two of them dealt with the crying baby. She couldn't afford to let that happen.

Making a split-second decision, she bent over the stroller. "Oh, he's adorable," she said.

The truth was the baby was quite unattractive at the moment. His face red and scrunched up, eyes watery, nose running and his mouth open with bawls of annoyance.

Mila refused to let it deter her. "Come here, precious," she cooed, imitating the behavior of her sappy aunt Nancy around babies. She gathered the messy little guy from the stroller. "What's the trouble, huh? Are you hungry?"

She felt ridiculous speaking to an uncomprehending baby in such a sickly sweet tone, but it was the only way she could think of to stick with Troy. And she was determined to stick with Troy.

She forced herself to keep from grimacing as she brought the baby's gummy face to her shoulder. Her tank top would wash, and so would her skin. She patted him gently on the back, surprised by the warmth of his little body and by the softness. He felt as though he didn't have a single bone or muscle.

His cries changed to intermittent sobs.

"Let's get going," the woman said anxiously. "This won't last long."

Mila refused to make eye contact with Troy, knowing he had to be angry at her pushiness. Instead, she marched past him, heading down the short hall to the doors at the end.

Two

Two women had invaded Troy's apartment, for two completely different but equally frustrating reasons. Well, maybe not equally frustrating, since he could get rid of Mila Stern in short order, just as soon as she put the baby down. Though, for the moment, the baby was quiet in her arms, and he was hesitant to mess with that.

Kassidy was bent over his sofa sorting through her shoulder bag, pulling out diapers, flannel blankets and tiny socks.

"He likes you," she said to Mila, straightening with a bottle in her hand.

"He seems like a sweetheart," said Mila.

Something pinged on Troy's radar. Mila's expression was perfectly neutral, and there was no reason for her to lie about something as innocuous as a baby. But for some reason his suspicions were up again.

"He can be a terror," said Kassidy. "Especially at night. It's going to take Troy a while to get used to all the crying."

"Hello?" Troy didn't like the sound of that.

The guest rooms were on the opposite side of the apartment from the master bedroom, but the kid seemed to have quite a set of lungs.

"I'm Kassidy Keiser, by the way," Kassidy said to Mila.

Mila looked surprised. She glanced to Troy. "So, you two are…married?"

"No," they both barked out simultaneously.

Drake let out a cry of surprise.

"Kassidy is my sister," said Troy.

Mila's glance went to Drake. "So the baby isn't yours?"

"No!" This time Troy beat Kassidy to the punch.

"I live in Jersey City," said Kassidy, taking Drake from Mila's arms. "That is, I normally live in Jersey City. But I've relocated for a while. Me and Drake. We'll be staying here with Troy until things calm down." She sat down on the sofa and popped the bottle into Drake's mouth.

The baby dug into the meal, his little hands clasping and unclasping as he sucked and swallowed.

Mila took an armchair, perching on the edge to watch. "What things need to calm down?" she asked Kassidy, concern evident in her voice.

Troy started to protest. Mila wasn't a guest. She had no business engaging his sister in chitchat while his lunch hour ticked away. He had a busy afternoon coming up, and he didn't intend to spend it starving.

"Or until I get used to it all, I suppose," said Kassidy. "And used to him." She smiled down at Drake, smoothing a lock of his dark hair. "Isn't he adorable?"

"You could have put him up for adoption," said Troy.

The baby was adorable. There had to be dozens if not hundreds of stable, loving couples who would want him. Kassidy was in absolutely no position to take on an infant. She could barely take care of herself.

But her eyes flashed angrily at him. "I told you, I promised."

"What a thing to say," Mila cut in, adding her own glare at Troy. "What kind of support is that? This is your nephew."

"He's not my nephew," said Troy.

"He will be," said Kassidy. "Legally, morally and in every other way there is. You better get used to it, Troy. Because little Drake here isn't going anywhere. Not anywhere."

Now Mila just looked confused.

"She's adopting him," said Troy, wondering why he bothered to explain. It was past time for Mila to leave.

"Where are his birth parents?" Mila asked Kassidy.

"His mother passed away," said Kassidy, her tone going soft and her hand smoothing over Drake's head for a second time. "She was a good friend."

The baby was blissfully oblivious to the discussion swirling around him. His hunger was being satiated, and that was all he cared about. Troy felt a pang of jealousy and then realized he could make that same decision for himself.

"I need to get lunch," he announced, checking the time on his wrist.

He had less than thirty minutes before he had to be back downstairs. The Bulgarians had hired Pinion Security for an important upcoming UN reception, and he needed to get the team set up.

"Help yourself to whatever you want," he told Kassidy. He dug into his pocket for a key card. "This will get you into the exterior doors as well as this apartment. You should know there are cameras all over the building." His gaze moved to Mila. "We can track anybody, anywhere, at any time."

She obviously understood. "You knew I was coming."

"We saw you hiding from Vegas on the elevator. We were curious."

"Sneaky," she said.

"Seriously? Me, sneaky?"

"You could have said something."

"Why would I say something?"

Kassidy's gaze was ping-ponging back and forth between them.

"I only wanted to talk to you," said Mila.

"And you did. And we're done." He gestured to the apartment's front door. "The control room will be watching you all the way out. So don't try anything."

"Who are you?" asked Kassidy.

Mila looked at Kassidy, but obviously hesitated over her answer.

"I thought you were his girlfriend," Kassidy continued as she lifted Drake to her shoulder and began patting his back.

"I'm applying for a job," said Mila.

"She means she's stalking me," said Troy.

"Welcome to the club," Kassidy said to Troy.

"Someone's stalking you?" Mila was quick to pick up on the inference.

"I don't know," Kassidy answered. "Maybe. I have these fans." She gave a little burst of laughter. "I guess if you're not dating Troy—"

"I'm not dating Troy."

"—then you wouldn't know I was a singer. I'm a singer. And I have some fans. Not a whole bunch of fans, but enough. And some of them have been sending me emails. They're a bit creepy."

Mila looked to Troy.

He gave a shrug to indicate he wasn't unduly alarmed. "I've forwarded copies to a profiler."

"Can I see them?" asked Mila.

"Sure," said Kassidy.

"No, she can't," said Troy. "She doesn't work here, and they're none of her business."

"Why doesn't she work here?" asked Kassidy.

"That's none of *your* business," said Troy.

"I'm serious," said Kassidy.

"So am I."

Kassidy turned to Mila. "Why don't you work here?"

"I'm trying," said Mila. "But your brother doesn't hire women."

Kassidy's blue eyes went wide and she stared at him with patent disapproval.

"That's not true," said Troy, wondering why he was feeling defensive. "I have three women working in this building alone."

"Not as security agents," said Mila.

Troy glared at her, sending the unmistakable message that she should shut up.

"Why not as security agents?" asked Kassidy. Using one hand to hold Drake, she dug into her shoulder bag. "I'll show you the latest emails."

"Mila is leaving, and I'm having lunch." Troy had to try at least.

"Go ahead and have lunch," said Kassidy. "I want a woman's opinion on this."

He turned his tone to steel. "Goodbye, Mila Stern."

"Don't you be a jerk, Troy," said Kassidy.

"I won't charge you," Mila said, rising to her feet and heading for Kassidy.

"Charge me with what?" He was baffled by the statement.

"Charge you for the time," she said.

"You *don't work for me*."

"This new one came yesterday," said Kassidy, holding out a sheet of paper.

Despite himself, Troy's curiosity was piqued. He hadn't seen this one. "Who's it from?"

Mila was quicker on the draw, taking the printout from Kassidy's hand.

"BluebellNighthawk," said Kassidy.

Mila was reading her way through it, and Troy went behind her to look over her shoulder.

The message rambled about Kassidy's hair and her eyes, her voice and a song she'd written that BluebellNighthawk seemed to think was about him.

"Is this the only new one?" asked Troy.

"Is there any significance to the word *window*?" asked Mila.

Troy stared down at her. "Why?"

"None that I can think of," said Kassidy.

"He uses it twice," said Mila. "And both times it's the end of a thought followed by an awkward transition."

Troy reread the note. "It's all awkward."

"True," said Mila, sitting back down in the armchair, still gazing at the printout.

Troy summoned his patience. They were going backward here.

"I'm starving," he said to both of them.

"So go have lunch," said Kassidy.

Mila merely waved him away.

* * *

Mila had managed to stay in Troy's apartment with Kassidy while he went downstairs for some meetings. She now had a hundred fan emails sorted into piles on the dining room table and had reconstructed Kassidy's recent concert schedule on a digital map on her tablet.

Drake cooed in his baby seat in the corner of the living room. Kassidy chatted on the phone to her business manager in the kitchen, the occasional word or burst of laughter filtering out.

Mila was matching the emails to the performance dates, and now she needed to link them all on the map. For that, she needed a scanner.

She glanced around and spotted an open door that looked promising. She rose to look more closely and discovered it was Troy's home office. Sure enough, she found a scanner on the corner credenza.

It looked straightforward enough, and she loaded in the documents.

"Can I help you with something?" Troy's deep voice came from behind her.

"No." She turned to meet his decidedly annoyed expression. "I think I've got it working."

"I didn't mean that literally." His frown deepened.

"What did you mean?" she asked conversationally.

She refused to let herself be intimidated by his scowl. Kassidy was living here with him, and she had invited Mila to stay and sort through the emails.

"I meant, what the hell are you doing in my office without permission?"

She held his gaze. "I'm scanning documents."

He advanced a couple of paces, shrinking the space with his presence. "I thought you'd be gone by now."

"You have cameras all over the place. You'd have known if I left."

"I don't monitor the control center."

"Your staff wouldn't notify you?"

He paused at that. It was obvious from his expression they would have contacted him immediately.

Their gazes stayed locked, and a tickle of awareness found its way into her pores. There was no denying he was a good-looking man. And masculine strength was definitely a turn-on for her. But it was odd that his belligerence wouldn't have counteracted those two traits. She wasn't blindly attracted to just any tough guy.

The scanner chugged and whined in the background.

"You need to leave," he said.

"You don't want to know what I found?"

"We both know Kassidy's in no real danger."

"We do?"

Mila wasn't ready to go that far. Though it did seem likely Kassidy was experiencing the harmless, if annoying, adoration that could be directed at any pretty young woman in the public eye.

"You've given it a nice try," he said. "You've given it a terrific try. You've gone above and beyond in trying to get me to hire you. I'll grant you that."

"Thank you. So, hire me."

"I'm not hiring you."

"Why not?" she asked.

He rolled his eyes with obvious derision. "You're stalling again."

"I'm serious. In this day and age, what possible reason could you have for not hiring women?"

"You want the truth?"

"I'd love the truth."

"Okay. Here it is. It's a simple equation of muscle mass."

She gave herself an extra beat to frame her response. She knew this was her last and only chance to change his mind. Simple, she decided. Simple and direct was her best bet.

"Skills can overcome muscle mass."

"Maybe," he allowed, surprising her.

She felt encouraged. "And don't discount knowledge and intelligence."

He squared his shoulders, not looking at all like somebody who was about to capitulate. "I don't discount knowledge and intelligence. I hire for skills. I hire for intellect. I hire for experience. I hire for proficiency. And when all of those elements are present, I then hire for strength and power."

"I have all of those things."

"How much do you even weigh?"

"A hundred and twenty pounds. Almost."

He shook his head in a pitying way. "Two guys come at you, big guys, five hundred pounds between them. What do you do?"

"Shoot them," she said without hesitation.

"You're unarmed."

Mila knew two could play at this game. "What about you? How do you control a situation where the other guys are armed and you're not?"

"I'm never not."

"You know what I mean." She stared levelly across at him. "There are times when even you, Mr. Two Hundred… whatever—"

"Two-fifteen."

"Mr. Two-Fifteen, all muscle and sinew, are overpowered by the opposition."

"Less often than you," he said softly.

Something had shifted in the depths of his eyes, and she felt the sexual awareness all over again. He'd moved closer as they spoke. Or maybe she'd moved closer. But she could smell him now, and he smelled good. Another couple of inches, and she'd feel the heat of his body.

She told herself she wanted to fight him, not kiss him. But she knew it was a lie. She'd been trained to face the honest reality of any physical encounter. Anything less put her at an absolute disadvantage.

"You're trying to distract me," she said.

"You're the one trying to distract me." He leaned in, closing the gap between them even farther.

"It's not on purpose."

"Of course it is."

"You think I can do that?" she asked, easing closer. "With you? With all that self-discipline you must have, I could distract you with sex?"

His expression faltered.

"If I can," she continued, "you should probably hire me, because that's something over and above what any of the muscle-bound brotherhood can accomplish."

"That's your strongest attribute?" he taunted. "I wouldn't think you'd want to brag about it." But his gaze kept hers trapped, and the air seemed to thicken around them.

She realized her mistake. "It's not my strongest attribute." As she spoke, she surreptitiously shifted her right hand around his side. "My strongest attribute right now is the knife pointed at your kidney."

"You don't have a knife."

"It's in its sheath. But I do have a knife."

He moved, and she instantly jerked her fist against him to show she could have stabbed him.

He grabbed her wrist, and his other hand went to her throat.

"You're dead," she told him.

"I'm bleeding out," he agreed. "But you're dead, too." His hand gently stroked the skin of her neck.

"Am I hired?" she asked.

"You're insane."

His voice was a whisper. His face hovered over hers. She smelled his skin, imagined the taste of his lips, the feel of his body enveloping hers.

He was going to kiss her. It was in the smoke of his eyes, the twitch of his fingers, the indrawn breath that tightened his chest. She shouldn't let him. She couldn't let him. But she knew she was going to let him. And it was going to be fantastic.

Kassidy's excited voice sounded through the doorway. "Mila?"

Troy instantly stepped back.

Mila snapped to reality. "In here."

"I've got a gig tonight," Kassidy sang. "It's a good one. The Ripple Branch on Georgia Avenue. They had a cancellation."

She appeared in the doorway. "Oh, hi, Troy." She focused her attention on Mila. "Can you come with me?"

"Love to," Mila immediately answered.

Kassidy barely took a breath. "You okay to babysit?" she asked Troy.

"What?" The question clearly took him aback. It was probably the only thing that stopped him from ordering Mila not to go anywhere with Kassidy.

Mila knew she shouldn't laugh at his obvious predicament, but it was tough to fight the urge.

"Drake should go to sleep by eight," said Kassidy. "And I don't have to leave until seven. I could have everything ready in advance. All you'd have to do is give him a quick bath, a bottle, and wind up his rainbow jungle toy. He loves watching it while he falls asleep."

"Sounds easy enough," said Mila.

"Go away," Troy growled under his breath. "You don't work here."

"Your sister needs protection."

"My sister needs a nanny."

"Before you fight with me, take a look at what I've found," said Mila. "I wouldn't call your sister's situation high risk, but it's not zero either."

"Nothing's zero," he said.

"There's something there," she said.

It was just out of reach, like the wisps of a dream. But

Kassidy's anxiety was real. The girl's instincts were telling her to protect herself. Mila didn't like to ignore instincts.

"You're so transparent," he drawled.

"Fine," said Mila. "Believe whatever you want. Hire me, don't hire me, but I'm going to the performance with Kassidy tonight."

"It's a free country," said Troy, his blue eyes going icy gray. "Call a nanny service before you go," Troy said to Kassidy. "I'm not your babysitter."

"It'll be easy," said Kassidy.

"I've got work to do."

Mila fought an urge to tease him, but she bit back the unwise words. She'd accompany Kassidy to the performance tonight and file a report with Troy in the morning. Maybe he'd read it. Maybe he wouldn't. Even if her work was exceptional tonight, it might not change his mind. There might be nothing she could do to change his mind about hiring her. But she wasn't going down without a fight.

In the ops control room, Vegas turned his head at Troy's entrance. He did a double take of Drake sleeping on Troy's shoulder.

"New recruit?" he asked.

"It's the apprenticeship program," said Troy, his hand splayed across Drake's diaper-covered bottom, easily balancing the baby's slight fifteen pounds.

Two dozen video screens decorated the walls, receiving feeds from fixed and mobile cameras, tracking devices and information from their international offices. This time of night, people were just arriving at work in Dubai.

"I take it this is the new nephew," said Vegas.

"He's not my—" Troy stopped himself. He supposed, technically, Drake was going to be his nephew. "There's a nanny on the way. She had car trouble or kid trouble or something."

All Troy knew for sure was that he was alone with Drake, and he didn't like it.

"Kassidy's out on the town?" asked Vegas, disapproval in his tone.

"She's working." Which he imagined was pretty much the same thing for Kassidy.

Troy had protected a lot of celebrities over the years. With a few notable exceptions, sports stars and film personalities were mostly professional. The lion's share of what made it into the tabloids was a part of their carefully crafted public image. Musicians, however, were a breed unto themselves. They kept late hours, drank and partied, and a lot of them truly lived the rock-and-roll lifestyle.

Vegas eyed Drake up and down. "I don't get it," he said. "It would be one thing if she got knocked up."

"You do remember you're talking about my sister." Troy wasn't sure why he felt compelled to defend her at this late date.

Vegas's brow went up. "Well, excuse me, but isn't this the baby sister who trashed three rooms at the Poco Hollywood Hotel?"

"She had help."

To keep the whole thing out of court, Troy had paid the bill.

"She's not exactly mother material," said Vegas.

Troy couldn't disagree with that. He briefly tightened his hold on Drake. Poor kid. This was likely to be a rocky ride.

"I'm thinking a full-time nanny," said Troy.

Vegas coughed out a chopped laugh. "One for each of them?"

Troy opened his mouth to defend her again, but he had nothing to say. There was no point in pretending Kassidy was in any position to raise a child. Why a terminally ill single mom had made his sister promise to take guardianship of an innocent baby was a mystery to him.

"I saw Mila leave with Kassidy." Vegas let the sentence hang.

"I didn't hire her," said Troy.

"Does she know that?"

"Yes."

Vegas gave a crooked smirk.

"She may not have accepted it yet," said Troy.

"But she's not equipped." It wasn't a question. If Mila had a company camera or communications device, Vegas would see it on his monitors.

"It's not an op," said Troy. "It's a performance."

"So you've analyzed the data."

"Not all of it. Not yet. It's fan letters. If Kassidy wants to flail around onstage in lingerie while she belts out pop tunes, guys are going to make comments."

"You think there's no danger?"

"Do you think there is?"

Vegas shrugged. "I doubt it."

"There. Good." Troy sat down on one of the rolling desk chairs. "What's going on in the Middle East?"

Vegas zoomed in on a camera. "Prince Matin had a late night, but he's up and around, and the car is out front of the hotel."

"Gotta love the partying spirit of the reformers," said Troy.

Vegas grinned. "He had a supermodel on his arm when he finally left the reception."

Prince Matin was in his early thirties, had plenty of money and was a genuine supporter of capitalism and an improved regulatory regime. He had the respect of his countrymen and an understanding of the West. That was a rare enough combination that nobody seemed to care what he did in his private life.

"Any new chatter about the protest?" Troy asked.

"It's been quiet enough. John's got five guys going undercover in the crowd. They're liaising with the city police."

"The minute the speech is over tonight, we put him behind the glass."

"That's the plan," said Vegas.

There were sensitivities around the podium being behind bulletproof glass, but they'd erected a barrier on each side of the stage, so only one dignitary would be exposed at any given time.

"The snipers?" Troy asked.

"Two of ours and five will be from the police department. Matin agreed to the bulletproof vest."

"That's a first."

Drake wriggled on Troy's shoulder, moving his head back and forth, and Troy readjusted his hold.

"What are you going to do if he gets hungry?" asked Vegas.

"The nanny should be here any minute." Troy extracted his cell phone and pressed the speed dial for the front reception.

"Yes, boss?" came Edison's voice.

"Any sign down there of Alice Miller from Total Tykes?"

"Nothing so far. Problem, boss?"

"Not yet."

But Vegas did have a point. Eventually Drake was going to get hungry.

"Shall I track her down?" asked Edison.

"Sure. See what you can do." Troy assumed Edison would start with the agency's phone number rather than a city-wide traffic cam search.

"Did Kassidy leave you a bottle?" asked Vegas as he double-checked a set of GPS markers in France.

Troy wasn't sure he'd understood the question. "Say again?"

"I take it the nanny is MIA. Check your refrigerator. I bet you find bottles of formula."

"She's a nanny, not a fugitive. She'll be here any second."

"Just giving you a contingency."

Drake wiggled again.

"Since when do you care about babies?" asked Troy.

"He seems a little restless."

"He's supposed to sleep for hours."

"Whatever you say." Then Vegas zoomed in on a screen. He went still and flicked a switch on his headset. "Boomer's on that job in Rio, remember? He's on the run."

Troy's focus was instant. "What happened?"

Vegas reached for the intercom to put the feed on the speakers, but Troy grabbed his arm. "You'll wake him."

Vegas nodded, withdrawing his hand to leave the sound coming to his headset. "Shots were fired."

"At *the band*?" Troy could barely believe it.

Vegas paused. "Nobody hit. They're in the bus headed for the hotel."

Boomer was at a Rio de Janeiro jazz festival with a California band. The festival attracted thousands, but it didn't have a history of violence. It had been considered a routine operation.

"They think it was probably celebratory gunfire," said Vegas. "But Boomer wasn't taking any chances."

"Good decision," said Troy.

"Roger that," Vegas said into his microphone. He flicked a smile. "No longer headed for the hotel. They happened onto a beach party. Boomer will pull in a couple of reinforcements."

"Gotta be a hundred parties there tonight," said Troy.

"I wouldn't mind an assignment in Rio," said Vegas.

"I'd take anything with palm trees right about now."

There were no windows in the DC control room, but the day had been cloudy and gray, October drizzle turning into November cold.

Troy's phone buzzed.

He could only hope it was Edison with good news.

"Yeah?"

"Troy? It's Mila."

Her voice took him by surprise. For some reason it seemed to resonate right down to his bones.

"What are you doing with my direct line?" he asked.

"Kassidy gave it to me."

Drake wriggled against his shoulder, and Troy lowered his voice. "Next time, call the switchboard."

"Sure." She went silent.

"Is something wrong?"

"I thought you'd like an update."

"What I'd like is a nanny."

"The nanny's not there yet?"

"No," he said.

"Where is she?"

"I have no idea. You want to come back and take over?"

"Kassidy is onstage. The crowd's going nuts. You know, Troy, she really is good."

"I know she's good."

"I mean *good*, good. There's something in the crowd. It's an energy, almost a fervor. This is about to go big-time, and you really do need to think about formalizing her security."

"Let me guess, you want to head the task force?"

"Sure."

"That was a joke, Mila."

"I'm not joking."

"You're angling for a job." He wasn't buying what she was selling.

"Is that deductive reasoning 101?"

"Ha-ha."

"Gotta go. We'll talk later." The line went dead.

Troy heaved a sigh and pocketed his phone while Drake kicked his little legs and whimpered in his sleep. Anybody could see this babysitting thing was all about to go south.

Vegas turned from the monitor screens to gaze at the baby. "You ready to talk about the formula contingency plan?"

Three

Mila and Kassidy crept into Troy's apartment at three a.m. after a fantastic performance. Kassidy had come back on-stage for two encores, and the club manager had already contacted Eileen Renard looking to set up future gigs. The social media buzz that had started during the evening continued even now.

"I'm trending," said Kassidy in an excited whisper as the apartment door swung shut behind her.

She scrolled through the screen of her phone while she kicked off her shoes and started for the living room. "It's mostly good."

"I'll go through the posts in the morning," said Mila.

She was dead tired right now, and as soon as she retrieved the rest of Kassidy's email printouts from Troy's dining table, she was headed home for bed. She'd taken dozens of photos of the audience and the outside crowds, and she'd add the new social media posts to the mix. She intended to get back to her situational analysis early tomorrow.

"Oh, look," whispered Kassidy, coming to an abrupt halt at the edge of the living room. "How sweet is that?"

Mila followed Kassidy's gaze to find Troy sound asleep on his sofa. He was flat on his back, Drake sprawled across his chest, eyes closed, his face pressed into the crook of Troy's neck.

"Sweet," said Mila. Though, even sleeping, she found Troy more imposing than sweet.

His eyes blinked once then came fully open, obviously alert.

"What happened to Alice Miller?" asked Kassidy.

"She left." Troy cradled Drake and sat up, glancing at his watch. "This one slept until five minutes after she drove away."

Troy's short hair was still neat, his shirt wrinkle-free, and he seemed completely awake and alert. The only flaw to his otherwise perfect appearance was the shadow of a beard. But it was sexy—made him look rakishly handsome.

"He'll be hungry soon," said Kassidy, moving to take Drake from her brother.

"He'll be chubby soon the way he eats," said Troy.

"That's what babies do," said Kassidy.

"That's not all they do," said Troy. "Don't go making more plans that include me. This diaper duty is not going to be a regular thing."

Kassidy hesitated, glancing uncertainly at Mila.

"What?" asked Troy.

"They really liked me," said Kassidy.

"She was fantastic," Mila added. "I meant what I told you on the phone."

The night had obviously been thrilling for Kassidy, and Mila hoped Troy didn't put a damper on it.

"Is there any money in this?" asked Troy as he relinquished Drake. "What I mean is, enough for a full-time nanny?"

"Eventually," said Kassidy. "I think. I'm sure." She didn't look all that sure.

Mila was no expert, but it seemed the money ought to rise along with Kassidy's popularity. There might be a lag time up front, but it had to be worth the financial risk of hiring a nanny so that she could continue to perform.

Drake let out a cry, and Kassidy rubbed his back, cradling him close, rocking her body to soothe him. "It's okay, baby," she crooned. She headed for the kitchen. "Let's get you a bottle."

Mila and Troy were left alone in the dimly lit living room.

He rose to his feet. "Is this the part where you remind me she needs a bodyguard?"

Mila didn't see an advantage to pressing him further about a job tonight. But she wasn't going to mince words, either. "What your sister needs is a proper security plan."

"Here we go," he said.

"No, we don't. That's a conversation for tomorrow. Right now, I'm taking my analysis and going home. Can you tell Kassidy I'll call her and let her know what I find?"

"What are you looking for?"

"I don't know yet," Mila answered honestly as she gathered the pile of paper. "I'll go through the photos and the social media posts, see what jumps out. Last we checked, she was trending, so there'll be plenty of material."

"Trending where?"

"Just here in DC."

He nodded thoughtfully. "How big was the crowd tonight?"

"Capacity." She stopped halfway to the door to stand in front of him. "Which I'm told is three hundred. And there was a lineup outside."

"What's the typical for the Ripple Branch?"

"On a Thursday, the manager says it's usually at two-thirds capacity."

Troy looked thoughtful. "So she had an impact."

"She had an impact."

"They'll want her back."

"Them and a dozen other places in the DC area," said Mila. "I did some rudimentary research on Eileen Renard. She seems legit, and she seems excited."

"You checked out Eileen Renard?"

"Yes."

"And you have pictures from tonight?"

"The audience, the lineup, staff, autograph seekers outside the back door."

"Do you have a list of the new offers for gigs?"

Mila pulled her phone from her pocket and lit up the screen to show him.

"You made a list," he said without glancing at it.

"Of course."

"You're hired."

Her brain stumbled. "What?"

"Temporarily."

"Did you just offer me a job?"

"You need to be quicker on the uptake than that, Mila."

"You can't blame me for being surprised."

"I want you to watch Kassidy."

Temporary wasn't her first choice, but she'd absolutely take it. It was an opportunity to show him what she could do.

"That's a smart decision," she told him.

Now he looked amused. "Not half-confident, are you?"

"I'm fully confident."

"Are you going to get cocky on me?"

No, she wasn't. "Confidence is different than arrogance. I was the one on the ground tonight. I saw what I saw, and my assessment stands."

"You think she needs a security strategy."

Mila was about to say she *knew* Kassidy needed a security strategy, but it had already been a long evening. "I do."

"We can talk about it in the morning."

Drake started to cry in the kitchen.

"And a nanny," said Troy. "We're definitely going to talk about a nanny."

Mila sat across from her sister, Zoey, beside the front window in the Benson Street Bakery. Steaming mochas and fresh-baked banana muffins sat on the table between them. Rain spattered on the glass. Pedestrians rushed past in the half light, while the morning coffee crowd lineup snaked through the center of the small space.

"Anything worth doing has a high barrier to entry," said Zoey, breaking off a bite of her muffin.

"Do you have to quote Mom this early in the morning?" Mila cut her muffin in half and spread it with a layer of butter.

Zoey grinned. "Didn't get a lot of sleep last night?"

"A couple of hours." Mila took another drink of the creamy coffee, thinking maybe she should have gone with espresso. But, man, this tasted good.

"He's hot," said Zoey, turning her phone to show Mila a picture she'd found of Troy.

"I don't care about hot," said Mila. Though there was no denying Troy's sex appeal. "He's a bit annoying. And he's definitely chauvinistic. But he's great at the job. I can learn a lot from him. And that's all I care about right now."

Zoey turned the picture back toward her, taking it in with moony eyes. "Will you introduce me?"

"No, I won't introduce you. You think I want my sister dating my boss?"

Mila's brain flicked involuntarily back to the moment yesterday in Troy's office when she'd almost kissed him. Or had he almost kissed her? It didn't matter. Her feelings were the same, and they weren't good. Maybe she *should* introduce him to Zoey.

Her sister was five foot eight, model thin, always dressed for success, and men buzzed around her like bees on a hive.

Right now, Zoey put on a conspiratorial grin. "I might be able to influence him in your favor."

"*You're* going to sleep *my* way to the top?"

"What are sisters for?"

"Not that."

Zoey laughed. "You want him for yourself?"

"No," said Mila, telling herself she had to keep any attraction to Troy under ironclad control.

"Hang on," Zoey said, studying Mila's expression. "You are interested in him."

"Not interested," said Mila.

But her sister was a lawyer, a skilled cross-examiner. There was no chance of getting away with an outright lie.

"Attracted, sure," she continued. "I'm female, and I have a pulse. But that's where it stops, and it's definitely not going any further."

"I guess you won't get him to take you seriously once he's seen you naked."

"He's not going to see me naked." Mila felt her face heat.

"Okay." Zoey drew out the word, obviously fighting a grin.

"Stop," said Mila. "We're talking about my career, not my love life."

"Let's talk about my love life."

"You have a love life?" Mila immediately realized how that sounded. "I mean, other than the dozens of offers you get every week."

"I met a guy," said Zoey.

"A guy, guy?" Mila asked in surprise.

Zoey had an active but very informal dating life. Her career came first, and she'd studiously avoided the demands a serious relationship would put on her. She was already the youngest person in her prestigious law firm to make associate partner.

"Is there another kind?" she asked.

"An honest to goodness potential maybe-you're-the-one kind of guy?"

Zoey hid a smile behind her coffee cup. "Yes."

Now Mila was baffled. "Then why do you want to meet Troy?"

"I don't. I wanted to see your reaction when I asked to meet him. He seems like your type."

"*Annoying chauvinist* is not my type."

"Rough and ready is your type. I know how you feel about those metrosexual guys."

"Only because I can't stand aftershave."

It seemed shallow to discount an entire classification of men. Mila didn't want to seem shallow. But she did prefer a man with a lot of obvious testosterone, one who looked at home in jeans and a canvas work shirt, one that she couldn't physically overpower in less than a minute. There was no particular reason for the preference. It was just the way her hormones worked.

"You also hate men in skinny jeans and cardigans," said Zoey.

"That's just good taste." Then Mila stumbled. "Wait. Your new guy, he's not into cardigans, is he?"

"Business suits. Silk ties."

"Not bow ties."

"Designer suits. Business formal."

"He's a lawyer?"

"He's a judge."

"Are you allowed to date a judge?"

"Sure. Of course, I can't date him and argue in front of him at the same time."

"But, otherwise…?"

"Otherwise, it's fine. Well, technically fine, from a professional standpoint, anyway." Zoey worried her muffin.

Mila might not be an experienced trial lawyer, but even she could tell her sister was holding back something important. "What aren't you telling me?"

"It's Dustin Earl."

"Dustin *Earl*?"

"Yes."

Mila gave her head a little shake. "Are there two of them?"

"No, just the one."

"You're *dating* the judge who approved the demolition of the Turret Building."

Zoey pursed her lips. "That building was over two hundred years old."

"That would be Preservation Society's point." Mila had heard it all from her mother.

"It was condemned," argued Zoey.

The structural integrity of the building—or even the merits of the decision—wasn't really Mila's point. "Mom's going to have a cow."

Their mother, Louise Stern, was also a superior court judge. She called Judge Earl a brash, maverick upstart with little appreciation for the long-range impact of his decisions. They disagreed on almost everything, but nothing more stridently than the fate of the Turret Building.

"Tell me about it," said Zoey, popping another bite of her muffin into her mouth.

"Are you going to tell Mom and Dad?"

"I'm not telling anybody."

"You just told me."

"You don't count."

Mila couldn't help but smile at that. "Gee, thanks."

"You know what I mean. You're not going to tell Mom or Dad, or Rand or Franklin."

Their oldest brother, Rand, was a decorated captain on a Navy cruiser somewhere in the Mediterranean. Franklin's Green Beret missions for the Army were secretive. But he was probably hunkered down in a jungle on some mountainside, monitoring drug kingpins or rebels.

Zoey continued, "And I knew you wouldn't freak out."

"True enough," Mila said as she worked her way through the oversize muffin. "I've got far too many other things pinging my worry meter."

Zoey's clandestine love life would have to take a backseat to Troy's reluctance and Kassidy's security.

"Things like Troy Keiser," Zoey said, the glint returning to her eyes.

Mila refused to take the bait. "If I don't get him to hire me permanently, I'll have to explain a professional failure to the family."

Zoey lifted her coffee cup. "If you fail, it'll take the pressure off me."

"Or the other way around," said Mila. "If they're freaking out about Dustin Earl, nobody's going to care that I've blown my dream job."

"You want to bet on that?"

"No," said Mila.

Not that she'd ever wish her sister ill. But she doubted even the infamous Judge Earl would be enough to distract her family from any kind of career failure.

If Troy turned her down, she'd have four drill sergeants

all shouting at her to get up off the mat, to regroup and try again. If a job with Troy Keiser was the best credential for her future career, then that was exactly what Mila was expected to achieve. No hesitation, no excuses, no giving up.

"I'm headed to Pinion Security right now," she said, polishing off the last of her coffee.

"Show him what you've got, little sister."

Mila had made up her mind to take it slow, take it steady and methodical in order to impress Troy. She wouldn't try to knock it out of the park in the first five minutes.

"There's nothing for me to do but paperwork this morning," she said. "And after that I have to find a nanny."

"A nanny?"

"Kassidy can't perform without someone to take care of Drake."

"And if she can't perform, she can't be in danger. And if she's not in danger, you can't save her."

Mila frowned, not liking the way that sounded. "My plan is to keep her *out* of danger. If there's no danger, I've still done my job."

"Troy Keiser probably won't be all that impressed if you keep her safe from nothing."

Much as she hated it, Mila knew Zoey's words were the bald truth. If Kassidy's fans were simply fans, it would be difficult for Mila to shine. Still, she couldn't bring herself to wish any danger on Kassidy. And the most foolish move in the world would be for her to see things that weren't there. She'd have to keep herself on an even keel, make sure she didn't look too hard for threats.

This morning, Troy had found himself second-guessing his decision to hire Mila. Second guessing wasn't like him. And he couldn't afford to do it. He was in a business full of split-second decisions, most of which were final, some deadly final.

"How did she convince you?" Vegas asked from across their shared office.

It was a utilitarian room, with a couple of guest chairs, computers, monitors, an old-fashioned whiteboard and a large rectangular work table in the middle. Their desks both faced the windows, side by side, looking toward the river.

"It was Drake who wore me down," said Troy. "I don't care who does it, but somebody's hiring a nanny."

"Kassidy can hire her own nanny."

Troy had to admit it was true. Not that he had a whole lot of faith in Kassidy's judgment. But she could use a reputable service. Last night's nanny seemed perfectly fine. Her only problem was leaving too early.

"Mila seems methodical," Troy said to Vegas, using the reason he'd settled on for himself. "I appreciate methodical."

"Do you think Kassidy's under any real threat?"

"I think Mila will find out. If it's nothing, terrific. Then once we have a nanny, Mila's gone."

Troy would let her go without a second thought. Her persistence might have seemed admirable last night, but she was just another investigator. He'd decided that a woman was probably good for Kassidy under the current circumstances, but once the threat assessment was complete, that would be the end.

"Have you set up the employment entry tests?" asked Vegas.

"No." Troy was surprised by the question. "This isn't a regular hire."

Successful completion of four stringent performance tests was required of every Pinion Security agent—tradecraft theory, technical skills, weapons proficiency and physical fitness. There was an overall 80 percent failure rate, even among ex-military members. The obstacle course was particularly grueling. There was no way a woman could complete it.

"So, you're lowering the standards?" asked Vegas.

Troy took in his partner's critical expression. "Yes. I'm

lowering the standards. For her. It's a one-shot mission, she's
not—"

"Don't you dare lower the standards," Mila's voice interrupted from the doorway.

Both men turned to the sound of her voice.

"This is a private conversation," Troy said, coming to
his feet.

"Then you should have closed the door." Her green eyes
were hard as emeralds. "I don't need to start at the ladies'
tee."

"You're a woman," said Troy. "And you're a temp. Testing you would be a waste of time."

"Then I'll do the tests on my own time." She paced briskly
into the office. "It'll be hard enough getting the other security
agents' respect without skipping the entry tests."

"You're not going to get their respect," said Troy. It was
the truth, and there was no point pretending otherwise.

"Not like this, I'm not."

"And you don't need it. You'll be working on your own
with Kassidy."

His concern that hiring her had been a mistake was back
in force. He should reverse the decision. He should do that
right now.

"Maybe." She rested both her butt and the heels of her
hands against the work table. "But it doesn't matter. I'll still
be around them."

Not if he fired her, she wouldn't.

He sized up the determination in her eyes and was reminded of the admiration he'd felt last night. She definitely
had tenacity going for her. Too bad it wouldn't be enough.
Even if she could shoot straight, she was too small and weak
to make it through the fitness course. And there was no way
to picture her in hand-to-hand knife combat. No way in the
world.

"Let her do it," said Vegas.

Troy turned to stare, astonished that Vegas had contradicted him. Vegas was normally reserved and more than circumspect.

"She'll fail," Troy told him in an unyielding tone.

"I won't," she said, straightening to square her shoulders and cross her arms over her chest.

It was obvious she was trying to be tough, but she was too attractive to pull it off.

"You're going to carry a two-hundred-pound dummy?" said Troy, naming only one of more than twenty obstacles.

"I know how to lift."

"A forty-foot rope climb? A twenty-kilometer road course?"

"I can run. I can climb. I can swim. And I can shoot. Don't make assumptions of what I can't do, Troy."

He wasn't assuming. If he let her skip the tests, the guys might not like it, but that was on him. If she took the tests and failed, then it was on her. She was either too dumb or too stubborn to understand the risks.

She walked toward him, lips pursing.

The closer she got, the more vivid his memory. He could see her in his apartment office, her cheeks flushed, her chest rising and falling, the awareness in her green eyes and that final moment when she'd realized he was going to kiss her.

He wanted to kiss those pursed lips right here and now. He didn't want her struggling through the obstacle course, stumbling with exhaustion, crawling through mud. He'd seen tough men reduced to tears over it. How would that help her gain the respect of her fellow security agents?

"No," he told her in a resolute tone.

"Yes," she said, stopping only inches from him, looking up into his eyes, hers glittering with icy determination. "Can't you see I'm trying to help you?"

"Can't you see I don't want your help?" She looked to Vegas, addressing her next question to him. "He's your partner. How do I change his mind?"

Vegas shrugged his broad shoulders. "Personally, I use thirty-year-old single malt."

"Done," Mila said without hesitation.

She made a crisp turn and left the office.

Troy glared at Vegas. "Really? You advised her to bribe me?"

Vegas gave an amused smile. "You should thank me. I was going to suggest she use sex."

"What?"

"I can see the way you look at her."

"That is *not* where this is going."

Sure, Mila was attractive. And maybe he wanted to kiss her. Maybe he wanted to do more. But that was simple hormones.

There was no denying she was sexy. But there wasn't a chance in the world he'd take a bad situation and make it even worse.

Besides, he assured himself, he liked his women soft and malleable, someone with a pretty hairdo, makeup and a silk dress. There were differences between men and women. As far as Troy was concerned, the more acute those differences, the better.

Sleep with Mila—yeah, right.

Sleep with an employee, not a chance.

And the idea that she could vamp him into changing his mind was laughable.

"We'll see," said Vegas.

"No, we won't see. I've made a decision."

"It's the wrong decision." Vegas looked completely serious. "You just parachute her in, without having her take the tests, and the guys will eat her for lunch."

"They're going to eat her for lunch anyway. That's why we don't hire women."

"Maybe we should," said Vegas. "If we'd hired one before now, this wouldn't be such a problem."

Troy clamped his jaw. He didn't have to say the words out loud.

Vegas's expression took on a shade of sympathy. "We've lost men before, too."

"But not through our own stupidity."

"We weren't stupid to hire Gabriela."

"We were stupid to get her killed on day five."

"Ops go bad sometimes," said Vegas.

"She never should have been in that house."

"It wasn't because she was a woman."

"Yeah, it was."

Vegas heaved a sigh. "It was a bad deal all around."

Troy dropped back down into his chair. "It was. And I'm not going to make the same mistake twice."

"Nobody's asking you to do that."

Troy stared at Vegas, but all he saw were Gabriela's big brown eyes. She'd been laughing as she left the office that day. She'd had a date coming up on the weekend, some guy she'd met at the gym. Troy remembered feeling sorry for him, knowing Gabriela was as tough as they came.

"The obstacle course isn't dangerous." Vegas interrupted his thoughts.

Troy switched his focus to the present. "Yes, it is."

"Okay, it is dangerous, but it's not deadly. And you are hiring Mila to protect your sister."

"I'm hiring her to read social media and find a nanny."

"She's not working in a bubble. And she's trained. She's got some experience. Give her a chance with the company tests. You know she'll get more respect for trying and failing than she will for not stepping up at all."

Troy opened his mouth to rebut, but a new argument didn't form. He realized that stopping Mila from taking the tests wasn't his best move. His best move would have been not have hired her in the first place.

He hated it when he screwed up.

Four

"Time," Troy shouted, and the lights came up in Pinion's basement shooting range.

Mila set the completely reassembled AK-47 down on the table and stepped back, mentally crossing her fingers that she'd gotten it all right. Target shooting was one thing, and she'd aced that part of the exam. She was also confident her reflexes had been fast and her aim accurate in the tactical house.

Troy approached the table and lifted the weapon.

"You should have warned me," she said.

"I did warn you."

"I meant that I'd be disassembling an automatic weapon under combat conditions."

He gave a ghost of a smirk. "It was recorded gunfire and flashing lights."

"I wasn't expecting combat field weapons. Who uses an AK-47 on the streets of DC?"

"Hopefully, no one."

"Then why test me on it?"

Had she known he was testing her as a combat mercenary, she'd have refreshed her memory on a whole bunch of topics.

"You wanted the standard tests. Pinion has offices in Europe, South America and the Middle East."

She couldn't help but move forward for a closer look. She wanted to ask him if she'd passed, but she also wanted to look confident by pretending not to be worried.

"Will you send me to South America?" she asked instead.

"You don't want to sleep on the floor of the jungle."

"I'm not a princess."

He barked out a laugh. "You don't have to be a princess to hate leeches and poisonous snakes."

"Do you hate them?"

"Yes."

"Do you put up with them?"

"Only when I have to." After an initial inspection, he worked the action of the gun.

She held her breath, but the click and clatter sounded normal. Thank goodness.

She kept her voice even and unconcerned, pretending she wasn't attuned to his every movement, expression and word. "What's your main focus in South America?"

Research had told her Pinion protected business executives and provided security to resource companies operating in areas with drug trade and guerrilla activity.

He walked the few paces to the shooting range and pushed a magazine into the gun. "Lately, it's been VIPs. Kidnappings are on the rise. Mine-site protection is pretty much standardized, and very effective. The drug lords don't mess with gems and minerals, and the guerrilla groups want the notoriety of a high-profile hostage as much as they want the insurance payout."

"Kidnapping insurance has been a mixed blessing."

He snapped on a set of earmuffs and raised the weapon to his shoulder. She followed suit, covering her own ears.

"You could put it that way," he shouted.

Then he pulled the trigger, and three shots rang out in rapid succession, hitting the center of a bull's-eye target fifty yards away.

"It's better if they have insurance," he stated in a raised voice, releasing the magazine and popping a cartridge out of the chamber.

"If there was no insurance, on aggregate, fewer people would get kidnapped." She pulled off the earmuffs.

"I'm insured," he said, placing the AK-47 back on the table and removing his own hearing protection. "And as a Pinion employee, you are, too."

"So you could send me to South America."

"Bushmasters grow up to ten feet long."

"Venomous?"

"Yes."

She wasn't even going to pretend she wanted to cope with a ten-foot snake. "Perhaps a nice city posting. Maybe Buenos Aires?"

He'd come closer as they spoke. "Not a lot of guerrilla activity in Buenos Aires."

His eyes were deep blue, intelligent with a trace of humor.

He was incredibly sexy. If he was anyone else, in any other circumstance, she'd be parting her lips, tipping her head with an invitation. Or maybe she'd just up and kiss him, forget waiting for him to make the first move.

"You passed weapons proficiency," he said softly.

"I know."

The back of his hand brushed hers, sending a rush of warmth along her arm. He didn't pull away, and neither did she.

"Is that bravado?" he asked, carefully watching her expression.

"I'm well trained."

She knew she should back away. She was sending signals she didn't want to send, waiting for something to happen that couldn't happen. Her brain was conjuring up his kiss in vivid detail. He had to be a fantastic kisser. A man didn't look like that, didn't smell like that, didn't have that predatory expression if he wasn't about to deliver an amazing kiss.

He tripped the backs of his fingertips up her bare arm.

Her stomach contracted. It fluttered. Her entire body stilled in anticipation.

The buzz of the fluorescents grew louder while the white light flickered rapidly in her peripheral vision. Troy's earthy scent blocked out the sharp tang of gunpowder. Her skin was heating, the moist air pressing against it like bathwater.

He bent his head.

She waited.

His lips brushed hers, and heat rocked to her core.

He groaned, leaning into her, his arms wrapping around her, his lips going firm against hers, parting, invading.

She kissed him back, her hands balling into fists, pressing them to his hips. This was reckless and dangerous and downright stupid, but she gave in to the insistent pangs of arousal as they coursed through her. She touched her tongue to his, marveling at the flood of sensation.

Her body tightened with desire. Her hips pushed against his thighs. His palms slipped down her back, cupping her rear, pulling her close, then lifting her to press her intimately to him, her thighs wrapping around his body. The kisses went on, heated and impatient as he turned to perch her on the table.

His hands slipped under her T-shirt, kneading her bare waist, making their way up. She could feel her nipples harden beneath her cotton bra, tingling in anticipation, waiting for his touch, desperate for his touch.

"This is bad," he rasped.

No, it was good. It was too good. It was ridiculously good.

"There are cameras," he said.

That got her attention.

She jerked back. "Here?"

He nodded.

"Is someone watching?"

"Probably Vegas."

She struggled to quash her hormones, to catch her breath, to summon up the guilt and embarrassment the situation warranted. She was kissing her boss. More than that, she was making out like a crazed teenager with the very man judging her professionalism.

Maybe this was a test. It was probably a test. She'd passed weapons proficiency only to fail miserably at self-control. She scrambled to salvage the situation, seizing on the first idea that hit her brain.

"About me going to South America?" She dredged up a coquettish smile and blinked up at him.

His eyes went flat along with his voice. "Are you kidding me?"

She brazened it out, walking her fingertips up his chest. "I speak pretty good Spanish."

He trapped her hand with his, squeezing it tight. "You're telling me this was persuasion?"

She looked him straight in the eyes. "Of course it was persuasion."

"You're lying."

"Are you sure?"

"I'm sure."

She lifted a brow. "You believe you're that irresistible?"

His expression flinched.

"Think about it, Troy." She gave a careless little laugh.

He grasped her chin, holding her head still, staring into her eyes.

Anxiety overtook her. She ordered herself not to crack, to hold onto her self-control. If he knew she'd melted like sugar in his arms, he'd kick her to the curb.

His jaw clamped tight, and the moment stretched into infinity.

"Don't you ever," he growled, "*ever* try to play me again."

She'd have nodded, but his grip was too tight.

"Got it?" he demanded.

"Yes," she whispered.

He turned abruptly away, and she all but sagged against the table.

"Anyone else see it?" Troy asked Vegas as he marched into the control room.

"No," Vegas answered.

"Delete it."

"Already done."

Troy halted, relief easing the knot in his chest. He didn't really know why he cared. It was no skin off his nose if the guys saw him kissing Mila.

"Thanks," he said.

"I did it for her."

"No kidding."

There was no reason to protect Troy's reputation. It was Mila who would suffer if anybody saw the footage. And she'd brought it on herself. Still, Troy didn't want to make her life even more difficult while she was here. Only a colossal jerk would do that.

"I don't know what I was thinking," he muttered to himself.

"I know exactly what you were thinking," said Vegas.

"I don't usually let women play me."

"Huh?" Vegas looked surprised.

"She's better at it than I expected." Troy's mind rewound to the shooting range. "A lot of women have tried. I can usually spot it coming a mile away. And her? *Her.* I had every reason in the world to suspect she'd try something."

"What makes you think she was playing you?"

Troy gave his partner a look of astonishment. "Intellect and reason. She's looking for a permanent job."

"Doesn't mean she'll use seduction."

"She admitted that she did."

Vegas peered at him. "She admitted she was playing you?"

It took Troy a moment to frame a response. "Is there something wrong with the way I'm speaking English?"

"Nothing wrong with the way you're talking," Vegas said, glancing to the monitors and punching a couple of computer keys.

Troy was hit with a sudden suspicion. "You didn't put her up to it, did you? You were just yankin' my chain yesterday."

Vegas raised his palms in a gesture of mock surrender. "I've got *way* better things to do with my time."

"So do I."

"That's reassuring. The footage is deleted. It's like it never happened."

"That's what I wanted to hear."

As far as Troy was concerned, the kiss had never happened. It had been tradecraft, that was all. Mila was a beautiful woman. She knew it and had seen an advantage in flirting with him. Under normal circumstances, if she was on an operation, he'd admire her skill.

"Did she pass?" Vegas asked.

"Yes."

Mila was definitely proficient in the use of firearms.

"Care to elaborate?"

"She's good with a gun. Her reaction time is acceptable, so is her judgment under fire."

"A ringing endorsement," Vegas drawled.

"What do you want me to say?"

"She scored 100 percent in the tactical house."

"Lots of guys do that."

"And we hire them."

"Are you making a point?" asked Troy.

"What are you going to do if she aces it all?"

"She's five feet four, less than a hundred and twenty pounds. There's no amount of training, grit or determination that gets her through the obstacle course."

"True enough," said Vegas. "Your sister is on her way down."

Troy glanced at the elevator camera feed to see Kassidy inside with a crying Drake in her arms. She looked exhausted, her purple hair messy and her makeup smeared.

"I'm glad we don't have audio," said Vegas.

"This is ridiculous," said Troy.

"Might be a good time to suggest she rethink her life plan."

On the monitor, the elevator doors opened. Down the hall, Drake's piercing cries echoed along the passage.

The sound grew inexorably louder until Kassidy came through the doorway.

"He's teething," she said.

"So you brought him *here*?" Troy's question sounded like an accusation.

"I needed to talk to you."

"We're trying to work here." Even as he admonished her, he found himself taking the blubbering Drake from her arms.

He had no desire to be anywhere near the shrieking, soggy, slimy baby, but Kassidy looked as if she was about to keel over. There was simply no other way to avoid imminent injury to both of them.

He put Drake to his shoulder, cringing as the kid's snotty nose came into contact with his neck.

"His gums are all red and swollen," said Kassidy.

"Can you give him something?"

Surely modern medicine had come up with a cure for swollen baby gums. Aspirin came to mind, or maybe a little whiskey. A little whiskey might also put the poor kid to sleep for a while.

"I *have*," Kassidy wailed. "More than once. It's supposed to numb his mouth. But it doesn't seem to help at all."

A numbing agent struck Troy as a decent idea. Still, Drake continued to cry in his ear.

"How's the nanny search coming?" he asked her.

"The service wants a deposit." Kassidy bit her bottom lip. "I was wondering…"

She looked sweet and defenseless in her pretty pastel blouse and yoga pants.

"No problem," he said. "I'll add it to the total."

"You don't have to say it like that," she snapped back.

"Like what?"

"Like you don't expect me to ever pay it back. I'm going to pay it back."

Vegas stepped in. "Have you ever paid anything back?"

Kassidy turned on him. "I'm earning money now. More money than ever. It just takes a while for it to get into the pipe. There are up-front costs, and…"

Troy tried jiggling Drake, figuring the motion might distract him.

Vegas arched a look at Drake. "And it's a pretty expensive new hobby you've taken on."

"He's not a hobby," said Kassidy. "He's a human being." She took Drake from Troy's arms as if to rescue him. "What is *wrong* with you people?"

"I said yes," Troy pointed out. "Tell the service to invoice me."

"They want a check up front."

"Fine. Whatever. Just find a good nanny."

Twin tears formed in Kassidy's big eyes, and Troy felt like a heel.

Before he could apologize, Mila appeared, taking in the scene.

"What's going on here?" she asked Troy. "What did you do?"

It was her turn to take Drake from Kassidy's arms.

"Me?" Troy asked.

"Why is everybody crying?"

"He's teething," he found himself answering.

Mila put a hand on Kassidy's shoulder. "Did something happen? Did you get another email?"

Troy jumped on the non-baby topic. "Another email?"

Kassidy was shaking her head.

"She desperately needs some sleep," Mila said to Troy. "She's got a gig tonight."

"And that has *what* to do with me?"

Mila frowned at him. "Nice."

"What nice? I just told her I'd foot the nanny bill."

Mila handed Drake back to Troy.

"You have *got* to be kidding," said Troy.

Out of the corner of his eye, he saw Vegas smirk.

"I'm putting Kassidy to bed," said Mila.

"I'm *working.*"

"I'll be back."

"You have five minutes," he told her.

She rolled her eyes in response, ushering Kassidy out the door and down the hall.

Drake's cries turned to blubbers.

"Well played," said Vegas.

"Shut up," said Troy.

"Do you think Mila will come back?"

"If she doesn't, I'm hunting her down."

Troy rubbed a hand up and down Drake's back, his sympathies engaged. He tried rocking the baby, hoping to lull him to sleep. The poor kid sure hadn't won any prizes so far in life.

Troy paused to listen outside his apartment door. He preferred to cook his own dinner, but if Drake was up and crying, he'd head down the block to The Devon Grill.

Silence.

He slid his key card into the lock, opened the door and crept cautiously into the foyer. All he could hear was the whir of the heating system, and then clicks as someone typed on a keyboard. He moved around the corner, bringing into view his living room and the dining room beyond.

Mila was at the dining table. Her head was bent over a laptop computer, and the space around her was littered with papers. Her hair was in its usual neat braid. Her blue T-shirt was stretched over her slim shoulders. And Drake was sleeping against her, balanced on her arm, his face tucked into her neck.

Troy moved quietly across the carpet to where she could see him, having no desire whatsoever to speak and wake the sleeping baby.

She caught sight of him and looked up. Then she pointed to Drake and put a finger across her lips.

"Where's Kassidy?" he whispered.

"Sleeping."

"No nanny?"

Mila gave a small shake of her head. "There's one coming by at seven for an interview."

"What about the last one? She seemed okay." In Troy's mind, expediency was more important than perfection in the circumstances.

"She only does occasional work."

"Oh. Well, could she come occasionally tonight?"

Mila smiled. "Hopefully the new one will work out."

Drake squirmed against her.

"Can you put him in his crib?" Troy asked.

"I tried a few times. He just woke right up again."

"We're waking him by talking."

She glanced down at the baby. "I guess I can't let him sleep forever."

Troy wasn't ready to discard that as a valid approach to child rearing. Babies definitely seemed easier when they were fast asleep.

Then she gave a grimace. "My arm's asleep."

He heaved a sigh and gently gathered Drake to nestle him against his own shoulder.

"Thanks," said Mila, rubbing her left arm.

She met Troy's gaze for a moment, and then seemed to remember the awkwardness of their morning. She quickly glanced down at the table.

"I've been working through some club records," she told him, moving some of the papers around, her words rapid, tone louder.

Drake wiggled some more against him.

"For Kassidy's last twenty gigs. I convinced the clubs to give me credit card records for ticket sales and drinks, and I'm loading the names into a database. So far, I'm not seeing any distinct patterns. And a lot of people pay cash at the door, so I don't know how far this will get us. But it's a start."

"Repeat customers?" he asked, moving so he could see her computer screen.

"Some. I've got more data to enter. Then I'll track down photos and see where facial recognition gets me."

Troy had to admit, it was a solid start to the investigation. He couldn't fault her work so far.

He gazed down at her profile, noting the cute slope of her nose, the translucence of her skin, the length of her dark lashes and the intense color of her full lips. He remembered kissing them. Even now, he could feel their heat, taste their sweetness, and he experienced that potent rush of hormones all over again.

She glanced up, looking instantly startled by the expression on his face.

He quickly cleared his throat, tamping down the desire to drag her into his arms. "Are you up for another test tomorrow?"

It took her a beat to answer. "Which one?"

"Tradecraft theory." It was a written test, and he wouldn't need to be in the room while she wrote it.

"That doesn't give me any time to study."

"You don't get to study."

"That doesn't seem very fair."

"This is about what you know, not what you can cram into your brain overnight."

"I'll be with your sister overnight."

"Shall we say ten a.m.?"

Drake began to vocalize in Troy's ear. The crying was going to start any minute.

"You're not going to give me any chance at all, are you?" she asked.

"I'm giving you exactly the same chance as anyone else. Is there a bottle around? I'm no expert, but I think this guy might be hungry when he wakes up."

Mila came to her feet and turned for the kitchen. "I don't believe you."

Troy followed. "That he'll be hungry?"

"Ha-ha." She passed through to the kitchen. "That you give all of your employees a pop quiz on tradecraft."

"I do."

She removed a baby bottle from the fridge and turned on the hot water. "You want me to fail."

"I expect you to fail. That's not the same thing."

She held the bottle to warm under the running water. "You also want me to fail."

Drake was whimpering now, taking in deeper breaths, obviously working up to something more impressive.

Troy went around the island, moving closer to Mila and the bottle, wanting to pop it into Drake's mouth just as soon as it was ready.

"I don't know what you think you'll achieve," he said. "Why put yourself through this?"

"I want a job."

"I've already told you I'm not hiring you permanently."

She looked up at him. "I'm trying to change your mind."

He fought against the distraction of her crystalline green eyes. He knew she thought this was simple. It was anything but.

"It won't work," he told her.

"We don't know that yet."

"One of us does. Honestly, Mila, save your strength. You can't talk me into it, and you can't seduce me into it."

She shut off the tap. "I don't want to get a job by seducing you or anyone else."

He lifted his brow in disbelief. "Then why did you try it this morning?"

"It was a lark. I was curious to see if it would work."

"It didn't," he lied. "I didn't give you a job." He could at least cling to that.

She handed him the bottle. "I'd have turned it down anyway."

"Now who's lying?"

She seemed to think about that. "You're right. I'm lying. I'd have taken it. Sad, isn't it?"

"That your moral fortitude isn't all that you'd like it to be?"

He doubted many people could make that claim. He sure couldn't.

Drake let out a cry. Instead of answering Troy's question, Mila handed him the bottle and headed back to the dining room table.

Troy moved the baby across his left arm as he walked, putting the bottle into Drake's mouth, wiggling it so that he latched on. It didn't feel as awkward as it had the first few times Troy had fed him.

"You're not going to answer, are you?" he asked her.

"Would you?"

He took the chair cornerwise to hers. "I've got no claim on moral fortitude." He made the decision to toss it back out on the table. "I kissed an employee this morning."

Mila didn't look up from the laptop. "She kissed you back."

"Vegas deleted the footage."

She nodded. "I really wasn't thinking about cameras."

"I'm always thinking about cameras."

She did look up then, an expression of skepticism on her face.

"Maybe not in that precise moment," he admitted.

He hadn't been thinking about anything but her.

"If the video got out, I'm not sure who it would be worse for, you or me."

"Worse for you inside Pinion. Worse for me anywhere else."

She gave a considered nod. "That sounds about right."

"I do have moments of intelligence."

For some reason, she glanced sharply up. "You have nothing *but* intelligence."

The compliment surprised him.

"That's why I'm here, Troy. I want to learn from you. I

looked at all of my options and realized you were the guy with the most to teach me."

Something flipped over in Troy's stomach. Her expression was open, honest and heart-haltingly gorgeous. And he couldn't think of anything more gratifying than teaching her everything he'd ever known about security and everything else.

But he couldn't let himself go there. He couldn't teach her the trade. He'd be teaching her how to die.

Five

In the wings offstage, Mila scrolled through the messages with hashtag KassidyKeiser and KassidyRocks. It was exciting to see them coming through by the minute, but disconcerting to try to keep up. She breezed past the comments on Kassidy's singing, her choice of songs and tonight's outfit. Mila couldn't help but smile at the female fans' oohs and ahhs over the sexily unkempt drummer.

Coming up on midnight, Kassidy was gyrating her way through the second set. The club was full again, with a line on the sidewalk outside. There were Kassidy Keiser posters on the wall, and they'd even printed some Kassidy Keiser drink coasters. Mila had a feeling that the nanny's salary was not going to be a problem much longer.

Eileen arrived by her side.

"T-shirts," she said to Mila in a loud voice above the guitar solo. "I'm ordering T-shirts and hats."

"Did you print the coasters?" Mila asked.

Eileen nodded. "And the posters." She pointed to the nearest one. "See the pattern of the purple spotlights?"

"I do," said Mila.

"I've got a graphic design company using that and a silhouette of Kassidy's profile to come up with a logo."

"Nice."

"It always helps when the talent is gorgeous."

"Kassidy is definitely pretty."

It was covered up most of the time with funky hair, exaggerated makeup and wild clothes. But Kassidy was a very beautiful young woman.

"She's going all the way," said Eileen.

Mila scanned the crowd. Everyone was on their feet, pressed up close to the stage. She was willing to bet they'd broken the fire code a few hours back. The club had to be making a killing.

She glanced back down at her phone, continuing through the endless stream of texts. Then a word popped out and she halted her thumb, scrolling backward.

A text from someone called MeMyHeart said, Drake's one lucky little boy.

A few pictures had been posted by fans online of Kassidy with Drake in his stroller. People could easily assume she was his mother. But to find his name? That would have taken a significant level of investigation.

Mila tapped MeMyHeart, finding a dozen other messages from the past hours. Judging by the message content, MeMyHeart was here. She scanned the audience, but it was dark and chaotic. Everyone out there would have a cell phone.

Her heart rate had kicked up, and her instincts told her to call Troy. But she stopped herself. Slow and methodical, that was still the best course of action.

Instead, she called Pinion's main number, getting Edison.

"It's Mila. Can someone check a cell number for me?"

"What's the reason?"

"They're tweeting about Kassidy, and it looks suspicious."

"Can do," said Edison. "Forward the tweet." He rattled off a number.

"On its way." She continued her visual scan of the audience, checking for expressions that seemed too intent on Kassidy, maybe not so much into the music.

"Hang on," said Edison. "Everything else okay there?"

"The place is rocking."

Edison chuckled. "Don't tell the boss I said so, but his sister is smokin' hot."

There was a crackle on the line, and then Edison's tone abruptly changed.

"Vegas wants to talk to you," he said.

"Sure," said Mila, moving slightly back in an effort to get away from some of the noise.

"It's a burner," said Vegas.

"The phone?"

"Whoever sent the tweet used a burner phone. But they're close, within a two-block radius, probably there."

"You read it?"

"Yeah. You want backup?"

"I'm not pressing the panic button," said Mila. "It could be nothing. I'll get as many pictures as I can."

"How's she doing?"

"Fantastic. You want me to bring you a Kassidy Keiser coaster?"

"No, thanks. But I'm picking you up."

"I've got my car."

"I'll tail you."

Mila hesitated. She didn't want to hand things over to Vegas just when they got a little interesting. But she didn't want to take chances, either. Her goal was to protect Kassidy, not to show off for Troy.

"Sure," she said. "I'm parked beside the stage door. I'm driving—"

"I know what you're driving." Vegas sounded vaguely insulted.

Mila wasn't sure how to respond. She decided to let it drop. "There'll probably be a crowd."

"I'll see you out there." He hung up.

She focused again on Kassidy, noting the almost imperceptible croak to her voice. She'd put in a really long night, singing some of her toughest songs. Her skin shone with sweat, and her heavy makeup was starting to crack along the edges. Her hair was messy, but then, it had started the evening that way. Unless you knew her well, it was hard to tell the difference.

Mila switched her attention to the crowd, raising her phone and snapping a multipanel panoramic shot. Then she focused on men who appeared to be alone. She made her way down the short staircase onto the floor, moving to the back, surreptitiously taking picture after picture. She slipped through the front entrance, nodding to the bouncers, and took in the crowd on the street.

By the time she made it back inside, Kassidy was bowing to a thundering ovation. Kassidy skipped her way offstage, blowing kisses to the audience, and the house lights came up a notch. Purely from the point of Kassidy's obvious exhaustion, Mila was glad they were skipping the encore tonight.

She pocketed her phone and jogged up the stage stairs, then along back of the curtain and down the dark, narrow hallway to the small dressing room. She took note of all the faces she was passing by, at least vaguely recognizing each of them as staff members.

The dressing room door was open, the space elbow to elbow. Eileen seemed excited, talking to Kassidy and one of the backup band members.

"Six months," said Eileen. "A trial on both sides."

The band member—Mila remembered his name was Arthur—spoke directly to Kassidy.

"What do you say, babe?"

Kassidy grinned. "I say we do it." Then she spotted Mila. "Hey, Mila. We're gonna sign a contract with Bumper. Eileen's putting together the tour."

Mila wasn't surprised by the news. Eileen had been talking about a tour all week long. Bumper was a solid backup band, and continuity obviously made sense for Kassidy.

"You ready to go?" Mila asked.

Kassidy heaved an exaggerated sigh. "I guess I have to."

"You look tired."

"I'm not. But it'll take a while to get to the car. Did you hear from Gabby or Troy?"

They'd found a nanny in Gabby Reed, who had started work two days ago.

"No news is good news," said Mila.

Kassidy slung her bag over her shoulder. "Catch you guys later," she called.

The three band members waved their goodbyes.

"Call me when you get up tomorrow," said Eileen.

"Toodle-oo." Kassidy waggled her fingers as they made their way toward the door.

Mila went first, cutting through one end of the kitchen to the delivery entrance. There she pushed open a steel door that led to a small concrete staircase. The alley behind the building was wide and decently lit, and a cheer came up from the assembled crowd that surged forward as Kassidy exited.

She put on a big grin and waved to them.

There were more people than last night, and Mila braced herself. She waded into the crowd with Kassidy on her heels. It was slow going. Fans stuffed papers and pens into Kassidy's hand and stuck their faces next to hers for selfies.

Mila's gaze darted from face to face, checking out body language and noting the objects in everyone's hands. Cell phones mostly, CDs, pens, nothing so far that looked dangerous.

Her gaze snagged on a thirty-something man with neat hair and a mustache. He was scowling, frowning at the people jostling around him. He looked out of place in a blazer and tie. But then she checked his hands and saw he had a CD.

"Mila?" Kassidy's voice sounded shaky behind her.

Mila whirled to find a large man squeezing Kassidy close, taking a picture of the two of them together.

Mila swiftly inserted herself between the two, elbowing the guy in the solar plexus, temporarily knocking the wind out of him. She looped an arm around Kassidy and threaded her way swiftly through the crowd toward the car.

Vegas met her halfway there, taking up a position on the other side of Kassidy.

"You two okay?" he asked as they keep moving.

"Under control," said Mila, hitting the button to unlock her SUV.

Without slowing her momentum, she reached out and pulled open the passenger door. She propelled Kassidy neatly into the seat and locked the door behind her.

"Is this normal?" Vegas asked as they rounded the front of the vehicle.

Flashes went off as fans took pictures through the vehicle windows.

"This is more people than usual," said Mila.

"Why didn't you say something?"

She turned to put her back to the driver's door. "I did say something. I told Troy the crowds were building. I told him her popularity was growing. And I recommended, on more than one occasion, that we formalize a security plan for Kassidy. He thought I was bucking for a full-time job."

"You are."

"I am. But that doesn't change my assessment of the situation."

"I'll talk to him," said Vegas.

Mila tried to keep the bitterness from her voice. "Because if a *man* says it, it has to be true?"

"Because I've got no skin in the game. Part of your job, Mila, is to make Troy listen when he doesn't want to listen."

"You don't think I've tried."

"Obviously not hard enough."

She told herself to control her temper. "You're asking the impossible."

"No, I'm asking the difficult. Did somebody tell you this job wasn't difficult?"

Mila counted to three. "No."

"Then, suck it up, princess. There are no awards for effort in this game."

"I'm not asking for an award." She understood that results were the only thing that mattered.

"Good," said Vegas.

"This is the biggest crowd so far." She scanned the sea of people. "It's the first time anyone's mentioned Drake. It's the first time Kassidy has been nervous. And I'll be making a full report to Troy in the morning."

"You do that," said Vegas, his tone completely even. He

glanced past her to where Kassidy sat in the passenger seat. "I'll follow you back."

Mila turned to the driver's door and used the key instead of the button, not wanting to risk unlocking Kassidy's side.

As she levered into the seat, she struggled against her disappointment. This had been a chance to impress Vegas. It was his company, too, and she got the sense that he was more open than Troy to hiring a woman. But she'd blown it.

Technically, she hadn't done anything wrong. But it was clear he thought she'd been sloppy. He thought she'd let the situation get out of control.

She slammed the door behind her, locked it, then gripped the steering wheel, swearing once under her breath.

"You okay?" asked Kassidy.

"Fine," said Mila, starting the engine. "You?"

"That was wild." Kassidy seemed more exhilarated than upset.

"I'm going to talk to your brother tomorrow. We definitely need some help."

"Where did Vegas come from?" asked Kassidy.

"I called him earlier."

"He seemed ticked off."

"He thinks I screwed up."

"*You?* How on earth did you screw up? You're the only one helping me. You want me to talk to him?"

Mila pulled the vehicle into Drive. "No. No. Don't worry about it."

"Seriously, Mila. If he's bein' a jerk."

"He's not being a jerk." The last thing Mila needed was Kassidy jumping in to defend her. "He was just surprised. I don't think he was expecting this kind of a crowd."

Kassidy gazed out her window as they cleared the alley and turned onto the street. "Neither was I." She gave a little giggle. "That was awesome."

"It *was* awesome," Mila agreed. "You were terrific on-stage tonight."

"I'm really lovin' the guys from Bumper. I'm glad they want to stick around."

"Who wouldn't want to stick around? You've got to be the best thing that ever happened to them."

"They're a really good band."

The SUV picked up speed, and the streetlights flashed by.

"It's a weird thing in the music biz," Kassidy continued. "A singer can be good, and a band can be good, but the combination can really suck. Or, apart the two are decent, but together they're fantastic. It's like complementary smells. You put cinnamon and sugar together, it's magic. Sage and butter, all good. But try sage and sugar, and it's yucksville."

Mila smiled at the analogy.

Kassidy covered her mouth with a yawn. "Do you like Gabby?"

"I do," said Mila, having become used to Kassidy's sudden changes in topic. The new nanny seemed very calm, very soft-spoken, but also very organized.

"What about Troy?" asked Kassidy.

Mila tensed. Why was Kassidy asking about Troy? Had Mila given herself away? She had tried to keep her emotions under wraps, been careful not to gaze at him, attempted to keep at least an arm's length between them.

"What do you mean?" she asked cautiously.

"Do you think he likes Gabby?"

Gabby? Was Troy attracted to Gabby? Mila hadn't even thought of that. Gabby was youngish, fairly attractive, not glamorous, more down-to-earth. Which was fine. There was nothing wrong with being down-to-earth.

"In what way?" Mila asked.

Kassidy stared at her for a moment. "As a *nanny*."

"Oh."

"What did you think I meant?"

"That's what I thought you meant."

"Did you think I meant *like*, like?"

"No, no." Mila determinedly shook her head.

"I don't think Gabby is at all Troy's type. He's always been, well, a player, really. He likes women tall and blonde, with long legs and high heels and fashions straight off a Paris runway."

Mila didn't care. She truly didn't care what the heck Troy liked in women. The farther she was from his type, the better. Though he had seemed to like kissing her. So, well, he wasn't completely immune to her as a woman.

Not that she wanted him to see her as a woman. She wanted him to see her as a security agent. No more, no less. That was *all* she wanted.

"Wait a minute," said Kassidy, a trace of excitement in her voice. "Are you interested in—"

"No!" Mila realized her protest was too quick and too sharp. "No. I work for him. That's all. Nothing more." She needed to get this right. "Hey, would I dress like this if I wanted him to notice me as a woman?"

Kassidy seemed to give it some thought. "Good point. Those boots? Wow. Give me a break."

Mila couldn't help but glance down at her feet.

She should have felt relieved, but she couldn't stop a twinge of disappointment. They were work boots, that was all. She had to dress sensibly to do her job. Surely Troy understood that.

Then she realized she was acting as though she cared. She didn't. Troy's opinion of her as a woman was completely irrelevant.

Mila finished her tradecraft exam with thirty seconds to spare. She clicked the done button and a scroll bar appeared at the bottom of the screen, counting off the time while the machine calculated her score.

The door to the small meeting room opened and Troy walked in, shutting it behind him.

He leaned against it. "Vegas says you downplayed the risks last night."

The scroll bar was 20 percent done. In about two minutes, she'd know her score on the exam.

"I didn't downplay anything," she said, dragging her gaze from the screen to Troy. "*You* wouldn't listen to me."

"You want to blame the boss?"

"I want to acknowledge the truth." She glanced back to the screen. Forty-seven percent done.

He moved toward her. "The truth is Kassidy was accosted last night."

"It was a fan taking a selfie." Mila stood so he wouldn't tower over her.

"We're putting together a formal protection plan."

"Great idea, Troy," she drawled. "Too bad nobody thought of it earlier."

He leaned in. "Do it. Say, 'I told you so.'"

"To the boss?" she finished for him before she could censor herself.

His blue eyes flared, and she immediately regretted the rash words.

"I'm sorry," she offered. "That was out of line."

"I have no idea what to do with you."

Before she could answer, he continued, "But we are upping Kassidy's protection. Vegas is going to take point."

"What?" Mila voiced her shock. "Wait. No. Kassidy is my detail."

"You're contradicting me."

"Yes."

"You have to be the most insubordinate person I have ever met."

She struggled to keep her temper in check. He was marginalizing her. He was marginalizing her solely because she was a woman.

"Don't do it," she told him, determined not to be replaced by Vegas.

He eased closer, his gaze searching hers, his hand just barely brushing her forearm.

"Don't do what?" His voice had dropped to a whisper.

He'd deliberately switched topics, and her attraction stirred. Oh, no. This was bad.

His blue eyes softened, and his full lips parted.

She felt a zip of reaction right down to her toes. The kiss was coming. She could taste it on her lips and feel it in her chest, hot and heavy, a demand that had to be satisfied.

Her hands twitched. She ordered herself to push him away. She could do it. She could have him flat on his back before he saw it coming. But instead she touched his arm, feeling the steel of his biceps, the heat of his skin, the brush of his T-shirt sleeve.

His lips werc on hers in a second. His hand splayed at the base of her spine, jerking her forward. She arched against him, tipping her chin, parting her lips, catapulting into instant paradise.

Man, he was a good kisser. The pressure was right, the angle was perfect and he tasted fantastic. Her hands tightened on his arms, anchoring herself while the world began to spin faster.

"This is ridiculous." Vegas's voice was like a splash of cold water.

Mila jerked back, but Troy kept her hips plastered to him.

"You're adults. If you want to do it, just—"

"We don't," Mila barked, feeling her face heat.

"—get it over with," said Vegas.

"We don't," Mila repeated, breaking Troy's hold and stepping away.

"Whatever." Vegas shook his head in obvious exasperation and moved to the computer.

Mila didn't dare look at Troy.

"You got ninety-eight," said Vegas.

She immediately perked up. "On the exam?"

"I sure wasn't grading you on the kiss." Vegas turned the screen toward her.

She took in the score and smiled. "Is that good? It has to be good."

"That's four questions wrong," said Troy.

"How do people usually do?" she asked.

"It's good," said Vegas.

"You're fine on theory," said Troy.

"And on planning," she felt compelled to add. "And in the field, and in reporting and analysis."

"When's Kassidy's next performance?" Troy asked.

His demeanor had switched to professional, remote. She told herself she was glad.

"Thursday," she answered. "Four days."

"I'll need your report by tonight."

She gave him a nod. "The mention of Drake is my biggest worry."

As far as Mila was concerned, that took the potential threat to a whole new level. Whoever MeMyHeart was had researched Kassidy's personal life and was trying to connect with her on a far more intimate level.

"I'm thinking three of us," she continued, speaking to Troy. "One outside, me backstage and one in the crowd."

"Vegas can—"

"I don't need Vegas," she interrupted.

Troy's eyes flared with obvious displeasure.

"Vegas can vet the plan, but he doesn't need to be on-site," she said.

Troy looked to Vegas.

"The guy wants to get close to her," said Mila. "He probably wants to date her. There's nothing to indicate he wants to do her harm. You've gone from zero to sixty in a heartbeat."

"You two work it out," said Vegas, backing toward the door. "I'll be in the control room, watching Prince Matin buy a new yacht."

"You don't get to dictate your own job," Troy said to Mila as the door closed behind Vegas.

"I can make recommendations." Mila didn't want to push

too far, but if she was shoved aside, she'd never be able to prove her worth. "Do other security agents make recommendations?"

Troy didn't answer.

She struggled to come up with a convincing argument. "Try this. Close your eyes and pretend I'm a man."

"That's not about to happen."

"Sit down."

He raised his brow, looking affronted. "Excuse me?"

She gave herself a beat, slowing things down, trying to work up an appropriate level of deference without compromising her bargaining position.

She sat down on one of the meeting table chairs. "Please, Troy. Have a seat so we can talk."

He watched her with what seemed like impatience.

"Please?" she repeated.

"This is ridiculous."

"Don't think of me as a woman."

"That's impossible." But he sat.

"All I'm asking," she said, measuring her words, watching the nuances of his expression for clues of what he thought, "is that you let me form a plan for Kassidy. If you don't like it, fine. If you think I'm incompetent, then hand it all off to Vegas. But give me a chance to show you what I can do. I'm just another security agent."

His gaze flicked to her lips. "No, you're not."

"Forget you ever kissed me."

"I can't."

"You have to."

"Maybe Vegas is right."

The statement threw her. "About what?"

"We should get it over with."

"We should…" Mila suddenly realized what he meant. "You think we should *sleep* together?"

"It might alleviate the tension."

"You did *not* just say that."

"Pretending you're a man isn't going to work."

Her voice rose with indignation, along with the slightest touch of panic. "Well, having a fling with my boss sure isn't going to work."

He sat back in his chair. "You're probably right."

"I'm absolutely right."

"But it would be fun."

She went momentarily speechless, and the two of them stared at each other. Their latest kiss replayed itself inside her head.

"Is this why you don't hire women?" she asked. "Because you can't keep your hands off them?"

For some reason, Troy laughed.

"I don't think it's funny."

"That's absurd. I have *enormous* self-control."

"As do I."

Abruptly, they both went quiet, their gazes locking.

A muscle ticked in Troy's cheek, and he drummed his fingertips against one knee.

She could almost hear the question echoing through his brain. It was the same question she was asking herself.

If that was true, then what had just happened?

Six

Mila and her sister, Zoey, rode side by side on a bike pathway along the Potomac. Sunday's frosty morning had turned into a sunny afternoon. Mila had a ton of work to get done on Kassidy's security plan, but clearing her head with fresh air seemed like a good idea.

"That's bloody inconvenient," said Zoey.

"That I'm attracted to my boss?" Mila asked as she downshifted her bike to start up a rise in the path.

"That he's attracted to you in return. I trust you to keep yourself under control."

"Why don't you trust him? You don't even know him. And he's an extremely squared-away guy." Sure, Troy had kissed Mila a couple of times, but it hadn't gone any further. In fact, he was the one who'd called a halt at the gun range.

"Guys are guys," said Zoey.

"I don't even know what that means."

They passed under a grove of golden aspens.

"It means," said Zoey, "in the moment, they don't have a lot of self-control."

"In the moment, apparently neither do I."

"You can't sleep with him." Zoey sounded worried.

"He offered. I said no. I already told you that. What I really need is a great protection plan for Kassidy. *That's* what will help him see me differently."

"How's it coming along?"

"Slowly," Mila admitted. "I'm beginning to think this MeMyHeart is using more than one alias to text and email."

A cold breeze wafted up from the river, and they went into single file to go around a group of people who were out walking.

Zoey pulled alongside again. "What makes you think that?"

"A few specific words: *watch*, *gaze*, *view* and *window*."

"That's creepy."

"At Troy's, she's on the ninth floor."

"He could have binoculars."

"I thought of that." Mila was going to recommend sheers or opaque shades for Kassidy's bedroom window. She was also going to get one of Pinion's technical guys to encrypt the baby monitor. It was password protected, but she didn't want to take any chances.

She was gradually meeting the other Pinion agents. It was clear they were surprised by her gender, but they were also polite and professional. A little too polite, but she supposed she couldn't expect to be one of the guys overnight.

"Does that change your security plan?" Zoey asked.

Mila nodded. "A broad-spectrum plan is different than a plan for a specific threat."

"Will that impress Troy?"

"Only if he agrees with my analysis. If he doesn't, it'll set me back."

A flock of ducks lifted off the river, quacking as they became airborne.

"Could you do two plans?" asked Zoey. "One for each scenario?"

"That'll show a lack of commitment and a lack of faith in my own analysis. The safe route is a broad-spectrum plan. The high-risk, high-reward approach is to go with my analysis and focus on the specific threat."

"If not for Troy—if you weren't second-guessing yourself based on his reaction—what would you do?"

"Specific threat," Mila said without hesitation.

There was something off about MeMyHeart. And Mila couldn't get the guy in the blazer out of her mind. He might have been just another fan, but there'd been something too intent in his expression. He might have been looking for an autograph for his CD, but he had also been annoyed. Had he been annoyed at Kassidy, at someone around her, at the situation?

"There's your answer," said Zoey. "Trust your instincts.

Don't let him get under your skin. Sure, he knows his stuff. But so do you."

"I wish I had more concrete facts. The last thing Troy wants to hear is that it's a woman's intuition."

"A woman's intuition—*anybody's* intuition—is the sum of concrete microfacts, filtered by your subconscious. Just because the conscious part of your brain hasn't yet figured something out doesn't mean it's not true."

Mila couldn't help but smile.

"What?" asked Zoey.

"I'm trying to picture Troy keeping quiet long enough for me to explain the psychological origins of intuition."

"I think your real problem will be keeping his primitive brain from drowning out everything else." Zoey affected a deep, pounding voice. *"Sexy woman, must have her."*

"I asked him," said Mila.

"Asked him what?"

"If he didn't hire women because he couldn't keep his hands off them."

Zoey grinned in the sunshine. "That won't help you get a job, but I like your style."

"It was an honest question."

It probably wasn't the wisest question in the world. But at the time, Mila had been serious. Kassidy had described Troy as a player. He obviously liked women, a lot of women, evidently.

A pulse of jealously pushed into her brain. She quashed it. Troy's sex life was entirely his own business. She only wanted him to take her seriously as a security agent. This sexual attraction to him would wear off. It had to wear off.

"Did he give you an honest answer?" asked Zoey.

"He did. He told me he had enormous self-control. He seemed sincere. You know, according to my woman's intuition."

"Then he's got it bad for you."

Mila found herself looking down at her incredibly ordinary figure, clad in gray yoga pants, a worn T-shirt, scuffed runners and a unisex windbreaker. Her hair was thrown into a ponytail, and she'd left the house without makeup. Again.

"Why?" she asked her sister. "It's not like I'm you."

Zoey rolled her eyes. "The sum of concrete microfacts, filtered by his subconscious."

"Telling him what?"

"That you'd give him healthy children."

"Whoa." Mila's bike wobbled, and it took her a moment to recover.

"Or that you could defend the family and the village. That you could skin and cook the mastodon. Our primitive drivers are our primitive drivers. We can't control them."

"I'm not skinning anything. And I don't think I'm interested in being any man's fit and healthy specimen of a child-bearing woman."

"Fair's fair," said Zoey. "You're always looking for a fit and healthy specimen of a man."

Mila had to admit it was true. "Am I shallow?"

"Not at all. Your primitive brain is telling you he can hunt and defend your children."

"My primitive brain is annoying."

Mila didn't *want* to want to sleep with Troy. But she did. There, she'd admitted it. She seriously wanted to sleep with Troy. At least she did at some primitive level.

Good thing her nonprimitive brain could override her instincts.

Mila was more than halfway through the Pinion obstacle course, and Troy couldn't help but be impressed by her grit. Her strength left something to be desired, but if he was grading on determination, she'd be getting full marks. Unfortunately for her, successful completion was all about timing.

It was a circuitous route over twenty wooded acres behind the company building. The standards allowed four hours to complete the challenging course. Most of their successful recruits did it in three.

Mila did well on the balance challenges. It was obvious she did a lot of running. And she'd done better than he expected on the mud and water obstacles. Her big challenge was strength. She was halfway up the rope-climbing wall, and her arms were shaking with the strain.

On the sidelines, he moved toward her, shouting up.

"You want to call it?"

She had a third of the course yet to go, and there was no way to make it in the time she had left.

"No," she shouted back, reaching for the next handhold.

"You're at three hours forty-two."

She didn't answer, instead took another step up.

"Are your hands numb?" he called to her.

The air temperature was barely thirty degrees. Her face was pale beneath the mud, her eyes looked too big and her expression was pinched with strain.

She kept climbing.

"Mila."

But then she was over the top. Part of him wanted to cheer, and part of him wanted to yell at her to give it up already. There was no way for her to succeed. Not now, and really not ever.

She planted her foot on a rope. Then she gripped with her hand. She moved the next foot, took the next handhold, and the next.

But then her foot missed a step, and she lost her grip. She dangled from one hand for a terrifying second before the rough rope slipped from her fingers.

She was falling, and Troy was running, desperate to catch her and at least partially break her fall. But there was too much ground to cover. He couldn't make it.

She hit the hay mound feet first, her legs instantly collapsing, dropping her onto her back.

"Mila," he cried out, skidding to a halt, dropping down on his knees. "Don't move."

"I'm okay," she gasped, blinking her eyes.

"You fell thirty feet."

"Crap."

"What hurts? Can you move your fingers and toes?"

"Yes."

"Yes, what?"

"Yes, I can move them." She started to sit up.

"Stay *still*." He needed to know if anything was broken.

"Was that legal?"

He didn't understand the question.

"Is there a limit on how far I can jump off the wall?"

"You didn't jump."

"Yeah, I did." She sat up. "That was a jump. Am I disqualified?"

"No. You fell, Mila. You need medical attention."

"I'll get it later." She tried to get to her feet.

"Will you *stop*?"

"Will you *back off*?"

"You could be hurt."

"I'm not hurt." She successfully staggered to her feet. "Will you quit coddling me? I'm not a woman. I'm a *security agent*. And I'm fine to carry on."

"You're down to fifteen minutes."

She squared her shoulders. "I know."

"You'll never finish."

She started walking toward the balance beam. Then she gave her head a shake and broke into a trot.

He wanted to stop her. Every instinct inside him told him she shouldn't be here. This was never intended for a woman. After the balance beam was a mud-and-wire crawl, and then it was a hundred push-ups, the dummy drag and a tire climb. And that was all before the final two-mile run to the finish line.

She was halfway through the wire crawl when the horn sounded. She stopped, groaned and did a face-plant into the mud.

Any sane person would be glad it was over. She didn't look glad. Then again, she didn't seem sane, either.

"Mila?" He approached her.

She didn't answer.

"Are you breathing?"

She gave a weak nod.

He stepped into the obstacle and parted two of the wires, making a hole for her. He wanted to reach out and help her to her feet, but there was no way for him to do both.

She came up on her hands and knees, then she slowly rose, the weight of the mud adding twenty pounds. She staggered to one side and he grabbed her, wrapping an arm firmly around her shoulders.

"You okay?" he asked.

"I'm disappointed." She swiped a hand across her face, removing some of the mud, smearing the rest.

She'd have looked comical if he hadn't felt so much pity for her.

"You did better than I expected," he told her.

"But not good enough."

"You didn't give up."

"No thanks to you." She smacked him in the center of the chest.

It didn't hurt, but there was a level of power to the blow that was impressive given her exhausted state.

"I was afraid you'd hurt yourself."

"Yeah, yeah. I know. I'm a girl. Therefore, I can't hack it."

"Nobody 'hacks it' through a broken leg."

"My legs aren't broken."

"I didn't know that."

"See?" She shrugged out of his grip and started walking. "Working perfectly."

She swayed again, and he looped an arm around her waist this time.

"Not perfect," he said. "But not broken."

"I'm just a little tired." She shook out her hands. "And a little dirty."

He couldn't help but smile at that. She was a mud slick

from head to toe. He didn't know how she'd get it all out of her hair.

"Can you point me to the showers?"

"We don't have a women's facility."

"I don't care."

"Well, I do." There was no way in the world he'd allow her to strip down in the men's locker room.

He helped her into a nearby company jeep for the quarter mile back to the course's start and finish line at the Pinion building. "You can shower in my bathroom."

She looked horrified. "I'm not going upstairs like this. I'll ruin your apartment."

He couldn't care less about his apartment right now. But she was probably right.

"Fine," he said as he drove down the road that circled the course. "We'll rinse you off in the locker room. *Fully clothed.* Then you can come upstairs."

"And flood your carpets?"

"They'll survive." He pulled up to the back entrance of the building.

Vegas was there to meet them.

"You did great," he told Mila.

"For a girl," she grumbled as she climbed from the vehicle.

Vegas held out a hand to help, but she pointedly ignored it.

"She's a little testy," Troy explained to Vegas.

She rounded on Troy. "Must you always frame my behavior as emotional?" She looked at Vegas. "She's a little *tired*, and a little *grimy*. And you're a little condescending!"

Vegas fought a grin. "You earned me fifty bucks."

She looked confused.

"I had you timing out at the wire crawl. I was the most optimistic of everybody."

Mila's eyes narrowed in her muddy face. "You *bet* on me?"

"Sure. A bunch of the agents did."

She shot an accusing look at Troy. "You, too?"

"He had you on the rope wall," Vegas interjected.

"*That's* why you tried to stop me there?"

Troy was insulted. "Yeah," he said dryly. "I was desperate for the fifty bucks."

She glared at him. But she had to know the idea was preposterous.

"Let's get you into a shower," he said. "You're a mess."

Her hand went to her drying cheek, and she rubbed ineffectively at the grit.

"You'd have to pay money for that at a spa," said Vegas.

"You just can't stop making the girl jokes, can you?"

Troy stepped back in. "And you can't control your hypersensitivity."

"I'm not—"

"Yeah, you are. Come on." He canted his head toward the door and started walking.

It didn't take her long to follow.

"You're going to have to let them tease you," he told her as she came up beside him, though he wasn't sure why he was giving her the benefit of the advice. "If a guy's short, he gets teased. If he's slow, same thing. If he's particularly strong, or if he knows gourmet food, or if he's a good shot. Whatever it is, positive or negative, it gets noted and acknowledged. You're a woman, Mila. It's not something they can ignore."

He reached out to open the door.

"What I can't get past," she said as they worked their way down a narrow hallway, "is that it's a showstopper. Sure, maybe it's not a strength in every circumstance. Mostly it's neutral. But around here, it's unforgivable."

"It's noticeable." He pushed open the locker room door and called out to see if anyone was inside.

Not that the guys would care about Mila walking in on them. But he didn't think she needed an eyeful.

There was no answer, so he led her inside.

She trailed after him. "So is red hair."

"And red hair will get you teased." He gestured to the

back of the locker room, the painted brick doorway that led to the communal showers. "Have at it."

She kicked off her shoes, stripped off her socks and carried them into the shower room.

He heard the water splash against the concrete floor.

"You're telling me I should chill out," she called.

He moved closer so that she would hear him. "I am."

"Why?"

"So people will know you have an appreciable sense of humor. They'll know you can take it. They'll know they don't have to walk on eggshells around you."

He realized he didn't have to stand outside and shout. She wasn't taking off her clothes. There was no social prohibition against seeing her wet. He stepped into the shower room.

Her eyes were closed under the spray, and she kept her voice raised. "I mean, why would you help me?"

"I'm right here."

Her eyes popped open. It was good to see her regular face again. Damn, she was gorgeous. Even with her hair plastered against her head and her tank top sticking—

He quickly dragged his gaze from her breasts.

"Why should I trust your advice? You don't want me here. You don't want me to win over any of your team."

"Maybe I'm just a nice guy."

"You're a tough guy. And you're a smart guy. But you're definitely not nice."

He supposed that was true. So why was he helping her? The potential answer was unsettling. "Maybe I'm trying to seduce you."

Watching the water cascade over her, he realized it was a completely plausible answer. It made him feel slightly better.

"It's not going to work," she answered tartly.

The outer door opened, and Troy turned toward the sound. "Female inside," he shouted out.

Then he realized how this was going to look. He quickly

made for the exit to explain the situation. It was Edison, and he seemed to accept Troy's story at face value.

When Troy returned to the shower room, the water was off. Mila had helped herself to a towel and was patting down her clothes. Her rinsed runners and socks were on the tile floor, and Troy retrieved them.

"Shall we go do this for real now?" he asked.

Later, as she came out of Troy's guest bathroom, Mila detected the unmistakable aromas of sausage, tomato, bread and cheese. Her stomach rumbled, drawing her down the short hallway to the living room.

She was dressed in a black cotton robe that fell past her knees and wrapped nearly twice around her body. When Kassidy arrived, she'd see if she could borrow something that was a better fit. She sure couldn't go home dressed like this.

She found Troy on the sofa, a pizza box and two bottles of beer on the coffee table.

"You ordered pizza." She couldn't quite control the reverence in her tone.

He tossed her a grin. "I hope you like sausage and mushroom."

"Love it." She made a beeline for the coffee table. "I swear, I could ki—"

She quickly checked herself. No, she couldn't kiss him for ordering pizza. That was entirely inappropriate.

"Whatever you were about to say," he drawled, searching her expression. "I wouldn't tell you no."

She busied herself settling on the opposite end of the sofa, making sure the robe completely covered her thighs. "It was nothing."

"You sure?"

She kept her gaze away from his. "I'm sure."

"Okay, I'll take your word for it." He stretched out to hand her a napkin. "But if you change your mind…"

"I won't."

"In that case, dig in."

She realized she was too starving to be proud. She reached out and peeled back the cardboard lid, helping herself to a generous slice.

Troy twisted the caps off the bottles of beer and slid one of them down the table in front of her.

"How are you feeling?" he asked.

"I'm fine," she answered automatically. Then she took a first bite of the pizza. It was delicious.

"What's sore?"

She swallowed, trying not to let the power of suggestion cause her to stretch out her aching muscles. "Nothing much. I'm mostly starving."

"Liar," he said softly. Then he helped himself to a slice.

It occurred to her that honesty would likely impress him more than bravado.

"Everything's slightly achy," she admitted. "But it won't take me long to recover. When can I go again? Maybe Wednesday, before Kassidy's next performance?"

Troy looked genuinely surprised by the question. "You want to try again?"

Did he think a single setback would make her give up?

"I absolutely want to try again."

"You nearly killed yourself out there."

"I'm a long way from dead." She took another bite.

She'd been going over the course in her mind, and she understood where she'd made some of her mistakes. Upper-body strength was her biggest problem. She needed to pace herself on some of the obstacles, kick her running speed up a notch to buy herself some more time. Then be really methodical on the climbing walls and hold something back for the dummy drag.

Troy watched her while they ate.

His perceptive gaze was unnerving, and she finally couldn't stand it anymore.

"What?" she asked him.

"I don't get you."

"There's nothing to get." She washed down the pizza with swallows of the beer.

"You could get another job," he continued. "Easily. You've got skills. You're not stupid."

"Thanks so much," she mocked, setting the bottle on a cork coaster on the coffee table.

He set down his own beer, sat up straight and eased slightly closer. "Why me?"

She straightened, matching his body posture and meeting his gaze. "Pinion is the best."

"I'm not going to argue with that."

"A topic of agreement?" She couldn't help but joke. "How long did that take us?"

But Troy remained serious. "Why do you need to work for the best?"

"Why would I want to work for second best?"

"Because it's a better option."

She shook her head. "For a Stern, it's not an option at all."

His brows went up. "Do tell."

She hesitated. The last thing she wanted to do was to bring him into her confidence. Her family dynamics were none of his business. And letting him see any vulnerability was a definite risk.

"You brought it up," he said.

"It's nothing."

"Let me be the one to decide."

"Why?"

"Because I'm your boss." He shifted, closing the space between them. "And you're trying to impress me. Maybe this will impress me. I like honesty, Mila. I don't like secrets."

She accepted his point. The motivations and psychological health of security agents were relevant to their job performance.

"My family prides itself on achievement," she said.

"Achievement?"

"High achievement. Like my mother, the superior court judge, or my father, the esteemed university professor with tenure, and my brothers. One's been captaining a military cruiser at a ridiculously young age, and the other is a decorated Green Beret. And then there's my sister, the lawyer, already on a partnership track at Cable, Swift and Bradner."

Troy seemed to consider her words. "You're the youngest."

"How did you know?"

"You're obviously playing catch-up."

"They all had a head start."

There was sympathy in his eyes, an apparent understanding. She hadn't expected that.

"What about you?" she asked.

"My company's doing great."

"Your family. What did they expect from you?"

"Ah, my family." He sat back, stretching his arm along the back of the sofa.

The arm wasn't around her, but it was close, and her body reacted with awareness. In fact, it was more than awareness. It was arousal. She took in his square chin, his softening eyes, his full, dark lips, the broad chest and firm abs beneath his black T-shirt. The temperature in the room seemed to move up a notch.

"Kassidy and me," he said. "That's all there is."

"Your parents?"

"Mine are both dead. Kassidy's mom is still alive, but, well, we don't talk about her."

"You're an orphan?"

He cracked a smile. "I'm thirty years old. I was in my twenties when I lost each of my parents."

Mila felt vaguely guilty for criticizing her own family. There wasn't anything to criticize, really. The flaws lay with her, not with them.

"Do you miss them?" she asked.

"We're not talking about me."

She felt a whisper of a touch and realized it was on her

hair. Troy was fondling her damp hair. Desire glowed in her belly, radiating out.

"Chilly?" he asked in a whisper.

"No."

His touch grew bolder, his broad fingers running against her scalp, along the length of her hair. "You're still damp."

Her skin tingled at his touch. "I'm drying."

He drew his hand through her hair again.

She knew she should push him away, but she couldn't bring herself to move. She was trapped by his blue-eyed gaze, mesmerized by the heat of his hand, enticed by his scent.

He cradled her cheek with his hand, shifting closer. His thigh brushed hers, and his thumb stroked the corner of her mouth.

She desperately wanted his kiss. She remembered every nuance of his mouth, the taste, the texture. Her imagination took flight. He'd press his lips to hers, kiss her deeply. His other hand would go to her waist, cradling her ribs, pulling her tight, or maybe slipping beneath the robe.

Her nipples tingled and tightened in response to the image. His fingertips were rough, just callused enough to be masculine. His hands were strong. He could pull her tight, envelope her in an overwhelming embrace. It would feel so good.

Then he spoke, and his voice was a low, pained growl, and she realized he hadn't moved an inch. "We have to do something about this."

She blinked him back into focus.

"I want you pretty bad," he continued. "And you're not shutting me down."

Her lips parted. She didn't want to admit it, but she couldn't lie to him, either.

"Don't look at me like that," he rasped.

"We can't," she managed. She needed him to take her seriously.

"What's the alternative?"

She didn't have an answer.

"If we don't," he said, "we'll go crazy."

She couldn't argue with that. She was already going crazy.

"We do it," he stated. "We get it out of our system. We move on."

She was tempted. Her body shifted toward him. She was inches, seconds from melting into his arms.

A boom reverberated through the apartment while white light flashed outside the windows.

In a split second, they were on the floor, Troy's body covering hers as the apartment plunged into darkness.

"What?" she gasped against the press of his shoulder.

Troy raised his head. "Don't move." He pulled up.

She sat, blinking against the dark room. Through the windows, she could see city light a couple of blocks away. Whatever had happened, it was local.

"It was an explosion," she said.

Was it a pipeline? A gas stove? A *bomb*?

"I'm going to check it out," said Troy.

She came to her feet. "I'm coming with you."

"Stay here." It was a clear order. He'd already moved across the apartment, and a small flashlight beam shone in the foyer.

"I'm not some delicate flower." No way, no how was she cowering up here while the men investigated the danger.

"You're also not dressed."

She tightened the robe around her. "So what, I'll—"

The apartment door banged shut.

"—find something to wear," she finished.

It only took her a moment to find the dining room table. She felt her way to her cell phone and turned on the flashlight.

Permission or not, she was borrowing some of Kassidy's clothes.

Seven

Troy and Vegas were on the rain-swept street with the majority of the Pinion staff on duty. Edison was inside with a few other men, starting the backup generator and making sure Pinion wasn't the target. Sirens whined, red and blue lights flashing in the dark as more police and firefighters arrived.

"A vehicle hit the electrical pole," said Vegas. "They're guessing a faulty wire, or the impact could have cracked the insulation on the transformer. Went up like a torch."

"The driver took off?" Troy asked.

As he spoke, his gaze caught a flash of orange leggings and a glittering top. His first thought was Kassidy had arrived home. But then he saw it was Mila. She was soaking wet, talking to a man in the crowd.

"Probably drunk," said Vegas. "Cops only heard from witnesses that it was a black SUV. Our security cameras might show more."

Mila handed something to the man. With a sinking feeling, Troy realized it was probably a Pinion business card. She was representing Pinion Security looking like *that*. Fantastic.

"Anyone gunning for us right now?" He wasn't particularly paranoid, but Pinion did gather its share of enemies.

"Nothing particular comes to mind," said Vegas. "Most of the messy stuff is offshore."

"That's what I thought." Troy watched Mila approach another man. He assumed she was introducing herself as a Pinion employee. "Good grief," he muttered.

"What?" Vegas glanced around.

"I'll be back."

Troy strode through the puddles, rain falling on his face, the lingering fire from atop the power pole flickering against the wet ground. The strobes of the police cars put Mila into light and then shadow, light and then shadow.

Her hair was soaked. Her shoulders were bare. And her boots, still saturated from the obstacle course and shower, were unlaced and flopping around her ankles.

He shrugged out of his jacket as he approached, wrapping it around her shoulders as he spoke into her ear.

"I thought I told you to stay inside."

"Thank you," she said to the man, handing him a card. "If you remember anything else, please give me a call."

"I'm investigating," she told Troy as the man walked away.

"It was a hit-and-run. Both the police and station fifty-one are here investigating."

"But who hit and who ran?"

"Put your arms in the sleeves." He latched the bottom of the zipper.

She quickly stepped back. "Don't treat me like a child."

"We have a dress code." He eyeballed her up and down. "You look ridiculous."

She closed his jacket around herself. "I didn't have much of a choice."

"You had the choice to stay put upstairs."

"This could have something to do with Kassidy."

He paused for a moment, thinking his way through the incident. He wasn't seeing it, but Mila had his curiosity going. "How?"

"Whoever hit the pole was distracted."

"Or drunk."

"Maybe. But it's a Wednesday night, and there aren't a lot of bars in the neighborhood. Someone might have been checking out the Pinion building to look for Kassidy, missed seeing the pole, set off the explosion then took off to protect his identity."

"You're reaching." It was a common mistake, particularly among rookies—looking at evidence in a way to fit a pet theory.

"It's a theory," she said. "I'm not married to it. But I'm not discounting it, either."

"You have evidence?"

"Two witnesses say it was a man. They describe him as a businessman."

Troy waited. "That's it?"

"There was a guy at the last gig. He was in a blazer. Something about him looked out of place."

"And you're thinking businessmen wear blazers."

"Exactly."

It was the first time Troy had been disappointed in her reasoning. He hadn't always agreed with her, but he'd taken her for logical and intelligent.

"There are a lot of blazers in DC," he said.

"And somebody's stalking Kassidy."

"Maybe." As far as he was concerned, they hadn't even established that much. Nothing had happened so far that couldn't be explained by an exuberant fan base.

Mila set her jaw. "I'm going to ask some more questions."

Troy scanned the small crowd of onlookers. Nobody set off his radar. Nobody looked suspicious. He was inclined to believe this was just a random accident that had nothing to do with either Pinion or Kassidy. There was little good, but little harm Mila could do by continuing to question bystanders.

"Zip up the jacket," he told her. "And next time, wear appropriate clothing."

"That wasn't my—" She seemed to check herself. She swallowed. "Yes, sir."

His passion rolled back in a rush. She looked sexy and sweet and vulnerable standing in the rain in his oversize jacket, determined as all get-out to do a good job. What was he going to do with her? How the hell was he going to keep his perspective?

He checked out the crowd one more time.

He didn't see any danger.

He turned away, crossing the street to where Vegas was on his cell phone.

Vegas tucked away the phone. "What was that all about?"

"She was handing out our business cards, looking like a rock star."

"Why does she look like a rock star?"

"Kassidy's clothes."

Vegas looked him up and down, clearly suspicious.

"No," said Troy. "She showered, and we ate some pizza."

"Uh-huh," Vegas said, still looking skeptical.

"I'm not lying."

"You just tried to zip her up nice and cozy in your jacket."

"So she wouldn't embarrass Pinion."

"I don't care if you lie to me. But don't lie to yourself."

"She's hot," said Troy. "She's sizzling. If she offers, I won't say no." He set his jaw, letting his expression serve as a challenge to Vegas.

"I couldn't care less about your personal life," said Vegas. "Just don't make stupid decisions when it comes to Pinion."

"You think she'd sue?" Troy's gaze moved back to Mila. He couldn't imagine her claiming sexual harassment.

"I'm not talking about a lawsuit." Vegas sounded disgusted. "I'm talking about you rejecting a good employee because you can't see past your own lust."

"She's a woman," said Troy.

His decision had nothing to do with her being attractive or not. Though she was intensely and incredibly beautiful. He watched the play of light on her face as she spoke. Her skin was creamy smooth, her eyes a deep green that seemed to go on forever, and her lips were plump, ripe and kissable.

He should have kissed her when he had the chance. If he'd kissed her hard enough, maybe they wouldn't even have seen the explosion.

"Troy?" came Kassidy's questioning voice, approaching them.

Drake was in her arms in a yellow raincoat. They'd obviously just arrived home.

"What happened?" she asked, looking around.

Troy couldn't help but smile at his nephew. The hood was

askew, and Drake was chewing on the plastic sleeve. His cheeks were plump and pink, and his eyes took in the chaotic scene of flashing lights and bustling bodies.

"Blown transformer," said Troy. "It was quite spectacular."

Though he wasn't buying into Mila's theory, he couldn't help glancing around. He'd be more comfortable if Kassidy and Drake were inside.

"The generator's running," he told her. "You should take him in and warm him up."

Mila appeared. "Have you got a minute?" she asked Kassidy.

"No, she doesn't," said Troy. The last thing he needed was Mila frightening or upsetting his sister. "Drake needs to get to bed."

Both women looked at him in obvious surprise.

"What? I can't know his routine?"

"It'll just take a minute," Mila said to Kassidy.

"She doesn't have a minute," said Troy. "And I need to talk to you. Vegas, can you take Kassidy and Drake upstairs?"

Kassidy's surprised glance went to Vegas. She looked decidedly uncomfortable. Troy guessed she knew Vegas wasn't her biggest fan. Too bad. Not everybody could adore her. Troy needed some time alone with Mila.

"Sure," said Vegas.

"I can take her upstairs," said Mila.

"I need you here," said Troy; his look told her to keep quiet and agree.

She opened her mouth, but he didn't let her get in another word. He grasped her by the arm and turned her away, walking her across the street.

"Don't forget I'm your boss," he said close to her ear.

"So, I'm hired?" Her retort was sharp and saucy.

"Temporarily." He let go of her arm, weaving between two police cars to the perimeter of the hubbub.

She kept pace. "You're overbearing, you know that?"

"I don't need you upsetting Kassidy."

"I'm not going to upset her."

"She doesn't need to hear your theory."

They made it past the emergency lights and into the shadows of the dark buildings.

He halted and turned to face her, slammed immediately by a wall of desire. His hormones might have gone dormant there for a while, but they were now waking up to the moments before the explosion.

"I was only going to ask her some questions," said Mila. "Jeez, Troy, give me a little credit. My theory is my theory. I'm pursuing it. But I'm not going to freak Kassidy out for no reason."

Troy knew she was talking. Her gorgeous lips were moving. But his brain had stopped making out the words.

She paused. "Troy?"

"We need to talk about this." It was getting worse. He could barely focus around her.

"We *are* talking about this."

"Not that. The other."

She seemed to regroup. "You mean sex?"

"I mean us. You and me, and how we're reacting to each other."

"We need to ignore that."

"You think that's the answer?" It sure wasn't his answer. He'd been trying to ignore it for days. Ignoring it only made it worse.

"I do," she said.

"It's not working."

"So we make it work. We're rational adults."

He wasn't so sure about the rational part. He took a step closer to her. "We were ready to tear each other's clothes off."

"But we didn't."

"Only because something blew up."

"I take that as a sign."

"You don't believe in signs."

She flexed the slightest smile. "True. But we were lucky. Another couple of minutes…"

Another couple of minutes, and Troy would have felt extremely lucky.

"We can't give in," she said. "It would be bad for you, and it would be really bad for me."

He started to argue, but she kept on talking.

"I need you to have confidence in me, to see me as a fellow professional, one of the guys."

"I'm never going to see you as one of the guys."

"Not if you see me naked."

A vision flashed through Troy's brain, Mila naked on his bed. "Too late."

She drew back in obvious surprise.

"In my imagination," he clarified. "I've seen you in my imagination."

"Well, *stop*."

"It's not that easy."

"Then it's a good thing you have self-control."

"You're saying no." He didn't like it, but he had to accept it.

"Yes. No. I'm saying no."

"But you weren't back there." For some reason, he needed to hear it. "I saw your expression. That was a yes in my apartment."

Silence stretched between them. The shouts of the firefighters and the lights of the accident scene seemed to fade.

When she finally spoke, her voice was low. Standing in the drizzling rain, she looked more vulnerable and desirable than ever. "Back there. Yes, it was a yes."

Troy wanted to drag her into his arms. He wanted to hold her tight then carry her back to his room, where he'd strip off her clothes and kiss every inch of her delectable body.

There was no way on earth he was ever going to think of her as one of the guys.

"I don't know where we go from here," he said.

She squared her shoulders. "We go back to work."

"And pretend it never happened?"

"It's the only thing that will work."

"That's not going to work, Mila."

It was never going to work.

Zoey hung her big shoulder bag on the back of the maple dining chair Sunday morning, plunking down across the table from Mila.

She glanced around the upscale family restaurant. "What are we doing here?"

"A muffin isn't going to cut it today," said Mila, closing her menu, having decided on a Southwestern omelet and wheat toast.

"You need comfort food? Pancakes? What happened? What's going on?"

Mila briefly considered the merits of pancakes. Carb loading wouldn't be the worst idea in the world.

"I'm having a do-over on the obstacle course today."

"Oh." Zoey drew out the word in a dire tone. Then she leaned forward. "I thought you might want to talk about the hunky boss."

"I don't."

"Will he be there?"

"He was last time," said Mila. "But I asked Vegas if he could supervise."

"What's going on with that?"

"Vegas?" Nothing was going on with Vegas. He was a decent guy, loyal to Troy, sure. But he didn't seem to have the same chauvinistic tendencies.

"Not Vegas. The boss."

"I've been staying out of his way since Wednesday night."

Zoey said she understood Mila's hesitation but, like Troy, she had wondered aloud about the practicality of bottling up their desire.

"How's that working?" Zoey asked. "Have your feelings changed at all?"

Mila wished she could say they had. But they were intensifying. Even seeing Troy from a distance made her heart beat faster, her knees go weak and her lips tingle with anticipation.

"I'll get over it."

Her sister gave a shake of her head and a disbelieving smile. "That's not the way it works."

"It will be this time."

Zoey gave a roll of her eyes. "Are you coming to Mom and Dad's next weekend?"

Mila cringed. She'd forgotten about the upcoming family dinner. Her brother Rand had arranged a video conference from the ship, so it was a mandatory invitation. She'd have to find the time.

"I thought I'd bring Dustin along," said Zoey.

"Very funny."

"I'm serious."

"No, you're not."

"Rand will help calm Mom down. We know Dad'll be no help in that."

"Are you actually serious?"

"I want to get it over with. The subterfuge is killing me."

"You don't like lying."

"I'm not exactly lying. But I'm leaving out volumes of information. And, yes, I hate it. I want to be honest and up front with myself and everyone else. Dustin's a fantastic guy, and I refuse to treat him like some shameful secret."

"He knows what's going to happen?"

Zoey rolled her eyes. "Yes, baby sister, he has met our mother."

Mila coughed out a laugh. "He must really like you."

Her sister's expression sobered. "He says he does. He sure acts like he does."

"If he's willing to brave Judge Stern, he must have it bad."

"I know I have it bad."

Mila considered Zoey's admission. She couldn't help wonder how it would feel to truly fall for someone.

She thought of Troy. But that was just lust. Aside from his good looks, intellect, work ethic and all-around sexiness, he was really quite annoying. She was under no illusion that her feelings for him were anything more noble than physical desire.

That being true, perhaps it *was* something she could get out of her system. Maybe sleeping with him wasn't the worst idea in the world. Perhaps he'd be a mediocre lover, and with that attraction off the table, he'd be just another guy to her. Maybe if she slept with him, she'd be able to focus on her work.

She realized Zoey was watching her with curiosity.

"Is this a happily-ever-after thing?" she asked, putting herself back on topic.

"I don't know." Zoey smiled. "I'm not ruling anything out."

"Wow. Maybe don't tell that to Mom up front."

Zoey laughed as the waitress arrived to pour coffee and take their order.

Mila decided to add a couple of pancakes, while Zoey stuck with a grainy muffin and coffee. The young woman walked away.

"Mom can't throw Dustin in jail or anything, can she?" asked Mila.

Zoey tore open a packet of artificial sweetener. "I like to think our judicial system has checks and balances against that."

"You *like to think*? You're a lawyer. Shouldn't you be certain?"

"I'm pretty certain. But, you know, well, there's always a chance of an unexpected verdict."

Mila tried to decide if her sister was joking because she wasn't concerned, or if she was covering up her worry with humor. It could go either way.

"What time do you do the obstacle course?" Zoey asked.

"Eleven. I'm going straight there from here."

"Think you'll make it this time?"

"I don't know. It's really tough, but I have a plan. And I know where I went wrong last time."

"If you finish, will he hire you?"

"I wish. It's more like if I don't, he definitely won't hire me. If I finish, I take away one of his reasons to turn me down."

"You know his other reasons?"

"Main one is that he doesn't like women." Mila realized how that sounded. "I mean, he likes women. But he seems to think they're more decorative than functional."

Zoey canted her head to one side, wrinkling her nose. "I wonder what he sees in you."

Mila tried not to be insulted. "Thanks a ton."

"We both know you're far more functional than decorative. And I've checked the man out on social media. His dates are all glam bombshells."

"My abs are better than theirs." Even as she spoke, Mila didn't know why she was arguing. She had no desire to be decorative.

"If you like a six-pack on a woman."

"I don't have a six-pack. They're healthy, that's all. I'm in shape." She lifted her coffee cup. "Maybe I'm his walk on the wild side."

"It doesn't fit the pattern."

"There doesn't have to be a pattern."

"There's always a pattern."

"Then what's your theory?" Mila challenged. "Why is he propositioning ugly little me?"

"Stop pretending to be insulted. If you wanted to be a bombshell, you'd wear makeup, buy some nice clothes, put on some heels. You know you could do it if you wanted to."

"I don't want to." Mila assured herself it was true. The last thing she wanted was for Troy to think she was pretty.

"I'll help. Anytime you want a makeover, just holler."

"I don't—"

"Hey, that'd be fun. Glam you up, throw him off balance, send the guy for a loop."

"I'd feel like a fraud. It would run counter to everything I'm trying to accomplish."

"I didn't say it would be smart. I said it would be fun. How about this? If you get to a point where you are absolutely *positive* there is no way *on earth* he's *ever* going to hire you, we do it."

"No."

"Give me a yes, sister."

"What would be the point?"

"Satisfaction."

"Wouldn't it just reinforce his belief that women are different after all?"

"You're not listening. It's a parting shot, justice, revenge— call it whatever you like. It'll keep him awake at night."

"You're really not a nice person."

"And for all your tough-girl act, you can be a real doormat."

"Excuse me?"

"Have a plan, baby sister. If it all goes bad, have a final move in your hip pocket that will give you some measure of satisfaction."

"Is that what you do?"

"Yes."

"And if Mom won't accept Dustin?"

"I'm not there yet. I'm nowhere near there yet. She will." Zoey paused, uncertainty clouding her eyes. "Eventually."

Mila was hit with a wave of guilt. "I'm sorry. That was a thoughtless comparison. What I meant is that I'm not there with Pinion Security, either. I'm a long, long way from giving up."

This wasn't about Troy. It was about a job, her career, her

professional success. Troy was simply the manifestation of her current challenge. She'd rise to it. A Stern always did.

Troy didn't feel a single scrap of satisfaction seeing Mila fail a second time on the obstacle course. Watching through the security monitor, via the cameras positioned around the course, he shouldn't have been pulling for her, but he was. Intellectually, he knew she'd have used her success as another argument in her quest for a permanent job. And he didn't want that.

But emotionally, he'd been with her on the run, through the mud, along the balance beam and over the wall. She'd made it farther this time, but she was still a long way from completion.

He assumed she'd come upstairs to shower, so he waited in the apartment. Kassidy was in her room, taking her own nap while Drake took his. He and Mila wouldn't be completely alone, but he would take what he could get. She'd been avoiding him for days now, as if she needed to put an exclamation point on her refusal to take their physical relationship any further.

He got it.

She was off-limits.

That didn't mean they couldn't have a conversation. For a woman who claimed to want a permanent job, she had a funny was of relating to the boss.

He parked himself in the living room, where he'd hear her knock. He surfed through some news channels, then picked up a technology magazine. He checked his watch, wondering what was taking her so long.

Finally, he called the control room to see if she was on her way.

The staff member on duty reported that Mila had returned from the obstacle course with Vegas. They'd gone into the locker room and hadn't yet come out.

Troy checked his watch again. More than half an hour had gone by. Why were they still in the locker room?

And then it hit him. Perhaps she'd been hurt. Maybe Vegas was administering first aid. She could have cut herself on the barbed wire in the mud crawl. Maybe she'd injured an ankle jumping off the rope wall. She could have dislocated a finger or gashed her arm. He'd seen all of those things and more happen on the obstacle course.

He was out the door and down the hall in a flash. He didn't have the patience to wait for the elevator. Instead, he bounded down the stairs, coming out on the main floor on the back side of the building. From there, it was a short trot to the locker room.

One of the security agents was coming through the door.

"Female inside," he warned Troy.

"She okay?" asked Troy.

"In the shower." The man grinned and waggled his brows.

Troy nearly slammed him into the wall.

But that would take time, and he wanted to find out what was going on.

He breezed through the door. A second staff member was washing his hands.

"Where is she?" Troy barked.

The man jammed his thumb toward the back of the facility.

As he walked, Troy could hear the shower running.

She was in the shower. She might be fully dressed, but he had a terrible feeling she wasn't. She was making a statement. She wanted to be one of the guys. No more showering in the boss's bathroom—she was going all out.

He rounded the corner and nearly plowed straight into Vegas.

Vegas stood, arms over his chest, feet planted apart in front of the shower room doorway.

"That's as far as you go," he said to Troy.

"Don't tell me she's—"

"Naked? Yeah, she's naked."

Troy took a step forward, ready to give Mila a piece of his mind.

"Oh, no, you don't," said Vegas.

Troy stopped himself. "Has she lost her mind?"

"The guys aren't going to bother her," said Vegas. "But just in case anyone's tempted, I thought I'd stick around."

"She could have come upstairs. She knows she should have come upstairs."

"You saw?" asked Vegas.

Troy hesitated over his answer, not wild about Vegas knowing he'd monitored her attempt. "I saw."

"She's disappointed."

"I know."

The security cameras monitored from a distance, but when the buzzer rang, her body language was pretty telling.

"I doubt she wants to talk to you."

"She wants to talk to *you*?" Troy knew he sounded jealous, but he didn't particularly care.

"I'm not talking to her," Vegas offered easily.

"Were you? Did you? What did she say?"

"She wants to try again."

Troy felt some of the tension leave his body.

She wasn't hurt. She wasn't demoralized. She was just as feisty as ever.

"There's no point," he said.

"Maybe not," said Vegas. "But she won't get any static from me."

Troy stood up a little taller. "You think I'm giving her static?"

"You do spend a lot of time telling her what she can't do."

"Well, she can't do that. It's not humanly possible."

"Hey!" came Mila's voice over the shower spray. "I can hear you talking."

Troy winced, and he did an immediate recap of the conversation. Had he been insulting?

Vegas smirked.

"Shut up," said Troy in an undertone.

"Go away," said Mila.

"Come out here," said Troy.

"I'm busy."

"I need to talk to you about Kassidy." It was partially true. It took Mila a moment to answer. "Fine."

The water shut off.

Troy looked to Vegas. "You can go guard the main door now. Don't let anyone else in."

"I don't think so."

"There's nobody left but me."

"You're the guy I'm guarding her against."

"Give me a break." Troy raised his voice. "Mila? Okay if Vegas leaves?"

"Up to him."

Vegas didn't move.

"He thinks I might try something."

"Not and live," she called back.

Vegas grinned.

"She says she can take care of herself," said Troy.

"I believe she can. Watch yourself."

"I'm not going to try anything."

"You'll want to. I'm just sayin' don't do it."

"Go away. As far as I'm concerned, she's one of the guys."

"Uh-huh." Vegas's voice dripped skepticism as he walked away.

Mila appeared in the doorway, her hair soaking wet, her bare shoulders covered in droplets, and a big towel covering her from chest to knees.

"What about Kassidy?" she asked.

Troy had to clear his throat.

"She's okay, right?" asked Mila.

"She's taking a nap."

Mila smiled, her sparkling eyes and the glimpse of her white teeth turning him on. "That's our girl."

He forced himself to concentrate. "I need an update."

"On?"

"On everything. Your investigation. The current security plan. Her upcoming performances. Anything you believe might be relevant."

"No problem." Mila crossed to a bench that held her wet clothes.

"How did those get out here?" He was trying to picture the logistics of her in the shower and Vegas in the doorway, and who knew who else coming and going.

"Vegas," she said.

"He saw you naked?"

"What if he did?"

Troy was advancing on her before he had time to think it through. "Tell me he didn't."

She met his hard gaze. "He didn't. He reached his hand around the doorway and I gave him my clothes."

"Are you sure he didn't peek?" Troy couldn't help but think, for himself, it would have taken ethics of steel to keep his eyes averted.

"Is this junior high? Of course he didn't peek. And the world wouldn't have come tumbling down if he had."

"Is that a yes or a no?"

"That's a mind your own business, Troy Keiser."

The color was high in her cheeks, and he was suddenly, blindingly reminded that she was naked under the towel.

Vegas had been right. Troy wanted to try something. He desperately and absolutely wanted to try something.

He curled his hands into fists and forced himself to take a step back.

"Get dressed," he managed through the roaring in his ears. "Meet me upstairs."

Eight

Mila had been smarter this time. She'd packed a change of clothes and another pair of boots in a duffel bag, knowing what she'd look like at the end of the obstacle course.

She stepped into her jeans and tugged a rust-colored T-shirt over her head. Her leather ankle boots were scuffed and worn, but they fit her like a glove and were both sturdy and comfortable. They gave her confidence.

She tied her wet clothes into a plastic bag and stuffed them into the duffel. Her hair was still wet, but she'd combed it out. She slung the bulky black bag over her shoulder, jazzed at the prospect of seeing Troy, even knowing her buzz of arousal was a seriously dangerous state.

She exited through the open doorway, finding Vegas standing guard.

"I hope that wasn't too inconvenient," she said as they walked side by side down the hall.

"I didn't mind," he answered.

He looked as though he didn't. And it helped. Vegas seemed both immensely capable and down-to-earth.

"I meant for everyone else," she told him. "It's hard to be one of the guys when you have to lock them out of their own showers."

"I doubt anyone had a shower emergency in the past fifteen minutes."

"You know what I mean."

"I do," he said.

He pressed the button to call the elevator.

"You did good out there," he told her.

"I failed miserably." She hadn't expected to magically pass, but she had hoped to improve her result more than she'd managed.

"You've got grit, Mila. They'll be impressed by that."

"Troy?" she couldn't help but ask.

"Troy doesn't want to be impressed. He's looking for reasons not to be impressed. But you already know that."

"I don't know what to do," she admitted. "It's…" She wanted to say complicated. She wanted to say impossible. But she didn't want to admit the depths of her discouragement to Troy's partner, of all people. "I really don't know what to do."

"If you sleep with him, you'll never be one of the guys."

Mila gaped at Vegas's blunt words.

The elevator door slid open, but she didn't move.

He touched her arm and guided her inside, coming with her. "If you don't sleep with him, both of you will go stark raving mad."

She felt her face heat with embarrassment. "What did he tell you?"

"Nothing. I have eyes. And I'm paid to be observant. And I saw the expression on your face that day at the shooting range. You turned away from Troy, but you were looking at the camera."

She could only imagine what she had revealed to a man like Vegas. "Are people gossiping?"

The elevator rose.

"Maybe," said Vegas. "Though not to me. They're more interested in seeing if you wimp out. And they want to see if Troy cracks on his no-women rule."

"I guess they all know about that?"

"They all know about that."

The number panel flashed past floor five.

"What about a different job?" Vegas asked. "Somewhere other than Pinion."

"Settle for second best?" She shook her head. "That's not in my makeup." And it wasn't in her family's makeup. A job at Pinion might be challenging. But it was what she wanted, and it's what she'd go after.

"You'll really try again?" Vegas asked.

She assumed he meant the obstacle course. "In a couple of days."

"Stay lower in the mud crawl. Use your core strength and save your arms. And don't do the whole course again for practice. Work on the technical parts, the low walls, the logs and the ropes. Don't waste your energy with bad technique."

The elevator came to a halt on nine.

She didn't know what to say. She was exhausted, sore and stupidly close to tears.

She swallowed. "Thank you."

"I'm just treating you like one of the guys."

"That's all I want."

"I know."

The door slid open.

"Don't sleep with him, Mila."

"I won't." She stepped into the hallway, vowing to take that advice.

Vegas gave a sharp nod as the door slid shut.

Her stomach danced with nerves as she made her way to Troy's front door. She knocked once, and he answered almost immediately.

When he didn't say anything, her heart began to thud deeply in her chest. His stance was tense, his gaze penetrating, and his knuckles were white where he gripped the door. Her first thought was that she was about to be fired.

"Uh…" she started haltingly. "You wanted to talk about Kassidy?"

He blinked, as if her words weren't making sense. Then his hand shifted on the door. "Kassidy, right."

"Should I come back later?" She'd like to come back later. She'd rather come back later. Whatever Troy was thinking, she didn't want him to say it out loud.

But he stepped back. "No. Come in."

"Is Kassidy up?"

Company would be a good idea. Would he fire her in front of his sister? Hopefully, Kassidy would take Mila's side.

"You have your laptop?" he asked.

"I do." She wondered where this was leading.

Was he going to suggest she update her résumé? Maybe he'd offer her a letter of reference. Should she take it? Should she beg him to reconsider? Should she slam out of here in righteous anger?

She pictured herself marching out the door. Then she pictured herself begging him to keep her. Then, unfortunately, the image turned to him kissing her, holding her, reassuring her that—

That what? That they'd be good in bed together.

"Let's do it in my office," he said.

Her stomach contracted. "Excuse me?"

He looked annoyed as he shut the door. "Bring your laptop to my office. I want to run through your analysis."

"On Kassidy?" she confirmed, still feeling as though she was changing gears.

"Of course on Kassidy. What is wrong with you?"

"Nothing."

"Did you hit your head out there?"

"I did not hit my head." She started for the office. "I bruised just about everything else," she muttered as she walked.

She wanted to blame him for that. She did blame him for that. The obstacle course was impossible. It was going to kill someone. Probably her.

She entered the room and plunked her duffel bag down on the floor.

"You okay?" he asked, his voice unexpectedly close and unexpectedly even.

She turned.

"Are you hurt?" he asked, scanning her face.

"I'm fine."

"Any falls this time?"

She shook her head. "Just the usual scrapes and bruises."

"You made it farther."

The statement took her by surprise. "You saw me?"

"Only on the monitor."

Had he watched her struggle? Had he judged her performance? Or had he merely happened to glance at the security monitor as the buzzer went off? There was no way to guess, and she wasn't going to ask.

"Did you laugh?" she asked instead, hoping to lighten the mood.

She was feeling better now that it looked as though she wouldn't be fired today.

"Only the first time, when you…face-planted in the mud." Then he sobered. "I didn't laugh. I was pulling for you."

"No, you weren't. You're going to hate it when I succeed."

"I think you mean *if* you succeed."

"I think I mean when."

Instead of answering, he touched her collarbone, brushing gently across her skin. "You have a gash."

"It's nothing."

He pulled on the neck of her T-shirt. "It's minor."

"Isn't that what I just said?"

"I needed to see for myself."

"Because you don't trust me?"

"Because I worry about you."

"I'm not made of glass, Troy."

His fingers feathered across her neck. "I wish you were. It would be so much easier if you were delicate, feminine, and I could protect you and you wouldn't challenge and protest every little thing I do."

"Is that what you like?" she dared to ask. "You like helpless women?"

"I thought I did." He was coming closer. "I thought I knew exactly the type of woman I liked. And then you came along. And now I have to question myself. I don't like questioning myself."

She told herself to back away, but she didn't move. "Are you looking for sympathy?"

"No."

"Good."

"I'm looking for an answer. Yes or no."

"To what?"

He took a step. Then he took her hand. He lined up their lips, canting his head to one side. "Yes or no?"

"No," she managed to whisper, clinging to good sense.

"You sure?"

"No." She wasn't sure at all.

He brushed his lips lightly against hers, starting a trail of desire that warmed her brain.

He paused.

She waited, thinking of his kiss, desperate for his kiss.

"Yes or no?" he repeated.

She groaned in surrender. Her hands went to his waist, and she crossed the miniscule space between them, pressing her lips to his in a hungry kiss.

Troy immediately wrapped her in his arms, pulling her tight, holding her flush against him.

It felt good. It felt so, *so* good. She gave in to the sensations, running her hands along his arms, up to his shoulders, feeling the strength and mass of his muscles. He shouldn't feel so overwhelmingly sexy. Sure, he was fit, and he was buff, but he was just a man. Why couldn't she resist him?

She reached for his buttons, kissing him deeply while her fingers worked his shirt. She separated the fabric, touching his skin, feeling its heat, the play of his muscles, the ridge of a scar, then another and another.

She broke the kiss, gazing down. She kissed the white line that crossed his left ribs.

He gasped, and his hand tunneled into her hair.

The sound of the door swinging shut beside them should have given her pause. But she was beyond caring. She tugged off her T-shirt, then stripped off her bra, putting them skin to skin and tipping her chin for his kiss.

He rumbled her name, bringing his lips back to hers. His hands stroked her bare back. He gathered her close, flattening her against him, the heat and friction building.

He turned them both, lifting her to perch her on the edge of his desk. She widened her thighs so he fit between. She looped her arms around his neck, steadying herself, letting her nipples rub against his chest, the tingles from the contact shooting spikes of desire through her stomach and lower.

He kissed her neck, moving to her breasts, drawing her nipple into his hot mouth.

She grasped the lip of the desk, holding tight as her head tipped back. A moan escaped from her lips. Heat suffused her body. Passion ramped up, blocking out sight and sound as her world contracted to Troy.

She felt him pop the button on her jeans, draw down the zipper. She kicked her boots free, and her jeans came off, followed by her panties.

She reached out to him, getting rid of his pants, desperate to bring them together. His palms cupped her rear, lifting her up, pulling her to him, hot and hard.

She curled to his body, kissing his chest, tasting the salt of his skin, inhaling his musk while his rhythm drew her upward into a spiral of pleasure. He drove her higher, and she panted his name over and over.

He took her mouth, his kisses hot and deep, his tongue tangling with hers, while his hands kneaded her flesh and he thrust and withdrew.

The world seemed to pause and hover at the edge of paradise.

"So good," he groaned, his body turning to heated iron. "Mila. Oh, Mila." His hug tightened, his arms like bands of steel holding her safe.

"Faster," she begged him, feeling the crescendo tingle its way through her limbs. "Please."

"Yes," he growled, increasing his speed. "Yes."

Her hands tightened on his shoulders, struggling for an anchor as passion threatened to pull her apart.

"Troy," she cried out as her body imploded.

His body shuddered in return.

Then his kisses grew gentle. He stroked her hair. He cradled her body, taking her weight against himself.

Reality returned to her.

She'd had sex with Troy.

This was bad. It was very, very bad.

They were naked. And he was still inside her. And heaven help her, it still felt fantastic.

"Oh, no," she moaned. "Oh, no."

He tensed.

She drew back. "We didn't just do that."

He glanced down to where their bodies were joined. "We didn't?"

"No." She slipped free, wiggling back on the desk. "It was an accident. We didn't think it through." Her brain was desperately scrambling for an out. "It's not like we had dinner and wine, candles and lingerie, a big bed and a night together."

"That was an option?" he asked.

She smacked him on the shoulder. "Work with me here. This *can't* have happened." She hopped off the desk, searching for her clothes. "You're my boss. I'm one of the guys."

She found her bra and her T-shirt. She glanced over her shoulder to find him perusing her backside. "Stop!"

"Mila, you've never been one of the guys."

"You know what I mean." She grabbed her panties from the floor and pulled them on, covering up.

She put on her bra and covered it up with her T-shirt. There, that felt better. Better still, she was climbing into her jeans.

Troy quickly got dressed, too, running spread fingers through his short hair, while Mila tightened the laces on her boots.

She came to her feet to face him. "This never happened."

He looked more amused than upset. "You're rewriting history?"

"It can't impact anything we do or anything we think.

We're going to review my notes on Kassidy and discuss her case on its merits. We're putting everything else out of our minds, and we are never, ever telling a soul."

"You mean, we're never telling anyone what didn't happen?"

It took her a second to wrap her head around his statement. "Yes. Exactly. It's like we both had the same fantasy, but it wasn't real."

He looked skeptical, and she didn't exactly buy into it herself. But it was her only hope.

Sitting beside and slightly behind Mila at his office desk, Troy watched her scroll through her analysis of Kassidy's last few performances. It was a struggle to understand the words. He was mostly listening to the sound of her voice, inhaling the wintergreen scent of her hair, and stopping himself from brushing the bare skin of her arm.

"So Edison checked the cell tower traffic for those exact times," she said. "I like Edison."

That got Troy's attention. "What do you mean you like Edison?"

"I mean he's a big help. So is Vegas. So is Charlie."

Troy hated the surge of jealousy that rose in his gut. "What have you been doing with Charlie?"

"I work well with your staff, Troy. We cooperate. I'm a team player. You should think about that."

"I am thinking about that." He hated picturing Mila talking, laughing, doing anything with members of his staff.

"They originated from the same burner phone."

"What? Who?"

She turned her head. "What's the matter with you?"

"Nothing." Unless you counted the fact that his brain was still reeling from having made love to her.

Yes, he'd made love to Mila. And it had been off-the-charts fantastic. He wanted to do it again. It was all he could do not to sit forward and wrap his arms around her. She was in fantastic shape, but also soft in all the right places. She smelled like paradise, and she tasted sweeter than fifty-year-old brandy. And she had about as much of a kick.

He couldn't help but smile in satisfaction.

She gave him a look of disgust. "Like I said, the guy in the blazer. He was back on Saturday night. He was texting, and I wrote down the times." She focused on the screen again, her voice going no-nonsense. "I jotted down as many as I could, then I correlated them to the information from the cell tower. I got a burner number. But the interesting thing is that some of the times coincided with posts to Kassidy from MeMy-Heart and BluebellNighthawk. It's one person."

"Lots of people have two accounts."

As far as Troy was concerned, all Mila had identified was a fan. Sure, she'd matched a face with two account names and a burner phone. But that didn't mean the guy wasn't a perfectly ordinary fan.

"He drives a black SUV," she said.

"Did you get the plate number?" Now *that* would be useful.

"He was too far away."

"So we have nothing."

"We don't have nothing. This is the guy who mentioned Drake. Charlie's coming with us on Thursday. He'll watch for the SUV. I'll watch Kassidy, and Edison will monitor the electronic traffic."

"Vegas is coordinating?"

Her shoulders tensed, and her voice went cold. "You can't even fake it, can you?"

He didn't know what she was trying to say, but he was sure he didn't like it. "I don't fake anything."

"Yes, Vegas knows about the plan. But he's not coordinating. This is my operation, Troy. I'm leading the investigation. I'm creating the strategy."

"As long as Vegas is there for quality control."

She pivoted the swivel chair. "You won't give me a chance, will you? You won't give me a single break."

A break? She wanted a break, after all those speeches insisting she be treated like one of the guys? Now she sat there with her big green eyes, her rosy cheeks, that soft skin and kissable mouth, wanting special treatment?

His voice came out harsher than he'd intended. "What kind of a break would you like, sweetheart?"

Her expression went hard. "Go to hell." She jumped to her feet.

He shot up with her, grasping her arm. "What makes you think I'm not already there?"

While he glared at her, his lungs labored, and sweat broke out on his brow. It didn't matter that they'd made love half an hour before, he was desperate to do it again.

"You think you can hold me?" she asked.

He wanted to hold her. That much he knew.

She unexpectedly slammed her fist into his solar plexus. "I can take care of myself."

The power behind her fist shocked him, and he staggered back.

She braced herself, stood ready, as if she thought he was going to hit her back.

He held up his palms to show her he had no intention of retaliating. He wouldn't hit her. He'd never hit her.

Her eyes narrowed, and her face screwed up in obvious disappointment. "No," she cried and took a menacing step forward.

"I am not going to fight you," he told her.

"Defend yourself."

"Stop."

She made a fist, and he grabbed and held her hand. But she was quick, she'd obviously anticipated his move, and she pivoted, putting him off balance.

"Stop," he shouted.

He wrapped his arms around her from behind, clamping down while she wiggled to get free.

The door suddenly swung open, and Kassidy appeared.

"Troy!" She gaped at her brother in obvious horror.

He immediately released Mila.

"What are you doing?"

"She attacked me."

Kassidy headed across the room. "What did you do to her?" She put a comforting arm around Mila's shoulders.

He was disgusted. Talk about having it both ways.

"I started it," said Mila.

"Too bad," said Kassidy, still glaring at him. "He's the man."

"No, he's *not* the man." Then Mila seemed to realize how that sounded. "I mean, he *is* a man. But we're both…"

Troy couldn't help himself. "Men?"

She glared at him. "Equals."

"He's got a hundred pounds on you," said Kassidy.

"Almost," Troy agreed.

"I'm faster," said Mila clamping her jaw.

"No, you're not," he countered.

"What are you two fighting about?" Kassidy asked.

Mila blinked, looking momentarily confused.

He couldn't remember, either.

"He's stubborn," said Mila.

"She's opinionated," he said.

"We were talking about your fans," she added.

"Yeah. Your fans. And your gigs. And your security."

"I have a plan." Mila shrugged. "And he's trying to give Vegas the credit."

"I am not." That wasn't remotely close to what he'd told her. "If you were a man," he said to Mila. *"If* you *were,* in fact, a man, I'd have Vegas sticking to you like glue."

She folded her arms across her chest. "Because I'm incompetent?"

"Will you two stop shouting?" Kassidy broke in.

Then he heard it. Drake was crying in the bedroom.

"Thanks a lot," said Kassidy. "I was hoping to get a cup of coffee first."

Troy experienced an unexpected and unwanted shot of guilt. It was his apartment, for goodness' sake. He wasn't allowed to raise his voice in his own apartment?

"I'll get him." Even as he made the offer, he wondered why he was doing it.

Maybe just to get away. Maybe to put some distance between him and Mila. He sure needed it.

For a while there, he'd thought making love to her would get things out of his system. He thought that if he stopped wondering about it, stopped speculating on what it would be like, stopped imagining her naked, he could stop obsessing over her.

That was a mistake. Making love to her was better than he could have imagined. She was more beautiful than he'd ever dreamed. The obsession wasn't gone. It was worse now than ever.

He paced his way across the living room, finding Drake in the dim bedroom, up on his hands and knees in his crib bawling his eyes out.

Troy gently lifted the baby, cradling him against his chest, stroking his hair.

"Poor thing," he crooned. "Who wants to wake up all alone in the dark?"

He laid the baby down on top of the dresser, which was the makeshift changing table. He'd gotten pretty fast at changing a diaper. Though Drake fussed, it was over quickly, and he was back in Troy's arms.

Troy patted Drake's back as he left the bedroom, heading for the kitchen and a bottle of formula.

"Who wants to wake up all alone in the dark?" he repeated in a soothing undertone, even as he pictured his own empty bed. "I wish I could tell you it gets better, little guy. But life is full of long, long, lonely nights."

Nine

Mila was working with two new pieces of information from last night's performance, and Vegas had assigned her a desk in the bullpen. Sitting next to Charlie, an irreverent, handsome twenty-something and the newest employee of Pinion, she was beginning to feel more like a member of the team.

Charlie didn't seem to have Troy's bias against women. He'd worked the street outside the club last night, photographing all of the black SUVs in the vicinity. Now he was working through facial recognition databases with the best picture she'd taken of the blazer guy. If they could get a name, they might match it to a license plate.

The man had been right up front by the stage this time. She'd been tempted to talk to him, but the last thing she wanted to do was tip her hand. She'd checked with the bartender, but the man hadn't bought a drink. Too bad—a credit card receipt or a glass with fingerprints would have been nice.

At the same time, she didn't want to fixate on him. She hadn't seen him send any messages last night, yet Kassidy had received seven from both MeMyHeart and Bluebell-Nighthawk.

It could still be someone else.

She was reviewing another long list of messages when something caught her eye.

"Hang on," she said to Charlie.

There were three other agents working in the room, creating a backdrop of telephone conversations, newsfeeds and the hum of equipment.

"What is it?" he asked, looking up from his monitor.

"It's on the MeMyHeart account. He says the usual stuff—she's beautiful, talented, looks good in pink. He does seem to have a thing for pink. But get this: 'when we're reunited, all together again, and you are my own.'"

"Creep level of about four," said Charlie.

"I'd give it a five. But here's the thing, the words *all together again*. Does that sound like more than two? Together again would be two. All together is more."

"Maybe."

"Maybe three?" She sorted her way through possibilities.

"Could be," said Charlie.

"Drake makes three."

Charlie looked up at her.

Mila quickly went back to her computer and scrolled through MeMyHeart's previous posts.

He'd mentioned Drake. He'd mentioned the baby more than once. Could he have meant the three of them all together? He'd also used the word *again*. Had the three of them somehow been together in the past?

A shiver ran up her spine. Could blazer guy have something to do with Drake? Were they coming at this backward? Could Drake possibly be the conduit to Kassidy?

She brought up blazer guy's picture and hit print. She had to show it to Kassidy.

"I'm going upstairs," she told Charlie.

"You got something?"

"Just a hunch. I won't be long."

"Anything I can do?"

She went for the printer. "Find me a name for blazer guy. That'll make my day."

"Working on it."

She paused with the printed picture in her hand. "Thanks, Charlie."

He looked puzzled. "Just doing my job."

"I mean, thanks for treating me like one of the guys."

He gave a small smile. "You are one of the guys."

The words warmed her heart.

He went back to his work. "I'll call you if anything comes through."

"Thanks."

She was on the third floor, and she took the stairs to nine, knocking on Troy's apartment door.

While she waited, she realized that it could be Troy who opened the door. It was almost noon, and he often had lunch in the apartment. She hadn't seen him since their disastrous lovemaking. She hoped she wasn't about to see him now.

What would she do? What would she say? More importantly, what would he do, and what would he say? Would he ignore it as she'd asked? Would he allude to it? Would he make a move?

If he made a move, she'd absolutely call him on it and tell him in no uncertain terms to keep his hands to himself. She wasn't about to become the boss's plaything.

As she thought about his hands—what they'd done to her, what they could do to her—her skin heated up and a gleam of desire began in her core. The man had magic hands, magic lips, magic—

The doorknob rattled, and she braced herself.

But it was Kassidy who opened the door.

Mila told herself she was relieved.

"Hey, Mila." Kassidy was jiggling Drake in her arms.

The baby grinned when he saw Kassidy, holding out his arms and leaning toward her.

"Oh, sure," Kassidy chided with a smile. "Go to Auntie Mila. Never mind that I'm the one who feeds, changes and rocks you to sleep."

Mila lifted Drake, settling him against her hip while he cooed and grabbed at the leather bag strap on her shoulder.

"Got a minute?" she asked Kassidy.

"You bet. Want a coffee? Gabby's making pancakes, breakfast for me, lunch for Drake. Have I told you that I love her? I love, love, *love* her."

Mila laughed. Kassidy had been singing the nanny's praises ever since she was hired. "You may have mentioned it once or twice. Drake eats pancakes?"

"Mostly he plays with them. But a little bit gets ingested."

"Yes to the coffee. No thanks on the pancakes."

Kassidy led the way to the kitchen. "What do you want to talk about?"

Mila extracted the picture of blazer guy from her shoulder bag. "Does this man look familiar?"

Kassidy accepted the picture.

"Hi, Mila," Gabby greeted from where she stood over a frying pan, flipper in hand.

She was in her early twenties, good-humored, down-to-earth. She had a diploma in early childhood education and had just become engaged to a chiropractor. She was willing to work flexible hours, and Drake adored her.

"Was that at the performance last night?" asked Kassidy.

Mila had been careful to keep Kassidy from getting unduly worried or upset. So she hadn't shared a lot of information with her.

"I saw him texting a few times that coincided with messages you received. It's a bit of a long shot, but if there's anything you can tell me about him?"

"Vaguely familiar," said Kassidy, squinting at the picture. "If he's been up front at the stage before, I probably remember him from that."

Kassidy handed the picture back and reached for Drake. "Come to Kassidy, sweetheart. Are you hungry?"

Gabby handed Mila a cup of coffee.

Mila inhaled the aroma. "Thanks." She took a drink.

Kassidy sat Drake in his high chair, fastening a clean bib around his neck.

"One more question," said Mila. It was even more of a long shot, but she wanted to be completely thorough on the Drake angle.

"Sure," said Kassidy.

"Did you know Drake's father?"

Kassidy froze. The color drained from her face.

"Kassidy?"

"No," Kassidy said brightly, giving Drake's shoulders a squeeze and smoothing his fine hair.

"Are you sure?"

"Of course I'm sure."

"You faltered there."

Kassidy looked up. "It was a rough time. The guy was a one-night stand. And then Drake's mom got sick. The whole thing was very upsetting."

"I'm sorry," said Mila, but her brain was ticking about a hundred miles an hour.

There was something about Drake's father, something that had Kassidy worried. It was an outlandish theory. But could the stalker be Drake's father? Could blazer guy be Drake's father?

Mila finished her coffee and headed back to the bullpen.

Charlie was gone, but Troy was staring at her monitor.

Her chest tightened at the sight of him. Her pulse jumped and butterflies formed in her stomach.

Troy looked up, his expression smooth and professional. She schooled her own.

"This is from last night?" he asked.

She moved to where she could see the screen. "Yes. That's the blazer guy I said I thought was suspicious."

"There's something…" said Troy.

"What is it?"

"He looks familiar."

"You know him?"

That was significant.

"I can't place him." Troy picked up the phone and dialed. "Take a look at the picture up on Mila's computer."

"Who's that?" she asked.

"Vegas," Troy told her. "Anything?" Troy said into the phone. Then he waited for a moment. "I've come across him somewhere before. Why can't I remember? It's definitely been a few years."

Another moment passed.

"Are you sure?" Troy asked Vegas. "Yeah. This might be something completely different. I'll be right there." He hung up the phone.

"What?" asked Mila.

"I know that guy. This might have nothing to do with Kassidy. It could be about me."

Mila wrapped her head around the theory. It was possible. The same way the Drake link was possible. She hated having so many tenuous threads.

"Kassidy might have crazy fans." Troy rose and started for the door. "But I've ticked off some very dangerous people over the years."

Mila followed, coming at Troy's theory from as many angles as she could muster. "Why target her?"

"To get to me."

"There are easier ways to get to you."

"Not really. I'm cautious. I'm prepared. I'm always armed."

"I don't mean get to you as in harm you. I mean upset you."

"I'm pretty upset."

They made their way down the hall to Vegas and Troy's office.

"It started when she was in New Jersey."

"So?"

"So, the two of you were estranged. You said yourself, you only saw her once a year."

"She's still my half sister. I've always stepped up when she needed it." He marched through the office doorway. "She's in my building. She's in my apartment." He spoke to Vegas. "We need to do a full sweep."

Mila looked for flaws. The notes to Kassidy were personal. The writer seemed to be obsessing about her and Drake, not about Troy.

"Where does Drake fit in?" Mila asked.

"He's incidental."

"He's mentioned in the posts. You're not."

"So what? He's part of her life, part of my life. This is a whole lot bigger than a rabid fan."

Vegas was on his cell, heading for the door.

"Don't let Kassidy out of your sight," Troy called to him.

"I'll go," said Mila.

"I want Vegas."

"I can handle it," said Mila, moving to follow.

But Troy grasped her arm to stop her. "This is above your pay grade."

"Excuse me?" She tried to shake him off, but his grip was tight.

"I'm not leaving this to you. You're inexperienced, you're temporary, you're—"

"Female?"

"I didn't say that."

"You didn't have to. You've said it a thousand times."

"This isn't about you being a woman."

"This is *all* about me being a woman. It's another of your knee-jerk reactions."

He glared at her in obvious anger.

"This might be about you," she allowed. "But it could still be about Kassidy and Drake. It could even be all about Drake."

"Drake?"

"Yes."

"Based on what? Evidence? Facts? Because I definitely recognize the guy. That means he's somewhere in my past."

"You don't remember where. It could be anywhere. Don't ignore everything else."

Troy's jaw tightened.

"There's a very good chance you're wrong," said Mila.

They stared at each other, their gazes locked. Emotions raced through her—frustration, annoyance, anxiety, exasperation. At least it wasn't sexual attraction. She had that going for her.

"Are you *looking* to get fired?" he ground out.

She kept her stare level and steady. "I was never hired."

"Kassidy likes you. That's the only thing you have going for you. You can stay and follow my orders, or you can leave, right now."

Mila wanted to leave. She'd take great emotional satisfaction from turning on her heel and walking away.

But that wouldn't help Kassidy. And it wouldn't help Drake. They were innocent in all of this. If Troy was wrong, if he fixated on the wrong problem, the two of them could be in real danger.

It was better to stay and do what she could, everything she could, even if it meant going behind Troy's back, following her own leads and risking his wrath.

Later in the week, Vegas sat in a leather armchair in Troy's living room. He had a computer printout in his hand, one ankle resting on the opposite knee. "I warned her not to sleep with you."

Troy stared back, anger warring with disbelief.

"Maybe I should have told *you* not to sleep with *her*."

"She *told* you that?" Troy was shocked to think Mila might have confided in Vegas.

"She didn't have to tell me a thing."

"Then you're guessing."

"Your judgment is clouded."

Troy's gaze flicked to the closed door of Kassidy's room. Mila was with her in there. She'd chosen to stay, and she'd agreed to take direction from Troy.

"My judgment is fine," he said.

"Why did you do it?"

Troy decided to brazen it out, force Vegas to put his cards on the table, if he had any cards. "What makes you think I did?"

"You might as well have worn a neon sign Sunday night. Jovial, relaxed, satiated. Too bad it didn't last."

Troy had no interest in this conversation, but he wasn't going to lie, either. "It was a mistake. It's over and done. It has no bearing on this."

"You don't want her to get hurt."

Troy felt the jab directly in the center of his chest. "I don't want anybody to get hurt."

"Especially not her."

"Can we end this conversation?"

Vegas shifted his leg and leaned forward. "Problem you've got is, it wasn't about sex."

Troy sat up straight. "I'm serious. This conversation is *done*."

"You have feelings for her."

"What do I have to do to shut you up?"

"You're protecting her."

"I'm *protecting* Kassidy."

"You're protecting Mila. It was bad enough when she was just another woman, just another Gabriela—"

"Shut up." Troy rose to his feet, his stomach twisting into a knot.

Mila wasn't Gabriela. But she was a woman. And Troy had learned from Gabriela. He *had* to have learned from Gabriela. Otherwise, Gabriela had died in vain.

Vegas set down his report and stood more slowly. "She's an asset."

"She's a *person*."

"So am I. So are you. So are Edison and Charlie."

Troy glared at him. "She's not like Edison and Charlie."

"Trust her," said Vegas. "You like her. You want her. I know you admire her. Now you've got to trust her."

"I *won't* kill her."

"This isn't about you."

"You're right. It's about her, and what's best for her. And what we do, who we are, is not best for her."

"That's not for you to decide."

"Yes, it is."

It was. Troy could decide to hire her, or he could decide to let her go. Letting her go was safe. Hiring her was fraught with risk.

Kassidy's bedroom door opened, and Mila appeared.

Troy watched as she approached, unable to look away, his emotions hovering at the surface. She was wearing her usual cargo pants, tan colored today. They were topped with an olive-green T-shirt that stretched across her breasts, covering her shoulders in cap sleeves. Her hair was braided, her makeup nonexistent, and her worn leather boots were as serviceable as footwear could be.

She was drop-dead gorgeous.

He had to stop himself from going to her.

"We need to leave for the club in about fifteen minutes," she told them.

"I'm coming," said Troy.

She gave a nod, as if she'd expected the decision.

"I'll take backstage tonight," Troy stated. "Vegas will be at the door, and Charlie will be outside."

"What about me?"

He wanted to tell her to stay here, to lie low with Drake and the nanny. As the thought flashed through his mind, he realized Vegas was at least partially right. Troy did want to keep Mila safe.

His feelings for her weren't just about sex, and they weren't just professional. He liked her far too much, and he wanted to protect her.

"I'll mix with the crowd," she spoke into his silence. Then she looked down at her outfit. "But I'm not going to blend in this."

"Don't spook the guy," said Troy.

She gave him a look of reproach. "I won't."

"I want to see him in action, walking, talking." It was the best plan he'd come up with. "Maybe that'll jog my memory."

"I'll go put on something sexy."

Troy's throat went suddenly dry.

"I'm sure Kassidy has an outfit I can borrow. Maybe blazer guy will buy me a drink."

"No." Troy didn't want Mila that close to the guy.

She frowned. "If he uses his credit card, we get his name. If I'm going to have the downsides of being a woman, I might as well have the upsides as well."

"No," Troy repeated.

"It's not a bad plan," said Vegas.

"Stay out of this."

"Have I recently resigned as your partner?" asked Vegas. "Because I used to have a say in operations."

"It's a dangerous plan."

"It's a *drink*," said Mila. "And Vegas will be right there. Not to mention you. Come on, Troy. Get a grip."

"We don't know who this guy is."

Even as he said the words, Troy realized he was outdone. Vegas had an equal say in company operations. Troy couldn't veto him. Besides, they were right. It was a reasonable plan. The danger was minimal. He didn't know what was wrong with him.

"That would be the point," said Mila, moving closer. "I can clean up. I can look like a girl. I could attract a guy's attention."

Troy opened his mouth, about to tell her she'd knock any guy with a pulse off his feet. He caught Vegas's knowing smirk in his peripheral vision.

"Okay," he said instead.

The answer seemed to take her by surprise. But she quickly recovered. "Give me ten minutes." She headed back to Kassidy's room.

Mila felt conspicuous dressed in Kassidy's short kilt skirt. It was deep blue and green tones, pleated and flirty, barely falling to her midthighs. She'd paired it with a cropped black angora sweater, the sleeves pushed up above her elbows.

Kassidy had layered on some dramatic makeup while

Mila had brushed out her hair. It was wavy now and looked slightly disheveled from the earlier French braid. She'd never attempted heels this high, but judging by the lingering looks coming her way, the outfit was working.

She hadn't spotted the blazer guy yet. But she'd had three offers of drinks from other men. Through her discreet earpiece, Vegas surprised her with his sense of humor in response to the pickup lines. Troy seemed less than amused, warning her away from the men. As if she was about to get swept off her feet by: "Hey, girl. This is your lucky day."

She camouflaged her lips with her hand. "I've done this before, Troy."

"Been picked up in bars?"

Vegas jumped in. "She means been hit on in bars."

Charlie coughed out a laugh before he obviously switched off his mic.

"That's what I meant," she confirmed.

"You go into bars alone?" asked Troy.

"Sure."

"Dressed like *that*?"

"It doesn't matter what I'm wearing."

"Guys are easy," said Vegas.

"Guys are hound dogs," said Troy.

"Nice to hear one of you admit it," said Mila.

"Your two o'clock," said Vegas, his tone turning serious.

She glanced toward the front door, confirming blazer guy's location before letting her gaze move onward, pretending to scan for the restroom.

"That's him," she said. "How long until Kassidy comes out?"

"Ten minutes," said Troy.

Mila watched while the blazer guy made his way to the bar. He spoke to the bartender, who poured him an ice water.

"Going in," she muttered.

"Go get 'im," said Charlie.

"Enough commentary," said Troy, his tone clipped.

Mila wanted to tell him to lighten up, but she was pretty sure that would only make matters worse.

She sidled her way up to the bar, setting down her clutch purse and leaning forward. She didn't have a lot of cleavage, but by strategically placing her arms and letting the V neck of the sweater gape, she made the most of what she had.

The bartender was there in a heartbeat. Unfortunately, blazer guy barely glanced her way.

"Get you something?" asked the bartender.

"Neapolitan martini."

"Vodka?"

"Yes."

"Preference on the brand?"

"Give me your best."

"You got it." The man smiled as he withdrew.

Mila turned her attention to the blazer guy, staring openly at his profile, waiting for him to turn her way.

He slanted her a glance but didn't turn, instead taking a sip of his ice water.

She slipped onto the bar stool, watching the bartender work and toying with a cardboard coaster.

"Eight minutes," said Troy.

"I don't think that's helpful," said Vegas.

"Ask him about his jacket," offered Charlie. "The designer or whatever."

Mila inwardly rolled her eyes. She moved her elbow and knocked her purse to the ground. It landed with a clatter, the contents spilling out.

That got his attention.

"My phone," she cried, clambering down, pretending to stumble and leaning into him.

He quickly grasped her arms, steadying her.

"I'm so sorry," she gasped. "It's these heels."

Predictably, he looked down to see the four-inch strappy black shoes, replete with winking rhinestones.

"Could you?" she asked prettily, gesturing to the mess.

He glanced to the stage, hesitating before answering. "Sure."

She put a hand on his arm. "Thank you *so* much."

Then she bent down with him, exploiting her cleavage.

"Nice," said Vegas.

"Is that how women do it?" asked Charlie.

"Careful," said Troy.

Mila wanted to ask why she had to be careful. They were in a crowded bar, and she had three bodyguards. It wasn't as though the guy could spike her drink.

He gathered up her lipstick, cell phone, wallet and keys, then rose and handed her the purse.

"Thank you," she repeated, giving him an overly encouraging smile. "I'm Sandy." She held out her hand.

Again, he hesitated.

"Jack," he told her, accepting the handshake.

"Lie," said Charlie.

Jack's hand was soft, almost limp. Not a tradesman, she concluded. His skin was pale, so he didn't work outside. And his shoulders and arms seemed slim. She doubted he had a physical job at all. Maybe he was an accountant or an office manager.

"Three minutes," said Troy.

The bartender put the drink down in front of her and she quickly took a swallow, then another and another.

"That's commitment," said Vegas.

"This is fantastic," she enthused.

The bartender gave her a smile.

"I wouldn't mind another," she mused, finishing the glass.

Jack didn't pick up on the hint.

Unfortunately, the bartender was quicker on the draw. "Coming up."

Mila took another tactic, gesturing toward a poster of Kassidy. "I've heard she's a good singer."

Something came into "Jack's" eyes—possessiveness, defensiveness and caution. This had to be their guy.

"Have you heard her before?" Mila asked.

"A couple of times." His tone was flat.

"You like her?"

His glare told Mila he would prefer she shut up and go away.

"Made of frickin' stone," Charlie muttered.

"Quiet," Troy ordered. "One minute."

The bartender set the fresh drink down in front of her. He looked to Jack. Clearly, he was picking up on the vibes she was sending out.

But Jack ignored him.

"On the house," the bartender told her.

"Thanks." But she extracted a twenty from her purse and pushed it toward him.

"I'm coming over to pay for the drink myself," said Vegas on a note of disgust.

The bartender took the bill. He looked to Jack and gave a pitying shake of his head.

The lights came up on the stage, and the opening bars of Kassidy's first song rang through the room. Jack immediately vacated his bar stool and made his way forward.

"Got him," said Vegas.

"Good effort, Mila," said Charlie.

"Coming up on stage left," said Vegas.

"Got him," said Troy.

Mila sighed her defeat and took a sip of the new drink.

"Dumb as a bag of hammers," said the bartender.

Mila gave a shrug. "Maybe he's got a girlfriend. Have you seen him in here before?"

"Once that I remember," said the bartender. "Three weeks ago. Same singer."

"Yeah?" Mila turned her attention.

"He wasn't with a girl that time."

"Did he stick to ice water?"

"Cheap," said the bartender.

"My take was that he lied about his name." Mila let the statement hang.

"You ask, and I'll give you *my* name, my address and phone number, and the keys to my apartment." The grin and waggle of his eyebrows turned the statement into a joke.

"You need help?" asked Troy.

"She's fine," said Vegas. "Focus on Kassidy."

Yes, focus on Kassidy. What was Troy's problem?

"You ever get that guy's name?" Mila decided to come right out with it.

"Don't tell me you're still interested." The bartender sounded incredulous.

"Only curious," said Mila. She took another sip of the drink. "Maybe it's my ego. I'd like to know what went wrong."

"What went wrong is that he's a prize idiot. That's what went wrong."

"Gotta agree with that," said Charlie.

"Back off," said Troy, sounding genuinely ticked off. "Jack's at the edge of the stage. He's texting."

Mila went for her phone. Edison had set it up so that she could intercept Kassidy's messages.

"Six, six seven," said the bartender.

"Cute," said Mila.

She brought up Kassidy's messages. Sure enough, there was a new one from MeMyHeart.

The bartender moved to serve another customer.

"New message, MeMyHeart," Mila said in an undertone.

"Can you read it?" asked Edison from the control room back at Pinion.

The bartender returned. "You need another drink?"

"No, thanks. This is fine." She decided to give it one final try. "So that Jack guy, he never paid for anything with a credit card?"

The bartender's eyes narrowed, suspicion coming into his expression. "You a cop?"

"Not a cop." She searched for a cover story. "I have a sister," she said, then took a drink to buy herself some time. "That guy, well, he lied to her, treated her like crap."

"You're looking for payback?"

"I am."

The bartender shook his head. "Wish I could help you. Believe me, if I could rack up some points with you, I would."

Mila couldn't help but smile at his candor. "I'd give you points if you could come up with something. Anything."

"Drank only water. Watched the show. Left alone. That's all I can tell you."

She came to her feet. "Thanks anyway."

"So, no chance I'm getting your number?"

"No chance," said Troy.

"Sorry," said Mila. "But you seem like a good guy."

"Good guy," the bartender mocked. "Always the good guy."

"See you later," she told him as she moved away.

"I won't count on that," he called from behind her.

"Keep right on walking," Troy said in her ear.

Ten

It was impossible for Troy not to see the way men stared at Mila as she crossed the parking lot at the end of the performance. He was surprised by how many fans stayed back to catch Kassidy leaving through the back door, including the guy who'd called himself Jack.

They didn't have a whole lot more information from tonight, except to be positive that Jack was Kassidy's problem fan. He was definitely the guy sending messages as MeMyHeart and BluebellNighthawk.

Troy was also certain he'd seen him before. Vegas didn't recognize him, nor did anyone else on their staff. But Troy couldn't shake the impression this had something to do with him and Pinion. Kassidy was somehow a pawn.

They decided that Charlie would tail Jack while Vegas took Kassidy in his car. Mila would debrief with Troy on the ride back to Pinion. They needed to plan their next move. And she needed to accept that it would be Troy's call, not hers.

She'd done decent foundational work, but real threats were involved. She hadn't accepted that the situation likely centered on Troy, and he wanted to duke it out with her in private. He couldn't let her challenge him in front of his staff.

If he used kid gloves, it undermined his authority. And if he fired her…if he fired her, she'd be gone from his life. And he wasn't ready for that.

She was thirty feet from his vehicle, looking cold without her coat, being stopped by a couple of men. The two guys had obviously been drinking and were leering at her. Why hadn't she covered up with her coat? It was barely fifty degrees. She had to be freezing.

He rocked away from the SUV, intent on sending the two jerks packing. But her glare warned him off. Was that an order? Had the woman just given him a silent order?

Then she was moving again, coming closer, her little skirt

swaying against her smooth, tanned legs, her wavy hair rising and falling with her steps. She was graceful, beautiful, stunningly sexy. He wanted to grab her and kiss her, hold her tight and show every man in this parking lot that she belonged to him.

But she didn't. And he had no right to touch her. And that fact was probably going to kill him before this was all over.

He opened the passenger door. "How are you not freezing?"

She shivered at the suggestion. "My jacket didn't go with the outfit."

"You've been finished with the barfly act for a while now." He couldn't help a glance at the two guys who were still standing in the middle of the parking lot watching her.

He gave them a *back the heck off* glare, holding it until they looked away.

"It's in Vegas's car."

"Why didn't you get it? Or ask me to get it? Or ask Vegas to get it?"

"Are you done?"

His grip tightened on the open door. "Done what?"

"Criticizing me? Coddling me? Whatever it is you're doing. Can we please get in now and start the engine, maybe warm up?"

He swore under his breath and shrugged out of his jacket.

"Oh, no, you don't," she protested, backing away.

He swiftly wrapped his jacket around her, pulling her toward him.

"I'm one of the guys, remember?"

She was way too close to be one of the guys.

He zipped her in as if it were a straitjacket. "Get in."

"Is that an order?"

The jacket was roomy enough that she wiggled her arms into the sleeves, pushing them up to reveal her hands.

"It's an order," he confirmed.

"Yes, sir." She gave a mock salute and turned.

He impulsively patted her on the butt. Then he cringed, bracing himself for instant retaliation.

She froze, but didn't hit him. "Are you suicidal?"

"I may be. Sorry," he added.

"You *can't* do that."

"I know." Then the joke all but leaped out of him. "It's the skirt."

She made an inarticulate moan of protest. "How can you *be* like that?"

"This is why women can't work at Pinion."

She shifted to face him. "Because you'll manhandle them?"

"Because we don't do politically correct."

"Try, Troy. Summon some strength and *try*." She plunked herself down on the passenger seat.

He slammed the door, cussing himself out as he rounded the SUV. What was the matter with him? *Don't touch her.* It was one objective, one rule. How hard could that be?

It was five long minutes before she spoke.

"We need a name," she said.

And he realized she hadn't been sitting there stewing over his behavior.

She popped open her little purse. "We have his fingerprints."

Troy glanced to her lap, and he couldn't help a smile of admiration. "That's why you dropped your purse?"

"That and to get his attention. Seriously, Troy. Is this not a hot outfit?"

"It's a very hot outfit."

He didn't like to recall how hot it was. Because that made him hot. For her. And he didn't dare let his mind go there.

"The man's got a thing for Kassidy. I know you believe this is all about you, but I could have been a block of concrete for all he cared."

"Or he's focused on revenge. Guys like that don't have normal reactions to anything."

"I'm not being conceited," she said.

"Who said you were?"

"It's not that I think I'm super attractive. I get that I'm pretty plain."

Troy would vehemently disagree with that statement.

"But men aren't that picky," she said.

"You're not plain."

She waved away the sentiment. "I have a sister who's a bombshell. Trust me, I know the difference. My point is this Jack guy truly does have an obsession for Kassidy."

"And *my* point is, you are incredibly hot in that outfit tonight. I can't stop picturing it. I can't stop thinking about you. I can't stop *wanting*—"

"Don't." Her voice was so soft, he barely heard it.

He jammed the brakes and swung the vehicle to the side of the road, putting it in Park and angling to face her. "I can't control it."

"You can."

"Can you?"

"Yes."

"You're lying. You said I have a tell. Well, so do you. When you lie, your knees get tight."

"That's not true." But she glanced to her knees.

"For most people, it's in the face. You say it's my left ear, and I believe you. So, tell me, Mila." He turned his head to show the left side of his face. "Am I lying?"

He gave her a moment to focus. And he gave himself a moment to focus. His chest tightened up, and a part of his brain yelled at him to shut up. But he didn't want to shut up. He had to say it out loud.

"I can't stop thinking about you. And it's not just sex."

"No."

"I know you want to be one of the guys. And I wish you could be one of the guys. But it isn't going to happen. I can't keep you, but I can't bring myself to send you away."

"Let me prove myself."

"It doesn't work like that." He'd give anything to banish

the knowledge, the sickening certainty that told him how this all ended.

"Then how does it work? Tell me how it works, and I'll do it."

"You want to know how it works?"

"Yes!"

"You *die*, that's how it works."

"Huh?" Her expression turned to complete confusion.

"Maybe not today. Maybe not tomorrow. But I send you into a situation, and you're overpowered, and it all goes south, and you end up like Gabriela, in a body bag."

"Gabriela?"

"No amount of skill…intellect…or conditioning can prepare you for the guy who's six feet four and can bench-press a compact car."

"Nobody can overpower everybody."

"There's a mathematical odds element."

She seemed to frame her thoughts. "Who's Gabriela?"

"A security agent. A former security agent."

"Did she…?"

"She died."

Mila put a hand on his shoulder. "I'm so sorry."

"It was my fault."

"I'm sure it wasn't."

"You don't know anything about it." He gave into the urge to cover her hand with his.

"I know you." Her gaze was penetrating and honest. "You know what you're doing. You don't take chances. You don't make mistakes."

He squeezed her hand. "Nobody's perfect. I'll mess up again. It's only a matter of time. And I couldn't stand it…" He couldn't stand it if she was on the firing line when he did.

The street was dark. The car was dark. The glow of the dashboard reflected the smooth skin of her cheek. She was so close.

He reached out, stroked the pad of his thumb ever so gently against her cheek.

"Troy, don't." But her face tipped into the cup of his palm.

He slid forward. He kissed her mouth. His hand burrowed into her hair. The scent of her surrounded him, and she kissed him back.

He moved closer still. Their kisses grew longer and deeper. He unzipped his jacket, his hand going to her waist, finding its way between her skirt and her sweater.

"So soft," he whispered as he touched her skin.

He kissed her cheek, her neck, the curve of her collarbone, pushing the sweater out of the way to kiss the tip of her shoulder.

"We can't do this," she told him in a strained voice even while she shrugged out of his jacket, moving closer, tugging his shirt from his waistband.

"We have to do this."

He touched the hem of her sweater.

She hesitated, and he waited.

She lifted her arms. He eased the sweater off, then unhooked her bra. Her breasts came free in the dash light, creamy smooth, topped with deep coral nipples. He palmed one, and then the other.

She moaned, and he pulled her to him, smoothing the heated satin of her bare back. He made a tactile memory of her shoulder, her ear, her parted lips. She drew his finger into her hot mouth, and desire ricocheted along his limbs.

Cars zipped past them on the arterial road that led to Pinion, motors whining, headlights flashing off the glass.

He kissed her again, pressing her back against the padded seat. He touched her thighs, swirling upward to her silky panties. He longed to tear them off. He was hot and hard and impatient.

Instead, he eased past their barrier, drawing them away from her, slowly peeling them down, across her thighs, her knees, her calves and over her heels. He gazed at her bare breasts.

She cradled his head, drawing him down. He kissed one pert nipple. He pushed up her skirt, his fingers parting her, feeling her heat and moisture. His breaths were labored, a rapid pulse pounding in his temple.

"You okay with this?" He forced himself to ask.

"Good." She gave a rapid nod. "Good."

He flicked the button on his pants. There was a condom in his wallet, thank goodness. He found it. He pushed his clothes out of the way, and he settled her on his lap, her legs straddling his hips.

The heat of her around him was mind-blowing. He wanted it to last. But then she moved, and he was all but lost.

He gripped her hips, planning to hold her still. "You can't."

She leaned into him, her breasts coming up against his bare chest. Her cheek went to his, and she whispered, "Watch me."

Then she flexed her hips, and he groaned loud.

"Mila, slow—"

"Too slow?"

"No."

She was going to kill him.

"Faster?"

"No. Yes." He wanted both. He wanted it all.

"I can do faster."

He tried to protest, tried to tell her, tried to explain that there was fast and then there was fast. But it all came out as a groan of despair as he fought hard for control.

"Oh, Troy." Her breathing was rapid, while whimpers started down in her chest.

He realized she meant fast. She meant very *fast*.

He stopped fighting it, letting himself go, taking over the rhythm of their lovemaking, anchoring her, going faster and harder while the headlights blurred and she cried out in ecstasy.

He followed her over the edge, his heart all but exploding with the effort. They slowed and stopped, wrapped tight in each other's arms. The heat was blasting from the car vents, and the two of them were covered in sweat.

She was limp against him, and he didn't know what to say. Should he apologize? Was she going to be angry? Disappointed?

Her hands went tight on his shoulders, and he braced himself for recriminations.

But her voice was breathy soft. "I guess we can't pretend that never happened."

Mila's breathing was still deep as she gazed at their naked bodies, latched together on the leather seat in the hazy glow of the dashboard lights. There was distorting reality, and then there was smashing it into a million pieces.

She couldn't pretend to be one of the guys when she'd just had wild, shameless sex with the boss. There was no dressing it up this time, and there was no glossing it over.

"I'm not expecting anything in return," she told him, feeling as though she needed to state that up front.

"You can have anything you want in return. Name it, and it's yours."

"That's not how I'm getting a job."

"Except a job." He softened the words with a light kiss on her neck. "I can't give you a job."

"So, anything except what I really want?" She could joke about it because she would absolutely never let him hire her that way.

"I was considering jewelry or clothes, maybe a trip. Hey, you want to take a trip? Maybe a weekend in Cancun?"

Another set of headlights flashed in the mirror. Then it stabilized, grew brighter, shining directly on the back window.

She all but leaped from Troy's lap. "Someone's stopping."

"Huh?" He swiveled to see.

"Get dressed," she called out, pulling down her skirt and

fumbling for her sweater that was wedged between the seat and the door.

At the same time, Troy yanked up his pants.

They heard a car door slam shut.

While he scrambled for his clothes, she jerked her arms into the sleeves of his jacket, stuffing her bra and panties under the seat.

Then she smoothed her hair, tucking it behind her ears.

Someone rapped on the driver's window.

Troy looked at her. He reached out to rub his thumb beneath her lower lip.

"Smeared," he said.

She quickly scrubbed her hand back and forth across her mouth and shrugged down deeper into the jacket.

Troy unrolled the window.

It was Charlie.

"You guys okay?" he asked, glancing past Troy to Mila.

She gave him what she hoped was a benign smile.

"We're fine," said Troy. "How did you do? Did you follow him home?"

Charlie straightened so Mila couldn't see his face. "I lost him at Metro Center. He parked and took the subway."

The statement surprised Mila. Had the man known he was being followed?

"He could be anywhere. I got the vehicle license. But it's registered to a numbered company. The corporate address is an abandoned building. This guy knows what he's doing."

"Can you trace it further?" Mila asked.

She was trying desperately to forget she was naked under her skirt, and that she'd just had the best sex of her life. Kassidy was what mattered here. They needed to figure out who this Jack guy was and his connection to her.

"Not tonight," said Charlie. "I'll be on it first thing tomorrow. You all okay? Car trouble?"

"We were arguing," said Troy. "The more we learn, the

more I think this has to be about me. She's convinced it's all about Kassidy."

"He's stubborn," said Mila.

"She's closed minded."

"Me?"

"Sometimes your first instinct is wrong."

"It's not wrong. It might be complex, but it's not wrong."

"Whatever," Charlie drawled. "I'll leave you to it." He gave two taps on the door and left.

Mila waited until the interior light came on in his car.

"You think he guessed?" she asked Troy.

"Guessed that you and I can't keep our hands off each other?"

"What else would I mean?"

Troy checked the rearview mirror. "Could be our incessant arguments are throwing them off."

She realized he was probably right. "Why do you suppose that is?"

"Because they think we hate each other."

"No. I mean us. I mean, how can we fight so much and then…" She pointed back and forth between them. "And then *that*?"

"Beats me," he said.

"Do you secretly like me?" The question was out before she realized how pathetic it sounded.

He didn't miss a beat. "I'm a man. I don't have to secretly like you to—" He squeezed the steering wheel, staring through the windshield. "Scrap that. Yes, I like you. I don't mean it to be a secret."

She hated how relieved she felt. She shouldn't need his validation. Sex could be sex without worrying about the whole emotional package. She certainly wasn't looking for the whole emotional package. She was only looking for a job.

"You know I'm not going to die. I'm no more likely to die than Vegas or Charlie."

He turned to look at her, genuine pain in his expression. "I can't talk about that now."

She gave a sharp nod. "Sorry. Yes. That was out of line."

"That's not what I meant."

"I'm not going to use this against you."

His voice went sharper. "That's not what I—" He stopped talking and buckled his seat belt. "It's late. Let's get you home."

She followed suit as he flipped on his signal light and pulled onto the road.

"My car's at Pinion," she reminded him.

"I'm taking you straight home."

"But—"

"No point in you having to double back at this time of night. Plus, you've been drinking."

"That was hours ago."

She didn't know why she was arguing. Why would she want to go to the Pinion office, warm up her car, then make the twenty-minute drive back to her apartment when Troy could simply drop her off?

"Shut up," he told her mildly.

"Shutting up," she agreed, leaning her head back against the seat and shutting her eyes. "Thanks."

"No problem." He made a right turn.

"You know where I live."

"I know where you live."

She'd put her address on her employment forms. But she'd had no reason to assume he'd checked them.

"Off the top of your head?" she asked.

"Off the top of my head."

"Why?"

"Because I read your file. And I'm capable of holding dozens of facts up there all at the same time."

She couldn't help but smile to herself. "Dozens?"

"Some days, I amaze myself. You know where I live. Fair's fair."

"Where you live is relevant, and it's also kind of cool."

"Cool?"

"A penthouse at the top of a fortress. I know why Kassidy feels safe there."

"She is safe there."

"I feel safe there. Then again, I also feel scrutinized when I'm there. You have a lot of cameras in that place."

"Not in the apartment."

"Thank goodness for that." She couldn't help remembering the first time they'd made love, in his office.

"Here we go." He pulled to the curb in front of her apartment building, setting the parking brake and shutting off the engine.

"Thanks," she said again. Her hand felt heavy as she reached for the door handle.

He angled his body, stretching his arm across the back of the seat. "You mind if I come up and have a look?"

The question took her by surprise.

"I'm not asking to spend the night." He glanced at his watch. "I'm getting up in three hours anyway. I just want to see where you live. I feel like you know me way better than I know you."

"Sure," she agreed.

Fair was fair. And there was no reason not to show him her apartment. In fact, she found she liked the idea. It could be that she was romanticizing the situation, but saying goodnight in her place felt better than saying it at the curb.

They walked to the front door. She inserted her key, and Troy held it open. The lobby was small—two elevators, a door to the staircase, a couple of armchairs and a planter.

Both elevators were parked at the lobby. Troy pressed the button and the doors immediately opened.

"Twelve," he said, reaching for the button.

"Did you study up on my employee forms?"

"I thought one day there'd be a quiz."

The door closed behind them.

"What else do you know about me?"

"Your weight. Your height. Your graduation date. And your mother's maiden name."

"Not my bank account numbers?"

He smirked. "Well, we did need them for direct deposit."

"I trusted you."

"You can trust me."

The doors slid open, and they began to walk again.

"I'm at the end," she said. "Or did you know that too?"

"Never took a look at the schematics."

"But you could?"

"Edison would have them for me in about five minutes."

She unlocked the apartment door, swinging it open on a living room, open kitchen and a door that led to the bedroom and bathroom.

"It's small," she warned, flicking the light switch.

He gazed around at the dove-gray sofa, the coral throw pillows, the white accent tables and the watercolor portraits. "Wow."

"Wow good or wow bad?"

"Wow, prettier than I expected."

"So, you're back to thinking I'm a girl."

"I always knew you were a girl." He stepped toward the longest row of paintings. "Who are these people?"

"I have no idea."

He turned. "You hung strangers on your wall?"

"Is that weird?"

"A little. I'd think you'd go with people you knew, or maybe celebrities or public figures."

She moved up beside him. "I like the artists. And the subjects…" She tried to put it into words. "They're people I'd like to know. Each of them strikes me as mysterious, enigmatic, someone who has a secret."

"You like secrets?"

"I like complexity. Are you hungry?" She realized she was starving. "Cookies?"

He smiled. "You have cookies?"

"Homemade, chocolate chip."

"You *baked* cookies?"

"Don't sound so surprised." She unzipped his jacket, draping it over a kitchen chair as she made her way to the cupboard.

"You definitely don't strike me as the homemaker type."

"Then aren't you learning a whole lot of new things?"

"I am."

She took the container from the bottom shelf. "I like cookies. I like them fresh. So I learned how to make them."

"Cookies sound terrific," he said.

She returned the few steps to the living room, taking a seat on the sofa and setting the cookie container on the glass-topped coffee table, removing the lid.

Troy perched beside her, peering in. "Those look great. And they smell delicious."

"Help yourself."

He did.

She took two, kicked off her shoes and curled her feet beneath her on the sofa. As she did, she remembered her underwear. It was still stuffed under the seat of his SUV.

"What?" he asked, studying her expression.

"Nothing."

"What's wrong?"

"I left some of my clothes in your car."

He did a slow blink, his expression going slightly intense.

She bit down on a cookie.

"I'll get them later," he said.

She nodded.

His gaze held hers as he took a first bite.

Then his eyes lit up in surprise. "Delicious."

The reaction warmed her. "I have many talents."

"I'll say." He took another bite.

He picked out a second cookie, then he leaned back, his shoulder brushing hers. "Tell me more about your overly accomplished bombshell sister."

Mila faked an offended tone. "Hoping to do a little comparison shopping?"

"Yeah, that's what I'm doing."

"Sorry, bud. Zoey has a secret boyfriend."

"A *secret* boyfriend?" The interest level in his voice rose.

"A judge who's at odds with my mother."

"Is it serious?"

"It might be. And when the secret comes out, it's all going to hit the fan."

"It's her life," he said reasonably.

"Maybe so, but we're a close family. And they have expectations."

"That your parents get to approve your boyfriend?"

"Not exactly." She paused to think. "Well, kind of. It's important to them that we still work as a team."

"Team Stern?"

"Yes."

Troy took her hand. "You're twenty-four years old."

"You got that from my employment form."

"I did. But it's true."

She watched his thumb stroke a circular pattern on the back of her hand. She felt his light touch delve to the center of her chest, tightening her heart, making her body feel heavy and wanting.

"What's your point?" she asked.

He was silent for so long that she didn't think he was going to answer.

"No point." He cradled her head, drawing it down to rest on his shoulder. "We're going to figure this out."

"Figure what out?" From what she could tell, there was a list.

"Your life. And how it relates to mine."

Her heart stuttered then thudded. He couldn't have meant that romantically. And if he had, she should be scared. But she wasn't scared. She felt safe with Troy. The only scary part was that she wanted to keep feeling this way.

Eleven

Mila had fallen asleep in Troy's arms. And he'd held her as long as he dared before carrying her to her bed and covering her with a quilt then letting himself out of her apartment. He'd stolen a couple of extra cookies, which he now savored with a cup of coffee at the island in his kitchen.

Drake had heard Troy arrive and cried out from his crib, so he was now settled in his high chair pretending to eat cereal rounds.

"Sorry about this, bud," Troy said conversationally as he booted up his laptop to check a video he'd taken from backstage. "But you're too young for cookies."

"Bah," said Drake.

"I can't disagree with that." Troy clicked the play icon, watching closely as the man who called himself Jack made his way toward the stage at last night's performance.

"Bah, bah," said Drake, slapping his hand on the plastic tray hard enough to rattle the brackets.

"Maybe when you're older," said Troy, popping the final bite of cookie into his mouth. "If Auntie Mila is still around, she might bake you cookies."

As he said the words, Troy realized that Mila wouldn't be around to bake cookies for Drake or anyone else. Before long, she'd realize Troy was never going to give in and hire her, and she'd walk out the door.

He swallowed. The thought that she'd never forgive him left a hollow spot in his chest.

Drake let out a squeal.

"Shh." Troy put his finger to his lips. "You'll wake your mommy."

Then he paused, searching his memory, realizing he couldn't recall Kassidy ever referring to herself as "Mommy." She called Mila "Auntie Mila." But she used her own first name with Drake.

Was she struggling with the title? Was she planning to change it later? Drake deserved to have a mommy. He also deserved to have a daddy. But there wasn't anything Troy could do about that. Kassidy's career was all encompassing, and there was no sign of a boyfriend on the horizon.

He was forced to wonder all over again about Kassidy's decision. Was it too late to back out of the adoption? Might she reconsider? Of all people, Kassidy should have an appreciation for a stable family life. Theirs had been anything but.

He remembered their little house on Appleberry Street, the attic that had been converted into two bedrooms. At seven years old, Kassidy had been short enough to stand up in hers, but Troy had gotten dressed every day for high school slouched over.

Their father was always away. Kassidy's mother was off in her own world, making amateurish clay pots or writing rambling letters to the government about some perceived injustice or the other. Troy had bolted from that dysfunctional home before his graduation cap hit the ground.

Drake squealed again. He didn't seem upset or angry, more jubilant than anything else.

Troy poured another handful of cereal onto the tray in front of Drake. The majority of the rounds would end up on the floor, but they kept the little guy entertained, and usually they kept him quiet.

The video had continued playing, so Troy pulled it back to the beginning, settling in with his coffee to watch. Jack ignored the waitresses. He ignored the crowd. His attention was completely focused on Kassidy.

He could see where Mila was coming from, but he also knew he recognized the guy. And that was both significant and worrisome. The mathematical odds of a fan posing a danger to Kassidy were slim. The mathematical odds of someone from Troy's past posing a danger to his family were a whole lot higher than slim.

He took in the man's expressions, his walk, his stance.

He'd heard a little bit of the guy's voice over Mila's microphone last night, but it wasn't clear enough to gauge.

Who on earth was this guy?

"There you are, pumpkin," said Kassidy, wandering into the kitchen in a printed satin robe.

"You're up early," said Troy.

Drake squealed.

Troy smiled. "He's happy to see you."

"Of course he's happy to see me. Does he need a bottle?" Her voice changed to high-pitched baby talk. "You want Kassidy to bring you a bottle?"

"Bah," said Drake, slapping with his hand.

Troy's curiosity got the best of him. "You don't want him to call you Mommy?"

Kassidy stubbed her toe on the counter. "Ouch!"

"You okay?"

"No. Ow. Darn, that hurts." She hobbled to the table, cringing as she lowered herself into a chair.

"Are you really hurt?"

"Just give me a minute." She scrunched her eyes shut and breathed deeply.

Drake kicked his feet, squealing in a tone that sounded annoyed.

"Kassidy?"

"Yeah?"

"Don't you want Drake to call you Mommy?"

"Sure. Yes. Eventually."

"Are you having second thoughts about the adoption?"

Her eyes popped open. "No! No, Troy. I'm *not* having second thoughts. Drake is part of this family. Get *used to it*."

Troy held his palms up in surrender.

"Can you get him?" she asked.

"Sure." Troy stopped the video and rose.

Kassidy might be frustrating, but none of this was Drake's fault. Troy unfastened the safety belt, and the baby was immediately climbing to his feet. Troy couldn't help but smile at the antics. The kid definitely knew his own mind.

Troy brushed off the stray cereal and lifted Drake into his arms.

"You're getting stronger," he told the kid.

"Bah."

"Soon I'll have to take you to the gym." Troy did a mock exercise with Drake's chubby arm. "I'm a pretty good drill sergeant. You'll be buff enough to get any girl you want."

Troy's thoughts turned to Mila, her struggles on the obstacle course. Her killer naked body wrapped around his.

"Then again," he said quietly, "sometimes the girl's buff enough to get you."

Drake tugged at Troy's lower lip.

"Can you picture it?" asked Kassidy.

Troy stared at his sister. Did she know what he was talking about? Had she guessed that he was powerless to resist Mila?

"What?" he asked cautiously, hoping he could come up with an explanation on the fly.

"The gym, with Drake, when he's older. Do you see yourself in his life?"

Troy felt a rush of relief. "Sure. Why not? If he doesn't have a daddy around, he's going to need me."

Kassidy blinked rapidly, her eyes shimmering with tears.

"Hey," Troy cooed. "What's this?" He moved to her.

"My toe," she answered, her voice thick. "No, it's not my toe. It's you, Troy. You're stepping up."

Troy hoisted the wiggly Drake. "You mean with this little guy?"

"Yes."

"I'll admit, I don't know what you're doing. I'm not sure it's the right thing. But I'll be here for you, Kassidy." He thought back again to the house on Appleberry. She'd been so incredibly young back then. "I probably should have been here for you a long time ago."

She shook her head, coming to her feet, unexpectedly

wrapping her arms around him. "You're here for us now, big brother. That's all that counts."

"I'm here for you now," he said, wrapping his free arm around her.

Mila woke up alone on top of her bed, still dressed in Kassidy's clothes, a comforter keeping her warm. It was nearly ten o'clock in the morning, and she had no idea how late Troy had stayed. He'd obviously carried her to the bed. The realization was both heartwarming and unnerving.

She wondered if he'd slept at all. She was guessing not. He was probably chasing down leads for his own pet theory, which meant she was already running behind on her work. Would he hold it against her? Would he see her falling asleep as a sign of female weakness?

She swung her legs off the bed and headed for the shower. She needed to redeem herself, to demonstrate her analytical abilities, to remind him she was more than just a good-time girl.

She twisted the shower taps to full and stepped into the spray. Last night had been a mistake. And she knew she should regret it more.

Okay, she should find a way to regret it at all. Because she didn't. Right now, making love with Troy was a warm, exotic memory. Forget regret—she wanted to do it all over again.

This was bad. It was terrible. She might have undone every bit of her hard work. Nobody was going to take her seriously now, least of all Troy. And if he told anyone else—

She felt suddenly cold. *Would* he tell anyone? Would he tell Vegas?

Vegas was her best ally at Pinion, and she'd promised him she wouldn't sleep with Troy. If Vegas lost faith in her, if he thought she was fickle, if he thought she was weak—

She groaned under the hot spray. She'd worked hard for this chance. She wanted to be strong and in control, to take on both physical and mental challenges. She wanted to work with a top team and keep others safe. But the chance was rapidly slipping from her grasp. She had to stop the slide.

She squirted some shampoo into her palm, pushing her brain back to Kassidy and Drake, and back to Jack.

Troy would be looking at the man's connection to himself. It followed that his staff would be looking there, too. Mila needed to come at it from Kassidy, or even from Drake.

Suds running down her neck, her earlier theory came to mind again. It was outlandish, but it wasn't impossible. Jack could be Drake's father. Kassidy might not even know.

She hadn't reacted to the picture of Jack. But she'd sure reacted to the question of Drake's father. Maybe she knew Drake's father was dangerous, but maybe she didn't know who he was.

A chill came over her. If that was true, she needed concrete evidence to take to Troy. Because if she was right, they needed to protect Drake as much as they needed to protect Kassidy.

She threw on a pair of jeans and a T-shirt. Her car was still at Pinion, but she didn't have any time to waste. She hailed a cab and went directly to the airport. She didn't have much to go on, only the name of the hospital and Drake's date of birth.

She'd try the hospital first. If that didn't work, she'd go to public records. She might be able to talk her way into getting at least partial details.

It took her two hours to get to New Jersey, and less than ten minutes to get shut down by the hospital staff. By midafternoon, she was fighting a losing battle with the department of vital statistics. Without parental permission, she was not getting her hands on Drake's birth certificate.

She tried to explain that his mother was dead, and his father was unknown. She even pretended the query was related to Kassidy's adoption, hoping they'd have Kassidy's name on file. She was told to get a lawyer and a court order.

Defeated, she left the building, pausing on the stone steps, traffic whizzing through the intersection in front of her.

"Problem?" asked a well-dressed man in his late thirties. He moved up the steps toward her, flashing a friendly smile.

"No problem." She looked away.

"Get what you were looking for?"

"I did," she answered, starting to walk.

He fell into step beside her. "It doesn't look like you did."

"And what exactly would that look like?" As soon as the question was out, she wanted to kick herself. She'd just played into his hand.

"You wouldn't look so defeated. You'd have kept walking."

"I am walking."

"And you'd be carrying a manila envelope." He nodded to a couple who were also exiting the building. "Like that one."

"It's in my purse."

"Your purse isn't big enough. My name's Hank Meyer. I might be able to help you out. For a small fee, of course."

"I'm not interested, Mr. Meyer."

"Call me Hank."

"I don't believe I will." She picked up her pace.

"There are other ways of getting records."

Mila held up her hand to hail a cab. "Illegal ways?"

The guy was either fleecing her or asking her to participate in the crime.

"Quasi-legal."

"There's no such thing as quasi-legal."

He pointed across the street. "There's an internet café right there on the corner. They take cash. You're in, you're out, there's not a single footprint."

"It's still illegal."

"They're called opaque records. You can see them. You can't download them. You can't use them for any business or personal purpose. But you can snap a screenshot with your cell phone."

A yellow taxi passed by, but it already had a passenger.

"What are you looking for?" asked Hank Meyer.

"None of your business."

"I'm only trying to help you."

"No, you're not."

He had an angle. She just hadn't figured out what it was yet. An internet café was public, so she'd be in no physical danger. And using cash protected her identity and credit cards—his most likely scam. Perhaps this was bait and switch. It started out with cash, but then a credit card was ultimately required.

Another cab came into view, and she waved at it.

"You don't like what I have to offer, you can walk away at any time."

She sighed in exasperation as the cab passed by. "You're wasting your time, Mr. Meyer. I'm not falling for it."

"What were you after?"

She frowned at him.

"Just in broad strokes. Birth, death, divorce? I can tell you're on the job."

"On the job?"

"A private investigator."

"I'm not... Okay, I am investigating."

"Then you're either young or new. You look like you're both. We walk across the street. You give me the name. Fifty bucks, you're in, you're out. It's not exactly legal, but nobody's throwing anybody in jail if you're caught. Scratch that. If I'm caught, maybe I get a fine. You're just an innocent bystander."

"Or maybe you're law enforcement and, by the way, this is entrapment."

He laughed at that. "Yeah. Plainclothes detectives deployed to the public records center to entrap otherwise law-abiding document thieves. Now that's a good use of public resources."

Mila hated to admit that he had a point. She also hated to admit she was tempted. Fifty dollars. For fifty dollars could she get a sneak peek at Drake's birth certificate?

"This is Jersey, ma'am. Believe me when I tell you law enforcement has way better things to do."

Another cab sailed past. Mila couldn't help but wonder if it was a sign. She couldn't see any genuine dangers in the man's offer. He was likely just trying to make quick money.

"Have you been doing this long?" she asked.

"Two years. Never had a problem. What kind of a record?"

"Birth certificate."

"Recent?"

"This year."

"Piece of cake." He gestured to the crosswalk.

She took a bracing breath. "All right, Mr. Meyer. But I should tell you I have a black belt in Krav Maga and a permit to carry concealed."

"I don't expect the computer to fight back," he said easily. "But good to know."

The walk signal changed, and Mila quickly stepped up. If she was going to do this, she'd rather get it over with.

She gave Drake's name, birth date and the hospital information to Meyer. Then she waited on the sidewalk, feeling like a convenience store robber. Thankfully, he was back quickly.

"Start walking," he told her.

"Did you get caught?"

He grinned. "No. I'm done, that's all. Do you need a copy? It's safer if you just look at it on my phone, then there's no digital link between us. But if you need me to send it—"

"I'll just look," she said.

"Smart." He handed her his phone.

She looked at the photo, and her heart stopped.

She looked up at him, wondering if this could be some colossal con or sick joke.

"What?" He looked genuinely concerned. "Are you okay?"

"This is it?"

"Absolutely." He pointed to Drake's name and then to his birthdate.

"It's…" She didn't know what to say.

"Fifty bucks," he reminded her.

"Yes. Yes." She dug into her pocket, extracting the fifty she'd placed there while he was in the internet café. "Thank you."

"Pleasure doing business with you." He took his phone and sauntered away.

Mila moved down the sidewalk, gripping an iron fence at the edge of a small park.

It was Troy.

Troy was Drake's biological father.

She had to call Kassidy. And Kassidy *had* to talk to Troy.

What on *earth* was the woman doing? And who was out there stalking her?

"Kassidy is shopping with Mila," said Troy. He was on his way up from the Pinion garage, back from a working lunch with the Bulgarian planning team. "I told her she could turn the extra bedroom into a nursery." He couldn't help but smile at the memory. "She was really excited."

"Mila's car is still here," said Vegas.

"That's weird." Troy had assumed Mila would grab a cab back to the office once she woke up.

Again, he smiled, remembering how peaceful she'd looked when he'd left her, remembering how she had felt sleeping in his arms. He knew he was going to have to figure this all out, and soon. But for a moment he just wanted to enjoy how close he felt to her.

"The nanny's here, and Kassidy's late."

"So call her."

"Gabby tried, but she kept getting voice mail."

"Did you try?"

"For the past hour. Same thing."

Troy paused, for the first time hearing the worry in Vegas's voice. "You think something's going on?"

"I think we can't locate Kassidy, and she's been out of touch for a few hours."

"Call Mila."

The women had to be together. It was the only thing that made sense. Kassidy wanted to decorate the nursery right away. She couldn't wait to pick out wallpaper and furniture.

"I've tried Mila," said Vegas.

"Where are you?"

"The office."

"On my way up. I'll try Mila myself." Troy stabbed the end button as he mounted the stairs.

He dialed Mila, but it went straight to voice mail. He left a terse message to call him. She shouldn't be out of touch like this. Did she need call-waiting? They'd buy her call-waiting.

He strode down the hallway, thinking his way through the situation.

"Does Mila still have her communications device from last night?" he asked Vegas. "Get Edison to ping it."

Vegas immediately called down to Edison.

Troy greeted Gabby, who was in the office with Vegas. "I take it Kassidy was supposed to be here?"

"Over an hour ago," said Gabby. "Usually she calls if plans change."

"When did you last talk to her?"

"Last night."

So Troy was probably the last one to see his sister that morning.

"Do you mind waiting in the apartment?" he asked Gabby. "If she calls or shows up, get her to contact me right away."

"Of course," said Gabby. "If there's anything I can do to help."

"That's the biggest help you can be."

"I'm sure there's a simple explanation."

"So am I," said Troy, believing it less and less as the minutes ticked past.

"Mila's earwig is in her apartment," Vegas said as Gabby left the office.

Troy's phone buzzed, and he quickly checked the display.

"Mila," he said to Vegas, putting it to his ear. "Where are you?" he demanded.

"Getting in a cab. I'm on my way to the office."

"Kassidy's with you?"

"No. I haven't been able to reach her. Why?"

"You're not shopping?"

"I had something I needed to check out."

Troy swore.

"What happened?" Mila sounded worried.

"We don't know. Kassidy's out of touch."

"How long?" Mila's voice went on alert.

"At least an hour, maybe more. We thought she was with you."

"I haven't seen her since last night. Listen, there's something going on here that we haven't—"

"Who on earth *is* that guy?" Troy had racked his brain to no avail. His fuzzy memory of Jack was the best lead they had. "I have to call Charlie."

"Sure." Mila paused. "I'll be there in ten minutes."

"Good."

Troy wasn't sure why he felt relieved at the thought of her presence. There wasn't anything Mila could do to help. Kassidy might still be safe. She might have gone shopping alone and had her phone battery die.

And if that wasn't the case, if something had happened to her, there was nothing Mila could do that the Pinion team wouldn't already have underway.

"Yes, boss?" came Charlie's voice on the phone.

"What did you find out about the numbered company?"

"Not much. It's hidden behind a holding company."

"Local or offshore?" The thought that this could be an international client made things even more urgent.

"Pennsylvania."

That news was a relief—a small relief. It meant it likely wasn't a violent enemy based out of South America or the Middle East.

"Lancaster," said Charlie. "Didn't you live there once?"

"Yes," said Troy. He'd lived there with his father, Kassidy's mother and Kassidy. Adrenaline suddenly slammed the truth into his system. "Ronnie Hart."

Vegas looked up sharply.

"Who's that?" asked Charlie.

Troy's hair stood on end. "Find me Ronnie Hart. Anything you can get." Troy's brain started to race. "Particularly real estate. Does he own or rent anything in DC, Maryland or Virginia?"

"On it. That's our guy?"

"He's our guy," said Troy, ending the call.

"What?" asked Vegas, coming to his feet.

"A neighbor." Troy blew out a breath, not sure whether to be relieved or terrified. "Ronnie Hart was a neighbor on Appleberry Street, a teenager back then. But he played with Kassidy. He really seemed to like her. She was only seven, and it was kind of odd, but I was too self-absorbed to pay any attention. Her mother and my father were in their own worlds. You know, the kid practically raised herself."

"He's got them," said Vegas, tucking a gun into the back of his pants.

Troy agreed. "It wasn't about me."

He desperately scrambled for memories. Was Ronnie dangerous or merely deluded? He wasn't an international criminal bent on revenge. But he sure wasn't in touch with reality, either.

Vegas hooked up his earwig, tossing one to Troy. "Let's go get them."

Mila burst through the doorway. "What do we know?"

"Ronnie Hart," said Troy, gearing up himself.

"You have a name?"

"A former neighbor of Kassidy's and mine. Looking back,

I recognize the seeds of obsession. He must have followed her here. And now he's probably kidnapped them."

Mila moved closer, voice going low. "I need to talk to you."

"You armed?"

"Yes. But, Troy, we need to talk."

"Not now. Edison is looking for an address. I want to be in the car when he gets it."

"Now," said Mila. "Right now."

Troy glared at her. There was nothing more important than finding Kassidy and Drake. Whatever she wanted to hash out between them could wait.

"Mila," Vegas called. He tossed her an earwig. "You're coming?"

"I'm coming," said Mila. "Two minutes," she said to Troy, her voice implacable.

"I'll get Charlie and meet you in the garage," said Vegas.

"What is *your problem*?" Troy demanded as the door closed behind his partner.

"I'm sorry to do this," said Mila.

"Then *do it* later." Troy took his phone in hand, ready to answer the second Edison called.

"I wanted to talk to Kassidy first."

Troy gritted his teeth, his muscles turning to iron with anxiety and frustration.

"It's Drake," said Mila. "I'm sorry to say it like this. But, Troy, he's your son."

The words didn't make sense. They made absolutely no sense whatsoever. His first thought was that it was a joke. But if Mila was joking right now, he'd throw her out on her ass.

"Drake's mother is Julie Fortune."

Troy staggered on his feet, and a roar came up in his ears. "Julie?"

"You knew her?"

"She was a backup singer. For Kassidy."

"And…"

"It was one night." He barely remembered it. "In New York last year."

His brain scrambled through the memory. The dates were right. And Julie and Kassidy seemed to be close. The pieces became instantly clear. Troy had a son. Drake was his son. His son was in peril.

"Troy?" Mila touched his arm.

He forcibly snapped himself out of it. "Let's go."

A million thoughts pounded his brain as he strode through to the garage. But he couldn't let it mess with his judgment. He had a job to do.

As he entered the garage, his phone finally rang.

"Yeah?"

"Good call, boss," said Edison. "Ronnie Hart owns a house in Virginia. I just sent the address to your phones and to the vehicle GPS system. It'll take twenty minutes to get there."

"Get our earwigs all up on communications."

"Doing that right now."

"Over and out," Troy said, breaking into a run.

Twelve

It was an unassuming house, a single-story bungalow, red brick with black shutters on a corner lot of a quiet street. They'd parked two blocks away. Charlie and Vegas took the back, while Mila and Troy approached from the street.

Brown leaves were scattered on the lawn. Two maple trees and some miniature shrubs offered little in the way of concealment, so they stayed to one side of the building.

"Hang back," Troy told her.

"Yeah, right," she scoffed.

Mila was using every ounce of her skill and training to make sure Kassidy and Drake came out of this uninjured.

"That's an order."

"What are you going to do, fire me?"

He glared at her.

"Wait, listen." Her stomach clenched. "Oh, man."

It was a baby crying. Drake was inside that house crying his eyes out in fear, possibly hunger.

"It's a good thing," said Troy, his body taut, eyes steely with concentration.

"I know."

It meant Drake was okay for now.

They came to a stop, crouched under a window. And Troy stood slowly to look inside.

"It's a bedroom," he whispered to her and to everyone on the communications system. "I can't see anyone."

"They're not in the kitchen," said Vegas.

"Drake sounds like he's in the living room," said Mila.

Nobody disputed the analysis.

"You want to storm it?" asked Charlie.

"Too much of a risk," said Troy.

"Let me knock on the door," Mila suggested.

"Why you?" asked Vegas.

"I look normal. The rest of you look like mercenaries."

"Bad plan," said Troy. "He'll recognize you from the club."

"He didn't pay that much attention," she countered. "And I looked pretty different last night."

Nobody said anything.

"Got a better plan?" she asked.

"Stealth," said Vegas. "I can pick the lock on the back door."

"I'm going to check the living room window," said Troy.

He motioned for Mila to stay put, then he crept along the front of the house, below the level of the windows.

She followed anyway.

"It's only a matter of time before the neighbors see us and call the cops," she said.

He looked back at her and scowled.

"She's right," said Charlie. "If the cops show up, we could have a bad hostage situation."

Troy rose slowly, peeping into the front window. Then he snapped back down. "They're in there. But they're too close together. If we storm it, we risk Kassidy and Drake." He looked at Mila.

"Stealth's not an option?" asked Vegas.

"Any sound and he might grab one of them."

"I can do it," said Mila, making up her mind. "I'll knock. I'm just a woman with car trouble and a broken cell phone. If I get in, I can separate them and buy you some time."

There was another silence.

"Best we got," said Vegas.

Troy stared hard at Mila, looking as though he was trying to see down to her soul. He wanted to know she could pull it off.

She held her hand out flat, showing him her nerves were steady.

"Okay," he agreed.

He took up a spot between two windows, flattening himself against the wall. "No unnecessary chances."

"I'll only take the necessary ones." She tucked her gun into the back of her pants, moved her hair so that it covered her earpiece, then marched up the three concrete steps to the front door.

She boldly pushed the doorbell and knocked loudly, trying to sound like someone who wouldn't easily go away.

"Hello?" she called. "Hello? I need some help out here."

She glanced at Troy as she waited.

His mind had to be reeling from both the situation and the revelation about Drake. But he looked stoic, professional, focused. The job was the job, and he was getting it done.

This was why she admired him, she realized. It was why she wanted to learn from him. It was why she was falling for him.

She forcibly banished the distracting thought, banging on the door again. "Hello? I need to borrow your phone."

Drake was still crying inside, and she couldn't hear anything else.

She cupped her hand over the small opaque window, making a show of peering inside. "My car's broken down."

"Come on," she muttered under her breath. "Open up."

Then the door cracked. "I can't help you."

"I'm so sorry to bother you," she rushed on. "I hope I didn't wake your baby. How old is he, by the way? I have a niece."

"You need to leave," said Ronnie Hart.

"I understand. I will. But you're the third house I've tried, and nobody's home. I've got an appointment. I'm meeting my sister. She's pregnant. It's an ultrasound. It might be twins. And I just need to get the auto club. *Please?*"

It took him a minute to answer. "What's their number?"

"Oh, you're a lifesaver." She made a show of digging into her pocket. Then she leaned suddenly on the door, popping it open, sending him stumbling back.

"Thanks so much." she said, pretending he'd opened the door himself.

He swiftly backed away, placing himself next to Kassidy. She was pale and shaking. She seemed emotionally wrung out, holding a crying Drake and looking as if she might drop him.

"Hi, there," Mila told her cheerfully, making eye contact, hoping against hope she wouldn't react. "Nice to meet you. Cute kid. Your husband is making a call for me."

Thank goodness, Kassidy kept quiet.

But Ronnie took Drake from her arms. Not good.

"I know the number's here somewhere."

She looked up, and Ronnie was holding a gun on Kassidy.

"What's with the gun?" she asked to alert Troy and the others.

"Move!" Troy ordered.

"I recognize you now." Ronnie sneered at her. "You were there last night, chatting me up. You two must be friends."

Troy moved cautiously through the doorway, his gun drawn, gaze pinned on Ronnie.

"Back off," Ronnie ordered. He cocked the pistol. "Tell the other two to stay in the kitchen."

Troy's gaze went to Vegas and Charlie.

"I mean it!" Ronnie shouted. His eyes were glazed, and his face was flushed. He dangled the crying Drake precariously under one arm, the gun in his other hand trained on Kassidy, who was only inches away.

"Stay back," said Troy, motioning to Vegas and Charlie.

"We know what's going on here," said Mila in the calmest tone she could muster.

Ronnie brushed the gun against Kassidy's temple.

"I know you like Kassidy. I like her, too." Mila tried a smile.

"You know *nothing*," Ronnie spat.

"Mila," Troy warned.

But she couldn't back off. She was closest to them, and she was the only one who didn't have a gun trained on him. She needed to keep his attention, stop him from fixating on the deadliness of the situation and keep him from deciding he had nothing left to lose. And she needed to send a signal to Kassidy.

"I love her singing," said Mila, shifting her weight and using the movement to propel herself forward. "You must love it a lot. I know you've been in the audience.

"She's working on a new song," Mila continued. "With some great dance moves." She did a couple of foot moves, using the momentum to take her even closer to them.

Then she looked hard at Kassidy, peering deep into her eyes, willing her to understand the message. "There's this one move."

"Shut up!" Ronnie cried.

She continued staring at Kassidy. "At the opening of the new song. It's quite spectacular."

Kassidy's eyes went wide, and the blood drained from her face.

"We should get her to do it."

"Everybody," shouted Ronnie. "Get out!" He shook Drake, who shrieked in terror.

Two big tears welled up in Kassidy's eyes.

"Now!" Mila yelled, diving through the air for Drake.

Kassidy dropped to the ground. The gun went off. Mila tore Drake from Ronnie's arms, spinning her body to land on her back and break his fall.

She ripped the gun from her waistband and trained it on Ronnie.

But Troy was already there. He had Ronnie pinned to the floor. He flipped him over, fastening his wrists together.

Vegas was lifting Kassidy, cradling her in his arms.

"Get her out of here." Troy's voice was hoarse.

"Everybody okay?" asked Mila, gun still pointed at Ronnie.

Troy stared at her. She couldn't tell if he was angry or relieved.

Vegas carried Kassidy out the front door, while sirens sounded and grew louder. Obviously, the neighbors had reacted to the disturbance.

"I'll take him," Charlie said to Mila, crouching to lift Drake from her chest.

"He sounds hungry," said Mila, glancing around. "See if Kassidy had a diaper bag."

"Seriously?" asked Charlie.

"Seriously," said Mila.

Babies' stomachs didn't know anything about hostage-taking incidents. And with all that crying, he was probably dehydrated.

"I'm not changing his diaper," said Charlie.

"Wimp," said Troy, hauling Ronnie roughly to his feet.

Hours later, Ronnie was in custody, Drake was fast asleep and Troy was desperately trying to make sense of his life.

In the dimly lit bedroom, he smoothed his palm over his son's silky hair, watching his little chest rise and fall beneath the powder-blue sleeper. Drake suckled in his sleep, his red lips pursing in a bow. His fingers wriggled and so did his toes. Troy couldn't fathom what a baby that young could possibly dream about.

He also couldn't fathom what miracle had brought him here. How had Troy ended up with a child? He was the last person in the world who deserved an innocent baby. He had no role models to draw on. He had an erratic, sometimes dangerous job. He hadn't read any books, done any research. He certainly hadn't done any of the work to get Drake to this point in his little life.

"You drew the short straw, buddy," he whispered, his voice unexpectedly breaking.

Damn.

"But you're here," Troy continued. "And I'm what you get. And we're going to make the best of it. Okay?"

He leaned down and gave Drake a kiss on the cheek.

He straightened. "Okay." He braced himself. "Okay, that's what we're going to do."

He could hear Mila's and Kassidy's voices murmuring in the living room. A doctor had checked out his sister. She'd been suffering from mild shock, but some dinner and a glass of wine seemed to help.

Now he needed to talk to her. He needed about a million questions answered. Their voices grew louder as he entered the room.

He stopped. He stared in disbelief at his sneaky sister, reflexively folding his arms over his chest.

"Troy," said Mila in a warning tone. "The interrogation can wait."

"I don't think so." He moved forward, taking one of the armchairs, cornerwise from Kassidy.

He knew he had to stay calm. She'd had an incredibly rough day. But he needed answers.

"I don't get it," he said to his sister. "Why the ruse? Why not tell me up front?"

Kassidy's voice shook a little. "I wasn't sure how."

He felt like a heel, but he couldn't back off.

"Honestly," she said. "I wasn't sure *if* I should tell you at all. I know you don't want a baby."

"It doesn't matter if I want a baby or not. I *have* a baby."

"Troy, take it easy," said Mila.

"Julie asked me to adopt him. She wanted him to stay with his family."

Troy guessed he could understand that.

"I was afraid." Kassidy swallowed. "I was afraid you'd give him away."

Troy opened his mouth to protest.

"No," she said. "I knew there was a chance you wouldn't want him. And I know you thought I'd make a terrible mother."

He couldn't argue that. When she'd first showed up on his doorstep with Drake, that was exactly what he'd thought.

"I was terrified." Her throat sounded clogged. "That you'd make me give him away to someone better. But I love him, Troy. I was there when he was born. I couldn't bear to give him to strangers."

Troy's chest tightened. "We're not giving him to strangers." He leaned out to take her hand. "He's my son, Kassidy. Of course I'm going to raise my son."

She gave him a watery smile. Beside her, Mila wiped her eyes with the back of her hand.

Troy wanted to smile at that. Mila had been a rock today, and now she was getting sappy over a little baby. He swallowed a lump of emotion himself. He supposed he understood.

"You did good today," he told Kassidy. "Really good. You kept your cool and helped save Drake's life."

A shudder visibly ran though her. He realized she was still pale, and there were shadows under her eyes.

"Get some sleep," he told her. "We've got a nursery to plan."

She managed a smile.

"And your room, too. I want you here as much as possible to help with Drake."

She gave a rapid nod.

"We're an unorthodox family." That was an understatement. "But we are a family."

"We can do better than we have in the past," she said.

"Absolutely," Troy agreed.

Kassidy slowly rose to her feet. "Okay. That's good. I'm going to bed now." She leaned over to give Mila a hug. "Thank you *so* much."

"Get some sleep."

"I will." Kassidy gave a chopped sigh and left for her bedroom.

His gaze came to rest on Mila.

She looked back.

"You want to talk now?" he asked, even as his energy drained silently away.

"Are you ticked off at me?"

"Little bit."

She'd taken an incredible risk. She'd ignored his direct

orders in the field. They'd had a good outcome, but the end didn't always justify the means. And the end could have been very different.

"Then, no," she said. "I don't want to talk right now."

But she surprised him by rising, crossing the room and setting herself down in his lap.

His entire body sang in contentment. He settled an arm around her shoulders.

She peeled off her shoes. "Let's argue later."

"Later works for me." He had no desire to argue with her just then.

She leaned her head against his shoulder, and he placed his palm on her warm stomach. She was so fit and tough, but she was still soft and smooth. How could anyone be such a perfect combination?

The curve of her backside was cradled in his lap, and it took about thirty seconds for his body to respond.

He rested his cheek against her hair and inhaled deeply.

"I know we always do this impulsively," he said. "We don't analyze it, and we don't discuss it. But I have to say, all relevant facts considered, I really want to carry you off to my bedroom and make love to you for the next twelve hours or so."

"Maybe we should discuss the pros and cons," she whispered.

"There are a lot of pros." He wrapped his hand around her rib cage and settled her more closely to his body.

"Such as?"

"Such as, you're beautiful, you're soft and sexy, you're smart and funny and bold as all get-out. And I love the way you smell."

She turned her face toward him. "I love the way you smell." Her palms slid up his chest. "And I love the way you feel. So strong. You make me feel safe."

"You are safe."

She tilted her chin, and he kissed her mouth. She tasted amazing. He kissed her again.

"There are also cons."

"Not tonight. The cons can sit this one out. The world can sit this one out. It's just you and me, Mila."

She smiled, her green eyes bright and deep as a glacial lake. "Okay."

She pushed herself up and stood.

He took her hand. She snagged the bottle of wine.

On the way past the bar, he picked up a couple of glasses.

He locked the bedroom door behind them, hitting the switch for the gas fireplace. The spacious room was filled with a soft orange glow.

"Nice," she said.

"You're what's nice."

He set down the wine and the glasses and pulled back the covers on the king-size bed.

She followed him over, removing her T-shirt and dispensing with her bra. He pulled off his own shirt, unbuttoning his pants. Then he paused while she stripped off her socks and her jeans and stood there in her white lace panties.

"You're gorgeous," he told her, tracing a line from her neck to her shoulder and down her arm. "Can I just stand here and look at you for a while?"

"Sure," she said.

He'd expected to be impatient. He was definitely aroused. But he didn't just want sex here. He wanted more. He wanted to know her like nobody else knew her. He wanted all of her, body and soul.

She traced a scar that traversed his abdomen. He knew it was the most prominent one. She looked expectantly up at him.

"Car crash. Chasing a guy through downtown Munich."

"Not a knife fight?"

"Knife fights are bad news. You want to stay out of knife fights."

"Did you catch him?" she asked.

"I did."

She traced another scar.

"My misspent youth," he told her.

"Poor baby." She leaned in to kiss it.

The warmth of her lips sent tendrils of desire skittering across his skin. He groaned and drew her into his arms.

"You feel even better than you look," he said.

"So do you."

"Kiss me."

She looked up at him. "Sure."

He brought his lips to hers, and the world truly did fall away. He lifted her onto the bed, stripped off the rest of his clothes, dispensed with her panties and drew her full-length into his arms. She was all limbs and motion, warmth and friction. He touched her everywhere, kissed her everywhere, watched the firelight play off the honey of her skin.

She was everything he wasn't. Her hair was soft as silk. Her lips were like rose petals. Her soft breasts filled his hands, and her moist body welcomed him into the apex of heat and softness. He wanted to stay here forever. He wanted Mila forever.

There was no way in the world he could see giving her up.

Finally, they were satiated and still. He lay there beside her, then rose up on one elbow to gaze at her. Her eyes were closed. Her breathing was even. If she wasn't asleep, she soon would be.

He was in love with her.

He'd never felt it before, but he was certain of it. He wanted everything for her, nothing but the best. He wanted her to be happy and safe, and he wanted her to be close to him—to him and Drake—forever.

He didn't know what to do about that, but there it was.

"You saved my son," he whispered.

"Hmm?" The word was barely a breath. Her hand twitched but then went still.

"Thank you, Mila."

* * *

Mila awoke feeling lighter and more confident. She emerged from Troy's bedroom, hearing his voice coming from the kitchen. It was obvious he was talking to Drake.

She stopped in the doorway, leaning on the wall. "Morning."

Troy smiled at the sound of her voice, looking up from his tablet. "Morning."

She walked into the room.

"Coffee?" he asked.

"Love some."

He rose to take a white mug from the bottom shelf. "Sleep well?"

"I did." She stroked the top of Drake's head.

He banged his heels against the high chair, selecting another round of cereal.

"Me, too." Troy handed her a cup of coffee.

"You want to say what you've got to say?" she asked.

She'd ignored his orders last night, and he had a right to be annoyed. He'd said as much before they'd made love last night.

"It's over," he said.

"I don't understand."

Didn't he want to lay down the law, tell her to never pull anything like that again?

"Let's move on."

"To what?" She didn't want special treatment. If she deserved a dressing-down, she'd take it.

"Last night," he said, his voice gentle, hand coming up to touch her cheek, "well, it made me realize…"

"That I can hack it?"

"That you're one in a million."

Her heart warmed. "So, you get it now? You see what I can do."

He gave a secretive smile, stepping closer. "I saw what you can do, all right."

"That's not what I meant."

"It was pretty fantastic."

She wrapped her hand around his wrist. "I meant on the job."

"Let's not talk about the job."

She took a step back. "I proved my point."

His voice firmed up. "That it wasn't about me? I did know Ronnie Hart."

"What? No. I'm not saying you were wrong. I'm saying I handled myself. I did the job. I *saved* Drake."

Troy's voice went flat. "You're saying you want to be rewarded?"

"To be acknowledged. I want what I've always wanted, Troy."

His hand dropped to his side. "A hundred guys could have done what you did."

It took her a minute to believe he'd said it.

"You're better than that, Mila. You're more than those hundred guys put together."

She stared hard at his implacable expression. "Oh, no, you don't. Don't you dare tell me I'm too good for you to hire."

"You are too good for me to hire. I want you in my life, not as some employee, as a woman, as the woman—"

"No," Mila cried out.

He couldn't do this. He wouldn't do this.

"Hear me out," he said.

Dread trickled through her. "What about last night?"

"Last night had nothing to do with any job."

"But—"

His expression turned sour. "You said you'd never sleep your way into a job."

She wasn't talking about the sex. She was talking about rescuing Drake and Kassidy. "I showed you what I can do. I proved to you I was just as good as any man."

"Did I ever, even once say I wanted you to prove something? Did I ever offer to hire you? Did I ever give you any false hope?"

"I thought…" She'd thought he'd come around. She'd thought after yesterday he'd be forced to see she could do it.

Drake kicked and vocalized in the background, tossing cereal rounds to the floor.

"I want you in my life, Mila," said Troy.

"But not in your company."

"I want you forever, not just until the first bullet—" He abruptly stopped, balling his hands into fists.

"You have no faith in me."

"I'm a realist. I can't pretend I'm not."

She set down her cup and backed for the door. "And I can't pretend I'm a failure."

"I never said—"

"I'm not a failure, Troy." A sharp pain gripped her chest, tightening in the hollow space around her heart.

She'd deluded herself. She thought because she loved him, he loved her back. And if he loved her, he had to respect her.

She was wrong. He'd never respect her. Nothing had changed. He would never change.

It was over. She might be a Stern, but she'd failed anyway. She'd absolutely failed.

"Why didn't you *tell me*?" Troy demanded, glaring at Vegas's back where he sat in the control room.

"Tell you what?" Vegas asked without turning.

"That she was here. That she came back."

Troy's world had functionally ended two weeks ago when Mila walked out. He went through his days by rote, missing her every single second.

"She's been back a bunch of times," said Vegas.

"What?" Troy stared at the monitor that was trained on the obstacle course where Mila was dragging herself through the mud.

Vegas turned in his swivel chair. "To practice. She never gave up on herself. She's hell-bent on finishing it."

Resentment rose in Troy, anger at Vegas for keeping him in the dark. "Who else knows?"

"Everyone."

Troy saw red. He didn't dare speak. He wanted to fire the entire company.

"They've helped her," said Vegas. "Charlie, Edison, me. We've all shared our best techniques."

"Nobody goes near her," Troy shouted. *"Nobody."*

"Boss?" Charlie asked from behind him.

"Better get out of here," warned Vegas.

"Why?" asked Charlie.

Then Troy faced him, and Charlie's eyes went wide.

"What were you doing with Mila?" Troy demanded.

Charlie held his palms up in surrender, backing into the hall. "Nothing. Nothing, boss. I just gave her a few pointers on the obstacle course."

"They like her," said Vegas.

"I like her, too," Troy shouted. "That's why I want to keep her alive."

"She's not going to die," Vegas stated with impatience.

"Not on my watch," said Troy.

"She's no more likely to die than you," said Charlie.

Troy all but growled at him.

But Charlie took a bold step forward. "You're wrong in this."

"That's *not* your call."

Had Charlie lost his mind?

"Can Vegas take you?" Charlie asked. "Hand to hand, can he not take you every single time?"

Troy wasn't walking into that trap. It wasn't the same thing.

"Does that make you useless?" asked Charlie.

"Watch your—"

"Take me?" Charlie spoke right over Troy. "I'm not that big. But I can shoot a gnat from five hundred yards. And Edison? Even I can take Edison. But give him some common cleaning products and a remote car starter and he'll level a city block."

"It's *not* the same thing," Troy ground out.

"It's exactly the same thing," said Charlie. He pointed to the video monitor. "We like her. We *need* her. Diversity makes us stronger, and we want her on the team. We voted."

"You *voted*?" Troy couldn't believe what he was hearing.

"It was unanimous."

"Since when does voting have anything to do with decisions at Pinion?"

"I certainly have a vote," Vegas said quietly.

Troy and Charlie turned to look at him.

"But you're wrong if you think it's the same thing," Vegas said to Charlie.

Troy was supremely thankful for Vegas's sanity.

"It's different with Mila," Vegas continued. "It's different because Troy's not in love with you, or with me, or with Edison."

"I'm not—" Troy stopped himself. Did he really want to deny it out loud?

"Here's the thing," Vegas said to Troy. "You can love all of her, or you can love none of her. You don't get to pick and choose."

Troy didn't accept that he was trying to pick and choose. He was only trying to keep her safe. Any man would do that for the woman he loved.

Vegas canted his head to the monitor. "Look at the clock. She's going to do it this time. She's going to make it through the obstacle course."

"There's no way." But Troy took in her position on the course and the time left.

Charlie whistled under his breath.

Excitement took over Troy's stomach.

"You blow it with that woman," said Vegas, "I really am going to knock you senseless."

"Better me getting hurt than her." Troy was distracted by the monitor.

Vegas came to his feet.

Troy glared at him, half expecting to get into a fight.

But Vegas took a step toward the door. "Somebody's got to be down there to meet her."

"That'll be me." Troy wasn't letting anyone else near her.

"Then you'd better offer her a job," said Vegas.

Everything inside Troy rebelled.

He couldn't. He wouldn't. Then again, how could he not?

"Your choice," said Vegas. "But if you don't, I will. There's no way Pinion is passing on a candidate with her scores."

"I'll go," Troy repeated.

"And?" Vegas prompted.

"And I'll hire her," Troy ground out.

He turned on his heel, brushing past Charlie to stomp into the hall.

How could she do it? She was about to defy the odds, to defy logic, maybe even defy the laws of physics. She was one in a million, one in a billion. She wanted what she wanted, and he was powerless to say no. He was madly, passionately, hopelessly in love with her.

Then his footsteps grew lighter as he trotted down the stairs.

He was offering her a job. And then he was offering her a ring. And then he was begging her to spend the rest of her life with him and with Drake.

He burst through the back exit, sprinting toward the finish line of the obstacle course. She was a quarter mile away, running her heart out as the seconds ticked down on the clock.

She was going to make it.

She *had* to make it.

Suddenly, her ankle gave way beneath her. She fell to the dirt, and his heart lodged in his throat. He had to forcibly stop himself from rushing to her aid.

She pulled herself to her feet. She staggered a few steps, losing precious time.

"Come on, Mila," he said under his breath.

She broke to a jog, then to a run, steadier with each step.

There was less than a minute left on the clock. He wanted desperately to give her more time.

Then she saw him.

Her steps slowed.

"No," he called out.

She stopped.

"No!" he shouted at her. "Go. Run. You can do it!"

He heard voices behind him and realized half the building had emptied to cheer her on.

A smile came over her face, and she started again, running faster. He backed off, over the line to wait for her to get there.

She closed in on it while the crowd counted down the seconds.

She made it across with six seconds left, and Troy punched a fist in the air. He grabbed her, hugging her tight around the waist, hoisting her muddy body into the air.

"You're hired," he told her. "You are so, *so* hired."

Then he kissed her while the crowd rushed around, patting her on the shoulders, congratulating her.

He slowly lowered her to the ground.

She was grinning from ear to ear.

"Charlie," he said, never taking his gaze off Mila. "Better get someone to build a new locker room."

"Yes, boss," said Charlie.

"Everybody else?"

"Yes?" they answered in unison.

"Get out of here."

There were good-natured chuckles as they all backed off.

"Mila," he whispered, brushing her muddy hair from her sweaty forehead.

"Yes, boss?" she answered.

"You'll take the job."

"Yes."

"And will you marry me?"

Her clear green eyes went wide in her muddy face.

"I love you," he said. "I love you so much."

She hesitated for a moment.

He stilled, waiting with apprehension.

"Can I do both?" she asked in a hesitant voice.

It was his turn to grin. "I'm sure hoping you will."

"I'm hired?" she confirmed.

He laughed. "You're also engaged."

"I don't know which will make my family happier." She came up on her toes to kiss him.

He couldn't seem to stop himself from pressing his luck. "Which makes you happier?"

She brushed her hand across his cheek. "That I get to love you, and be with you, and share your entire life."

"Good answer, my love. We are going to make one heck of a team."

* * * * *

"I need to tell you..." Her words were still little more than a whisper.

"What do you need?"

Her eyes widened again as his face got within inches of hers, and she exhaled, something that sounded a hell of a lot like satisfaction. His gut twisted. Despite her lies and betrayal, the messy ending to their relationship and the long year on a different continent—despite it all—he wanted her.

"The job," she said in a voice that didn't even make it to a whisper. "I want the job, Byron."

And she didn't kiss him, didn't tell him she was so sorry she'd picked her family over him. At no point did she apologize for lying to him.

"Right, right."

She couldn't be more clear. She was here for the job.

Not for him.

* * *

His Son, Her Secret
is part of the Beaumont Heirs series:
One Colorado family, limitless scandal!

HIS SON, HER SECRET

BY
SARAH M. ANDERSON

Published in Great Britain 2015
by Mills & Boon, an imprint of Harlequin (UK) Limited,
Eton House, 18-24 Paradise Road, Richmond, Surrey, TW9 1SR

© 2015 Sarah M. Anderson

ISBN: 978-0-263-25277-4

51-0915

Award-winning author **Sarah M. Anderson** may live east of the Mississippi River, but her heart lies out West on the Great Plains. With a lifelong love of horses and two history teachers for parents, she had plenty of encouragement to learn everything she could about the tribes of the Great Plains.

When she started writing, it wasn't long before her characters found themselves out in South Dakota among the Lakota Sioux. She loves to put people from two different worlds into new situations and to see how their backgrounds and cultures take them someplace they never thought they'd go.

Sarah's book *A Man of Privilege* won the 2012 RT Reviewers' Choice Award for Best Harlequin Desire. Her book *Straddling the Line* was named Best Harlequin Desire of 2013 by CataRomance, and *Mystic Cowboy* was a 2014 Booksellers' Best Award finalist in the Single Title category as well as a finalist for the Gayle Wilson Award for Excellence.

When not helping out at her son's school or walking her rescue dogs, Sarah spends her days having conversations with imaginary cowboys and American Indians, all of which is surprisingly well tolerated by her wonderful husband. Readers can find out more about Sarah's love of cowboys and Indians at www.sarahmanderson.com.

To Joelle Charbonneau and Blythe Gifford, who took me under their wings when I was new and clueless, held my hands when I stumbled, and who even became friends with my mom. Thank you for being guides on my journey, ladies!

One

"This place is a dump," Byron Beaumont announced. His words echoed off the stone walls, making the submerged space sound haunted.

"Don't see it as it is," his older brother Matthew said through the speaker in Byron's phone. It was much easier for Matthew to call this one in, rather than make the long journey to Denver from California, where he was happily living in sin. "See it as what it will be."

Byron did another slow turn, inspecting the extent of the neglect as he tried not to think about Matthew—or any of his older brothers—being happily engaged or married. The Beaumonts hadn't been, until recently, the marrying kind.

Yet it hadn't been so long ago that he'd thought *he* was the marrying kind. And then it had all blown up in his face. And while he'd been licking his wounds, his brothers—normally workaholics and playboys—had been pairing off with women who were, by all accounts, great for them.

Once again, Byron was the one who didn't conform to Beaumont expectations.

Forcibly, he turned his attention back to the space before him. The vaulted ceiling was arched, but the parts that weren't arched were quite low. Cobwebs dangled from everything, including the single bare lightbulb in the middle of the room, which cast deep shadows into the corners. The giant pillars supporting the arches were evenly spaced, taking up a huge amount of the floor. Inches of dust coated the low half-moon windows at eye level. What Byron could see of the outside looked to be weeds. And the whole space smelled of mold.

"And what will it be? Razed, I hope."

"No," Byron's oldest half brother, Chadwick Beaumont, said. The word was crisp and authoritative, which was normal for Chadwick. However, the part where he lifted his daughter out of his wife's arms and onto his shoulders so she could see better was not. "This is underneath the brewery. It was originally a warehouse but we think you can do something better with it."

Byron snorted. Yeah, right.

Serena Beaumont, Chadwick's wife, stepped next to Byron so that Matthew could see her on the phone. "Percheron Drafts has had a great launch, thanks to Matthew's hard work. But we want this brewery to be more than just a craft beer."

"We want to hit the old company where it counts," Matthew said. "A large number of our former customers continue to be unhappy about how the Beaumont Brewery was sold away from our family. The bigger we can make Percheron Drafts, the better we can siphon off our old customers."

"And to do that," Serena went on in a sweet voice at direct odds with a discussion about corporate politics, "we need to offer our customers something they cannot get from Beaumont Brewery."

"Phillip is working with our graphic designer on incorporating his team of Percherons into all of the Percheron Draft marketing, but we have to be sensitive to trademark issues," Chadwick added.

"Exactly," Matthew agreed. "So our distinctive element can't be the horses, not yet."

Byron rolled his eyes. He should have brought his twin sister, Frances, so he would have someone to back him up. He was being steamrollered into something that seemed doomed from the start.

"You three have *got* to be kidding me. You want me to open a restaurant in this dungeon?" He looked around at the dust and the mildew. "No. It's not going to happen. This place is a dump. I can't cook in this environment and there's no way in hell I would expect anyone to eat here, either." He eyed the baby gurgling on Chadwick's shoulder. "In fact, I'm not sure any of us should be breathing this air without HazMat masks. When was the last time the doors were even opened?"

Matthew looked at Serena. "Did you show him the workroom?"

"No. I'll do that now." She walked toward a set of doors in the far back of the room. They were heavy wooden things on rusting hinges, wide enough a pair of Percheron horses could pull a wagon through them.

"I've got it, babe," Chadwick said as Serena struggled to get the huge latch lifted. "Here, hold Catherine," he said to Byron.

Suddenly, Byron had a baby in his arms. He almost dropped the phone as Catherine leaned back to look up at her uncle.

"Um, hey," Byron said nervously. He didn't know much of anything about babies in general or this baby in particular. All he knew was that she was Serena's daughter from a previous relationship and Chadwick had formally adopted her.

Catherine's face wrinkled in doubt at this new development. Byron didn't even know how old the little girl was. Six months? A year? He had no idea. He couldn't be sure he was even holding her right. However, he was becoming reasonably confident that this small human was about to start crying. Her face screwed up and she started to turn red.

"Um, Chadwick? Serena?"

Luckily, Chadwick got the doors open with a hideous squealing noise, which distracted the baby. Then Serena lifted Catherine out of Byron's arms. "Thanks," she said, as if Byron had done anything other than not drop the infant.

"You're welcome."

Matthew was laughing, Byron realized. "What?" he whispered at his brother.

"The look on your face…" Matthew appeared to be slapping his knee. "Man, have you ever even held a baby before?"

"I'm a chef—not a babysitter," Byron hissed back. "Have you ever foamed truffle oil?"

Matthew held up his hands in surrender. "I give, I give. Besides, no one said that starting a restaurant would involve child care. You're off the hook, baby-wise."

"Byron?" Serena said. She waved him toward the doors. "Come see this."

Unwillingly, Byron crossed the length of the dank room and walked up the sloping ramp to the workroom. What he saw almost took his breath away.

Instead of the dirt and decay that characterized the old warehouse, the workroom had been upgraded at some point in the past twenty years. Stainless-steel cabinets and countertops fit against the stone walls—but these walls had been painted white. The overhanging industrial lighting was harsh, but it kept the room from looking like a pit in hell. Some cobwebs hung here and there, but the contrast between this room and the other was stunning.

This, Byron thought, *had potential.*

"Now," Matthew was saying as Byron looked at the copper pipes that led down into a sink that was almost three feet long, "as we understand it, the last people who used this brewery to brew beer upgraded the workroom. That's where they experimented with ingredients in small batches."

Byron walked over to the six-burner stove. It was a professional model. "It's better," he agreed. "But this isn't equipped for restaurant service. I can't cook on only six burners. It's still a complete teardown. I'd still be starting from scratch."

There was a pause, then Matthew said, "Isn't that what you want?"

"What?"

"Yes, well," Chadwick cleared his throat. "We thought that, with your being in Europe for over a year…"

"That you'd be more interested in a fresh start," Serena finished diplomatically. "A place you could call your own. Where you call the shots."

Byron stared at his family. "What are you talking about?" But the question was a dodge. He knew *exactly* what they were thinking.

That he'd had a job working for Rory McMaken in his flagship restaurant, Sauce, in Denver and that not only had Byron been thrown out of the place over what everyone thought were "creative differences" but that Byron had left the country and gone to France and then Spain because he couldn't handle the flack McMaken had given him and the entire Beaumont family on his show on the Foodie TV network.

Too bad they didn't know what had really happened.

Byron's contact with his family had been intentionally limited over the past twelve months—his twin sister Frances notwithstanding. Nearly all of the family news had filtered down through Frances. That's how Byron had learned that Chadwick had not only gotten divorced but had then also married his secretary and adopted her daughter. And that's how Byron had learned Phillip was marrying his horse trainer. No doubt, Frances was the only reason anyone knew where Byron had been.

Still, Byron was touched by his family's concern. He'd more or less gone off the grid to protect them from the fallout of his one great mistake—Leona Harper. Yet here they

were, trying to convince him to return to Denver by giving
him the blank slate he'd been trying to find.

Chadwick started to say something but paused and
looked at his wife. Something unspoken passed between
them. Just the sight of it stung Byron like lemon juice in
a paper cut.

"You wouldn't have to get independent financing,"
Serena told Byron. "The up-front costs would be covered
between the settlement you received from the sale of the
Beaumont Brewery and the capital that Percheron Drafts
can provide."

"We bought the entire building outright," Chadwick
added. "Rent would be next to nothing compared to what
it would be in downtown Denver. The restaurant would
have to cover its own utilities and payroll, but that's about
it. You'd have near total financial freedom."

"And," Matthew chimed in, "you could do whatever
you wanted. Whatever theme you wanted to build upon,
whatever decorating scheme you wanted to use, whatever
cuisine you wanted to serve—burgers and fries or foamed
truffle oil or whatever. The only caveat would be that Percheron Drafts beer would be the primary focus of the beverage menu since the restaurant is in the basement of the
brewery. Otherwise, you'd have carte blanche."

Byron looked from Chadwick to Serena to Matthew's
face on the screen. "You guys really think this will sell
beer?"

"I can give you a copy of the cost-benefit analysis I prepared," Serena said. Chadwick beamed at her, which was
odd. The brother Byron remembered didn't beam a whole
hell of a lot.

Byron could not believe he was considering this. He
liked living in Madrid. His Spanish was improving and he
liked working at El Gallio, the restaurant helmed by a chef

who cared more about food and ingredients and people than his own brand name.

It'd been a year. A year of working his way up the food chain, from no-star restaurants to one-star Michelin establishments to El Gallio, a three-star restaurant—one of the highest-ranked places in the world. He had made a name for himself that had absolutely nothing to do with his father and the Beaumonts, and he was damned proud of that. Would he really give all that up to come home for good?

More than anything, he liked the near total anonymity of life in Europe. There, no one cared that he was a Beaumont or that he'd left the States under a swirling cloud of gossip. No one gave a damn what happened with the Beaumont Brewery or Percheron Drafts or what any of his siblings had done to make headlines that day.

No one thought about the long-running feud between the Beaumonts and the Harpers that had led to the forced sale of the Beaumont Brewery.

No one thought about Byron and Leona Harper.

And that was how he liked it.

Leona...

If he were going to move back home, he knew he'd have to confront her. They had unfinished business and not even a year in Europe could change that. He wanted to look her in the face and have her tell him *why*. That's all he wanted. Why had she lied to him for almost a year about who she really was? Why had she picked her family over him? Why had she thrown away everything they'd planned—everything he'd wanted to give her?

In the course of the past year, Byron had worked and worked and *worked* to forget her. He had to accept the fact that he might not ever forget her or her betrayal of him—of them. Fine. That was part of life. Everyone got their heart ripped out of their chest and handed to them at least once.

He didn't want her back. Why would he? So she and her father could try to destroy him all over again?

No, what he wanted was a little payback.

The question was how to go about it.

Then he remembered something. Before it'd all fallen so spectacularly apart, Leona had been in school for industrial design. They'd talked about the restaurant they'd open together, how she'd design it and he'd run it. A blank slate that was theirs and theirs alone.

It'd been a year. She might have a job or her own firm or whatever. If he hired her, she would work for him. She would have to do as he said. He could prove that she didn't have any power over him—that she couldn't hurt him. He was not the same naive boy who'd let love blind him while he worked for an egomaniac. *He* was a chef. *He* would have his own restaurant. *He* was his own boss. *He* was in charge.

He was a Beaumont, damn it. It was time to start acting like one.

"I can use whomever I want to do the interior design?"

"Of course," Chadwick and Matthew said at the same time.

Byron looked at the workroom and then through the doors to the dungeon of the old warehouse. "I cannot believe I'm even considering this," he muttered. He could go back to Spain, back to the new life he'd made for himself, free of his past.

Except…

He would never be free of his past, not really. And he was done hiding.

He looked at his brothers and Serena, each hopeful that he would come back into the family fold.

This was a mistake. But then, when it came to Leona, Byron would probably always make the worst choice.

"I'll do it."

* * *

"Leona?" May's voice came through the speaker on her phone.

Leona hurriedly picked up before her boss, Marvin Lutefisk, head of Lutefisk Design, could hear the personal call. "I'm here. What's up? Is everything okay?"

"Percy's a little fussy. I think he might have another ear infection."

Leona sighed. "Do we still have some drops from the last round?" She could hardly afford another hundred-dollar trip to the doctor, who would look at Percy's ears for three seconds and write a prescription.

But the other option wasn't much better. If Percy got three—now two—more ear infections, they would have to talk about putting tubes in his ears, and even that minor outpatient surgery was far beyond Leona's budget.

"A little bit…" May sounded unconvincing.

"I'll…get some more," Leona announced. Maybe she could sweet-talk the nurses into a free sample?

Just like she'd done nearly every single day since Percy's birth, Leona thought about how different things would be if Byron Beaumont were still in her life. It wouldn't necessarily solve her health care issues, but her little sister May treated Leona as if she had the means to fix any problem, anytime.

Just once Leona wanted to lean on someone, instead of being the one who took all the weight.

But daydreaming about what might have been didn't pay the bills, so she told May, "Listen, I'm still at work. If he gets too bad, call the pediatrician. I can take him in tomorrow, okay?"

"Okay. You'll be home for dinner, right? I have class tonight, don't forget."

"I won't." Just then, her boss walked past her cubicle. "Gotta go," she whispered and hung up.

"Leona," Marvin said in his nasal tone. Unconsciously, he reached up and patted his comb-over back into position. "Busy?"

Leona put on her best smile. "Just finishing up a client phone call, Mr. Lutefisk. What's up?"

Marvin smiled encouragingly, his eyes beaming at her through thick lenses. He really wasn't a bad boss—that she knew. Marvin was giving her a chance to be someone other than Leon Harper's daughter, and that was all she could ask. That and the chance to get her foot in the door of industrial design. Leona had always dreamed of designing restaurants and bars—public spaces where form and function blended with a practical application of art and design. She hadn't really planned on doing storefronts for malls and the like, but everyone had to start somewhere.

"We've had an inquiry," Marvin said. "For a new brewpub on the south side of the city." Marvin tilted his head to the side and gave her a look. "We don't normally do this sort of thing here at Lutefisk Design but the caller asked for you specifically."

A trill of excitement coursed through her. A restaurant? And they'd asked for *her* by name? This was good. Great, even. But Leona remembered who she was talking to. "Are you comfortable with me being the primary on this one? If you'd rather handle it yourself, I'd be happy to assist."

It hurt to make the offer. If she was the primary designer instead of the assistant, she'd get a much bigger percentage of the commission and that could be more than enough to cover Percy's medical costs. She could pay off some of May's student loans and…

She couldn't get ahead of herself. Marvin was very particular about the level of involvement his assistants engaged in.

"Well…" Marvin pushed his glasses up. "The caller was very specific. He requested you."

"Really? I mean, that's great," Leona said, trying to keep her cool. How had this happened? Maybe that last job for an upscale boutique on the Sixteenth Street Mall? The owner had been thrilled with the changes Leona had made to Marvin's plan. Maybe that's where the reference came from?

"But he wants you to survey the site today. This afternoon. Do you have time?"

She almost said *hell, yes!* But she managed to slam the brakes on her mouth. Years of trying to keep her father happy when he was in one of his moods had trained her to say exactly what a man in a position of authority needed to hear. "I need to finish up the paperwork for that stationery store…"

Marvin waved this away. "That will keep. Go on—see if this is a job worth taking. Charlene has the address."

"Thank you." Leona gathered up her tablet computer—one of her true luxuries—and grabbed her purse. She got the address from Charlene, the receptionist, and hurried to the car.

A brewpub. One that was on the far south side of the city, she noted as she programmed the address into her Global Positioning System. There wasn't any other information to go with the address—like which brewery this was for—but that was probably a good sign. Instead of doing an upgrading project, maybe this would be a brand-new venture. That would not only mean more billable hours but the chance to make this project the showcase she'd need when she started her own firm.

The GPS estimated the pub's location was about forty minutes away. Leona called May and updated her on her whereabouts and then she hit the road.

Thirty-seven minutes later, Leona drove past a small sign that read Percheron Drafts as she turned into a driveway that led to a series of old brick buildings. She looked up at the tall smokestack in awe. White smoke puffed out lazily, but that was practically the only sign of life.

Percheron Drafts…why did that name sound familiar? She'd heard it somewhere, but she didn't actually drink beer. She was going to have to fake it for this meeting. She'd have time to do the research tonight.

The GPS guided her underneath a walkway, around the back of the building and told her to park on a gravel lot that had weeds growing everywhere. Ahead she saw a ramp that led down to an open door.

Okay, she thought as she turned the car off and grabbed her things. So maybe the building was old, but this certainly wasn't an already established restaurant. Heck, she didn't even see another car parked here. Was this the right place?

She got out and put on her professional smile. Then— like something out of a dream—a man walked through the doors and up the ramp. The sunlight caught the red in his hair and he smiled at her.

She knew that walk, that hair. She knew that smile— lopsided and warm and happy to see her.

Oh, God.

Byron.

Percheron Drafts… It suddenly clicked. That was the name of the brewery the Beaumont family had started after their family business had been sold—and she only knew about that because it was her father who'd forced the sale.

Panic kicked in. He was coming toward her, his lean legs closing the distance rapidly. If he got too close, he'd see the baby seat in the back of her car.

Her head began to swim. She wasn't ready for this. He'd walked out on her. He'd believed her father over her and simply disappeared—just like her father had said all Beaumont men did. Beaumonts took whatever woman they wanted and when they were done, they simply abandoned them—and kept the children.

She'd known she'd have to confront him eventually. But now? Right freaking *now*?

She wasn't ready. She hadn't lost all the baby weight and, as a result, she was wearing the only kind of business-casual attire she could afford—the kind from discount stores. She couldn't even be sure that Percy hadn't spit up on her blouse this morning.

When she'd imagined facing the man who'd broken her heart and abandoned her, she'd wanted to look her very best to make him physically hurt. She hadn't wanted to look like a rumpled single mother struggling to get by.

Even if he was the reason she was exactly that.

But she couldn't let him see into the back of the car. If he didn't know about Percy, she wasn't going to tell him until she'd had time to come up with a plan. Because what if he did the Beaumont thing and demanded her child? She could not lose her son. She couldn't let Byron raise the boy to be yet another Beaumont in the line of Beaumont men. She had to protect her baby.

So, against her better judgment, she walked toward him.

Oh, this wasn't fair. It just wasn't. Byron's hair had gotten a little longer and he wore it pulled back into a low ponytail, which took all of the natural curl out of it—except for one piece that had come free. His lanky frame had filled out a little, giving him a more muscular look that was positively sinful in the white button-up shirt he wore cuffed at the sleeves.

He looked good. Heck, he looked better than good. And she looked...dumpy. Damn it all.

They met in the middle of the parking lot, stopping less than two feet from each other. "Leona," he said in his deep baritone voice as he looked at her. His eyes were a deeper blue now—or maybe that was just the bright sun. God, he was *so* handsome.

She would not be swayed by his good looks. Those looks lied, just like he did.

"Byron," she replied. Because what else could she say here? *Where have you been? I had your son after you left me? I don't know if I want to kiss you or strangle you?*

This was no big deal, she tried to tell herself. It was just the former love of her life, the father of her son—suddenly back after a year's absence. And apparently hiring her for a job. A flash of anger gave her strength. If he was back, why hadn't he just called her? Why did he have to hire her?

Unless…he hadn't come back for her.

He'd left without her, after all, jetting off to Europe. That'd been as much information as Leona had been able to get out of Byron's twin sister, Frances. Europe—as far away from Leona as he could get without leaving the planet. Or so it had felt.

And now he was back and hiring her. For a job she desperately needed. This was not him sweeping back into her life and making everything right. This was not him needing her.

So she did not flinch as he looked her up and down as if he expected her to fall into his arms and tell him how damned much she'd missed him. She would not give him the satisfaction. Yes, the past year had been the hardest year of her life. But she wasn't the same silly little girl who believed love would somehow conquer all. The past year had shown her how tough she could be. It was time for Byron to realize the same thing.

But it was difficult to keep her head up as his gaze traveled over her. He'd always done that—looked at her as though she was the most beautiful woman on the planet. Even when they'd worked together at that restaurant and the cream of the high-society crop had come into the restaurant every single night—even when other women had thrown themselves at his Beaumont name—Byron had always had eyes only for *her*.

She shivered at the memory of the way he used to look at her—at the way he was looking at her right now.

"You cut your hair," he noted.

Her mouth opened, the truth on the tip of her tongue— she'd cut it because Percy liked to yank it while he was nursing. She clamped down on that impulse. The words sat in the back of her throat, a lead weight that held her tongue still. She would give him absolutely nothing to use against her. She would not let him hurt her again.

"I like it," he hurried to add when she couldn't think of a single reasonable thing to say in response.

She blushed at the compliment. Her fingers itched to tuck the short bob behind her ears, but she held fast to the straps of her bag. She was not here for Byron, just like he hadn't been there for her. She was here to do a job and that was final. "Do you really need an interior designer or did you call me away from my job just to note I've changed my style?" *Since you left.*

She didn't say those last words out loud, but they seemed to hang in between them anyway.

Byron took another step toward her. He reached up. Leona held her breath as he trailed the very tips of his fingers over her cheek. It was almost as if he couldn't believe she was really here, either.

Then he reached down and picked up her left hand. His thumb rubbed over her ring finger—her bare ring finger. "Leona…" he murmured, his voice husky with what she recognized as need. He lifted her hand to his lips and kissed it.

Everything about her body tightened at the sound of her name from his mouth, his lips on her hand—tightened so much that she had to close her eyes because if she looked into the depths of Byron's beautiful blue eyes for one second longer, she'd be lost all over again.

It'd always been this way. There'd been something about Byron Beaumont that had pulled her in from the very beginning—something that should have sent her running the other way.

After all, her father had been drumming his hatred of all things Beaumont into her head for as long as she could remember. She knew all about Hardwick Beaumont, her father's nemesis, and his heirs. How the Beaumonts were dangerous, how they seduced young and innocent women and then cast them aside as if they were nothing.

Just as Leona had been seduced and cast aside.

So she did not give. She ignored her body's reaction to Byron, ignored the old memories that the mere touch of his lips brought rushing back to her. She kept her eyes closed and her focus on the job.

The job she needed because she was raising Byron's son on her own. A son he did not know about.

She needed to tell him.

But she couldn't. Not yet. Not until she figured out what he was doing here. Not until she knew where she stood with him. She was no longer young and innocent and she was not someone who would forget a year's worth of heartache and loneliness with the whisper of her name, thank you very much.

God, what a mess.

A tense second passed between them and then Byron dropped her hand. She felt him step away from her and only then did she open her eyes.

He now stood several feet away, looking at her differently—harder, meaner almost.

Another flash of panic hit her—did he already know about Percy? Or was he just mad that she wasn't falling at her feet in gratitude for being acknowledged?

"I need a designer," he said quietly. He didn't sound angry, which was at direct odds with the way he was looking at her. "I'm going to be opening up my own restaurant."

"Here?"

"Here," he agreed, sounding resigned to it. "It's a massive job and I—" she saw him swallow "—I wanted to see if it was the kind of thing you were still interested it."

"You're going to stay in Denver?" The question came out with more of an edge than she meant it to, but that was the thing she needed to know. If he were going to stay in Denver, then…

Then he'd have to know about Percy. They'd have to figure something out, something involving child support and visitation and…

Well, not their relationship. There was no relationship. That part of her life was over now.

And if he were opening up his own restaurant—her mind spun around the facts. Her father, Leon Harper, would find out that Byron had come home.

Oh, *God*. Her father would get out his old axes and grind them all over again. Her father would shove his way back into her life, ignoring all the ways she had tried to extricate herself from her parents. Her father would do everything he could to destroy Byron—again.

Her father would do everything to punish *her* again.

"Yes," Byron said, turning away from her and looking up at the old buildings. "I've come home."

Two

Byron walked into the darkened room that, somehow, would become a restaurant. Somehow. "Here we are. The dungeon."

Behind him, he heard Leona cough lightly. "Is that the theme you're working with?"

"No."

What the hell was he doing? Touching her face? Kissing her hand? That was not part of his plan. His plan was to hire her, get his restaurant going and kick her right back out of his life—this time, on his terms. She hadn't needed him. He didn't need her. Except for design purposes.

But that's not what had happened because something as simple as seeing Leona Harper again—and seeing that she wasn't wearing a wedding ring—had blown all to hell his simple plan to get simple answers.

There was nothing simple about Leona. A fact she'd made abundantly clear when she'd closed her eyes—when she'd refused to even look at him.

"Pity," she sniffed. "You wouldn't have to change a thing."

He grinned in spite of himself. Leona had always been something of a contradiction. She was, in general, a quiet woman who avoided confrontation. But when she'd been alone with him, she'd let out the real her—snarky and sarcastic with a biting observation ready at all times. She'd made him laugh—him. He'd thought he was too jaded, too cynical to laugh anymore, to feel much of anything anymore. But he'd laughed with her. He'd had all these feelings with her. For her.

He'd loved her. Or thought he had. But maybe that'd all been part of the trick, a Harper trapping a Beaumont. She hadn't told him who she was, after all, until it was too late.

"So if you're not going with torture chamber," she went on, "what do you want?"

"Whatever."

"Be serious, Byron." If he hadn't been looking at her, he wouldn't have seen the tiny stamp of her foot that set off eddies of dust.

He paused. "I am being serious. You can do whatever you want. I can cook what I want. The only caveat is that the beverage menu has to feature our beer. The restaurant can be whatever it wants."

Clutching her tablet to her chest, she gave him a long look that he couldn't quite make out in the dim light. "You have to have some idea of what you're interested in," she finally said in a soft voice.

"I do. I've always known what I wanted." He turned away from her. This was a bad idea. But then again, it was Leona—she'd always been a bad idea. "But I'm used to not getting it."

She gasped, but he kept walking back toward the soon-to-be-kitchen. He couldn't let her get under his skin. He never should have asked her here. He was safer in Spain, where she was nothing but a memory—not a flesh and blood woman who would always push him past the point of reason.

The reasonable thing to do was to keep as much space between the Beaumonts and the Harpers as possible. That's the way it'd always been, before he'd unwittingly crossed that line. That's the way it should have stayed.

He dragged open the doors to the workroom and flipped on all the lights. "This needs to be upgraded considerably," he said. He couldn't fix the past, couldn't undo his great mistake. But he could stop making it over again. He just had to focus on the job—it was the reason they were both here. He needed to find a way to be Byron Beaumont in a place where his last name permanently branded him, and he needed to make sure that Leona Harper knew she would never exert any power over him ever again.

She followed him into the cleaner space. "I see." She took several pictures with her tablet. "Do you have a menu yet?"

"No. I only agreed to do this yesterday. I thought I'd be on my way back to Madrid by now."

"Madrid? Is *that* where you went?"

Of course she wouldn't know. She probably hadn't bothered to look him up at all.

But there was something in the way she said it—as if she couldn't believe that was the answer—that made him turn back to her. She stared at him with big eyes and this time, there was no hiding that look. She was stunned—confused? She was hurt.

Well, that made two of them "Yes. Well, I spent six months in France first. Then Spain."

Her eyes cut down to his left hand—his ring finger. "Did you…"

He tensed. "No. I was working."

She exhaled. "Ah." But that was all she said. He was about to turn away when she added, "Where did you work?"

"George, you remember him?"

"Your father's old chef?"

For some reason, the fact that she remembered who George was made Byron relax a little. It wasn't like she'd forgotten him. Not entirely, anyway. "Yes. One of his old friends from Le Cordon Bleu gave me a job in Paris. Then I heard about an opening at El Gallio in Madrid and took the job."

Her eyes widened again. "You were at El Gallio? That's a three-star restaurant!"

He relaxed more. She remembered. Even though her reaction was probably all part of the same ruse to undermine the Beaumont family, he couldn't help himself.

For months, he and Leona had talked about restaurants—how they'd love to travel and dine at the world's best establishments and then open up their own. She'd design everything and Byron would handle the food, and it'd be so much better than working for Rory McMaken, the egotistical bastard.

Leona spoke, pulling him out of the past. "You're leaving behind El Gallio to open your own restaurant *here*?"

"Crazy, right?" He looked around the workroom. "Don't get me wrong. I loved Europe. No one there knew or cared that I was a Beaumont. I could just be Byron, a chef. That was..." *Freeing.*

He'd been free of the family drama, free of the long-standing feud between the Beaumonts and the Harpers.

"That must have been amazing," she said in a wistful tone. Which was so at odds with how he remembered the way things had gone down that he turned back to her in surprise.

"Yeah. I wasn't sure I wanted to come back to all of this. But this is an opportunity I can't pass up. It's a chance to be a part of the family business on my terms."

"I see. So you've decided to be a Beaumont, then." Her voice was quiet, as if he'd somehow confirmed her worst fears.

He would not let her get away with using guilt on him. Guilt? For what? He was the injured party here. She'd lied about who she was—not once, but for almost a year. And then she'd cast him aside the moment her father asked her to. Hell, for all he knew, that had always been the plan. It'd only been after he'd left the country that Leon Harper had managed to sell the Beaumont Brewery out from under the Beaumonts. Maybe he'd told Leona to split one of them off—divide and then conquer.

Right. If anyone should be feeling guilty here, it was her. He'd never lied about his last name or his family. He'd never made promises and then broken them. Thank God he hadn't actually asked her to marry him before she betrayed him.

"I've always been a Beaumont," he answered decisively. "And we are not to be trifled with."

He shouldn't have said that last bit, but he couldn't help it. He was the boss here. She worked for him. Emotionally, he didn't need her. If she was getting any ideas about turning the tables on him, she'd best forget them now.

She looked away.

"Anyway," he went on, focusing on the job. *His* restaurant. "I'm starting from scratch and I wanted…" Unexpectedly, his words dried up. He wanted so much, but like he'd said, he'd gotten used to disappointment. "I know there was a time in our past when we talked about a restaurant."

Even though she was studying the tips of her shoes very closely, he still saw her eyes close.

He remembered that look of defeat—he'd only seen it one other time—when her father, Leon Harper himself, had shown up at Sauce and gotten Byron fired and demanded that Leona come home with her parents right now or else. Leona had looked at the ground and closed her eyes and Byron had said "babe" and…

Well. And here they were.

"If you don't want the job, that's fine. I know that Harpers and Beaumonts don't work well together and I wouldn't want to make your father mad." He didn't quite manage to say *father* without sneering.

He watched her chest rise and fall with a deep breath. "I want…"

Her words were so quiet that he couldn't hear her. He stepped in closer and took a deep breath.

Which was a mistake. The scent of Leona—sweet and soft, roses and vanilla—was all it took to transport him to another time and place, before he'd realized that she wasn't just someone with the last name of Harper, but one of *those* Harpers.

He leaned forward, unable to stop himself. He'd never been able to stay away from her, not from the first moment she'd been hired at Sauce as a hostess. "What do you want, Leona?"

"I need to tell you…" Her words were still little more than a whisper.

He touched her then, which was another mistake. But she took what control he had and blew it to bits. He cupped her face in his hand and lifted her chin until he could look into her hazel eyes. "What do you need?"

Her eyes widened again as his face moved within inches of hers, and she exhaled, something that sounded a hell of a lot like satisfaction. His gut clenched. Despite her lies and betrayal, the messy ending to their relationship and the long year on a different continent—despite it all—he wanted her.

"The job," she said in a voice that didn't even make it to a whisper. "I need the job, Byron."

She didn't kiss him, didn't tell him she was so sorry she'd picked her family over him. At no point did she apologize for lying to him. She just stood there.

"Right, right." She couldn't be clearer. She was here for the job.

Not for him.

Her heart pounded and she wasn't sure she was still breathing.

Byron had dropped his hand and turned back to the stove, leaving her in a state of paralysis.

If he was going to stay in Denver, he had to know and the longer she didn't tell him—well, that would just make everything worse.

Somehow. She wasn't sure how things could get much worse, frankly. Byron hiring her to design a restaurant— and then switching between unbridled lust and a cold shoulder?

That thought made her angry. Why did he have to hire her to see her? He could have called. Sent a text.

The anger felt good. It gave her back some power. She was not a helpless girl at the mercies of the men in her life, not anymore. She'd gotten away from her father and had a son and done just fine without Byron. So what if all he had to do was look at her and her knees turned to jelly? Didn't matter. He'd left her behind. She was only here for the paycheck. Not for him.

She could not tell him about Percy, not when she couldn't be sure what version of Byron she would get. She'd spent the past year carving out a life that made her as happy as possible—a job she liked and a family she loved, with May and Percy. She'd spent a whole year free to make her own choices and live her own life. She'd stopped being Leon Harper's wayward oldest daughter, and she'd stopped dreaming of being Byron Beaumont's wife. She was just Leona Harper and that was a good thing.

Now she had to remember that.

"Well," she started, then cleared her throat to get her voice working properly. "I guess what I need is a menu. It doesn't have to be specific, but are you going to serve burgers and fries or haute cuisine or what? That will guide the rest of the design choices."

"Something in the middle," he replied quickly. "Accessible food and beer, but better than burgers and fries. You can get that anywhere. I want this to be a different kind of restaurant—not about me, but about the meal. The experience." He looked out at the depressing room that she was somehow going to transform into a dining hall. "A different experience than *this*," he added with a shake of his head.

"Okay, that's a good start. What else?"

"Fusion," he added. "I was cooking things in Europe that I didn't cook here. Locally sourced ingredients, advanced techniques—the whole nine yards."

She took notes on her tablet. "Any ideas for the actual menu items?"

"A few."

She waited for him to elaborate, but when he didn't, she looked up again. "Such as?"

He didn't look at her. "Why don't you come by the house tomorrow and I'll make you a tasting menu? You can tell me what might work and what doesn't."

She should say no. She should insist that their interactions be limited to this dank building. "The house?"

"The Beaumont Mansion. I'm staying there until I get my own place." He pivoted and fixed her with a look that she'd always been powerless to resist. "If you can tolerate being in the lair of the Beaumonts, that is."

"I tolerate you, don't I?" she snapped back. She would not allow him to make her the bad guy, and she would not let him paint her as the coward. He was the one who'd run off. She was the one who'd stayed and dealt with the fallout.

She didn't know how she'd expected him to respond, but that lazy smile? That wasn't it. "Shall we say six, then?"

Leona mentally ran through her calendar. May had class tonight—but tomorrow night she should be able to stay with Percy.

"Who else will be home?" Because no matter what had happened between Leona and Byron, that didn't change the larger fact that the Beaumonts and the Harpers got on much worse than oil and water ever had.

He shrugged. "Chadwick and his family live there full-time, but they eat on their own schedule. Frances just moved back in, but she's rarely home. A couple of my younger half siblings are still there—but again, everyone's on their own schedule. Should be just us."

For a brief, insane second, she entertained the notion of bringing Percy with her. But the moment the thought occurred to her, she dismissed it. The Beaumonts were notorious for keeping the children from broken relationships. That's what her father had always told her—Hardwick Beaumont always got rid of the women and kept the babies, never letting the children see their mothers again. That's what Byron had said happened to him and his siblings. It wasn't until later in his life that he'd gotten to know his mother.

At the time, that story had broken her heart for him. He'd been a lost little boy in a cold, unloving house. But now she knew better. He hadn't been looking for sympathy.

He'd been warning her. And she was more the fool for not realizing it until it was too late.

She was done being the fool. No, she would not bring Percy. Not until she had a better grasp on Byron's reaction to the idea of having a five-month-old son. Not until she knew if he would decree that the boy would be better off a Beaumont instead of a Harper.

Byron had to know about his child eventually, but she could *not* lose her son.

"All right," she finally said. "Dinner tomorrow night at six. I'll draft a few ideas and you can provide feedback." Her phone chimed—it was a text from May, reminding Leona about her class tonight. "Anything else?"

The question hung in the air like the cobwebs hung from the ceiling. Byron looked at her with such longing that she almost weakened.

Then the look shifted and anything warm or welcoming was gone and all that was left was an iciness she hadn't seen before. It chilled her to the bone.

"No," he said, his voice freezing. "There's nothing else I need from you."

That was an answer, all right.

But not the one she wanted to hear.

Three

"Your sauce is going to burn."

This simple observation from George made Byron jump. "Damn." He hurried over to reduce the heat under the saucepan, mentally kicking himself for making a rookie mistake.

George Jackson chuckled from his perch on a stool—the same place he'd been sitting for the past thirty-five years. Mothers and stepmothers came and went, more children showed up—being a Beaumont meant living in a constant state of uncertainty. Except for the kitchen. Except for George. Sure, his brown skin was more wrinkled and, yes, more of his hair was white than not. But otherwise, he was the same man—one of the very few, black or white, who didn't take crap from any Beaumont. Not even Hardwick. Maybe that's why Hardwick had kept George around and why Chadwick had kept him on after Hardwick's death. George was constant and honest.

Like right now. "Boy, you're a wreck."

"I'm fine," Byron lied. Which was pointless because George knew him far too well to buy that line.

George shook his head. "Why are you trying so hard to impress this girl? I thought she was the whole reason you left town."

"I'm not," Byron said, stirring the scalded sauce. "We're working together. She's designing the restaurant. I'm preparing food that might be on the menu in said restaurant. That's not trying to impress her."

George chuckled again. "Yeah, sure it's not. You Beaumont men are all alike," he added under his breath.

"I am absolutely not like my father and you know it," Byron shot off, checking the roast in the oven. "I've never married anyone, much less a string of people, and I certainly don't have any kids running around."

George snorted at this. "Be that as it may, you're exactly like your old man. Even like Chadwick, sitting up there with his second wife. None of you all could be honest with yourselves when it came to women." He seemed to reconsider this statement. "Well, maybe not Chadwick this time. Miss Serena is different. Hope your brother doesn't screw it up. But my point is, you all are fools."

"Thanks, George," Byron replied sarcastically. "That means a lot, coming from you."

From a long way away, the doorbell rang. "Watch the sauce," Byron said as he hurried out of the kitchen.

The Beaumont Mansion was a huge building that had been built by his grandfather, John Beaumont, after prohibition and after World War II, when beer had been legal and soldiers had come home to drink it. The Beaumont Brewery had barely managed to stay afloat for twenty years, and then suddenly John had been making money faster than he could count it. He'd built several new buildings on the brewery campus as well as the mansion, a 15,000 square-foot pile of brick designed to show up the older mansions of the silver barons. The mansion had turrets and stained glass and gargoyles, for God's sake. Nothing was ever over-the-top to a Beaumont, apparently.

Byron had always hated this house, the way it made people act. The house was toxic with the ghosts of John and Hardwick. This was not a house that had known happiness. He couldn't understand why Chadwick insisted on raising his family here.

Byron hadn't even bothered to unpack the rest of his

stuff because he wasn't going to be here long enough to settle in. He'd get a nice apartment with a good kitchen close to the Percheron Drafts brewery and that'd be fine. In the meantime, he'd spend as much time in the one room that had always been free from drama and grief—the kitchen.

He almost ran into Chadwick, who was coming downstairs to answer the door. "I've got it," Byron said, sidestepping his oldest brother.

Chadwick made no move to go back upstairs. "Expecting company?"

"It's the interior designer," Byron replied, happy to have that truth to hide behind. "I've prepared a sampling of dishes for her so we can build the theme of the restaurant around them."

"Ah, good." Chadwick looked at him, that stern look that always made Byron feel as though he wasn't measuring up. "Anything else I should know?"

Byron froze and the doorbell rang again. "George is making apple cobbler for dessert tonight," he said.

Then—weirdly—Chadwick smiled. It wasn't something Byron remembered happening when they were growing up. Back then, Chadwick had been imposing and their father's clear favorite, and Byron had been the irritating little brother who liked to play in the kitchen.

"If you need another opinion, let me know," Chadwick said, turning to head back upstairs. But that was all. No judgments, no cutting words—not even a dismissive glance.

"Yeah, will do," Byron said, waiting until Chadwick had disappeared before he opened the door.

There stood Leona. Something in his chest eased. It wasn't as if she was dressed to kill—in fact, she looked quite businesslike with a coordinating skirt and jacket. For the first time, he realized how much she'd changed in the past year—something that went much deeper than just her hair. *Maybe*, an insidious voice in his head whispered, *she's moved on and you haven't*.

Perhaps that was true. But there was no missing the fact that he was glad to see her. He should hate her and all the Harpers. Not a one of them were to be trusted.

He needed to remember that. "Hi. Come in."

She paused. Despite their year-long relationship, he'd never once brought her back to the mansion nor had she ever asked to visit. That had been part of what had attracted him to her—she had no interest in the trappings of Beaumont wealth and fame.

He hadn't realized her disinterest was because she had her own money. Maybe George had been right. Byron *was* a fool.

"Thank you." She stepped into the house and he closed the door behind her. "Oh," she said, staring up at the vaulted ceilings and crystal chandeliers. "This is lovely."

"Not my style," he admitted. "This way."

He led her down the wide hallway that bisected the first floor, past the formal dining room, the receiving room, the men's parlor, the women's parlor and the library. Finally, they reached the hallway that led around the back of the dining room and down the six steps to the kitchen.

The whole time, they walked silently. Byron didn't know much about the Harper house—it wasn't as if Leon Harper would invite him over—but he was sure this level of wealth wasn't unfamiliar to Leona and he had no desire to rehash old memories of his parents slamming doors after yet another disastrous meal.

Byron opened the door to the kitchen. "Here we are," he said, holding the door for Leona.

She stepped into the warm room. Early-evening sunlight glinted through the windows set above the countertop. The room had an impressive view of the Rocky Mountains. The light reflected off the rows of copper pots and pans that hung from racks, bathing the room in comfortable warmth.

Leona gasped. "This is *beautiful*." She looked at him, her eyes full of understanding, and in that moment, he nearly forgot how she'd lied and broken his heart. This was *his* Leona, the one he'd shared his deepest thoughts and feelings with. "Oh, Byron…"

"And George," George said, straightening from where he'd bent over to check the oven.

"Oh!" Leona took a step back in surprise and ran right into Byron. Instinctively, his arm went around her waist, steadying her—and pulling her into his chest. Heat—and maybe something more—flowed between them and he suddenly had to fight the urge to press his lips against the base of her neck, in the spot where she'd always loved to be kissed.

She pulled away from him. "George! I've heard so much about you! It's wonderful to finally meet you in person."

Then, to Byron's surprise—and George's, given his expression—Leona walked right up to the older man and hugged him.

"Yeah," George said in shock, shooting Byron a look. "I've heard—well," he quickly corrected when Byron shook his head. "It's good to finally meet you, too."

Byron exhaled in relief. George was the only person who knew the entire story about Leona—he hadn't even told Frances the whole thing. God only knew what the older man might have said to Leona.

"George is advising on the menu," Byron told her when she finally released George from the hug. "He'll be dining with us tonight."

"Oh. Okay." For some reason, Leona looked…disappointed?

Had she been thinking this would be an intimate dinner for two? She wasn't dressed for it—she looked as though she'd come directly from work. There would be no hot dates. Not now, not at any time in the future. If that's what she was angling for, she was in for a surprise.

A timer went off and Byron pushed that thought from his mind. He had food to prepare, after all. "This is going to be a tapas-style meal—all small plates," he explained, directing Leona to a stool across from George's normal perch. "Chadwick has all the current Percheron Drafts in stock so we can pair them up." He opened up one of the three refrigerators in the room, the one with all the beverages. "Which would you like to start with?"

Leona blinked at him. "I don't drink."

He stared at her. This was a new development. They'd always shared wine with a meal. Odd. "All right," he said slowly, snagging a White Horse Pale Ale for himself. "Then I'll get you some water."

Then he got to work. He plated the braised lamb shoulder, the *croquetas de jamón serrano*, the coq au vin, the ratatouille, the herb-crusted swordfish and the duck confit. He ladled the vichyssoise soup into a small bowl, and did the same with the bowl of Castilian roasted garlic soup and the gazpacho. George sliced the French bread and the homemade root vegetable chips fried in truffle oil.

Leona took a picture of every dish and made notes as Byron explained what the dishes were. "I don't know if I should have a hamburger and fries on the menu," he told her as he spooned the hollandaise sauce onto the asparagus spears. "What do you think?"

"It's a safe dish," she replied. "If you can handle having it on the menu…"

Byron sighed. "Yeah, yeah. Food for the masses and all that."

They all sat down. Leona looked at him. Was she blushing? "It's been a long time since you cooked for me."

Before Byron could come up with a response, George said, "Yeah, same here." He took a bite of the duck confit. "I'll give you this, boy. You've gotten better."

"Oh?" Leona said.

"When he started in my kitchen," George went on, "he could barely make cereal."

"Hey! I was what—five?"

"Four," George corrected him. He turned his attention back to Leona. "He wanted more cookies and I told him he had to work for them—he had to wash dishes."

Leona beamed at George. Then she shot a reproving glance at Byron. "He never told me that."

"Oh, he didn't do it at first. But the boy always had a weak spot for my chocolate chip cookies. He came back a few weeks later, after…" George trailed off thoughtfully.

Byron knew what the older man was thinking about—that Byron's parents had fought horribly at dinner, screaming obscenities and throwing dishes. A plate had nearly hit Chadwick in the head and Byron and Frances had ducked to avoid flying soup. He and Frances had been crying and their father had yelled at them.

Byron had run away from the noise. Frances had come with him and they'd wound up in the kitchen. It was the safest place he could think of, somewhere his father would never go. Frances had no interest in working for a cookie and a glass of warm milk, but Byron had needed…something. Anything that would take him away from the stress and drama, although that's not how he'd thought of it at the time. No, at the time, he'd just wanted to feel like everything was going to be okay.

Washing the dishes required enough focus that it had distracted him from what he'd seen at dinner. And then he'd gotten a cookie and a pat on the shoulder and George had told him he'd done a good job and next time George would show him how to bake the cookies himself. And that had made everything okay.

"I washed the dishes," he told Leona. "The cookies were worth it."

"You did an absolutely lousy job, I might add," George said with a chuckle.

Byron groaned. "I got better. Here, try the gazpacho." He ladled a few spoonfuls into Leona's bowl. "It's not quite as good as it was in Spain—the peppers aren't as fresh."

George scoffed as Leona tasted the soup. "Boy, don't tell them what they don't know. She never had the stuff you were making in Madrid."

"Mmm," Leona said, licking her spoon. Byron found himself staring at her mouth as her tongue moved slowly over the surface of the spoon. She caught him looking and dropped her gaze. He swore she was blushing as she cleared her throat and said, "He's right. As long as we can say 'locally sourced ingredients'—preferably with the name of the farm where you get your vegetables—that's what foodies value."

"We can do that. There's enough space around the brewery that I could also have some dirt hauled in and grow my own herbs and the like."

Leona's eyes lit up. "Would you? That'd be a great selling feature."

Byron liked it when she looked at him like that, even though he knew damned well that he shouldn't. But sitting here with her, talking about a restaurant they were going to open within months...

He'd missed her. He'd never stopped missing her. And as much as he knew he couldn't let himself fall under her spell again—couldn't risk getting his heart broken a second time—he just wanted to wrap his arm around her shoulders and hold her to him.

She would burn him. That he knew. That was the nature of the Harpers whenever they were around the Beaumonts.

But watching her savor the meal he'd cooked for her, talking and laughing with George...

He wanted to play in the flames again.

Four

Everything was, unsurprisingly, delicious. Leona especially liked the *croquetas*—she'd never had them before. Yes, the evening was full of good food and comfortable conversation. It should have been relaxing—fun, even.

The only problem was, she still hadn't told Byron about Percy. And, as George regaled her with story after story of Byron learning how to cook the hard way, she couldn't figure out how to break the news to him without running the risk of losing Percy.

Byron served three desserts—an almond cake that was gluten-free, peaches soaked in wine and yogurt, and a flan flavored with vanilla and lavender. She looked at her notes. A vegetarian dish, gluten-free options—with the hamburger, he'd have a menu that met most dietary needs.

"You like peaches, right?" he said as he set half of a peach in front of her.

"I do," she told him. Seemingly against her will, she looked up at him. Byron stood over her, close enough that she could feel the warmth of his body. He remembered that peaches were her favorite. There'd been a time when he'd cooked for her, peach cobblers and grilled peaches and peach ice cream—anything he could come up with. Those had been things he'd made just for her.

"Thank you," she told him, her voice soft.

"I hope the wine sauce is okay." He didn't move back. "I didn't know…"

"It's all right." She used to drink wine, back when he'd

make her dinner and pick out a bottle and they'd spend the evening savoring the food and the rest of the night savoring each other. But she hadn't drunk a thing while pregnant and then she'd been breast-feeding and pumping and who had the money for alcohol anyway?

He stood there for a moment longer. Leona held her breath, unable to break the gaze. All of her self-preservation tactics—clinging to the memory of being cast aside by a Beaumont, just like her father had warned her, and the very real fear that Byron would take her son away from her—they all fell away as she looked up at him. For a clear, beautiful second, there was only Leona and Byron and everything was as it should be.

The second ended when the door to the kitchen flew open with a bang. Byron jumped back. "George!" a bright female voice said. "Have you seen— Oh, *there* you are."

Leona looked over her shoulder and her heart sank. There stood Frances Beaumont in a stunning green dress and five-inch heels. "Byron, I have been texting you all… day…" Frances's voice trailed off as she saw Leona. They'd met a few times before. Frances had liked her then. But that felt like a long time ago.

Byron cleared his throat. "Frances, you remember—"

"Leona." Frances said the word as if it were something vile. Then she grabbed Byron by the arm and hauled him several feet away. "What is *she* doing here?" Frances added in a harsh whisper that everyone in the room had no trouble understanding.

Leona turned her gaze back to the luscious desserts. But her stomach felt as if a lead weight had settled into it.

"She's helping with the restaurant," Byron whispered back in a quieter voice.

"You're *trusting* her? Are you insane?" This time, Frances made no effort to lower her voice.

Leona stood. She did not have to sit here and take this assault on her character. Byron was the one who'd abandoned her, not the other way around. If anything, she shouldn't trust *him*. She didn't.

"I'll show myself out. George, it was a pleasure meeting you. Byron, I'll look over my notes and come up with some suggestions." She met Frances's glare as she gathered her things. "Frances."

"I'll walk you out," Byron offered, which made Frances hiss at him. But he ignored his twin and held the door for Leona.

"Good meeting you, too," George called out after her. "Come back anytime."

Which was followed by Frances gasping, "George! You're not helping…"

And then Leona and Byron were down the hall, the sounds of the kitchen fading behind them. They walked in silence through the massive entry hall. The evening had been, up to this point, an unmitigated disaster. Byron's cooking was amazing and, yes, George was just as sweet as she'd always pictured him.

But Byron had this habit of looking at her as if he wanted her, which didn't mesh with the otherwise icy shoulder he'd given her. He confused her and after everything he'd put her through, that seemed like the final insult.

She could not let him get to her, just like she couldn't let Frances's undisguised hatred get to her. Byron had left. He'd done exactly what his father had done and simply walked away. He didn't care for her—certainly not enough to fight for what they'd had.

She simply could not allow herself to care for him. It was not only dangerous to her heart, but also to Percy's well-being. She had to protect her son.

Thus resolved, she expected to say goodbye to Byron at the front door and call it a day. But Byron opened the door and stepped outside with her, pulling it shut behind her.

She walked past him, shivering in the chilly autumn air. She would not lean into him and let his warmth surround her. She did not need him. She did not want him. She could not let him ruin everything she'd worked so hard for and that was that.

Once the door was shut, he took a step into her. He wasn't touching her, not yet. "I'm sorry about Frances," he said in a quiet voice. "She can be a little…protective."

A part of Leona—the old part that cowered before her father—wanted to tell Byron it was all right and she'd smooth things over. But that part wasn't going to save her son. So she didn't. "Obviously." He looked confused, as if he couldn't guess that his sister would have been less than helpful in tracking Byron down. "I have no interest in re-living the past. That's not why I'm here."

She didn't know what she expected him to do—but lifting his hand and cupping her cheek like she'd said something sweet wasn't it. "Why are you here, then?"

"For the job." To her horror, Leona felt herself leaning forward, closer to his chest, to his mouth. "Byron…"

But before the words could leave her lips, a noise that sounded like a herd of elephants came through the door. Byron grabbed her by the arm and led her away. "I'll walk you to your car," he said.

As they walked, his hand slid down her arm until his fingers interlaced with hers. It wasn't a seductive gesture, but it warmed her anyway. He'd always held her hand whenever they were alone, whether they were watching a movie or watching the sun set over the mountains. She leaned her head against his shoulder as they walked. If only things had been different. If only…

She jerked to a stop less than five feet from her car. And the telltale car seat in the back.

"What?" Byron asked.

"I just…" She fumbled around for something to say and came up with nothing.

So she did the only thing she could think of to distract him.

She kissed him.

It wasn't supposed to be sexual, not for her. It was supposed to distract him while it bought her enough time to think of a better exit strategy.

But the feeling of Byron against her drove all rational thought from her mind. She melted into him. His hands settled on her waist and, as the kiss deepened, the pads of his fingertips began to dig into her hips. He pulled her into him. Her bag dropped to the ground as she looped her arms around his neck and held him tight.

She hadn't allowed herself to think about this, about how he used to make her feel. She'd made herself focus on how much she hated him, hated how he'd abandoned her—she hadn't allowed herself to remember the good parts.

Heat flooded her body and pooled low in her stomach as she opened her mouth for him. She wanted this, wanted him. She couldn't help it. She'd never been able to stay away from him. Some things never changed.

"I missed you," he whispered against her neck before he kissed the spot right under her ear.

Her knees wobbled. "Oh, Byron, I missed you, too. I—"

Suddenly, he pulled away from her so fast that she stumbled forward. His hand went around her waist to catch her, but his attention was focused on something behind her.

The car.

"What's that?" he demanded, taking a step toward the backseat of the car.

"What?" Again, her voice was wobbly. Everything about her was wobbly because this was the official moment of reckoning.

"That's a baby seat." He let go of her. "You have a baby

seat in the back of your car." This statement seemed to force him back a couple of steps. He cast a critical eye over Leona.

She wanted to cower but she refused. She was done cowering before any hard gaze, whether it was her father's or her former lover's. So she lifted her chin and straightened her back and refused to buckle.

"You—you've changed."

"Yes."

"You had a *baby*?"

She had to swallow twice to get her throat to work. "I did."

Byron's mouth dropped open. He tried to shut it, but it didn't work. "Whose?"

Leona couldn't help it. She wasn't cowering, by God, but she couldn't stand here and watch, either. She closed her eyes. "Yours."

"Mine?"

She opened her eyes to see that Byron was pacing away from her. Then he spun back. "I have a baby? And you didn't tell *me*?"

"I was—I was going to."

"When?" The word was a knife that sliced through the air and embedded itself midchest, right where her heart was. "And what? You had to kiss me? This I have to hear, Leona. I have to know the rationale behind *this*." He crossed his arms and glared at her.

No cowering. Not allowed. "I— You— You left me. I can't lose him."

It was hard to tell in the dim light from a faraway lamppost, but she swore all the color drained out of Byron's face. "Him?"

"Percy. I named him Percy." She bent over and retrieved her tablet from her bag. After a few taps, she had the most recent picture of Percy up on the screen. The little boy was sitting on her lap, trying to eat a board book. May had taken the photo just a couple of weeks ago. "Percy," she said again, holding the tablet out to Byron.

He stared at the computer, then at her. "I *left*? I left you pregnant?"

She nodded.

"And you didn't think it was a good idea to let me know you were pregnant? That you had *my son*?" His voice was getting louder.

"You left," she pleaded. Now that he knew, she had to make him see reason. Why hadn't she assumed he'd be this mad at her? For a ridiculous second, she wanted to beg for forgiveness, say whatever it took to calm him down— whatever it took so that he wouldn't take her son from her.

But she wouldn't beg. Not anymore. She'd fight the good fight. "You were gone by the time I got away from my father and I was afraid that your family would take Percy away—"

Byron froze midturn. "Wait—what?"

"I got away from my father. I took my little sister with me. May. She's watching Percy now."

Byron moved quickly, grabbing her by both arms. "Your sister? Is watching *my son*?"

"*Our* son, yes—"

He half shoved her, half lifted her up and carried her to the car. "Take me to him. Right now."

"All right," she said, retreating to grab her bag and fishing her keys out of the pocket.

They drove in painful silence. Her apartment was out in Aurora, which meant a solid thirty minutes of feeling Byron's rage from the passenger seat.

She was miserable. Just when she had a moment of hope, thinking maybe there was still something between them, something good—and it hadn't lasted. It would never last with Byron. It would always be like this—the two of them straddling the thin line between love and hate.

If only she wasn't a Harper. If only he wasn't a Beaumont. If only they'd been two nameless nobodies who could fall in love and live happily ever after in complete obscurity.

But no. It wasn't to be. He hated her right now because she'd kept quiet.

They pulled into the apartment complex parking lot. "You live here?" Byron asked. She could hear the confusion in his voice.

"Yes. This was all we could afford."

"And your parents? Your father?"

She got out of the car. "Please don't mention my father around May. She's…still nervous about him."

"Why?"

"Just…don't." Because she didn't want to go into why her parents were terrible people right after she'd finally told Byron about the baby. She grabbed her bag and locked the car. "This way."

Byron followed her up the two flights of stairs to the third floor of the apartment complex. "Here we are," she told him, unlocking the door.

"Oh, thank goodness you're home," May said from the couch, where Percy was crying. "I really think he's got another ear infection and—oh!" She recoiled in horror at the sight of Byron.

"It's all right," Leona told her little sister. "I told him."

May stood, cradling Percy in her arms. "He didn't come to take Percy, did he?"

"No," Byron said a little too loudly. "I just came to meet my son."

May's gaze darted between Leona and Byron like a rabbit trapped between a fox and a rock. And Byron was definitely the fox. "It's okay?"

Byron stepped up next to her. "Hello, May. It's nice to meet you. I'm Byron Beaumont."

Percy looked at Leona and held out his chubby little arms. May couldn't seem to do anything except stare in openmouthed horror at Byron.

"Let me have him," Leona finally said. She laid her bag on the kitchen table and took Percy from her sister and whispered, "It's going to be okay."

May attempted a smile and failed. "I'll just go. To my room." She all but sprinted down the hall. Seconds later, her door clicked shut.

"Hey, baby," Leona said, hugging Percy tight. "Aunt May says you have another ear infection. Do your ears hurt?"

Percy made a high-pitched whine in the back of his throat.

"I know," she agreed. "No fun at all." She looked over at Byron, who was gaping at the two of them. "I'm going to go find his ear drops. Do you want to hold him while I look?"

If possible, Byron looked terrified at this suggestion. "He has red hair."

Leona smiled down at her son. He had his fingers jammed into his mouth and he was getting drool all over her work blouse. "Yes, it's coming in redder. He takes after you."

Byron took a step back. "He takes after me," he repeated in a stunned whisper. "How old?"

"Sit down. I need to get his drops. Then we'll talk."

Almost robotically, Byron walked over to the couch and sat heavily.

"Percy, baby, this is your father," she whispered to her son as she sat him on Byron's lap. "Just hold him for a second, okay?"

"Um…" came the uncertain reply.

Leona moved quickly. She hurried to the bedroom and stripped out of her suit. She grabbed a clean pair of yoga pants and a long-sleeved tee and then rushed to Percy's room. "May?" she called out. The walls were thin enough that her sister should have no trouble hearing her. "Where are the drops?"

"I couldn't find them," May replied through the wall. "Are you sure he's okay?"

"He's Percy's father," Leona replied quietly. "He has a right to know."

There was a pause. "If Father finds out he's back…"

Yeah, that was a problem. Leon Harper would not take kindly to Byron's return any more than he'd taken kindly to Leona leaving with May. They'd reached an uneasy truce in the family since Percy had been born, but Leona didn't want anything to set off her father. She didn't even want to think about how low he might sink to get even with the Beaumonts.

She did a hurried check of the medicine cabinet and then checked her bedside table—ah. There they were—on the floor. They must have gotten knocked off and rolled under the bed. Leona fished the bottle out and held it up to the light. The little bottle was only one-fourth full, but that would have to do for now.

When she got back to the living room, Percy was leaning back against Byron's chest, starting up at him with curious eyes. "Here," she said, sitting down next to them. "I need to put the drops in."

She tilted Percy onto her lap. "Mommy's going to count to ten, ready? One…" She put the drops in and counted very slowly.

Byron rested his hand on Percy's feet, and then picked up one foot and held it against his palm. "This is really happening, isn't it?" he asked in a shaky voice.

"…Ten," she said in a happy voice. "That's such a good boy! Let's roll over." She lifted Percy so that he faced her.

"Yes," she told Byron, "it all happened." Then she began to count brightly again.

All of it—finding out Byron was exactly like all the other Beaumonts, realizing her father was right, keeping Percy far away from any Beaumont, long nights worrying how she was going to make it all work—it'd all happened.

Without Byron.

When she got to ten again, she sat Percy up. He was half on her lap, half on Byron's lap, safely stuck in the space between them. He looked up at Byron and smiled a drooly smile.

Byron managed a weak grin and then stroked Percy's hair. "How old?"

"Almost six months. I was three months pregnant when…" She couldn't bring herself to say, "when you left." At least, not out loud.

"I don't— You didn't—" He took a deep breath. "Why didn't you tell me? I mean, I could have helped out. I could *know* him."

She sighed. She'd long since put the events of that night behind her—or so she'd thought. But the pain felt as fresh as it ever had.

"He's a good baby," she said, desperate to avoid the hurt of remembering. "He's teething and that leads to a lot of ear infections, but that's about the only problem. He's happy and he eats well. And we…we do all right. He's got his own room here." Which was why they were so far out on the edge of Denver. The rents were cheaper, so they could afford a three-bedroom apartment. "I work for Lutefisk Design and May is finishing up college. She watches him when she doesn't have classes, but when she does, we have him in a day care. He likes it there," she added.

Percy squirmed against them. "It's his bedtime," Leona explained when Byron tensed. "You could help me get him ready for bed. If you want."

"Yeah," Byron said. "Sure."

She picked Percy up and carried him into the small bedroom. They'd found most of the furniture at resale shops. They had a crib, a glider and an old dresser that doubled as a changing table.

Leona laid Percy out on the changing table. With Byron watching, she changed the baby's diaper and got him into a clean set of footie jammies. Then she lifted him up. "Sit," she told Byron. To his credit, he sat in the glider and held out his hands for the baby. He didn't look less shell-shocked, but she appreciated the effort.

Leona leaned over the small basket that held the books. "How about…" Percy reached his hands out for the worn copy of *Pat the Bunny*. "All right," she agreed. "Can you read to him while I wash my hands?"

"Yeah. Sure."

She hurried to the bathroom, which was on the other side of May's room. In the distance, she heard Byron's deep voice read the simple story.

May's door opened and she popped her head out. "He's not staying, is he?"

"May," Leona said in a quiet whisper. "No, I don't think he's staying."

May shot her a disbelieving look. "You don't *think*? Leona, you know what he's like. He's a Beaumont. What if he wants to take Percy with him?"

Leona washed her hands in the bathroom. That was the question, wasn't it? Byron had the weight of the Beaumont name and family fortune behind him. And what did Leona have? She had May and Percy. She knew what lawyers could do to a woman. Her own father had regaled the family with tales of how he'd left his first wife penniless after she'd been seduced by Byron's father.

"I don't think he'll do that," she told May, who hovered in the doorway as if she expected to have to bolt at any second. Once, Leona would have said yes, Byron would take the boy and she'd never see her baby again.

But now? At dinner tonight he'd been the Byron she'd once thought she'd known. Caring, attentive, thoughtful. Heck, he'd even apologized for Frances's behavior. Those were not the actions of a man out to destroy her.

Of course, that had been before he'd seen the car seat. She had absolutely no idea what he was thinking now.

"I'm sorry," May said. "I'm just worried."

"I know." Leona dried her hands and gripped May by the shoulders. "I won't let him take Percy. I promise."

May's eyes watered. "I don't want him to hurt you again."

Leona pulled May into a tight hug. "I won't let him," she promised.

"Leona?" Byron called out. "We're done. Now what?"

At the sound of Byron's voice, May hurried back to her bedroom and shut the door.

Leona paused to take a deep breath. She couldn't let Byron break her heart again. She couldn't lose her son. And if they could keep her father out of it, that'd be great, too.

Sure. No problem.

Byron was rocking Percy, whose eyes were half closed. "Hi," he said when she entered the room.

Despite it all, she smiled at him. To see him holding Percy—she had dreamed of this moment.

This was what she'd wanted before that horrible night when it'd all fallen apart. For the months they'd been seeing each other, she'd thought about Byron being a father—being a husband. Helping with the babies, because of course they'd have children together. She and Byron were different than their families. Better. Electric. They were going to love each other for the rest of their lives.

Then he'd left before she'd gotten the chance to tell him she was pregnant and Leona had put those old dreams away.

She couldn't help it. Part of her still wanted those dreams, even knowing how much of a Beaumont he was.

But that vision of them growing old together was just that—a vision.

It could never happen.

Five

Byron's head was a mess as Leona took the boy—his son!—from him. No, *mess* was too generous a word for the muddle of emotions and thoughts all struggling to be heard.

He had a son—that was the first thing he had to make sense of. He had a son and Leona hadn't told him. She had lied to him again—maybe he shouldn't be so damned surprised. After all, she'd had no problem hiding her family from him before. Why was it so shocking that she would hide his son from him now?

It was obvious she loved the boy. She'd been sweet and gentle with him and this thing right now—nursing—was obviously something they did every night.

Byron walked back into the main part of the apartment. The place wasn't fancy—a standard apartment with beige walls, beige carpeting and beige countertops in the kitchen. A set of patio doors indicated that there was a small deck outside. There were a few pictures on the wall, all of May and Leona and Percy. Mostly of Percy. None of Byron. But then, why should there be?

He realized he was standing in the kitchen, opening the cabinets, drawers and the fridge, looking for something to cook. He always retreated to the kitchen when he was upset, even when he'd been a little kid.

Cooking was predictable. There was comfort in the routine. If he followed the recipe, he knew how the dish would turn out.

Leona had apples. Byron could make applesauce. There—

that was a good plan. That was him taking care of his son. Everyone had to eat.

He peeled the apples and got them simmering in the pot. Then he debated the ingredients—would Percy like cinnamon or would it be too strong for him? Would Leona want the applesauce to be unsweetened? In the end, Byron went with a little lemon juice to brighten the flavor.

As he cooked, he tried to think. Why hadn't she told him? It wasn't as though he'd gone off the grid. Yes, he'd been in Europe but he'd been findable. Frances, at least, had always known where he was. He'd kept his email address. He hadn't disappeared. Hell, even a birth announcement would have been okay, but there'd been nothing. Just another lie.

He needed answers—and while he was thinking about it, he still needed to know why she thought he'd left her and what did she mean, she and her sister had "gotten away from" their father?

She'd *gone* with her father. Leon Harper was her father and she hadn't told Byron that truth. And when Harper had demanded Leona come with him, she had. She'd left Byron standing on the sidewalk, in the rain, his heart in shards at his feet.

If she'd dumped him, he could have dealt with it. He might have still wound up in Europe, but if she'd said "Gee, Byron, this just isn't working, we should see other people, it's not you, it's me and we can still be friends" or whatever, he'd have moved on.

But she'd lied to him. She was the daughter of the man who was hell-bent on destroying Byron and his entire family. By all accounts, the man was doing a hell of a job at it, too. The brewery—a hundred and sixty-six years of Beaumont history and ownership—was gone, all because of Leon Harper. And his daughters.

Byron knew what betrayal looked like. He knew his father had cheated on his wives. He knew that at least one of the ex-wives had cheated on Hardwick. Byron knew there was always a risk that any relationship could go wrong. The Beaumonts didn't have exclusive rights to dysfunctional marriages.

But when he'd been with Leona, he'd managed to convince himself that he was different. That they were different. Byron and Leona had loved each other.

Or had they?

She'd lied to him before. Twice. Was she lying again? Even if she was, would he be able to tell the difference?

Apples were not going to solve that mystery. He had more pressing issues to deal with.

Percy was his son. Byron wanted to be there for the boy, to let Percy know that Byron loved him in the big ways and the little ways. All the ways Byron's own father had never loved Byron.

But how was that going to happen? He was still living in the mansion—he didn't even have his own place. And getting a restaurant off the ground wasn't a nine-to-five job, that was for damned sure. Not now, not ever. How could he make sure he was a part of Percy's life?

The sauce was halfway done when Leona came into the kitchen. She was wearing leggings and a T-shirt but there was still something about her. There'd *always* been something about her.

"Ah," she said when she saw the bubbling apples. She gave him a small smile. "I should have known."

"Applesauce. For Percy," he explained. "Just apples and a little lemon. I didn't know if cinnamon would be too much for him."

"It smells wonderful. He loves apples."

They stood there silently for a minute.

"It's not a big batch. Do you have a container for it?"

Leona dug out a plastic bowl and Byron moved all the

dirty dishes to the sink. Yes, he needed answers. But honestly? He had no idea where to start. So he didn't. He did the dishes instead.

The uncomfortable silence lingered for a few more minutes as he washed the knife and the cutting board. Leona dried. Finally, she broke the silence.

"We should come up with a plan, I guess."

"A plan?"

"Yes. If you're really going to stay—"

"I am," he interrupted, stung by the insinuation that he'd bolt.

"Then we need a plan." She swallowed, her gaze focused on the sink. "A custody plan. I know I can't keep Percy from you, but I'm not going to just give up custody."

"You already kept him from me." She winced but he refused to feel bad for her. "And I didn't say you had to give up custody. But why didn't you tell me?" he demanded. "Why did you keep this from me?"

"I thought…" She dropped the dish towel on the counter and turned away from him. "I thought you didn't want anything to do with me. Your phone was disconnected and you were in Europe—pretty damned far away from here."

That was true. But it was the way she said it that confused him. He looked at the back of her head as if he could peer inside and find the answers he was looking for. "You could have sent an email."

"I could have," she agreed. Her shoulders heaved with a massive sigh. "I should have. But I was afraid."

"Afraid? Of what?"

She turned to him, her wide eyes even wider. "Of you, Byron. Of all the Beaumonts."

He gaped at her. Before he could remind her that he was not the one who'd lied, she went on, "And we left home with only as much as we could carry, and I had to get a job. Being pregnant wasn't as fun as it seems on television and

May had classes and...and you weren't here. And I guess I convinced myself that you weren't coming back and it was just me and May and Percy on our own. It was better that way. We didn't need anyone else."

He dried off his hands and placed them on her shoulders. "I could have helped. Even if...even if I didn't come back, I still could have helped. Child support or whatever. You shouldn't have had to do this on your own."

She dropped her head and he heard her sniff. "Well, you're here now. I can't change what happened in the past but if you're going to stay—"

"I am," he told her again.

"Then, yes. Child support and custody visits. But I can't lose him, Byron." Her voice broke over this last bit. "Please don't try to punish me by taking him."

The anguish in her voice—her assumption that he'd exact some sort of twisted revenge... He spun her around and lifted her chin until she had no choice but to look him in the eye. Child support and custody visits were all very clinical-sounding things, like the few hours a year that he was shipped off with Frances and Matthew to visit their mother, who'd then spend most of the visit trying not to cry.

That's not what he wanted. He was not his father, for God's sake. He was better than that.

Except, was he? He'd gotten a woman pregnant and then left her in the lurch, completely alone with no other resources. Yeah, he'd thought her father would still be paying the bills and yeah, she'd rejected him, but when the facts of the situation were laid plain, he'd left her alone just when she'd needed him most.

She was right. That was exactly what Hardwick Beaumont would have done.

"I'm not going to take him away from you," Byron told her, feeling the certainty of the words. "Because you're both going to come live with me."

* * *

Leona's mouth fell open in shock. *"What?"*

Byron's grip tightened on her shoulders. "I don't have a place yet. You can either move into the mansion with me or help me pick something out—whatever you think is better. But you need to move in with me as soon as possible."

Maybe this wasn't happening. Maybe none of it was happening—not Byron returning, not him kissing her, not him reading a bedtime story to Percy. She could be hallucinating the whole kit and caboodle.

Sadly, the way he was holding her, the look in his eyes? She knew she wasn't hallucinating a damned thing. And that was a problem.

"You want me to pack up and come with you?"

The tendons in his neck tightened. "I want my son with me. And if that means you have to be with me, then so be it."

Ah. So he didn't want her, not really. He would put up with her if that got him what he wanted, though. His words cut like a dull butter knife—painful and ragged.

She'd promised May she would not let Byron hurt her again.

She hated lying to her sister.

Still, Leona was making remarkable progress. She didn't agree to Byron's demands just to keep the peace, and she didn't dissolve into useless tears and, most important, she didn't do both of them at the same time. Those days were done. She might not be able to be strong enough to protect her own heart, but she had to protect Percy.

So she cleared her throat. "What if it's not a good idea for us to live together?"

His eyes narrowed. "Why not?"

She couldn't look at that hardness, couldn't bear to feel the pain again. So she closed her eyes. She couldn't help it. "Look, I know we had something once but it fell apart."

"But—" he started to interrupt.

She cut him off. "And it doesn't even matter who did what. If we live together…we'll have to face those choices every single day."

Every day she'd have to wake up knowing that Byron was mere feet away, not oceans and continents. Every single day she'd have to look him in the eye to discuss what Percy had done and every single damned day, he'd probably cook her a meal and she'd love it.

And every day—every minute—she'd wonder when it was all going to end.

Byron pulled her in closer and she felt his hot breath on her ear. "You listen to me, Leona Harper." Panic blossomed in her stomach at his cold tone. "Maybe it doesn't matter who did what, maybe it does. That doesn't change the fact that I have a son and I am *not* going to stand aside a moment longer because you think it might be awkward around the breakfast table. You *will* move in with me and, until further notice, we *will* raise our son together."

An unspoken *or else* hung in the small space between his lips and her ear.

She would not cry, by God. She wouldn't do it. Not in front of him. Not in front of any man. Not anymore. She was an adult responsible for her sister and her son and she would *not* give.

"I can't afford very much. That's why we live here."

"I will pay for it," he replied firmly.

"But—"

"No buts, Leona. You've had to cover everything for a year. It's my turn to step up to the plate. It's the least I can do."

God, that sounded so good. She could live with him, let him take care of her, of Percy, with his part of the Beaumont fortune. She wouldn't be teetering on the edge of genteel poverty anymore. Things like doctor's visits and ear drops wouldn't be monumental mountains she struggled to climb. Byron had the ways and means to make that part of her life easy.

Of course, if she'd wanted easy—if she'd wanted to step back and let someone else call all the shots in her life—she'd still be living under her father's roof. She'd still be subjected to his rantings and ravings about the Beaumonts in general and Byron in specific.

Yes, that was easier. But it was not better.

She couldn't allow herself to be dependent on a man again, especially a man who'd already left her high and dry once. Byron could not be trusted, not on a kiss and a promise. Because this time it wouldn't just be her heart in danger. It'd be Percy's, too.

"May," Leona managed to say without her voice cracking. "She watches him. I can't just leave her." It was the best defense she had. May was twenty, yes—but she was a fragile young woman who was not ready to be thrown out on her own because a billionaire's son demanded it.

"Percy loves her," she offered, hoping that would help.

It didn't. Byron sighed wearily. Then, unexpectedly, his grip loosened. He didn't lean back, though—he just skimmed his hands up and down her upper arms. "Is that the deal? I have to provide accommodations for your sister before you'll move in with me?"

Once, they'd talked about moving in together. She'd been staying over at his place more and more—which had run the risk of drawing her father's attention to her activities. She'd known then that when her father found out, it would be a problem. But Leona hadn't cared because waking up in Byron's arms was worth the risk.

Of course, once she'd been sure that he'd marry her right away, when she told Byron she was pregnant. It wouldn't have mattered who her father was because Byron loved her and she loved him. She'd been sure that once she told him the truth he'd realize she hadn't been trying to hide anything. She'd just wanted someone who didn't care about her last name. She'd thought she'd found that man.

She was still paying for that mistake. She couldn't afford any more.

"I won't move into the mansion."

"Fine. I was going to look for a place close to the restaurant anyway." His hands were still moving up and down her arms and dang it all, she was leaning into his touch. "Is that all right with you? Or do you need to be closer to your job?"

She leaned her forehead against his shoulder. It wasn't much of a choice, not after he'd demanded that she uproot her whole life to be with him for the sake of their son. But he'd still thrown her a small bone. "The office is downtown. As long as we're not too far out, it should be about the same travel time."

"I'll make some calls in the morning. We'll move as soon as possible."

What was she going to tell her sister? *No, I'm not going to let him break my heart again, but by the way—pack up everything you own because we're all going to set up house together.*

May would be furious.

Still, Leona didn't think she could refuse. What were the alternatives? Byron was not interested in coming by to visit Percy here and, as far as she could tell, the only other possibility was Byron suing for custody. She couldn't let that happen—where would she get the money to defend herself? Lawyers weren't cheap, that she knew. She couldn't ask her parents for help, either. If her father knew Byron wanted the boy... It'd be an all-out war.

And if she lost? Once, she'd thought she knew Byron. But he'd turned out to be more of a Beaumont than she ever would have guessed. She had no idea what lengths he would go to, and she didn't really want to find out the hard way.

It was a risk she couldn't take. It'd be a short-term solution, she tried to tell herself. Just until they could get a formalized custody agreement arranged.

Byron's arms went around her, holding her to his chest. "I don't want to punish you, Leona," he said. None of the coldness was left in his tone. "But he's my son, too."

"I know." That's what she wanted to believe.

"It won't be bad, will it?" He swallowed. "At least, better than living with your parents?"

She shuddered at the thought. "We'll have to have rules. No fighting or anything in front of the baby."

"Okay," he agreed. "But I'm not looking for a fight."

If only she could believe that. There was one other important detail that had to be settled before she agreed. "We'll sleep in separate bedrooms. Just because we're living together doesn't mean I want you back."

His hands stilled and then he snorted. "This is for Percy. You can have your own bedroom. I don't expect you to sleep with me." There was a brief pause. "It'd probably be best if we keep things simple between us until we decide on what to do next."

"Agreed," she said. Which completely disregarded the fact that, at this very moment, he was holding her in a highly not-simple way. Could she really expect either of them to maintain a respectable distance? "Simple is better."

"And you'll keep helping me with the restaurant?"

"Yes." The absolute last thing she could do now was quit her job. Even if Byron was covering the rent, she still needed to maintain her independence. He might not be looking for a fight—and she wasn't exactly spoiling for one, either—but if things went wrong, she needed to be able to pick up and start over again.

Again.

He swallowed. "And your parents? Don't take this the

wrong way, but I don't want my son anywhere near your father."

"They're not a part of this. I cut ties when we left."

He leaned back and looked her in the eye again. "Why did you leave? I mean, we'd talked about getting our own place or you moving in with me—but you wouldn't do it then."

The corners of her mouth turned down as she pushed back against tears. She hadn't moved in with Byron before because moving in would mean telling him who she really was and she hadn't wanted to risk it. Looking back, she should have. But instead, she'd convinced herself that once she finished college and got a job—that would be the time to leave home. But she didn't explain any of that. Instead she said, "May and I had to get out. My father was... unbearable." She shuddered again at the memory of her father's completely unfiltered rage.

"Did he hit you?" Byron demanded, a fierce look in his eyes.

"No." But there are other ways to make a person hurt. "He threatened to have me declared unfit and to take the baby after he was born."

"He did *what*?"

"Because it was you." This time, she couldn't push the tears back. "Because of who you are. He wanted to make sure you'd never get the baby."

For years, her father had berated Leona, her sister, her mother. All of them bore the brunt of his rage. And she'd put up with it for far longer than she should have because she hadn't known any better.

Until she'd met Byron. Until he'd shown her that there was a different way to live, that people could actually care for each other. If only she'd been brave enough before...

But then again, now she knew Byron's true colors. She

could have escaped her father only to be stuck with a man who'd abandon her anyway.

Still, it had been those times with Byron that had given her the courage to leave home, single, pregnant and with May. She'd realized then that she had to get out while she could, before Leon Harper got ahold of her son.

Byron was staring at her in total shock. "He would, wouldn't he?"

She nodded.

A moment passed as he gaped at her. "Then there's only one thing to do," he finally said in a shaky voice.

No, she wanted to say, even though she didn't know what that one thing was. She knew she wasn't going to like it, wasn't going to want it.

"We have to get married."

Six

This was his life now, he realized. Proposing marriage in whispers to a woman who was crying, all so they wouldn't wake the baby. "Why hasn't he done it yet? Why hasn't he taken Percy away from you?"

"I don't know."

"It's the only way to keep Percy safe, Leona, and you know it."

If they weren't married, what was to stop her father from charging in like a bull elephant at any second? Byron had been out of the picture for a year. He didn't know the specifics of family law, but he was pretty sure his absence would count against him. He would beat Leon—he was the boy's father—but it would be a long, exhausting battle.

Memories of his mother mixed in with all the current confusion—not just the screaming fights, but how his father had had all of her things loaded into a moving van before he'd served her with divorce papers. How his mother had never quite recovered from being kicked out, from being steamrollered in court and losing her children.

Could Byron let that happen to Leona? Could he live with himself if she was the collateral damage in yet another Beaumont-Harper legal battle?

He should. She'd lied to him—twice. And not about whether or not she'd spent too much money or hated his cooking or any of those petty things other people lied about. She'd lied about who she was and the fact that she'd given birth to Byron's son.

And yet… He couldn't do it. Because Leona was right about one thing—it didn't really matter who'd done what a year ago. He couldn't bear to think of her being destroyed like his mother had been. That was a risk he wasn't willing to take.

He could barely think right now. Babies and apartments and a wedding. A ring. And a restaurant. Couldn't forget that.

And applesauce. He turned to the stove—yeah, it was done. He shut the burner off to let it cool. For some insane reason, he wondered if Leona had chocolate chips. If ever there was a time for cookies, this was it.

He turned back to Leona. She stood there looking as if he'd threatened her to within an inch of her life. Maybe he had. But what were his options? He could not let Leon Harper get his claws into Percy. Everything else was secondary.

"At least until we're sure your father can't take over," he rationalized. "And you can still have a private bedroom. I…" He took a deep breath. "I cared for you a great deal. I hope that we can at least be friends."

She dropped her gaze and he had the distinct feeling that he was making things worse. "Friends."

"For Percy's sake."

"Can I…think about it? Tomorrow's Friday. We probably couldn't get an appointment to get married for a week or two anyway."

"Sure." He tried to sound friendly about it, but he didn't think he made it. "But I'll start looking for places tomorrow." Because even if she didn't marry him, they still needed to live together.

But she'd marry him. She had to.

He should go. He'd just asked her to move in and marry him within the space of a few minutes, and the pull to make cookies was only getting stronger. She needed to think, too. "When will I see you tomorrow?" he asked.

"I have to go to the office and update my boss on the project and draft a few ideas for you. I promised," she added with a watery smile.

"Lunch, then? I'll have something ready for us."

"Not at the mansion, right?" Another small shudder went through her.

"No," he readily agreed. He didn't want another run-in with Frances. "At the restaurant."

"All right. Tomorrow around noon."

He transferred the applesauce into the container and sealed it. "For Percy," he said, holding out the still-warm sauce.

"For Percy," she agreed.

She didn't sound happy about it.

Byron went straight to the kitchen. It was late, though—George was already gone. The normally warm, bright room was dark and quiet, except for the echo of his footsteps off the tiled floors.

He flipped on the lights and assembled ingredients. Chocolate chip cookies were a must. For lunch tomorrow, he told himself. And he could try a few sandwiches. It was reasonable to think that he'd want to have a simple lunch menu.

He fell into the familiar routine of creaming the sugar and folding in the chips while the oven preheated. He didn't even have to think about this recipe anymore.

Had he really asked Leona to marry him? Because she'd given birth to a son—*his* son, the one with matching red hair?

He needed a ring. He hadn't bought one the first time around. A ring would show her he was serious about this.

"There you are."

Byron spun to see Frances standing in the doorway. Instead of the gown she'd been wearing earlier, she was in a pair of pajamas—thick, fleecy ones with a bright turquoise plaid pattern. She looked fifteen years younger than their twenty-nine years.

"What's wrong?"

"Nothing," he lied. "Does something have to be wrong?"

Frances gave him a knowing smile. "You're baking cookies and God only knows what else at ten at night? You and I both know that something's wrong." A shadow darkened her face. "It's Leona, isn't it? I can't believe you hired her, Byron. Do you enjoy getting jerked around?"

He slammed a bowl down on the island countertop.

"Jeez," Frances said, giving him a long look. "Spill it."

He didn't want to but Frances was his twin. They couldn't keep secrets from each other if they tried. "You're going to tell me why you suddenly moved back home?"

An embarrassed blush raced over her cheeks. "I made a bad investment."

"You're broke?"

"Don't tell Chadwick. You know how he is," she pleaded. "I can't stand to hear another 'I told you so' from him."

"Frannie…"

"Whatever," she said, brushing away his concern with a cynical shrug of her shoulders. "I'll be fine. Just getting back on my feet. But that's neither here nor there. Now spill it. You're baking cookies because…"

He took a deep breath. If he did it fast… "I have a son."

Frances's cynicism fell away. "You *what*?"

"Just like our old man, huh? Get a woman pregnant and then bail on her," he said bitterly. "Leona has a baby boy named Percy. He's got red hair." That probably wasn't the most important thing to know about the boy, but Byron felt it was the thing that sealed the deal.

"Who else knows?"

"Her family." Frances made a face of revulsion. "She

lives with her sister, who watches Percy. They don't have anything to do with their father."

"Oh, I see. And this is what she told you? Because we all know how very trustworthy she is. Do I need to remind you that this is the woman who didn't even see fit to tell you she was Leon Harper's daughter, even after you'd started sleeping with her?"

"No, you do not need to remind me of that," he snapped. "It doesn't change the fact that Percy is my son." He realized he was whisking the cookie batter with more force than was required. He made himself set the bowl down.

"And you're sure," Frances asked.

"Yes."

She shook her head in some combination of disbelief and pity. "God only knows what she's been saying about you. And her father? You have to get that kid away from her."

"I told her we had to get married. Immediately." Frances gasped in true horror.

"Are you nuts? You want to marry into that family of—vipers?"

"That's why I have to marry her—to make sure Harper can't take Percy away from us."

"Listen to you. *Us*. There is no *us*. There's you and a woman who broke your heart and then hid a baby from you." Unexpectedly, her eyes watered. "I already lost you for a year. You weren't here because of *that* woman. No one else understands me like you do. I missed having my twin here."

The last thing he needed right now was more guilt. "I missed you, too. But I'm back now," he told her.

Frances sniffed. "Isn't there another way? Do you have to marry her?"

"Yes." He got out the scoop he used for the batter and began to dish it out onto the baking mats. "It's the only way to make things right."

Or more right. After all, he hadn't spoken of undying love, of treasuring her forever. This was a marriage of necessity. They would have separate rooms. Her sister was going to live with them.

"You need to be careful, Byron."

He wanted to say, when was he not careful? But he knew what Frances would say to that—if he'd been careful the first time, he'd have realized that Leona Harper was Leon Harper's daughter. And, of course, if he'd been careful, he wouldn't have had a child he never knew.

But he hadn't been careful. He'd just wanted her. It hadn't mattered whose daughter she was. It hadn't mattered that every time he tried to ask about her family, she changed the subject. What had mattered was that they were together.

Well. He was finally going to make that come true. They would be together—for the sake of their son, if nothing else.

"I'll call Matthew. He'll get the lawyers going on it." There. That was a perfectly reasonable thing to say. After all, if he'd learned anything from his father, it was that marriages were temporary and a man with a fortune should *always* have a prenup.

"That's not what I meant."

"I know." He scooped out the second-to-last cookie's worth of dough and then offered the bowl to Frances. That'd always been her favorite part, licking the bowls. "Look, I just found this out tonight. I'm still trying to get my head wrapped around it."

She took the bowl and sat on a stool, swiping her finger through the batter. "Is he cute? Your son?"

Byron thought about the pale blue eyes, the shock of red hair and the drooly smile. "Yeah. Really cute."

Frances shook her head, but at least she was grinning as she did so. "You should see the smile on your face. Congratulations, Byron—you're a father."

Seven

"We're *what*? You're *what*?" May stared at Leona.

"I'm going to marry Byron." *I think*, she mentally added.

May's mouth opened, closed and opened again. "When? Oh, to heck with when. Why?"

"He's Percy's father. And no one wants Father to get involved in a custody battle. If I'm married to Byron, Father can't take Percy from us." These were all perfectly rational reasons for this sudden change of course. But rational had nothing to do with the way Leona's stomach was in a knot that might never get untied.

"And what about me?" May demanded, her eyes flashing.

It was, hands down, the angriest Leona had ever heard her little sister. Any other day, Leona might celebrate this development—May was speaking out instead of meekly taking whatever life dished out.

But it wasn't helping Leona's unmovable knot. "You can come with us. We'll get a bigger place—more than enough room for you to have your own space." May looked at Leona as if she'd grown a third head. Leona decided to change tactics. "Or you can stay here. I know this is closer to your college…"

"What about Percy? I don't want to live with a Beaumont, but I'm the one who takes care of him."

Leona winced at the dismissive way May said *Beaumont*. "I know. We'll find a way to make it work."

May looked doubtful, but she didn't say anything else. Instead, she turned and headed back to bed.

Leona went to her room and lay down on the double bed, but she didn't sleep. Her mind raced through all the options. Marrying Byron. Moving in with him. Being a family, at least during the day. Sleeping in separate bedrooms.

What other options did she have? Every time she asked herself that question, she came back to the same answer. None. But she kept asking it, just to be sure.

The separate bedrooms thing was nonnegotiable. It had to be. Even now, she could feel his lips on hers, feel a year's worth of sexual frustration begging to be released by his hands.

Sex with Byron had been fun and magical and wonderful. In his arms, she'd been special.

Was it wrong to want that back in her life? No, that wasn't the right question. Was it wrong to want that with Byron—again?

But separate bedrooms it was. Because she could not confuse sex with love. Fool me once, shame on you. But fool me twice…

She was no fool. Not any longer.

Finally, exhausted, she turned her attention back to the only thing that could possibly distract her from Byron—the restaurant. She needed some ideas for tomorrow.

She drifted off to sleep thinking about Percherons.

Byron shook the tablecloth out over the small metal bistro table he'd snagged off one of the mansion's patios. Then he set up the matching chairs around it. He'd brought a candle because…well, because. Once upon a time, he'd planned a romantic candlelit dinner where he would ask for her hand in marriage. The ring he'd picked out this morning felt as if it was burning a hole in his pocket.

But he'd finally decided that the dungeon was too musty

to eat in and it was far too windy outside to have a flame burning, so he let it rest. Candles were not required.

He had a picnic basket filled with three kinds of sandwiches, potato salad and gazpacho. He'd packed the almond cake from last night and had two bottles of iced tea. This wasn't his ideal meal, but as he was quickly learning, he had to go with the flow.

Just another tasting, he tried to tell himself as he set out the silverware. No big deal.

Except it was huge. He'd called Matthew—this situation seemed too important to discuss over a text—but Matthew hadn't picked up, which wasn't like him. So Byron had been forced to leave a vague, "Something's come up and I need to talk to you," message.

Byron had also called a Realtor and laid out his specifications. And he'd even called the county clerk to find out what he needed to get married.

Now he had to wait. He and Leona could get married next week, but he needed the prenup first.

Finally, after what felt like a long wait but was actually only a few minutes past noon, Leona's car rolled up. She sat behind the wheel for a few moments. Byron got the feeling she was psyching herself up.

Then she got out of the car. She was wearing another suit—the consummate businesswoman. But there was something more about her, something that had attracted him to her from the very first time he'd laid eyes on her. After all this time, he still couldn't say what that something was.

Whatever it was, he wanted to pull her into his arms and not let go. He'd hired her for a very specific reason— to make sure she knew she couldn't hurt him. But instead? He'd found out just how much he couldn't trust her.

He would not give in to the physical temptation that Leona represented. This marriage proposal wasn't about sex. It was about doing whatever it took to make sure his son was safe.

"Hi," she said. She looked at the outdoor table.

Was she nervous? Fine. Good. He didn't want her to think she held all the cards. The sooner she realized he was calling the shots, the better.

He stood and put his hands on her shoulders. She tensed and he swore he felt a current of electricity pass between them. But he wouldn't give in and pull her into his arms. He couldn't let her affect him. Not anymore. "Have you given any more thought to my question?"

Leona notched an eyebrow at him. That was better, he thought. He loved it when she was snarky and sarcastic—not shell-shocked. "I don't remember your asking me anything. I seem to remember more of a direct order."

Byron pulled the small, robin's-egg-blue box out of his pocket. Leona gasped. "Ah. Yes. That was a mistake." He opened the box. The sunlight caught the emerald-cut diamond and threw sparkles across the tablecloth. "Leona, will you marry me?"

If only he'd asked her a year ago…but even as he thought that, he remembered how she'd hidden her name, her family from him. Would she have said yes, if he'd asked her then? Or would she have laughed in his face? Would it have changed everything—or would it all still have happened exactly the same way?

Anything snarky about her fell away as she gaped at the ring, then him, then back at the ring. She reached out to touch the box but pulled her hand back. "We need to discuss work," she finally said in a firm voice. "Mr. Lutefisk is very particular about his employees having personal conversations while they're on the clock. He'll be calling to check in about an hour from now. He's letting me handle this project on my own, but he keeps close tabs on all of his employees' projects."

What a load of crap. She was stalling and he didn't like it. "Leona. This isn't just a 'personal conversation.' This is our life—together."

She gave him a baleful look that, despite all of his best intentions to not let her get to him, made him feel guilty. Then fire flashed through her eyes. "I work. This is my job. You can't think that hiring me and proposing means you get to control every minute of my life, Byron. Because if so, I have an answer to your question. I don't think you'll like it."

In spite of himself, he grinned. "When did you get this feisty?"

"When you left me," she snapped. "Now are we going to discuss the job for which you hired me or not?"

The accusation stung. "That's not how I remember it going down," he said, frustration bubbling up.

She shrugged out of his grasp and sat down at the table as if she was mad at the chair. "I'm not talking about it now. I. Am. Working."

"Fine. When can we discuss nonwork stuff?"

"After five."

"When can I see Percy again?"

She looked up at him, her jaw set. "Ah, now *that* was a question. Lovely. You can see him tonight, after five. I assumed you'd come visit him." Byron gave her a look and she rolled her eyes. "As you can see, I'm not trying to hide him from you. Can we please get to work?"

"Fine." He'd let it go for now. But he left the ring on the table, where it glittered prettily.

Leona pulled out her tablet and handed it over. "We have three basic choices for the interior—we can try to lighten it up, keep it dim, or go for broke and make it very dark."

Byron looked at the preliminary colors she'd chosen. One was a bright yellow with warm red accents. The next was gray with a cooler red and the last choice was a deep red that would look almost black in the shadows. "I like the yellow. I don't want the restaurant so dim that people have to use their cell phones to read the menu."

"Agreed," she said. She flicked the screen to the next page. "I thought we'd want to play off the Percheron Drafts in the name—Percheron Pub?"

"No."

"White Horse Saloon?"

He gave her a dirty look.

"No, I didn't think so." She grinned back. This was better—this was them as equals. This was what he'd missed. He had the sudden urge to lean over and kiss her like he'd kissed her last night, right before his world had changed forever. "I also considered bringing in the European influences. What do you think about Caballo de Tiro?"

"That's—what?" He thought for a second. "Workhorse?"

"Draft horse, literally. Which fits the brand and also highlights the Spanish influences you're bringing."

He glanced at her and saw she wore a satisfied smile. "You like that one, don't you?"

"It is my favorite, it's true. I wasn't sure if you'd get the translation."

"I picked up enough French and Spanish to get by." He gave her a look. "At least, enough to cook and fend off advances."

She glanced back at the ring. "Oh?"

He could hear that she was trying to sound disinterested, but she wasn't quite succeeding. "It was…well, I guess the good news was that no one cared that I was a Beaumont. That was great, actually. But a lot of people were intrigued by the American with red hair."

Which was a huge understatement. In Paris and then Madrid, not a week went by when he didn't leave work to find a beautiful woman—or occasionally a beautiful man—waiting for him.

"I guess that was probably fun." Leona was now staring at her plate, pushing the potato salad around with her fork.

"Actually, it wasn't."

She opened her mouth to say something but then changed her mind. "Right. We're working. What do you think of the name?"

He sighed. "Right. Working." Besides, he didn't exactly want to tell her that, at several points during his self-imposed exile, he'd decided to take a particularly lovely woman up on her offer, just to get Leona out of his system—only to back out before they got anywhere near a bed.

He forced himself to focus. This restaurant was his dream, after all. Caballo de Tiro—it had a good ring to it, and wasn't too complicated to pronounce.

"I thought we could bring in touches that suggest a draft horse—wagon wheels that are repurposed as chandeliers, maybe a wagon set up outside—it's reasonable to think parents might bring their children," she added. "A wagon could be both decoration and something to distract kids."

He flipped back to the colors. "So you'd paint the walls this color yellow, have red accents—"

"The tablecloths, napkins, that sort of thing, yes."

"And accent with weathered wood?"

"And leather," she added, leaning over to flick to another screen, which had several chairs pictured. "Rich brown leather for the seating. And maybe a few harnesses that will serve as picture frames on the walls. The whole experience would be warm and comfortable—formal without being stuffy."

"I like it. Let's go with that. Caballo de Tiro."

Leona looked pleased. "That was easy. I have some other ideas…"

Byron tried not to sigh. The restaurant was important, but he felt as though he was spinning his wheels. He wanted to get back to everything else—how Percy was, if she'd marry him or if she'd fight him every step of the way—and what, exactly, she'd meant by saying *he'd* left *her.*

She shot him a look. "You hired me, after all."

"I know," he groaned. "But five o'clock seems like a long time off."

"Byron, focus. I need the specs of the kitchen and then I need to call contractors and get a timeline set up, and my boss wants that as soon as possible. I'll formalize the sketches of the interior and exterior a bit more and…"

Byron's phone rang. "The Realtor," he said with relief. At least one thing was happening quickly. "You eat and then we'll talk ovens."

"Deal," she said.

The rest of the afternoon passed in a blur. The Realtor had a list of single-family homes ready, and she wanted Byron to come in on Saturday. Leona wanted to discuss kitchen appliances and table placements.

It was enough to give a man whiplash. It'd only been a few months ago that he'd settled into his cramped Madrid apartment, working late nights cooking for a world-famous chef and wandering the city alone, trying to lose himself in another culture.

Trying to forget about Leona Harper.

Now he would be running his own restaurant and living with Leona while they raised their son.

For a brief moment, as Leona talked about bathroom sink options, Byron wanted to go back to Madrid. Right now. This was insane, that's what it was. Proposing to Leona so he could ensure he'd never lose custody of his son? Going to look at houses tomorrow? Debating what "message" bathroom faucets "communicated" to customers?

Living with Leona—the woman who'd nearly destroyed him? Whose father had done everything to ruin his family?

But a Beaumont would not cut and run or admit defeat.

His father had not been much of a father, but Byron remembered the last conversation he'd had with Hardwick Beaumont. His father had been sitting behind his massive desk, a look of disgust on his face as he took in Byron's flour-dusted pants. "Son," he'd intoned as if he were passing a death sentence, "this cooking thing—it's not right. It's not what a Beaumont does. It's servant work."

It hadn't been the first time Byron had considered running away. He'd just wanted to cook in peace and quiet, without being constantly harassed about how he wasn't good enough. He'd been all of sixteen and thought he'd known how the world worked.

But, being sixteen, he hadn't. Instead, he'd mouthed off. "You want me to go? Then I'll go. I don't have to stay here and take your insults."

He'd expected to be disowned, frankly. No one talked back to Hardwick Beaumont, especially not his disappointment of a son. Hardwick's lips had twisted into a sneer and Byron had braced himself.

Then, to his everlasting shock, Hardwick had said, "A Beaumont does not cut and run, boy. We know what we want and we fight for it, to hell with what anyone else says." He'd leaned forward, his hard gaze locked on Byron. "If I ever hear you talk about giving up again, I'll make sure you have nothing to give up. Do I make myself clear?"

"Yes, sir." Byron had been pissed at the threat, but underneath, he'd also been confused. Had his father—what? Given him permission to keep rebelling?

He had turned and started to walk out of Hardwick's office when his father had called out, "The rack of lamb last night—was that you or George?"

It'd been a huge success, as far as Byron had been concerned. Even his half siblings had enjoyed the meal. "I cooked it. George supervised."

There'd been a long pause and Byron hadn't been sure

if he'd been dismissed or not. Then Hardwick had said, "I expect you to present yourself as a Beaumont in the rest of the house. I don't want to see flour anywhere on your clothes ever again. Understood?"

"Yes, sir."

And he hadn't left home. He'd stayed and put up with his father's crap about how he did servant's work and gotten better and better at cooking. Every so often, his father would look at him over the dinner dishes and say "that meal was especially good." Which was as close to a compliment as Byron had ever gotten out of him.

He hadn't thought about that chat, such as it was, in a long time. Not too long after that, Hardwick had keeled over dead of a heart attack. Frances scolded Byron about the flour in his hair, but no one had accused him of embarrassing the Beaumont name by insisting on doing servant's work. He hadn't had to fight for what he wanted anymore.

He'd *stopped* fighting for what he'd wanted.

Including Leona. Instead of fighting for her, he'd run away to Europe.

Well. Things had changed. He was in charge now and he knew what he wanted. He wanted Leona to marry him and he wanted to be a part of his son's life.

It was high time to start acting like a Beaumont.

Finally, it was five o'clock. Leona had made him look at color samples and shaped plates and steak knives and he didn't even know what all. Whatever was her favorite was what he went with—she was the designer, after all. What he cared about was the food.

He rinsed the lunch dishes in the sink and packed everything back into his car—except for the ring. That he put in his pocket. She'd left it on the table, and it made him nervous to have a twenty-thousand-dollar piece of jewelry sitting around.

She would wear it. She would accept his proposal.

This thought was followed by a quieter one, which barely whispered across his consciousness.

She would be his.

And why not? They were going to live together. They were going to get married. Why shouldn't he reclaim what he'd once had? As long as he could have her without letting her get under his skin like she had the first time. He'd always loved being with her. They were good together. He wanted to think they still could have that same magic in bed.

He could enjoy Leona but this time, he would not let his feelings for her blind him to the truth. She was still a liar. He had to keep his guard up, that was all.

She walked to her car door. "You want to follow me out? Assuming you're coming home with me…"

The ring was going to burn him clean through. "Yes, I'm coming home with you."

She looked at him then, her lips curved into a small smile and again he had to fight the urge to kiss her.

Oh, to hell with fighting that urge.

He closed the distance between them in three strides and pulled her into him. She made a small squeaking noise when he kissed her, but he didn't care.

He kissed her like he'd dreamed of kissing her for a long, cold year—like he'd kissed her last night. She might not be good for him—not now, not ever—but he couldn't stay away from her.

After a moment, she kissed him back. Her arms went around his neck and her mouth opened for him and he swept his tongue inside, tasting her sweetness.

He broke the kiss but he didn't let go of her. "Since we're off the clock," he whispered against her ear.

Her chest heaved against his for a moment as she clung to him. Then, apparently with great effort, she pulled away.

"Byron," she said in a warning tone. "You can't keep kissing me like that."

"Is there another way you'd like me to kiss you?"

"No—I mean—it's just—you made it pretty clear that you only wanted to marry me for the baby's sake. And we are going to have separate rooms and…" She took a deep breath. "And you cared for me once. But not anymore."

He pulled the ring out of his pocket. "Would it be bad? Between us, I mean."

"I just need to know what to expect, that's all. One minute you're mad at me and the next you're cooking for me and saying I'll have my own room and then you're kissing me and offering me a ring—is it a family ring?"

He slipped the diamond out of the case and held it in the palm of his hand. "No. I bought it this morning." Something that wasn't tainted by her family name or his. Something that was theirs and theirs alone.

"Oh, okay. I guess it doesn't matter."

That made him smile. "It matters. I don't even know what Percy's full name is—is it Harper or Beaumont?"

"Percy Harper Beaumont. You're listed on the birth certificate as his father. But I gave him my name as a middle name."

She'd given the boy Byron's name. For some reason, that made him happy. He stepped back into her and lifted her head up so he could look her in the eye. "Thank you for that."

Her eyelids fluttered. "You're doing it again," she murmured.

"Leona." He cupped her face in his hands and waited until she looked him in the eyes. "You know what I want. The question is, what do you want?" As he recalled, she was the one who'd asked for a separate bed yet had also kissed him back twice now.

"We need to get going," she replied, completely ignoring

his question. "May will worry." And with that, she turned and walked back to her car.

Byron stared after her for a moment and then shoved the ring in his pocket.

Beaumonts fought for what they wanted...to hell with what anyone else said.

Leona was about to learn how far he'd go to get what he wanted.

Eight

Leona fumbled with the keys in the lock of her apartment door. She didn't know why she was more nervous bringing Byron home with her this time, but she was. Even now, he stood too close to her, watching her. Waiting, no doubt, for an answer to his question.

If only she knew what she wanted.

"May?" She called out when she finally got the door open. "We're home."

Percy made a shrill noise. "Hi, baby," Leona said, walking into the living room and picking him up. "Did you miss me?"

May stood and said, "The doctor prescribed more drops. They're on the changing table."

"Thanks," Leona said.

There was an awkward pause as May glared at Byron without actually looking at him. "Right. I'll be back late."

"Have fun," Leona called after her as May grabbed her jacket and her purse.

That only got her a dirty look. Then May was gone.

Byron sighed. "I actually asked the Realtor if she could find us a place with a nice one-bedroom close by. I get the feeling May might not want to look at me every day."

"I'm not sure if she's going to move or not," Leona told him. If she didn't, Leona would have to keep paying rent on the apartment. Which might not be a bad plan—if it didn't work out with Byron, she could come back. "Here, hold Percy. I've got to change."

Byron sat down on the couch again and took the baby. Today, he looked slightly more confident. Or, at the very least, he looked less panicked. "How's my boy today?"

Percy made a face at him.

Leona hurried back to her room and changed into one of her prettier casual tops and a pair of jeans. She was not dressing for Byron's approval, not really. She was just being…comfortable.

Yeah, right.

When she got back to the living room, she found Byron and Percy stretched out on the floor together, both on their tummies. Byron was smiling at Percy, encouraging him. Leona wanted to stand there and watch them. This was what she'd dreamed of before Byron left her—having him all to herself, with no Beaumonts and no Harpers around to complicate things. They were going to have a family one day—they'd talked about it.

And then he'd gone and proved himself to be a Beaumont just like all the rest. He'd left her, like her father had always warned her Beaumonts did. And now he was back, issuing orders and expecting them to be followed to the letter.

She couldn't trust him. All this stuff he was doing—the ring, the apartment, talking about being a family—all of it was because he thought he wanted it. It had nothing to do with what she wanted. And the moment he changed his mind, it could all be taken away from her again.

She wanted to tie herself to a man she could count on, a man who would not treat her as if she were a ball and chain around his neck like her father treated her mother, and yet would also not treat her as if she were disposable and forgettable like all Beaumonts treated women.

She wanted stability and happiness and safety for herself, her son and her sister.

There'd been a time when she'd thought Byron was all of that and more.

She could not make that mistake a second time.

She focused on the safety and happiness of her son because right now, that was the thing that drove every other action. She would sacrifice her own heart to save his. "Having fun?"

"I was curious to see if he'd roll over," Byron replied, propping himself up on his elbow.

"He hasn't gotten that far yet." She sat down on the floor on the other side of Percy. "How are your ears, baby?"

Percy made a grunting noise as he tried to push himself up. "I know," she told the baby. "It's so hard to look around when you're on your tummy."

She rubbed his back and looked at Byron. He was staring at her as if he'd never seen her before. "What?"

"You haven't answered my questions—any of them."

"Ask me again," she told him, steeling herself to making it official.

"Will you move in with me?"

Letting Percy have this—a loving relationship with his father? Even if it meant torturing herself with her greatest love and her greatest mistake every single day for the rest of her life?

It was no contest.

"Yes."

"Will you come with me tomorrow to look at places? You can bring Percy, too, since he's going to be living there. He might have an opinion."

She couldn't help but grin. It was a thoughtful thing to say. If only everything he said and did was that thoughtful. "Yes."

He stared at her for a moment longer. There was something in his eyes, something deep and serious. "Will you marry me?"

She needed to say yes. For Percy. But… "I need to know what this marriage will actually be before I agree to it."

He raised an eyebrow. "Like what?"

"Will you see other women?"

"No." He didn't hesitate at all, which was good, she guessed. There was a pause. "You?"

"No. I have too much on my plate to even think about dating."

That got her a nice smile. "So we're agreed. No seeing other people. What else?"

Just the small matter of the facts. And the fact was that Beaumonts always cheated. Hardwick Beaumont always took the kids. Beaumonts were not to be trusted, no matter what.

"If it doesn't work out," she asked in a quiet voice as she picked up Percy and held him to her chest, "you won't take him away from me, will you?"

Byron sat up, as well. He leaned forward and kissed the top of Percy's head and said, "I am not my father, Leona."

She didn't reply. The silence seemed to stretch, pushing him away from her.

"And what about you?" His voice had turned colder. "If it doesn't work out, you won't take him and disappear? I will not stand for another lie, Leona. Because if you betray me again…" The words trailed off, but there was no give in his voice.

A cold chill ran up her spine. The threat was implicit. If she did something he didn't like, he would make her suffer for it.

"I never lied." It sounded weak to her own ears. "I told you my last name."

"Is that what you tell yourself? It wasn't a bald-faced lie, therefore you're completely innocent? How touching." He held out his arms for Percy.

She held her baby so tightly that he started to fuss. Byron sighed, the only acknowledgment of her feelings. "I want things to be different, you know. I don't want to be my parents." He came and sat beside her. Percy squirmed in her arms and she had no choice but to hand him over to Byron. "I know exactly what my father did to my mother," he went on in a quiet voice. "I would never, ever do that to you or to Percy."

She shouldn't believe him, shouldn't trust him. But he said it with such conviction that she couldn't help it. She looked down at her son, who was happily trying to suck on all his fingers at once. "I need help with him. If May doesn't move down with us, we'll have to find a day care for him and that's not cheap. The drops for his ears aren't cheap, and I didn't know how I was going to pay for Percy's surgery to get tubes, either. For the ear infections."

"I'll take care of it. All of it." He said it in an almost dismissive way, as if he'd never had to worry about money.

Well, maybe he hadn't. After all, she hadn't, either—not until she'd walked away from her father and his fortune. There'd been a very real price for her independence, but it'd been one she was willing to pay to keep Percy happy and safe.

Would she really give up that hard-fought independence and let Byron call the shots just because it was best for her son—even if it wasn't anywhere close to what was best for her?

No, she would not panic. She forced herself to breath and keep her head on her shoulders. "What about your family?"

"What about them?"

She gave him a hard look. "You saw how Frances reacted to me. If we get married, are they going to be…difficult about it?"

He grimaced. "Things have changed. It's almost like we all finally figured out that Hardwick is really and truly dead and we don't have to be what he thought we were anymore. Even Chadwick is different now. He smiles and everything."

"I wish my father realized that, too," she said wistfully. If only they could all just go on with their lives without a decades-old feud to haunt them.

Percy made the high whining noise that signaled he was getting hungry. "Oh, I should be making dinner."

She started to get up, but Byron was quicker. "Let me. What else does he eat?"

"He liked the applesauce," she called after him as he headed for the kitchen. "And yogurt and cereal. But it's still mostly baby food at this point."

Byron ducked his head around the kitchen door, a jar of what looked like green beans and mashed potatoes in his hand. "This stuff?" He made a face.

"Yes, that stuff," she replied, trying not to be defensive about it. "That's a good brand—all organic, no added anything."

After giving her a dismissive look, Byron disappeared back into the kitchen. Leona stood and checked Percy's diaper. "I have a feeling," she told the baby as she carried him back to the changing table, "that he's going to start from scratch."

She wasn't wrong about that. By the time she got Percy changed, Byron had peeled potatoes boiling and a can of green beans heating. "I don't like using the canned stuff," he told her in his chef voice. "I'll pick up some fresh or frozen ones for him."

"You don't have to…" He cut her off with a look. She sighed in resignation. "Fine. Go ahead."

In forty minutes, they sat down to mashed potatoes and green beans—Percy's being slightly more mashed together than theirs—and pan-fried chicken in a parmesan crust. "This is delicious," she said in between spooning Percy's dinner into his mouth and taking bites of her own. Percy agreed by thumping the top of his high-chair tray with both hands and opening his mouth for more.

"Good," Byron said, watching Percy swallow another mouthful. "I used to cook for the new kids, you know. When my dad would remarry and his new wife had babies. Dad expected us all to like the same things he did, but it was hard for a four-year-old to really get into steak au poivre, you know? George always had something else for us, but we had to eat it in the kitchen so neither of our parents would catch us." He looked at his plate. "That was a long time ago."

"That sounds a lot like dinners in my house growing up."

Byron looked at her. "We never really did discuss your past. You always changed the subject." He stabbed at his chicken viciously. "And I never caught on."

She couldn't tell who he was madder at—her or himself. "I knew who you were—it was hard to miss that last name. But I..." She sighed. "I wanted something different than Harpers versus Beaumonts. I wanted to see if you were really what my father claimed you were. I wanted to know if you liked me for me, not because I was heiress to a fortune."

She'd never gotten the chance to say those words out loud to him. Everything had happened so fast that night... "I just wanted to be something more than Leon Harper's daughter."

Byron set down his fork. "You were." He stood, picked up his plate and headed back to the kitchen. "You were..."

Leona leaned forward to catch the end of that sentence because it seemed important. But when she didn't hear the ending, she got up and followed Byron into the kitchen. "What?"

"Nothing," he said gruffly, scraping his plate into the trash and running hot water into the sink.

"Byron." She stood next to him and put her hand on his

shoulder in an attempt to turn him toward her. He didn't budge. *"What?"*

"You should have told me," he replied, grabbing his plate and scrubbing it furiously. "It wouldn't have mattered if you'd told me yourself. Instead I had to learn it from your father."

Guilt, which had been creeping around the edges of their conversation for the past few minutes, burst out into the open. "I wanted to. But I didn't want to risk ruining the best thing that had ever happened to me."

For a second, she thought he was going to give her that smile, the one that always melted her. But then his face hardened. "You didn't trust me."

She stared at him as a new emotion pushed back at the guilt—anger. "First off," she snapped, "I'm not the one who bailed. I was right here, dealing with the fallout of you abandoning me. I went on with my life when all I wanted to do was run and hide, too. I did not have that luxury, Byron."

Byron opened his mouth to protest, but she cut him off. "Secondly, this is exactly why I haven't said yes to your marriage proposal. At least this time it wasn't an order, but I simply do not know when you're going to switch from doting father to angry ex-lover."

Percy began to fuss, no doubt unhappy about being left behind while everyone else was in the kitchen. However, for the first time in her life, Leona didn't rush off to pick him up.

"And finally, you didn't trust me, either. Four days, Byron. That's how long it took to get away from my father—and you were gone. *Gone.* You couldn't even stick around for a damn week to wait for me." Unexpectedly, her throat closed up, but she would not crack. "So you'll forgive me if I want a little more reassurance that you're not going to up and disappear again, that you're not going to marry me only to dump me and take my son."

"You need me," he said in a quiet voice.

Percy let out a wail of impatience. Leona heard a spoon clatter to the ground.

"I need child support," she corrected him. "I need a job. You have yet to prove to me that I need *you*."

And with that, she turned and walked out of the kitchen.

Nine

It was hard to focus on bathing Percy with Leona's words ringing in Byron's ears. Wasn't offering to marry her enough reassurance that he wasn't going to disappear and take the baby? Marriage was… Okay, maybe it wasn't a permanent legal bond, but it was not something to be taken lightly. Once they were legally wed, it wasn't as though he could just walk off with the boy. Didn't she see that?

Besides, where were the reassurances *he* needed? The promises that she wouldn't lie to him again? Or that she wouldn't sic her father and his horde of lawyers upon Byron and his family? The reassurance that she wasn't just waiting until he let his guard down all the way to hit him where it would hurt the most—Percy? She'd already lied to him twice. Even if that had been a series of massive misunderstandings, it didn't change the fact that she had lied to him for months and months. How could he trust her, really?

Of course, he didn't get far in these thoughts because Percy slapped at his bathwater, splashing it into Byron's face. The baby made a trilling noise as a toy boat floated past him. There was more splashing. Byron's shirt was getting soaked and Percy was not getting any cleaner.

Just then, Percy twisted to reach the boat and Byron lost his grip. "Whoa!" he cried as Percy's head dunked under the water.

Immediately, Leona was next to him, pulling Percy upright. "I'll hold him," she said and amazingly, she didn't sound panicked. "You wash."

"I'm sorry," Byron said as Percy sputtered and coughed. He let out a disgruntled cry but stopped when Leona nudged the boat back in front of him.

"It's okay," she said softly and Byron was surprised to see she was smiling. "It'll get easier."

"If you say so," he said, scrubbing Percy's legs as fast as he could.

The argument—well, it wasn't quite an argument, but it'd certainly been more than a discussion—hung in the air between them. As they finished Percy's bath and got him ready for bed, Byron thought about what Leona had said. That she hadn't told him who her family was because she didn't want to be a Harper.

Did he believe her?

For the past year, he'd been operating under the assumption that she'd misled him on purpose, that she'd intentionally withheld the information so she could use her family name against him at the right time. And hadn't the right time been that awful night?

But maybe...maybe that's not what had happened.

He ran through his memories again—of Rory calling him out and, when Byron mouthed off, firing him. Of taking a swing at Rory because, damn it, he'd put up with enough of that man's crap over the year and a half he'd worked there and that was not how it was supposed to end.

And then Bruce—the pastry chef Byron had counted as a friend—had grabbed him from behind and physically hauled him out of the restaurant and thrown him down on the sidewalk, just in time to see Leona getting into Leon Harper's chauffeured vehicle.

Except...had she? Or had Leon shoved his daughter into the car? It'd been dark and rainy and Byron had thought...

Had it been part of the lie? Or was she now telling the truth? Was she being truthful about the lies she'd already told? Was that even a thing?

This was what she did to him. She spun his head around and around until he didn't know which way was up anymore.

While Leona nursed Percy, Byron furiously washed and dried the dishes, trying to remember exactly what Leon Harper had done in the minute before he'd gotten up into Byron's stunned face and taunted him.

That's when Leona came back into the kitchen.

"He go down okay?" Byron asked, because it seemed like the thing a parent would ask about.

"I gave him something for his ears. Hopefully he'll sleep for at least a couple of hours."

"Hopefully?" A couple of hours did not seem like enough.

Leona gave him a tired smile. "That's why we were looking at tubes."

"Yeah, I guess." He dried another dish. "How many ear infections has he had?"

"I've lost count. May gets up with him sometimes, but he usually just wants to nurse."

Byron's gaze dropped to her chest. She wasn't wearing a bra and he could see the outline of her nipples poking through the thin fabric of her shirt. Lust hit him hard and low as his mind chose exactly that moment to remember the kiss from earlier this evening and the one from last night.

"A-*hem*," she said, crossing her arms.

"Sorry," he replied, focusing all his attention back on the pots and pans.

Leona sighed. "Are you sure we should live together?"

He tensed. Damn it, this was going from bad to worse. "As opposed to what?"

"As opposed to a regular custody agreement where we each have Percy for a week or two and then trade, with child support and the like." She paused. "It might be better that way."

"Better for who? Not better for Percy—not when your father can take him. No way."

She grabbed a towel and one of the few remaining pots. "Byron, I don't want this to be hard."

"Hard?" He snorted. "I hate to burst your bubble, but nothing about this is easy."

"Fine," she snapped. "All I'm saying is that you're obviously still mad at me and I don't want Percy to grow up in a household where his parents are constantly sniping at each other. That doesn't make me the bad guy here."

"I didn't say you were the bad guy. And I'm not mad at you." He was, however, getting pretty pissed at himself. He couldn't be doing a worse job fighting for what he wanted if he tried. His father was probably rolling over in his grave.

If Hardwick Beaumont were still here, he'd slap Byron on the shoulder and say, "Stop screwing around. She's just a woman, for God's sake. You're a Beaumont. Act like one."

Except Byron didn't want to be a Beaumont if it meant bending Leona and Percy to his will just because he could. He didn't want to rule by force and fear.

She glared at him. "No, but you don't have to say the words, Byron. Your actions speak quite loudly."

"Oh, yeah? Then what does this say?" He grabbed her by the arms and hauled her to him. The kiss was not sweet or gentle—it was hard and unbending. He might not be able to get her to say yes to his proposal, but he was damned sure she wasn't going to say no.

After a moment, she bent. Her head slanted sideways and she opened her mouth for him with a sigh. He deepened the kiss. Could he kiss her like this without getting lost in the soft sweetness of her body?

Because that's what she was now, all soft and warm in his arms. His pulse beat out a faster rhythm. When she broke the kiss, he let her. "What are we going to do, Byron?"

"We'll do a trial run. I'll get us a place and you and Percy can come stay for a little while—say a week or two. You won't have to pack up all your things here. And if it doesn't work…" He paused and swallowed. He didn't want to admit it might not work. He didn't want to be wrong. But he had to give her something, a fallback to prove that he wouldn't hold her hostage once he had her and Percy with him. "If it doesn't work, then we'll go to your plan."

He could do that. He could trust her enough to bring her under his roof. And once he had her there, then he could figure out which part of her story was the truth—or if she was still lying to him.

For some reason that could only be described as self-destructive, he wanted to take her at her word.

She leaned back to look at him. "And if it does?"

Her eyes were wide—but not with fear. Instead, she looked hopeful. And hope looked good on her. He lifted his hand and stroked her cheek. "If it does, I'll ask you to marry me again."

She leaned into his touch and exhaled through slightly parted lips. He'd kissed her to end the argument and remind her that he was in control, but instead of it dampening his desire for her, it'd only ramped it up. He needed her—only her. No one, not even sensual European women, could satisfy him like this woman did.

"Two weeks?" she said softly, staring into his eyes.

He could get lost in her light brown eyes. As corny as the sentiment was, it was true. "Yeah," he said, his head dipping to meet hers. "That sounds good."

"Mmm," was all she could say because by then, Byron was kissing her and she was kissing him back and there weren't any more words, any more negotiations. There was just him and her, the way it had been. The way it should still be.

The kiss deepened when she touched his lips with her

tongue. It was a hesitant touch, as though she wasn't sure what would happen next.

Byron knew what he wanted to happen. He wanted to sweep her off her feet and carry her back to the bedroom and spend the rest of the night remembering what they'd once had. He didn't want to think about betrayal and lies. He just wanted *her*.

He swept his tongue into her mouth and felt her body respond. Old memories—good ones of the first time he'd kissed her—came rushing back. She'd been hesitant then, too. Now he knew it was because he was a Beaumont but back then he'd thought it was because she was sweet and innocent and afraid he'd push her too far. So he'd just kissed her good-night against the side of her car before she drove home alone.

Which was what he should do now. He should kiss her long and hard and then remove himself from the apartment. He should go home and take care of business himself instead of burying his body into hers over and over again. He shouldn't push his luck. Hell, he didn't have much luck left to push.

But Leona ran her fingers through his hair and leaned back, exposing her neck as she moaned, "Oh, Byron," and he was lost. He would always be lost to her.

He kissed her on the spot just under her ear and was rewarded with a shudder of pleasure. "Tell me what you want," he whispered. "Do you want me?"

She didn't answer right away, so he kissed her again. Their tongues tangled as heat built between them. Every moment he spent holding her made it that much harder to walk away and soon he would barely be able to walk at all. But he didn't care. If she brought him to his knees, so be it.

"Tell me," he demanded again. This time he took a step forward and pivoted, leaning her up against the counter. He slid his hands under her bottom and lifted her. Her body felt *so* good in his hands. "Tell me you want me." As he said it, he tilted his knee forward and pushed her legs apart.

She hadn't let go of him, hadn't pushed him away. Instead, she trailed her lips over his jaw and down his neck.

He stepped into her and tilted his hips so his straining erection rubbed against her very center. Leona gasped at the contact. She jolted upright, her eyes even wider as she stared at him.

This was it—the absolute last moment he could walk away from her tonight.

He thrust against her a second time without taking his eyes off hers. Her mouth dropped open into a perfect O and he couldn't help himself. He kissed her, unable to restrain the passion that was driving him forward over and over again.

She wrapped her legs around his waist, holding him tight. "You," she whispered in his ear. "I want you."

That was all he needed. He lifted her off the counter and carried her down the short hallway to her bedroom. Each step drove him against her, harder and harder, so that by the time he managed to kick the door shut behind them, she was moaning in his ear. "Byron—oh, Byron."

He all but threw her onto the bed. "Babe," he groaned as he covered her body with his. A nagging thought in the back of his brain told him it'd be a good idea to take this seduction and bedding slowly—that he should do it right.

But then Leona dug the tips of her fingernails into his back and the sensation drove any lingering rational thought from his mind.

He sat back on his knees and pulled her up enough that he could strip off her shirt. Then he traced the pads of his fingers over her skin and around her nipples. The little pink buds stiffened at his touch and he grinned.

Leona lay back, her hands over her head. "It's not— You're not weirded out, are you?"

"Nope. Your breasts are amazing. Your body is *amazing*." He flicked his fingers over the hard tips.

"It's not the same," she said and he heard the concern in her tone. "Everything changed. I'm not the same girl you remember."

"I know." He snagged the waistband of her pants. "You're better. You're a woman now." With that, he pulled.

Her pants peeled right off her legs and then she was in nothing but a pair of white cotton panties. Keeping one hand on her breast, he moved down. He pushed her legs apart and lowered himself onto her. He pulled the panties aside and kissed her on her sex. "Not so different," he murmured. He inhaled her scent deeply and everything he'd tried to forget for a year came crashing back on him. "Oh, babe," he said before he licked her.

Leona's body shook at his touch as she moaned. Her legs tried to close around him but he used his free hand to hold her open as he worked on her body. "Yeah, that's it," he whispered against her skin as her back arched. "You're so beautiful."

"Need…more," she ground out through clenched teeth.

"All you had to do was ask." He released his hold on her breast and trailed his hand over her stomach until he got both hands into the elastic waistband of her panties. He pulled them down and Leona kicked free.

She was completely open to him now. She held her hands over her stomach but he pried them away. There, permanently etched into her skin, were pale pink lines that hadn't been there before.

"Byron," she said in a trembling voice, as if she were waiting for pain to hit.

"Beautiful," he murmured as he kissed the stretch marks. She'd brought his son into this world with her body and he wanted to show her just how much he appreciated that.

So, even though he was about to bust out of his jeans, he

took the time to kiss all of her stretch marks before moving lower a second time. He pressed his mouth against her again. This time, he didn't do tender or gentle. This time, he was hell-bent on bringing her right up to the edge and then pushing her over. He looped his arms around her legs and pulled her up so he had a better angle.

She tangled her fingers into his hair, pulling it loose from the low ponytail. "Oh, Byron," she gasped quietly.

"You still need more?"

"Please," she got out in a high voice filled with need. "*Please*, Byron."

He couldn't help but grin. "*This* is how much I missed you," he murmured as he slipped a finger inside of her. She moaned in pleasure as he stroked her and licked her and kissed her.

"Yes," she whispered. She let go of his hair and pulled his face up so she could look him in the eye. "More. Need *more*."

"This?" he asked, slipping a second finger into her. "Is this what you want?"

Her mouth dropped open again, but she shook her head no.

"Tell me what you want, Leona. I need to hear the words." He didn't know why, but he did. No misunderstandings this time—just the truth between them. The truth he'd never been able to deny.

"I want you—all of you," she whispered. "Make love to me, Byron. *Please*."

He hopped off the bed to shuck his jeans. He had a condom in his wallet. He dug around until he found it, which took a few minutes because Leona had leaned forward and pressed her lips to his tip. He groaned in the small space between the pleasure of her mouth on his erection and the pain of needing to hold back his climax. "Babe, please."

As she lifted her eyes to look at him, her other hand

cupped him. Too much—she was too much. "Babe," he said in warning. He didn't want to lose it before he'd shown her how good it could still be between them and he didn't know how much time they had before the baby awoke or her sister came back. "Let me do this for you."

With his last bit of self-control, he pushed her away—at least, far enough away that he could roll the condom on. Then he climbed back onto the bed, back between her legs, and lowered himself to her. "You still like it like this?" he asked as he tucked her knees under his arms and pinned her to the bed.

"I think so. I'll let you know." Then she licked his lips and he couldn't hold back any longer.

He fit himself against her and plunged into her body. She was so wet and ready for him, as though she'd been waiting for just this moment, too. He buried himself in her and kissed her and thought, *I've finally come home.*

"Yes," she hissed as he drove into her again and again. "Still like that. Harder."

"Yes, ma'am," was all he could say. He had to focus on holding off his climax until she'd come. He had to show her how good he could be for her—to her.

So he thrust in harder and harder until the bed was squeaking and she was moaning and all he could see and feel and hear and taste was Leona. His Leona.

"Oh—oh!" she gasped as he gave her everything he had. Her body clenched down on his and her head came off the pillow and as the climax took her, he kissed her and kept thrusting while she rode it out.

Then she fell back onto the bed and his climax began to roar through his blood. Then—unexpectedly—something changed. The sensation surrounding his erection shifted. Deepened.

He tried to pull out but it was too late. He'd come—and the condom had broken.

Oh, hell.

"What?" Leona panted when Byron pulled away from her.

"I lost the condom," he said in a state of shock.

"Oh." Leona hopped out of bed and basically ran for the bathroom.

Byron sat down heavily on the edge of the bed and threw the remains of the useless condom into the trash. For the love of everything holy—he'd barely gotten used to the idea of being a father to one. Was he already on his way to being a father of two?

Stupid. He shouldn't have used an old condom, shouldn't have kept it in his wallet. He shouldn't have taken Leona to bed, not yet.

But this was how it always seemed to happen with her—he couldn't help himself. He'd wanted to show her how good they could be together and instead?

He'd set them both up for another pregnancy scare. What a freaking mess.

Maybe she was right. Maybe they shouldn't live together, shouldn't get married. Because this was how it was going to be. They'd always be walking the thin line between love and disaster.

The only difference was that, at least this time, he knew when they'd crossed that line.

Leona walked back into the bedroom, head down, arms crossed over her bare breasts. "Come here," he told her, pulling her onto his lap.

She sucked in a shuddering breath. "Might not be anything, after all."

"Might not," he agreed, trying to sound optimistic.

"This doesn't change the plans," she added. "Two-week trial."

"Are you sure?" He kissed her cheek. "Because, right up until the end there, I was... Well, I don't know if I'm going to be able to keep my hands off you." That got him a small smile. "I don't know if I'll *ever* be able to keep my hands off you, Leona," he said in all seriousness as he stroked her hair. "Not even for two weeks."

"I wish…"

"Yes?"

She leaned into him and sighed. "I wish I knew if that was a good thing or bad thing."

"Parts of it were very good. Great, even."

She giggled, but just then a small cry came from the other side of the wall. "Oh—the baby!" Leona said, shooting up and gathering her clothes. She was dressed in seconds and rushing out of the room.

Byron grabbed his shorts and his pants and pulled them on. He didn't know if he was staying here tonight or not. Not, he decided. He didn't have another condom and he couldn't risk the temptation of Leona again, not when there was still a chance that the condom failure might be nothing, after all.

He finished dressing and then peeked his head into Percy's room. The only light spilled into the room from the hallway. Leona sat in the dark, holding Percy to her breast. This time, he noted the things he'd need to get for his new place—the crib, the dresser, the glider.

But he also watched Leona and Percy. One of Percy's hands lazily waved around in the air, as if he wanted to grab on to something but was too sleepy to know what. Leona smiled down at him, her eyes full of love as she offered her finger for him to grip.

Byron had missed so much. The whole of her pregnancy, the delivery, Percy's first smile—all of it was gone into the past. But starting right now, he could make up for that. He could be here for the first time Percy rolled over, the first time he stood and took a step.

He wanted to be a better father than the one he'd had. That's all there was to it.

Behind him, the front door opened. May walked back into the apartment, already glaring at him. "You're still here?" She looked him up and down and sniffed in distaste.

Byron shrugged his shoulders at Leona and then walked over to where May was standing. He kept his voice low so he wouldn't wake Percy. "We're going to look at some real estate tomorrow. You're welcome to join us."

"I'm not going to uproot my life for you," she spat at him. "Not after what you did to Leona."

He kept his calm. Mostly because he didn't want to upset the baby. "I could find you a place of your own nearby if you wanted to stay close to Percy."

At this, May softened a little bit. "Why would you do that?"

"Because he loves you and your sister loves you," Byron replied. "And I want them to be happy."

Whatever small foothold he'd gained with May disappeared. "Then just stay away from them. From all of us," she hissed.

"I wish I could," he muttered as May sidestepped him and headed for her room. "I wish I could."

But he knew he couldn't.

Ten

They met outside the brewery. Leona was exhausted. Between the three times Percy had gotten her up in the middle of the night and the wild dreams she'd had about Byron, she'd gotten very little rest.

But here she was anyway, picking Byron up at the restaurant site instead of the Beaumont Mansion so his family wouldn't see him leaving in her car.

"How are you?" he asked as he climbed into the passenger seat. But before she could answer, he'd pulled her into a light kiss.

In the back, Percy shook his rattle.

"Sorry," Byron said, clearly not sorry at all.

And that, in a nutshell, was her problem. If she were to find herself pregnant again, she'd *have* to marry him.

An insidious voice in her head that sounded a lot like her father whispered, *Maybe that was his plan the entire time. Get you pregnant again to force your hand.*

She shook that thought out of her head. "Tired. He woke up a couple more times last night."

Byron frowned. "How long do those drops take to work?"

"A couple of days. Where are we going?"

Byron gave her the address and they headed out. "Do I take it May's still not interested in relocating to stay closer to you two?"

"No, not particularly." Which was the diplomatic way of saying it. At breakfast, May had been quite upset that

Leona was spending the day with Byron—and was taking Percy with her.

They drove in silence. The weight of what had happened between them last night hung heavy in the air. She could always buy the plan B pill, just to make sure she didn't get pregnant—but she didn't want to do that without discussing it with Byron, and she had absolutely no idea how to begin that conversation.

So, instead, she would look at real estate with a man she still wasn't convinced she should live with. Because last night he'd told her in all seriousness that he wouldn't be able to keep his hands to himself.

She liked to think she was no fool. Oh, sure, she had made some foolish choices. But this?

Living together meant sleeping together, no matter what either of them said about separate rooms. If she agreed to this trial, they'd be together in every sense of the word.

Part of her thought that was a grand idea. It's what she'd wanted, after all, back before she got pregnant the first time and Byron abandoned her and it all blew up in her face. The other part of her couldn't get past the part where Byron had abandoned her.

Even though Byron had laid her out last night and made her orgasm like no time had passed between them, she wasn't sure what she wanted to happen next. She wanted Byron but…she had to put her son first.

Of course, Percy should know his father. That was non-negotiable.

God, her head was such a mess. Maybe if she'd gotten more than four hours of nonconsecutive sleep she'd be able to think.

They arrived at the Realtor's office, and she came out to greet them. "Hi! I'm Sherry!" the woman said in a way-too-bright voice. Leona winced. It was still far too early for this level of enthusiasm. "I don't want you to have to unstrap that little cutie so we'll just head out, okay?"

"That's fine," Byron said. "We'll follow you?"

"Sure!" Sherry said with a blindingly white smile.

Leona turned to Byron. "What did you tell her?"

"Nothing." He gave her a sly grin. "Just that I was a Beaumont and I expected a high level of service. That's all."

"Oh, Lord," Leona muttered, following Sherry's car out of the parking lot. "Let the upselling begin."

Byron chuckled.

They drove into Littleton, which was not a town that Leona had spent a lot of time in. Her family lived in Cherry Hills in an old mansion behind a gated fence.

Although Littleton looked like a nicer place than the section of Aurora where she and May lived, it didn't come close to Cherry Hills. At least, not until the Realtor made a couple of turns and May found herself driving past a country club. "Byron?" she asked. "I thought you were just going to get us an apartment or something."

"Or something," he agreed as the Realtor pulled into the driveway of a truly stunning house. From the outside, it looked as if it was maybe half the size of her family's mansion—and easily five times the size of her current apartment, if not more.

Leona opened her car door and gaped. The house was built to look like a log cabin, but this was no primitive home. The red tile roof gleamed in the morning sunlight and the foundation plantings were lush—obviously well watered despite the lingering drought conditions.

"Here we are!" said Sherry with an even bigger smile.

"How much?" Leona demanded.

Sherry blinked and said, "It's $1.3 million, but it's been on the market for a few months so I think there's negotiating room."

"No."

Sherry's megawatt smile faltered. "I'm sorry?"

"No," Leona said, ignoring the Realtor and turning back to Byron, who had the nerve to look innocent. "This was supposed to be a temporary thing, a three-bedroom apartment—not a—" She turned back to Sherry. "How many square feet?"

"Nine thousand, if you account for the maid's room over the garage."

Nine thousand square feet of luxury. Not a cozy little apartment. This place had a maid's room, for God's sake. This felt wrong. Everything about it was off. She'd spent the past year scrimping and scraping. She didn't want this situation to even suggest that she could be bought—that her affection was for sale. That's what her father would do if he admitted he'd screwed up. He'd throw an insanely expensive gift at her and expect that to make everything okay.

Well, this was not okay. Her affection could not be bought and that was final. Yes, she wanted stability for Percy but this was so far beyond stable that it wasn't funny. "*No*, Byron. This isn't what we agreed on."

She started to get back in the car, but Percy began to fuss and before she could do anything, Byron had the back door open and was unbuckling the baby. "You want out? This place has a swing set in the back," he told the boy. "And a big lawn where you can run around and we could even get a puppy! Would you like a puppy, Percy?"

Percy squealed in delight, although Leona was sure he didn't really grasp what *puppy* meant. She glared at Byron. What the hell was he trying to do here—bribe a six-month-old?

"Come on, little man," Byron said. He shut the back door and walked to the front of the car. "Let's wait for Mommy."

Leona had several choice things she wanted to say, but Percy squealed and clapped his hands and he looked... happy. She was stuck in a very real way. She couldn't drive off without her son—but she didn't like this bait and switch. It felt as though Byron was steamrollering her and she didn't like it. If she wanted to be steamrollered, she'd go home and her father would be happy to run roughshod all over her.

"We're only looking," Byron said. He turned to Sherry, who was not wearing any kind of smile at all. "We have other places to look at that are at other price points, correct?"

"Yes!" Sherry replied enthusiastically.

Byron leaned down and kissed the top of Percy's head while he kept his eyes fastened on hers.

"Fine. But I don't have to like it," Leona snapped as she got out of the car.

"Duly noted. I want to see the kitchen."

Sherry unlocked the house and led them inside. The place had a grand feeling to it, but it wasn't the same sort of cold, sterile feeling Leona's parents' mansion had given her—or, for that matter, that the Beaumont Mansion had given her, kitchen notwithstanding. Instead of severe colors and harsh lighting designed to make everything look as expensive as possible, this entryway was filled with the warmth of the early-morning sun.

"Oh," she couldn't help but whisper.

"Beautiful," Byron agreed. "Which way's the kitchen?"

Sherry went on and on about the specifications of the house—the number of bedrooms and bathrooms and the view and so on. All Leona could do was trail along behind them, trying to take in the magnitude of the place.

She hadn't allowed herself to be disappointed with her apartment because she'd been desperate and only had so much money. It was the best she could do on short notice and, for that, she was grateful for it.

But for the first time in a year, she allowed herself to think about living in a place that was above good-enough.

Byron spent twenty minutes in the kitchen, examining the appliances and discussing a "work triangle" with the Realtor, who was back to full-on perkiness. While they talked, Leona held Percy and they walked through the living room again. Wide French doors opened onto a tree-lined yard. And, as Byron had promised, there was a swing set—although this was closer to the equipment one would find in a park.

They toured the four bedrooms, including a master suite that had a huge whirlpool tub, and then they looked at the office. "This would be yours," Byron said in a low voice as he opened the door for her.

Leona couldn't help but gasp. The room was mostly windows and looked out onto the green expanse of the golf course. Behind that, the mountains broke rank and raced up to the sky. The morning light gleamed deep purple off the mountains' sides. There wasn't a parking lot or Dumpster in sight.

"It's beautiful," she whispered.

"I thought that, if you ever quit working for that Fish guy—"

"Lutefisk," she corrected, staring at the built-in bookcases and filing cabinets that made up the interior wall.

"Yeah, him. If you wanted to quit working for him, you'd need an office space for your business."

She'd always talked about opening her own design firm—how she'd design his restaurant and then build her clientele from there. She turned to face him. "You remembered."

"I never forgot. Not you," he replied, holding his gaze with hers. "I want to make it up to you."

She wanted to believe that—to believe him. But Percy squirmed in her arms and she thought of all the long months without Byron, of being completely on her own.

"By buying me an extravagant house?" She forced herself to walk back out into the hall, away from the beautiful office and the stunning views.

"I've got to live somewhere—somewhere that doesn't involve my extended family," he replied, following her out. "And you requested your own space, did you not?"

Sherry gave them a sideways glance. "Let's go check out that playground!" she said, leaning forward to speak directly to Percy.

"I requested separate bedrooms. Not a freaking nine-thousand-square-foot mansion, Byron. It feels like you're trying to buy my loyalty. Or at least my complicity. And I don't like it."

He stared at her. "What on God's green earth are you talking about?"

"It just feels like this is something my father would do. Throw a lot of money at a problem—"

"You are not a problem," he interrupted. "Percy is not a problem."

"No? Maybe not right now, but how long before you remember you're still mad at me? Or when Percy has a rough day, a rough night and won't stop screaming? Then it'll be a problem, all right. *Mine.* When the going gets tough, you'll get going."

Sherry poked her head back around the corner. "Everything all right?" she asked.

Byron fixed Leona with a hard glare. She fought the urge to step back, to agree with him—to go along to get along. Those days had passed. She had to stand firm—this was her life, too. So what if the house was beautiful? So what if it had everything she could ever want in a home?

It would still be bought and paid for by Byron. He'd control the money, the house—and her. She was only useful as long as Percy needed her. Oh, Byron could dress it up with a pretty office or whatever, but still—she'd be dependent on him. And after she'd left home, she'd vowed to never be dependent on another man for as long as she lived.

After all, if it was his house on his terms, what would happen to her if it didn't work out? Would he show her the door? He might not disappear into the night again—but there were other ways to be abandoned. Wasn't that what his father had always done? Hardwick had never gone anywhere, but as soon as he'd tired of his wife, out she went without a penny to her name. If that wasn't abandonment, she didn't know what was.

She couldn't handle the rejection, not a second time. So she stood firm. She didn't back down and she didn't apologize for having an opinion. She was in control of her destiny, damn it all. If only destiny would stop throwing her curveballs.

Byron turned to the Realtor, who waited with an expression that made Leona think of a golden retriever.

"We'll take it," he said decisively.

Another freaking curveball.

Destiny had a funny sense of humor.

Eleven

The next thing Byron knew, Leona was stomping away from him. Why was she being so damn stubborn?

He had the entire buyout from the sale of the Beaumont Brewery sitting in a bank account, completely untouched. Seventeen million dollars— plus compounded interest— was waiting for him and if he wanted to buy himself a nice house, then damn it, he *would*.

He thought Leona was just going to cool off in a different room—but then he heard the front door slam.

"Leona!" he yelled, running after her. He got the front door open as she was belting Percy into his seat. "Leona, wait!"

She shot him an incredibly dirty look, but she did not wait. She got into the car and fired it up.

Before Byron could give chase, his phone rang with the tone he'd selected for Matthew. What the hell… He had to talk to Matthew. If anyone could fix this mess that Byron kept making worse, it was his older brother. So, with a groan of frustration, he let Leona go.

"Yeah," he said.

"For the love of God, tell me you're *not* backing out of the restaurant." Byron could almost see Matthew pinching the bridge of his nose in frustration.

The Realtor poked her head out. "Is everything okay?" she asked, as if the answer wasn't obvious. "Did your wife change her mind about the house?"

"Hang on," Byron said. Then, to Sherry, he said, "No,

we'll still take the house. But I have an important—and private—call to take, if you don't mind."

The Realtor's eyes lit up with commissioned dollar signs. "Oh, of course! I'll be inside."

Byron waited until the door shut. "No, I'm not backing out of the restaurant. And hello to you, too. Where the hell have you been? I called you three days ago!"

"You didn't say it was an emergency and Chadwick didn't call in a panic, so I figured it could keep. I unplugged for a couple of days."

"Since when do you unplug in the middle of the damned week? I thought you were always working."

"Not always. Not anymore." Something in his voice changed. "I took a trip with Whitney. We got married."

Byron was almost too stunned to speak. "Seriously?"

"Yes," was the terse reply.

"Well, congratulations, man. I would have come out for it."

"I know. But we wanted to keep it quiet."

Byron snorted. Usually, Matthew was all about maintaining the family image—public relations was his thing. But he'd gone and fallen in love with former wild-child star Whitney Wildz who, in real life, was a very private woman named Whitney Maddox. Matthew would do anything to protect her from the paparazzi. Including, apparently, getting married in complete secrecy.

"Did you at least tell Mom? You know she'll be heartbroken if you got married without telling her."

There was a short pause before Matthew said, "I flew her out for it. She was our witness."

"Good." And it was. Their mother had had enough heartbreak in her life. Byron didn't want to add to it. Still, the fact that Matthew had seen fit to invite their mother but not Byron or Frances stung, if only a little.

"So, yes," Matthew went on, "I am capable of unplugging for a little honeymoon with my wife. She's working with a horse, and I've got an hour to deal with the priority issues. If you're not bailing on the restaurant, what's up?"

Okay, so even if Matthew had gotten married without telling Byron, at least he was still a priority. "I have a problem."

"I'm listening."

Was there any good way to say this? Probably not. "You remember how I wanted you to invite Leon Harper to Phillip's wedding reception?"

"And his family, if I recall correctly. A request that struck me as so odd that I looked into Harper a little more. Apparently he has two daughters." Matthew sounded as if this were no big deal.

"And you remember how I went to Europe for a year?"

"Paris and then Madrid, yes. Are you telling me these two facts are connected?"

Byron kicked at a pebble in the driveway. He just had to get this out. It was his mess, but he needed help cleaning it up. "Three days ago, I discovered that Leona Harper—Harper's oldest daughter—gave birth to my son about six months ago. His name is Percy."

There was a stunned silence on the other end of the line—a silence that lasted more than a few moments.

Byron couldn't take it. He plunged ahead. "I've asked her to move in with me and—"

"Into the mansion?" Matthew spluttered. "Are you *insane*? A Harper living in the Beaumont Mansion?"

"As I was going to say before I was interrupted," Byron said, trying not to snap at his brother, "I'm buying a house for us. And I've asked her to marry me. For our son's sake."

Again, there was another painful silence. "Jesus, Byron," Matthew finally muttered. "I'd have thought, after our father left bastards scattered to the four winds, that you would have been a little more careful than that."

The condom failure from last night popped into his mind. "I was careful. But sometimes things don't work like they're supposed to. I need a prenup. We have to get married as soon as possible to make sure her father can't declare her incompetent and take my son away."

"No," Matthew replied flatly. "You absolutely *cannot* marry her. She's Harper's daughter for God's sake! Frances didn't tell me the details, but she made it pretty clear that someone had broken your heart and that's why you left."

"I am well aware of what happened. But I am not leaving any bastards to be scattered to the winds. He's my son and I'll do whatever it takes to keep it that way. Even marry a Harper."

"Are you into pain or something? You enjoy being Harper's punching bag? Because if you tie your horse to his wagon, that's all you're ever going to be," he groaned in exasperation again. "I don't think there's a prenup in this world strong enough to stand up to Harper's sharks. He could use you to take down the entire family. He already took our business from us, Byron."

"I know that," Byron snapped.

"Oh, for God's sake. Just take the boy. Legally, I mean. She didn't tell you about the baby, I take it?"

"No, but I'm not going to—"

"So we'll sue for full custody on the grounds that she's unfit to be a mother. And for the love of everything holy, do *not* sleep with her again."

Byron winced. He couldn't bring himself to deny it, but he couldn't confirm it, either.

"You already have, haven't you?"

"Yes."

Matthew let out a long, low growl of pure frustration. "Did you at least use protection?"

"We did. It failed. Again."

There was a noise in the background that could have

been Matthew kicking or throwing something. "You have *got* to be freaking kidding me. Come on, Byron! Stop thinking with your dick for once!"

"I am not thinking with my dick, damn it. I am trying to make things right. I thought you'd appreciate that—isn't that what you do? I got her pregnant. I wasn't there when the baby was born. I missed the first six months of my son's life. I'm trying to make up for lost time. I don't care what you think about her—Leona and Percy are already my family. I want to make it official. And if you won't help me, then I'll do it myself."

Another long silence. Byron would bet money that Matthew was now rubbing his temples and grimacing comically.

"Does Harper know you're back?"

"I don't think so. Leona took her sister and basically ran away from home after I left. They don't have any contact with their parents. But she was worried her father would try to take the boy."

"He wouldn't win," Matthew said decisively. "You're the boy's father." Then, a moment later, he added, "There's no doubt about that?"

"None. The boy looks like me. Red hair and everything."

Matthew sighed heavily. "There'd need to be blood tests to confirm, but you must realize Harper wouldn't win. You're the child's father. You don't have to marry her to protect the baby."

"But he'd try," Byron insisted. "Harper would sue anyway and that would be almost as bad. He'd drag Leona through court and smear her name in every patch of mud he could find. Not to mention how much it'd cost to defend against him." When Matthew didn't immediately respond, Byron added, "You know what Dad did to Mom."

"Yeah, I know."

"I'm not saying the situation is ideal," Byron went on. "But I can't let that happen."

"And—despite all the facts of the matter—you trust her not to turn you over to her father? Not to use this kid to bankrupt the entire Beaumont family?"

Byron hesitated. Deep down, he believed that she wouldn't turn back to her father again. But...did he really trust her not to rip his still-beating heart out of his chest and hold it up for him to see? Especially after the way she'd driven off and stranded him here with the Realtor, all because he wanted to buy a nice house?

"That's not a good silence over there," Matthew observed.

Byron started pacing. "We're still working through a few issues." There. That was something that Matthew would understand.

"A 'few issues,' huh? And you want to marry a 'few issues'? Man, you are nuts."

"It runs in the family," he shot back. "You're the one who wanted me to get arrested to distract the press so you could canoodle in private with an actress."

"That's not exactly what happened, but that's neither here nor there," Matthew replied calmly. "So what do you want me to do?"

"I want a prenup that protects the rest of the family from Leona's father and guarantees that she and I will always have joint custody of Percy."

"You always did act impulsively," Matthew said in an offhand way. "Running off to Europe, now getting married. What's the kid's full name?"

"Percy Harper Beaumont."

Matthew sighed heavily. "And her middle name? I assume she's still Leona Harper at this point."

Byron had to think about that. "Margaret. And before you ask, mine is still John."

"I hadn't forgotten. Okay, fine. I'll talk to the lawyers and get them working on something. But for the love of God, don't marry her until the prenup has been signed, sealed and delivered, okay? If I were you, I'd think long and hard about marrying her at all. Even if you think this is a short-term solution and even if you have a prenup, the divorce would be a huge mess." Byron swore he heard Matthew shudder. "The press would eat this for breakfast, lunch and dinner. We need to keep the whole thing as quiet as possible."

Byron looked back at the house, where no doubt the Realtor was on her phone. "Understood. But I'm buying the house anyway."

"Fine. Dare I ask how the restaurant is coming along?"

"Uh…"

"Byron," Matthew said in warning.

"No, it's coming along fine. I hired Leona to do the interior design."

There it was again, that noise that sounded like Matthew was breaking something. "Are you *kidding* me?"

"That's what she does," Byron quickly defended. "That's what she went to school for. She's got a lot of really good ideas—we're going to call it Caballo de Tiro, which is Spanish for draft horse. I've been testing out menu options and we've started lining up contractors. It's going to be great. Really."

"Caballo de Tiro?"

"It plays off the Percheron Drafts name but pulls in the European influences," Byron explained.

"Yes, I get it. So let me see if I have this straight—you hid in Europe for a year to get away from a woman, only to come back and hire her, move in with her, and marry her—all at once?"

"Don't forget the baby."

"Oh, no—who could forget the baby?" Matthew scoffed.

"Got any other surprise children hidden anywhere? Didn't leave anyone knocked up in Spain, did you?"

"No."

"You're sure?"

"Didn't sleep with anyone, if you must know. So yes, I'm sure. No more surprises."

"Fine," Matthew huffed, making it plenty clear that it was anything but. "I'll deal with the lawyers. Stay out of the headlines, Byron."

"Thanks," Byron said, but Matthew had already hung up on him.

He stared at his phone. Well. That had probably gone as smoothly as possible.

Now he just had to convince Leona that this house and a wedding were all for the best. No matter what Matthew said, Byron knew that marrying her was not only the right thing to do, but the best for all parties involved. And he had to do it all without letting her break his heart again.

No problem, right?

Yeah, right.

If there was one valuable lesson that Byron had learned growing up as a Beaumont, it was that money talked. Loudly.

He told Sherry that he'd pay full price—and full commission—if everything was settled within two weeks and she kept quiet about both his new address and the people with whom he'd be living. Within a week, he was the proud owner of a fabulous family home. Now he just needed the one thing that money couldn't apparently buy—a family.

His life was a strange dichotomy right now, and he wasn't having much luck merging the two halves back into a recognizable whole.

During the daylight hours, he worked side by side with Leona. They met with contractors, finalized design plans and ate, of course. Byron kept tweaking the dishes or trying something that might work better—something that Leona might like better. They had long discussions about rotating menu items, which local sources to use for beef and herbs and exterior landscaping. She had no problem talking to him during the day.

But at night? At night she kept the distance between them. Even when he came over to the apartment to play with Percy, she made sure she was far more than an arm's length away.

"I can move into the house next week," he told her a week later. He was lying on the floor of her living room, rolling a ball to Percy and making happy noises when the baby got anywhere near it. He could hear music coming from May's room, where she'd basically locked herself every time Byron came over. "I've got some basic furniture, but I wanted you to pick out what you liked."

From where she sat at the kitchen table, staring at her computer she glared at him. "I am not moving into that ridiculous house."

"And you have yet to give me a good reason why not," he shot back at her. "I don't see what the big deal is. You already agreed to move in so that we could raise our son together. I provided an adequate living space."

She snorted and continued to scroll.

"And I'm basically giving you a blank check to decorate it any way you want. Explain to me again how this makes me the villain here." When she said nothing, he sighed.

She shut her computer with a bit more force than was necessary. "You want to know what the problem is? Aside from the fact that I already told you once and you didn't pay any attention?"

"I am not trying to buy your complicity," he replied, trying mightily to keep his voice calm. "I'm not trying to buy your loyalty. I'm trying to provide for my family. I thought that's what you wanted."

She dropped her head into her hands. "Byron..."

Percy squealed as the ball went rolling wide to the right. "Whoa, buddy—now what are we going to do?" Byron asked him.

Percy flopped over and tried to crawl toward the ball, but when it turned out to be only unproductive wiggling, he howled in frustration.

"You can do it!" Byron said encouragingly to the baby. Then he looked back at Leona. Her head was still in her hands. Was she crying? "Leona?"

He got up off the floor and gently kicked the ball closer to Percy. Then he went to her. She *was* crying. Damn.

"I just want to know that you're going to be here," she whispered, her voice muffled by her hands. "And I don't."

Oh, come on. He fought this sense of frustration. "Leona. We have a child together. I'm buying a house for us—not even a rental. And in case you've forgotten it, we're working on this restaurant that will keep me in the greater Denver area. Are these the actions of a man who's going to bail?"

"No," she sniffed. "But that's not what I asked for, none of it is."

"I asked you to marry me. What other reassurances do you want? Do I have to open a vein and sign my name in blood?"

As if on cue, May's music got louder. Leona's shoulders tightened in response. But she hadn't answered yet.

He found a knot in her muscles and began to rub it. "I don't mean to add to the stress. You know that, don't you?"

"I do." Her voice, however, wasn't terribly convincing. But then she tilted her head to the side, stretching her shoulders for him. He found another knot and began to rub that one. "Oh, that's good."

It'd be better if Byron could lay Leona out on a bed.

Then he could give her a proper massage, one that would work out all the knots. Maybe that was what she needed— to know that he would take care of her in every respect, not just the material ones.

Her body started to relax under his touch and, as he focused on the base of her neck, she let out a low moan of relief. That moan took all of his noble intentions and did something less than noble to them. A full body massage was just what she needed, complete with candles and massage oil. Yeah, it'd be better if he could take his time and get her body nice and relaxed and then…

No, stop it. The last time he'd thought with his dick, he'd wound up using a compromised condom. Plus he'd sort of promised Matthew he would keep his damned zipper zipped until the prenup was signed.

Besides, there was that little issue of her making him guess what the hell was holding her up. What did she mean, she wanted to know he'd be there? How was he not showing her that? He didn't get it.

Percy fussed and she got up to get him. One thing was clear. Byron was going to have to figure it out—and fast.

Twelve

Leona tried to focus on choosing a font for the restaurant's name while Byron got Percy changed and read him a story, but it didn't work. Byron had figured out the bedtime routine in only a few short days, really. He could probably handle Percy on his own now, except for the nursing part. Which was great. Really, it was.

But whenever she thought that, it made her sad, too—and she wasn't sure why. All she knew was that the words on her computer screen kept blurring together.

Byron was involved. Byron was helping out. Byron was making all sorts of wonderful-sounding promises.

But did he really need her? Would he keep his word or would he disappear again? Could she trust him—or any Beaumont—not to take her son and leave her behind?

She kept thinking back to the way Frances had reacted to finding Leona in the kitchen. Was it a huge stretch of the imagination to think that, when Byron wasn't with Leona, his family was trying to convince him not to marry her—to just take the baby instead?

She didn't think so. And that made it hard to take Byron at his word. Once, he'd believed her father and his poisonous lies instead of trusting that Leona would come to him.

He could be perfect right now and she'd still be afraid that he'd kick her out of his life a second time.

Her head was such a wash of emotions that she couldn't form a single, rational thought. The house was huge and lovely, it was true. By any objective measure, it was perfect. So what bothered her about it?

She'd once dreamed of Byron asking her to marry him, of settling down with him and raising a family. A year after she'd given up on that dream, it was suddenly happening. She wouldn't have to worry about money or doctor's bills or making rent. Moving in with Byron would solve so many problems. She should be happy.

And yet, what price would she pay for stability? Or even just the illusion of stability?

She would have to give up her independence to a man who didn't want her—who only wanted a mother for his son.

It was a damned high price to pay.

She wiped her eyes again when she heard Byron finishing his story. This part of the nightly ritual—and the morning companion—was something that had always been hers and hers alone, and right now she needed the reassurance of the routine.

She walked into Percy's room and stood there, watching. Byron hummed something low as he rocked Percy back and forth. The whole thing—the baby boy with bright red hair in his father's arms, a look of peace on both of their faces—it was almost too much for her. Her eyes began to water again.

"Ready?" Byron asked in a quiet voice.

"Yes." She had to be, after all. This was for her son.

Byron stood and Leona took the glider. He carefully lowered Percy into her arms. "Good night, little man," he whispered. "I'll see you tomorrow." Then he looked at Leona. "I'll wait for you, if that's okay with you."

She nodded. He had never left while she was nursing Percy—usually he did something in the kitchen, even if it was just the dishes.

She lifted her shirt and Percy latched on. For the next

few minutes, she didn't have to think about moving and marriages and work and Byron. This was her time with her son. He still needed her. She hoped Byron realized that, too.

She might have dozed off while Percy was nursing because the next time she looked down, he'd fallen asleep with a trickle of milk running down the side of his face. She wiped him up and carried him over to his crib.

Surprisingly, Byron was not in the kitchen. And he wasn't in the living room. He wasn't in the bedroom, either, and she highly doubted he'd gotten anywhere near May's room.

Then she realized that the door to the patio was open. He was outside? She grabbed a cardigan to fight off the evening chill and headed out.

Byron was in one of the two sad little deck chairs that May had found at a thrift store, staring out at the night sky. The apartment faced the east, so they could actually see some of the stars over the Great Plains. "What are you doing out here? I'd have thought you'd be elbow deep in a soufflé or something."

He grinned and held out a hand. "Just thinking."

"About?"

"About how it could have been different. Between us."

She should sit down in the other chair. She shouldn't take his hand, not when she was mentally and physically exhausted. She should try to keep some kind of distance between them, some layer of protection from his considerable charms.

But she took his hand and he pulled her down so she was sitting across his lap. "Different how?"

Byron swept her short hair away from his face and rested his chin on her shoulder. She curled into him, into his warmth. "When I first asked you out—almost two years ago—you knew who I was, right?"

She nodded. She didn't want to revisit what had gone

wrong before. Not tonight. But the sky was beautiful and Byron was warm and one of his hands was tucked around her thigh and the other was rubbing against her back and the moment was…peaceful.

"But you went out with me anyway."

"After you asked me three times." Their voices were quiet, their heads close together. It felt intimate to sit like this.

"And…" He took a deep breath. "And if I'd asked you to marry me before *that* night, would you have said yes?"

The corners of her mouth pulled down. "Saying yes would have meant having to face who I really was."

"And it would have been a problem, it's true. Not a deal-breaker, though. But that's not what I'm asking. I'm asking if you would have said yes."

She stared at the stars. A plane from the airport cut across the sky, rising higher and higher. *Not a deal-breaker.* Was he being honest? Or would he have accused her of trying to trap him, when she told him she was *that* Harper and pregnant with his child?

"If you'd known who my father was from the beginning, would you have asked me out three times?"

He shifted, cupping her chin in his hand and lifting her head until he looked her in the eye. "I don't think I could have stayed away from you."

Even though the angle was awkward, she hugged him to her. That was all she'd wanted—to be Leona, and to be good enough. She'd almost had it, too—before it'd been torn away.

"And I can't believe you would have spent a whole year making me fall in love with you if it'd been a trap set by Harper."

She looked up at him. Their faces were close, so close. But he didn't kiss her and she didn't kiss him. "I *made* you fall in love with me? Is that what you thought?"

The last time he'd brought feelings into the conversation, it had been the extremely noncommittal "I cared for you once." Nothing about love, not then and not now.

This new confession, at least, was something that felt less like an evasion. Even if it was still a slight.

He touched his forehead to her, a sweet touch that made her lean into him even more. "All I'm doing is asking you now. I know a lot has happened in the past year but…" He pulled his keys out of his pocket. She was surprised to see that the ring was on the key chain. That didn't seem like the best place for a diamond. "I'll admit that I haven't done the best job of it."

She snorted, but she couldn't tear her eyes off the ring. It was a stunning piece—the emerald-cut diamond was huge. When he'd first pulled it out, she'd been too surprised to do much of anything but gape at it. He'd dropped a fortune on it, that much was clear. Just like the house, it'd seemed like *too* much. But now, flashing only occasionally, it didn't seem as overwhelming.

"I'd been planning on asking you for a few months before… Well, I'd been waiting for the right moment. And I missed my window then. But now? Now is the right time."

He jostled her from side to side as he worked the ring off the key chain. Then he settled her back on his lap and held the ring up for her.

"I thought you said I could decide after we made it through two weeks," she said in a breathless voice.

"Oh, don't worry," he chuckled. "If you want to wait the two weeks, I'll ask again."

This time, she physically picked up the ring. It was the first time she'd touched it. It felt warm in her palm—Byron's warmth. She closed her fingers around the ring. It was a heavy thing, but it didn't feel like a lead weight dragging her down. The corners of the rectangular stone dug into her fingers. She swallowed nervously. "And what if the two weeks don't go well? Then what?"

"I'm still going to live in that house. I like the kitchen," he said with a grin. But then the grin faded. "If we can't live together, I hope you'll consider letting me get you a place closer to me. I don't want to waste time I could be spending with my son in traffic."

She thought about this. She had no attachment to this apartment. And if Byron was helping with the rent, she'd love to get a place that had a yard for Percy to play in. She didn't need a mansion, no matter what Byron said. But she'd like to raise her son in a house.

"I guess that sounds reasonable." She wrinkled her nose at him. "But not a palace." Because if it fell apart, she wanted to try to keep things the same for Percy, and that meant keeping him in the same house as long as Leona could afford it.

"Does that mean you'll come to the house for the two weeks? You'll give it a shot?"

She uncurled her fingers and handed him back the ring. "I'll come to the house. Ask me again in two weeks."

Byron hugged her fiercely. His one hand moved up and down her back while the other did the same on her thigh. She twisted against him because her one shoulder was being compressed by the strength of his embrace—but that brought her chest in contact with his. Her nipples—unencumbered by a bra and sensitized by the cool night air—responded with far more enthusiasm than was strictly proper.

He brushed her short hair back from her cheek and looked at her tenderly. "Whatever happens, I'm here for you. I'm here for the long haul. You know that, don't you?"

She desperately wanted to believe that, wanted to believe all the pretty promises he'd made her. But she didn't know if she could. Not yet, anyway. He was here for the long haul, for Percy, that she believed. After all, the Beaumonts always kept the kids. He'd never desert their son.

She just wished she could believe that he wouldn't desert her—again.

She should have already bought a pregnancy test, but she just couldn't bring herself to do it. Another unplanned pregnancy was something she didn't have time for and she'd made a conscious decision that she wasn't going to think about it until it became apparent one way or the other. She simply did not have the time or energy to waste on what-ifs at this point.

Something about the way he was rubbing her back shifted and instead of just stroking her, he was pushing her toward him. It wasn't as if there was a lot of distance between them to begin with—she was sitting on his lap—but every millimeter closer to his lips felt more intimate—more sexual—than it had before.

She knew she was going to kiss him. She knew she wanted him to kiss her back—wanted all the things that she hadn't allowed herself to dream of for the past year.

She wanted him. She always had. Even when he'd first asked her out and she knew exactly who he was and knew exactly why she should steer clear of him—she'd wanted him then.

There was only one problem.

"We can't," she breathed. "Percy—May…"

"Shh," he said in a gentle voice. His hand slid over the outside of her thigh and down the inside. "Let me take care of you."

His fingers dipped down, rubbing against the seam of her yoga pants until she jolted in his arms. "Byron…"

His other arm circled her waist even tighter, pinning her to him. A single finger moved down farther, testing and pressing lightly until she gasped when he hit just the right spot.

"Shh," he said again, rubbing small circles over that spot. "You have to be quiet, babe. Let me do this for you."

She tucked her lower lip under her teeth and nodded. With a wicked grin, Byron pressed harder.

Leona tried not to make a sound, but Byron used his chin to tilt her head back and then he was kissing his way down her cheek, her neck—right to that place below her ear that had always made her shiver with need, even before she'd been able to name what that need was.

She must have made a noise because the hand around her waist squeezed tighter and the hand between her legs stopped moving and Byron whispered against her skin, "Are you being quiet?"

She bit down even harder on her lip and nodded.

"If you can't be quiet," he went on, his words little louder than a breath, "I'll have to stop. Do you want me to stop?"

Before she could shake her head no, he scraped his teeth over that place. She managed to keep the moan locked down in the back of her throat, but there was no stopping the way her body shook for him.

She clutched at his forearm, the one that was moving against her. The muscles in his arms, thick and corded, moved under her hands. He'd always been so strong, moving with a coiled grace both in the kitchen and out of it. Whether he was handling his knives or handling her, he knew exactly what he was doing.

Her hips shifted down onto what was quite clearly a growing erection. "That's it," he murmured. His single finger made lazy little circles over the seam in her pants, which rubbed against her.

She could feel her muscles tightening, feel him bringing her closer and closer to an orgasm. She clung to Byron as his finger moved faster. Her legs started to lift in response to the strain of trying to keep quiet, but Byron used his elbow to keep them down. "Do you need to come?"

he whispered against her neck, his breath caressing her bare skin.

She nodded, struggling to breathe without uttering a sound. She wanted him inside of her, wanted to feel the weight of his body pinning her to the bed. She wanted to be his. God, how she wanted to be his.

"Say it," he said, and for the first time she heard how ragged his breathing was. "Tell me you need to come."

"I…" He pressed against her and held firm. Her body pulsed around his and she was afraid if she tried to talk, all she'd do was scream.

"Say it," Byron said again. "Say how much you need me to let you come."

"I need to come. *Please.*"

Her words came out as a garbled moan, but at least Byron understood the gist of it. Without hesitation, he pressed and rubbed harder and faster until Leona came apart in his arms. Her back arched so far that, if he hadn't been holding her, she would have fallen right off his lap.

But Byron held her close as the waves of orgasm rolled through her. His touch against her sex slowed and then the pressure lightened until he was gently stroking her. When she fell forward against him, he curled both arms around her as she struggled to get her breathing back to normal. Byron stroked her hair, his arms strong around her. She could still feel his erection hard against her bottom. "You're so beautiful, babe. I want to do that to you every night."

"*Just* that?"

He laughed. "I'll get some new condoms or whatever you want to use, I'll cover it. Because *that*," he added, pausing only to kiss her on the lips, "was only the beginning."

Thirteen

Byron didn't have much to pack. He'd only taken a few suitcases with him to Europe. Everything else had gone into storage and it had stayed there when he'd moved back into the mansion.

The beds had been delivered yesterday. For some reason that was beyond his grasp getting mattresses only took a matter of days but the rest of the furniture Leona had ordered would take a couple of months. The baby furniture had also come quickly, but that was because Byron had refused to take no for an answer.

He'd arranged for the rest of his things to be delivered on Monday—his pots and pans and his knives—things that wouldn't have exactly cleared security for the flight over to Paris. He had some basic furniture that would fill the gaps until the rest was delivered.

He was loading his T-shirts into a bag when someone knocked on his bedroom door. He cringed—he didn't want to go around with Frances again. "Yes?"

But it wasn't Frances who poked her head into the room—it was Chadwick. "Hey," he said, looking stern. "Got a moment?"

It was hard to see how this visit would be a good thing. Chadwick had always been the cold, serious favorite of their father, so Byron hadn't even tried. He'd been George's favorite and that was what had mattered. As long as Byron didn't screw up any of Chadwick's plans, they existed in relative harmony.

Harmony that looked like it was about to be broken. "Sure. What's up?"

Chadwick shut the door behind him before he pulled out the chair at the antique writing desk and sat. *Not good*, Byron thought.

Chadwick watched as Byron tried to keep packing his bags. They'd never been close. Byron was eight years younger and Chadwick and Phillip—Byron's other, older half brother—had always been locked in a battle of wills with Matthew. Byron and Frances had been an afterthought, if anyone had thought of them at all.

Finally, Chadwick spoke. "Is there something you need to tell me?"

Damn. The only real question was who had talked— Frances or Matthew? Byron would put his money on Matthew. He ran the new Percheron Drafts with Chadwick. "Actually, I'm planning on getting married."

Chadwick's eyebrows jumped up, but he didn't say anything. He just waited.

Damn it all. Byron forced himself to keep a casual tone. "And I bought a house, so I'm going to be living there from now on." He tried to smile in a jokey manner. "I appreciate the hospitality, though."

Chadwick waved his hand dismissively. "Anytime. This will always be your home as much as mine."

Byron shrugged and started loading his socks into another bag. "So, the future bride," Chadwick went on. "Anyone we know?"

"Frances met her once. She's an old girlfriend. We broke up before I went to Europe but now that I'm back, we're together again." Which was true, in the strictest sense of the word. He was not lying. He was just omitting. Big difference.

A guilty thought hit him. That was what Leona would have thought—what she *had* thought.

Hell.

"I see," Chadwick said in a severe tone that made it clear he was disappointed with Byron's answer. Damn it, someone had squealed. "So the fact that our lawyers want to run a prenup with a *custody* agreement past me has no bearing on the situation?"

Oh, hell—the lawyers. On the bright side, at least Matthew hadn't ratted Byron out. But that probably just meant that he, Matthew and Frances were all in the doghouse for holding out on Chadwick.

"I didn't think it was relevant. I was merely taking steps to protect the family business."

"Ah." Chadwick lounged casually in the chair. He was wearing a suit, of course. Byron had trouble remembering a time when Chadwick hadn't worn suits. He probably even showered in the damn things. "Forgive me, but I fail to see how the fact that you've fathered a child is not relevant. For that matter, I don't see why you felt it was necessary to protect the family without actually telling any of us about it. Forewarned is forearmed."

Byron slumped onto the bed in defeat. "Fine. I didn't want to tell you because I knew you'd freak out on me."

"I do not 'freak out,'" Chadwick replied. "We're not children anymore. It's not like I'm going to ground you. If you have a situation and you think it might affect the family, you can tell me."

Byron had his doubts on that one. "I'm planning on marrying Leona Harper. She had our son six months ago. I only found out about him when I hired her to design the restaurant."

Byron wasn't actually sure what Chadwick freaking out would look like. As it was, he sat in the chair without moving—without even blinking. The only change was that the blood drained out of his face.

Byron waited. He supposed this was always going to happen—sooner or later Chadwick would have found out.

But he'd kept this part of himself secret for so long—with only Frances knowing anything about his entire relationship with Leona, both the good and the bad—that to announce it felt wrong.

"*Leona* Harper?" Chadwick actually sounded a little shaky. "As in, *Leon* Harper?"

"She's his oldest daughter. She has a younger sister, May."

Chadwick began to tap one finger against his pant leg faster and faster. "You're marrying into the Harper family?"

"I knew you'd freak out."

"I am absolutely not freaking out," Chadwick announced in a too-loud voice. "I'm just— She's an old girlfriend of yours?"

"We saw each other for about a year," Byron admitted. "She knew who I was, but I didn't make the connection until her father showed up at the restaurant where we both worked. I thought it was over. That's why I left."

"And the baby?"

"I didn't know she was pregnant when I left. She didn't know if I was coming back."

Chadwick suddenly leaned forward and dropped his head into his hands. "And just so I'm clear on the situation, this is the same woman who's designing our restaurant?"

"Yes." Byron had to make this sound better than it did, so he added, "She cut ties with her father shortly after we broke up. But she's concerned—legitimately, I think—that Harper might pull some stunt to try to get custody of the baby. That's why I want to get married as soon as possible—as soon as the ink is dry on the prenup."

"Harper," Chadwick muttered. "Of all the people in the world, you had to go fall for the old goat's daughter." His head popped up and he glared at Byron. "Do you have any idea what that man will do when he finds out you're back?" He shuddered.

"That's why we needed the prenup and that's why I didn't tell anyone. We need to get married as quietly as possible so Harper can't screw it up."

Chadwick gave him a mean look. "You haven't told anyone?"

"Well, Frances and Matthew. But that's it." Chadwick continued to glare. "And Leona's sister, May. She's been almost like a second mother to the boy. Percy."

Chadwick looked hurt. "I see. And you're sure about this marriage?"

Byron had learned his lesson with Matthew. He didn't pause. Pauses were dead giveaways. "I am."

Chadwick thought for a moment. "She didn't tell you who she was? The first time?"

"No."

"And you trust her?"

Byron hesitated, but only for the blink of an eye. "That's irrelevant. This is about making sure my son is never taken away from me by anyone—especially Harper." And that? That was the truth.

"I want to meet her and this child." If Chadwick had freaked out—and Byron was sure that he'd deny it until his dying breath—he was back to his normal, authoritative self.

"Not yet."

Chadwick gave him another harsh look. "Not even a family dinner, with Serena and Catherine? I wouldn't try to scare her."

Byron appreciated the sentiment, but he didn't miss the way Chadwick said *try*. He explained, "She grew up listening to her father tell horror stories about Hardwick—how he always took the children and left their mothers penniless. She was afraid I would do the same thing to her."

"Have you considered that option?"

"No," he said forcefully. "She's *not* her father. She has no interest in the old feud and I have no interest in using our child as leverage. Whatever happened between Harper and our father is ancient history, as far as we're concerned. We just want to get on with our lives without Leon or Hardwick's ghost watching over our shoulders." Man, that sounded great. He wished he believed it 100 percent.

But he couldn't help thinking of the fact that, while Byron was making all sorts of truthful promises that he was here for the long haul, Leona had done very little in the way of reassuring him that she wasn't hiding anything else from him. First, she hadn't told him about her last name. Then she'd kept his son a secret. What else would she be willing to hide?

Unexpectedly, Chadwick cracked a smile. "We're all trying to exorcise Hardwick's ghost, aren't we?" He shook his head. "First Matthew gets married in secret, and now you. At least make sure your mom is there, okay?"

Byron felt himself deflate with relief. His mother had never been sure exactly where she stood with Chadwick, but the fact that he was thinking of Jeannie was kind, bordering on sweet. "Are you giving me your blessing?"

"It's not mine to give, really." He stood and put a hand on Byron's shoulder. "You always were the independent one, going off to do whatever you wanted, whenever you wanted to. I have to admit, I was jealous that you never got wrapped up in the family drama."

Byron stared up at his brother. Chadwick had been jealous of him? "Seriously?"

"Seriously. Trust me, trying to be like Hardwick was nothing but a recipe for disaster. You've got to do what you need to be happy." He grinned. "I think you might have figured that out sooner than the rest of us."

"What about you? Are you happy now?"

Chadwick gave Byron's shoulder a squeeze and then turned to the door. Before he opened it, he said, "I am. If you marry her—"

"I will."

"—then we'll stand behind you. You, Leona and the baby will have the full support of the Beaumont family if Harper tries anything."

Byron let out a breath he hadn't realized he'd been holding. Out of all his siblings, he'd figured Chadwick would have pushed the hardest to take a Beaumont baby away from anyone Harper. After all, Leon had come after Chadwick the hardest.

"Thanks, man. I appreciate it."

Chadwick gave him another uncharacteristic grin. It was so weird to see that man smiling regularly. "You're welcome. That's what family is for. And make sure we have your new address." He opened the door but paused. The smile fell away and once again, Byron was looking at a stone-cold businessman. "But don't make me regret it."

"I won't," Byron promised.

This time, there would be nothing to regret.

Leona was in a constant state of anxiety. The contractors were ripping apart the future kitchen of Caballo de Tiro, plumbers were roughing in bathrooms and the electricians were pulling old knob-and-tube wiring out of everything. Leona was in charge of overseeing all of it and every ten minutes someone had to ask her about something. While it was nice not to have to defer to Mr. Lutefisk all the time, the sheer weight of being responsible for every single decision wore her down.

Normally, when she got off work, she'd head home, change and do the mom thing with Percy. But this week she went to pick Percy up from either day care or from May and then she and the baby and Byron went wandering around cavernous furniture stores, where Byron deferred to her judgment in every instance.

When she was done with *that*, Leona headed back to the apartment where May would give her the coldest of cold shoulders. Safe to say, May did not approve of a single choice Leona was making at this point.

And of course, Leona was still getting up with Percy every night. He should have been over his ear infection by now, so Leona tried letting him cry himself back to sleep—only to have May burst into her room in the middle of the night and demand she do her job, accusing her of forgetting about her child in this rush to a new life with Byron.

By the time another two weeks had passed, Leona was little better than a high-functioning zombie. She had no idea what clothes she'd packed for her two weeks at Byron's house and if someone had asked her, she couldn't have told them what she'd packed for Percy, either. She wasn't even all that sure what day it was.

But what made it worse was that there hadn't been another time when she and Byron could be completely alone. The best she'd gotten was holding his hand while they debated the merits of this sofa versus that one.

She'd gone a year without having him in her bed on a regular basis. She should be able to handle another two weeks without him bringing her to orgasm.

But she couldn't. Not when she kept looking up from her work and catching him watching her with a small, suggestive smile on his face. Not when he'd brush a hand over her shoulder or across her lower back whenever he passed her. And certainly not when he'd lean in close and whisper in her ear how pretty she looked today, how much he was looking forward to the day she moved in.

He'd always watched her, always *seen* her in a way that no one else had. And that hadn't changed. And, just like it always had, knowing Byron was watching her—thinking of her—made her want him.

But desire was not love. It wasn't. Just because Byron had gone a couple of weeks without suddenly turning into a Beaumont and blaming her for everything didn't mean it wouldn't happen again. So what if he was being sweet and attentive? So what if he was helping out with Percy? So what if those little touches and glances sent her pulse pounding with need?

Her selfish physical wants were the least important thing going on right now. She wanted to believe this was the real Byron, the one she'd loved once. She wanted this to be a snapshot of what their lives together would be. She wanted more than a marriage in name only with separate bedrooms and separate lives.

She wanted to love him. Even more than that, she wanted him to love her.

And that was exactly the kind of thinking that had gotten her into this mess in the first place. She'd wanted a storybook love for the ages, one that ignored the distinctive realities of Harpers and Beaumonts and birth control.

So what she wanted did not matter. What she needed was a happy, stable home for her son and a viable backup plan for when Byron lost interest in her. She'd had a year with him the first time.

She didn't know how she was going to make it to Saturday without collapsing. Saturday was the day she would load Percy into the car and head for the big house in Littleton.

Somehow, Saturday arrived anyway. Leona wasn't completely sure how she'd held out this long. The fact of the matter was that she'd been too damned busy working to do much of anything but collapse into bed when she could. Even then, Byron haunted her dreams, always kissing her and touching her yet still leaving her unsatisfied. She didn't know what the female equivalent of blue balls was, but she had a *bad* case. The only thing that kept her from losing her mind was the fact that she'd probably already lost it and just didn't remember when.

They had separate bedrooms for a reason. A very good reason. She could not let him break her heart again and she especially could not let him break Percy's heart.

But did that mean she couldn't let him relieve a little of her tension? Or was that the shortest path back to pain?

She had the bags loaded into the car and a snack of raisins packed for Percy. All that was left was a final look around to make sure she hadn't forgotten anything.

And, of course, dealing with her sister. "I can't believe you're really going to *him*," May said from the couch where she was pouting.

Leona sighed. She didn't want to fight with May, but she was tired of being made to feel like a traitor. "You don't know him like I do, May."

"That's the understatement of the year."

Leona almost smiled at the sarcasm. "It won't be bad. I promise."

May looked sullen. It was not a flattering look on her. "But he already left you once. What happens when he bails again?"

"He won't." Leona said it with confidence, but she couldn't ignore the little voice that insidiously whispered the same doubt in the back of her head.

What would happen if he left again?

May shook her head. "Well, I guess I'll be here, waiting to help you pick up the pieces *again*."

Even though she had Percy on her hip, Leona impulsively hugged May. "I know, honey. That's why I love you." May sniffed and hugged her back. "You're going to be just fine."

"Sure." She did not sound enthusiastic about this pronouncement.

"Come out next week. Percy will want to see you. And so will I."

"Will *he* be there?"

"It's a big place. You won't have to see him if you don't want to."

May nodded and then kissed Percy's head. "All right."

And that was that. Leona walked out of the apartment that had been her home for a year without another look back. She loaded Percy into his car seat and began the long drive. For all her apprehension and resistance to the idea that she and Byron should live together, now that she was actually doing it, she had the oddest feeling of...

Of coming home.

That feeling only got stronger when she pulled into the drive. Percy had fallen asleep during the car ride. Byron came out to greet them.

"You're here," he said as if he didn't quite believe she'd actually made the trip.

"We're here," she agreed, getting out of the car. "He's just waking up."

"That gives me time to do this, then." The next thing Leona knew, Byron had wrapped his arms around her and kissed her so hard that it nearly bent her backward. There was nothing slow or sensuous about this kiss—this was pure heat. God, how she'd missed this.

When the kiss ended, Byron grinned down at her. "Been waiting to do that for weeks."

"Oh, my." She blinked in the bright sunshine and gave him a lazy smile. "You're the one who insisted on ordering furniture, you know."

"Don't remind me." He gave her a slightly less passionate kiss and then stood her back up on her feet. "Have you decided?"

She fought the urge to rub her eyes. "About what? I'm here."

Byron reached over and caressed her cheek. "About where you're sleeping tonight."

Her skin flushed hot under his touch. "Oh. That."

"Yeah, that." He grinned. He picked up her left hand and kissed it.

This shouldn't be a huge deal. After all, she was physically moving in with him at this exact moment in time and they'd already done *things*. And it would be a relief to have him take care of her. But could she do it? Could she resume a physical relationship with him without losing her heart a second time?

Byron stepped in closer and slid his hand around the back of her neck. The touch was possessive—and hot. "Tell me," he said, his voice dropping an octave, "that you want me in your bed tonight."

There was nothing between them except some easily removed clothing. Heat, languid and powerful, built between them and her body ached for his. As tired as she was, she couldn't wait to be awake in bed tonight. There were no contractors listening to every word they spoke, no siblings to cast judgment. Now, finally, it was just Leona and Byron and this need between them. Figuring out if she could trust him again would have to wait until the morning.

And Percy. The baby fussed sleepily. But Byron didn't let go of her, not just yet. Instead, he leaned forward and pressed a kiss right below her ear. "Tell me you want me, Leona."

"I do," she said breathlessly. His lips brushed against her sensitive skin and her whole body screamed out for his. She couldn't say no if she wanted to. "I want you in my bed. After Percy goes to sleep."

Byron released his hold on her, trailing his fingers down her neck and her shoulder. She shivered under his touch. "I'll get your bags. Welcome home, Leona."

Fourteen

For the first time in what felt like weeks, Leona took a day off. She did not think about supporting beams or color schemes. She did not have discussions that revolved around which toilet seats were more pleasing to the eye or which kind of leather made better chairs and couches. She didn't even defend her relationship to anyone.

Instead she spent the day playing with Percy on the playground set and eating the delicious lunch of roasted broccoli, sweet apple sausage and macaroni and cheese—homemade, not from a box—that Byron had fixed for them.

The afternoon nap didn't happen—Percy was far too excited by the new playground and the big house and Byron to even think about lying down for an hour and missing out on all the fun. Which meant that, by dinnertime, he was a tornado of unhappiness. Anything or anyone who touched him only made things worse.

"Is he sick?" Byron asked, the concern writ large on his face as Percy screamed and tried to twist out of his arms.

"No, just tired," Leona said, dodging a handful of applesauce. "He skipped his nap. This is what happens with no nap." She tried to grin at Byron, but the exhaustion and the screaming were wearing her down. "I've dealt with worse."

Byron paled as he looked down at the raging ball of adorable fury in his arms. "It gets *worse*?"

A flash of fear hit her. Was this it? Would Byron change his mind? Up until this point, he'd only seen the mostly calm, totally cute side of Percy. He hadn't been getting up at all hours of the night because Percy wouldn't stop crying and he'd never seen an epic meltdown like this.

She tried to steel herself. If he was going to back out, better to do it now. She hadn't even unpacked her bags. They could pick up and be gone inside of fifteen minutes.

The thought made her ache. Byron had made a promise and she couldn't bear the thought of him breaking another one. Especially not this one.

"Okay, yeah," Byron said, looking at her with wide eyes. She thought he might be on the verge of panic, but at least he was doing an admirable job of keeping it contained. "Naps. Every day. Got it."

She felt a real smile taking hold of her lips. "If we can get some food into his tummy, I can nurse him and he'll go to sleep early."

Byron's eyebrows lifted. "Will he sleep all night?"

"Probably not," she admitted. "But hopefully for a couple of hours."

Byron exhaled heavily, which momentarily distracted Percy from his howling. "And you've been doing this alone for *how* long?"

"Five months," she replied. "But I had May with me."

Despite the squalling baby, the flying baby food, the fact that she was exhausted—Byron gave her the kind of look that seared her with heat. "And now you have me."

She was really too tired and coated in too much applesauce to feel this attractive. But that's what Byron did to her. That was why she'd eventually agreed to go out with him, why she'd never been able to call it off despite knowing that it couldn't end well. He made her want to melt into his arms and let the rest of the world fall away.

And he knew it, too. His gaze intensified and he leaned forward. "An early bedtime, you say?"

The warmth spread from her lower back all the way up

to her face because she wanted to have him in every way possible. "Very early."

"Come on, Percy," Byron said, enthusiastically scooping up another spoonful of applesauce. "Yummy, yummy!"

An hour later, Percy had eaten enough applesauce to count, had a soothing bath with only minimal screaming, and was sleepily listening to Byron read him a story. Leona decided to try out the new shower—it was hard to feel sexy with sauce in her hair. The bathroom had a huge two-person whirlpool tub and a separate shower. Byron had gotten some thick white towels and the basics of toiletries. Good enough.

Leona shaved her legs and let the hot water run. Today had been much better than she had expected it to be, but still, a few hours of Percy screaming had taken its toll.

She knew she wasn't going to fall into a deep slumber the moment her head hit a pillow. All day long Byron had been giving her that look—the same look he'd been giving her for weeks now, only a hundred times more potent. That look said he couldn't wait to rip all her clothes off and do bad, bad things to her.

And truthfully? She wanted—needed—to have some bad things done to her. For a year, she'd locked down her sexuality. She'd been so danged busy—untangling her life and May's life from her parents' nose-to-the-grindstone rules, being pregnant, getting a job and being a mother. She hadn't had time to even think about sex. And who would she have had sex with, anyway?

A year's worth of sexual frustration threatened to swamp her. Being touched by Byron every two weeks or so was simply not enough.

But what was he going to do tonight? Somehow, she didn't think it would be a quick and satisfying coupling before they both passed out. As tired as she was, the anticipation was more than enough to keep her awake. Before, he'd been patient with her, kind and loving and he'd never pushed her to do anything wild or kinky—all of which had made her feel very safe.

But since he'd come back? Since he'd held her still on his lap and whispered into her ear that she couldn't make a noise until he demanded she tell him she wanted him to let her come?

That was something new. Something *bad*. And, God help her, it excited her.

She hurried through the rest of her shower and threw her clothes back on. She didn't even get her hair dried. When she got back to Percy's room—which was across the hall and down one doorway from the master suite—Byron was just finishing up another story. Leona smiled at the small pile of books that had grown next to the chair. "Sorry," she murmured. At the sound of her voice, Percy twisted and started to fuss.

"We're fine," Byron assured her as he stood. "Have a good shower?"

She nodded, feeling the water drip off the ends of her short hair. When she took her seat, Byron placed Percy back in her arms and whispered, "I'll be right back."

Which turned out not to be the entire truth. The minutes passed slowly as Percy nursed himself into an epic milk coma and she continued to think.

What was she doing with Byron? She'd made this big fuss—this promise to herself—that there would be separate bedrooms. That she would not fall into his arms again.

And yet, Byron had basically reduced her to a quivering mass of need in the middle of the driveway. There'd been a time when she'd coveted the overnights in Byron's bed. It had felt like the ultimate act of rebellion—not going home to her father's house at the end of a date, but curling up under the covers with Byron and knowing she would have to come up with some kind of believable lie to cover the fact that she was sleeping with a man—and a Beaumont at that.

Oh, the lies she'd told to be with Byron. She'd claimed she'd had to work late, that a friend of hers had asked her out to the bars and gotten too drunk to get home safely, that the roads were bad. Whatever she could make sound believable so her father wouldn't start sniffing around.

Maybe she'd known it wouldn't last. Byron would find out, or her father would—it was only a matter of time. She wanted to think that she'd been preparing for the confrontation, that she would have stood up for herself and for Byron and finally shaken her father off.

But then Percy had happened.

She looked down at her sweet baby boy, touching his face. She could marry Byron. It wouldn't guarantee that they'd live happily ever after, necessarily, but it was an important step in cementing their status as a family. And it'd make it that much harder for her father to steamroller his way back into her life.

Yes, she could marry Byron. That wasn't the question. The question was, did she want to?

Would you have married me, if I'd asked a year ago?

That's what Byron had wanted to know. And she hadn't answered him.

But deep down, she knew. She knew that, had he asked—if she'd been carrying his child and he'd asked her to be his forever—she would have said *yes*.

When Byron appeared in the doorway, Leona startled and glanced at the clock. It'd been over twenty minutes since he'd left. She started to get up—Percy was pretty passed out—but Byron motioned for her to sit. Grinning, he stood and watched as Leona finished up and patted Percy on the back. What a change from the first time he'd seen her do this, when he'd fled to the kitchen to make applesauce.

She carefully put Percy into his new crib. The baby was

so passed out he didn't even stir. *Sleep, sweetie*, Leona prayed. *Sleep for Mommy and Daddy*.

Byron came in to stand next to her, his arm around her shoulders. There was an intimacy to the moment. For the first time since Byron had walked back into her life, she truly felt they were in this together. It was such a relief that she wrapped her arm around his waist and held him tight.

Byron checked to make sure the baby monitor was on and then whispered in her ear, "Come with me."

Desire spiked through her. Only Byron could to that to her—turn her on with three little words.

He led her out of the bedroom and up the hall to their bedroom. How weird was that? *Their* bedroom. She'd slept over at his place, a small apartment in an exclusive downtown complex, back when they'd been dating. But that'd been his. She'd always had her own room, her own bed to go back to.

Then the room registered. Byron had been busy while she'd been with Percy. The drapes were closed and the room was alight with the soft glow of candles, easily fifteen or twenty. Where had he gotten so many candles? They were on the mantel over the fireplace, on the dressers, and contained in tall glass jars on the night tables. The whole room glowed. It was one of the more romantic things she'd ever seen.

"Wow," she said. "This is beautiful."

"I'm glad you like it. Turn around."

She gave him a look, but it had no effect on him. Instead, he leaned in close enough to kiss her. But he didn't. He waited, his gaze searching her face.

The anticipation sending spikes of need through her body ratcheted up another notch. She turned around.

"I wanted to do this the other night," he said, pulling her shirt over her head and pushing her pants down so quickly that she barely had time to register that she was in nothing but her panties.

"What?" she asked, nervousness and excitement fighting for control over her stomach. The fact of the matter was, she didn't know what he was going to do to her. But she was pretty sure she was going to like it.

Then the piece of black silk slipped over her eyes.

Fear flashed through her, temporarily pushing the anticipation into panic. "Byron?"

The tips of his fingers traced the contours of her back, soft and gentle. "I just want you to feel this," he said, his voice right against her ear. His breath warmed her skin. "I won't do anything you don't want me to," he promised as he brushed her damp hair away from her neck. His fingers moved over her shoulder—the lightest of touches that held so much promise. Her skin broke out in goose bumps. "If you want me to stop, I will."

She felt exposed. She couldn't see what Byron was doing and she wasn't sure what, exactly, he wanted to do. Essentially, she was at his mercy.

He seemed to know what she was thinking. "Do you trust me?" She heard rustling.

Did she?

Before, when they'd become lovers, he'd taken his time with her. She'd been the kind of inexperienced that only virgins could pull off, but Byron had never rushed her. Once, they'd been making out hot and heavy on his couch. He'd gotten her top off and his shirt, too and Leona had finally decided to go through with it—right until he'd unbuttoned her pants. Then she'd had this moment of terror that he was a Beaumont and she was a Harper and what the hell was she thinking?

So she'd put the brakes on. Byron had hovered over her, his eyes closed and his chest heaving with effort and she'd panicked because she'd never allowed herself to get into this kind of situation, never before been this vulnerable with a man, especially not a Beaumont. Beaumonts were known for their womanizing ways—would that include forcing the issue?

And then he'd sat back and put on his shirt. And when she'd gotten dressed again, he'd pulled her into his arms and kissed her sweetly and asked what she wanted to do tomorrow night. There'd been no guilt, no pressure. She'd felt warm and safe and loved then.

Just like she felt now.

"Yes," she told him. "I trust you."

"Good," he said. He led her over to the massive king-size bed and said, "Lie down on your stomach."

Even though she couldn't see him behind her blindfold, Leona cocked an eyebrow at him. "Please," he added. She did as he requested. "Scoot a little more toward the middle," he instructed. But he didn't get on the bed, either.

"When do I get to know what it is you've got planned with all these candles and this blindfold?"

He chuckled. Then she felt the mattress shift as Byron kneed onto the bed. She could feel him getting closer, feel the warmth of his breath against her ear. "Very soon, babe. Don't tell me the anticipation isn't driving you crazy."

She shifted her hips, trying to take the pressure off the one place in particular where the anticipation was, in fact, driving her completely nuts. "All right, I won't tell you then. I will tell you, however, that you're being a tease."

She felt the bed shift under him as he moved. She couldn't help it—she tensed. "I consider it turnabout for fair play. Do you know what it did to me to watch you for the past two weeks?" He straddled her legs and said, "Lotion," which her brain hadn't quite made sense of when suddenly there was warm liquid being slicked onto her bare back.

She tensed. "Just massage lotion," Byron repeated.

There was a pause, then his strong hands began to work over her body.

"*This* is what you wanted to do the other night?" she murmured into the pillows as he found a knot in her shoulders and began to rub. "Oh, that feels good."

"I did," he said, his voice thick. "You've been pulling some long days and long nights and a three-minute shoulder rub didn't seem enough. I wanted to take care of you.

"You've changed," he went on. "You were always so quiet, back when you started at the restaurant. For a hostess, you always seemed almost…afraid of people. Like you had to force yourself to smile at them. It was like you didn't want to be noticed."

Leona relaxed under his touch. "I didn't, at first. But you noticed me anyway."

"I did," he agreed, attacking a particularly tight knot in her shoulders. She heard the click of the cap, then he applied more lotion. "I could see then that there was something else going on with you, under the surface. And these past few weeks? Watching you manage the construction and juggle everything? It's been like…" Unexpectedly, he leaned forward and kissed her in the middle of the back. "It's been like watching the woman I always knew was there finally emerging. You're strong and confident and decisive. And I like it."

Oh, my. Even though she still had the silk tied around her eyes, she turned her head to look back at him. "You do?"

This time, when he leaned down, his whole chest pressed against her back. He'd taken off his shirt, she realized when his bare skin came into full contact with hers. "I do. You were always different with me—you relaxed and you were sharp and snarky and I liked it. I liked you." His hands moved over her arms, stretching them out against the bed. "But after a while, it hurt me to watch the woman I loved retreat behind that wall of willing invisibility. I wanted…"

He sighed and pushed himself into a sitting position. This time, instead of kneading her shoulders, he trailed his fingers up and down her back in long, sure strokes. "I wanted you to be free enough to be yourself in the daylight, not just at night with me."

She had no reply for that. None at all. Was that how he'd seen her? Someone trapped behind a wall of subservience, someone dying to break free? She'd never thought of herself in those explicit terms—but had Byron been wrong? He'd been her first love, her first rebellion—and the reason she'd left behind a toxic home life when she couldn't bear the thought of her father treating her baby like he treated everyone else.

"I didn't have to *be* anyone else when I was with you," she said in a quiet voice. "That's why I couldn't stay away from you."

Byron's strong hands were suddenly stroking down until he found the waistband of her panties. He traced the edge for a moment before his hands moved to her thighs. Then he pushed his fingers under the thin cotton fabric. "I'm glad you couldn't," he said as he gripped her bottom.

Leona sucked in air as he massaged her. There was something else in his touch, something that bordered on possessive. *"Oh,"* she moaned as he dug the pads of his fingers into her skin.

She wasn't sure she could relax, not with him working on her like this. The more he loosened up the muscles in her back, the more tense other things seemed to get. The tension inside of her coiled down, tighter and tighter, until she was having trouble keeping her hips still.

Just when she was sure she couldn't take much more, he scooted up. She could feel his erection now, pressing into her bottom, hot and hard and for her. She thought he'd do something else, but instead he went back to work on her shoulders.

All she could do was moan when he hit a particularly tense spot. She let go of the stress of the past few weeks. Her body felt warm and limp under his touch.

He moved again and she expected more oil, but instead he leaned down and kissed her in the middle of her upper back. "How are you doing?"

"Better," she whispered as his mouth moved lower and he trailed kisses down her spine.

She didn't know what he would do next and he was clearly in no hurry to do it. By the time he sat back up and his hands left her body again, she was on the verge of begging for release. Anything he wanted—loud, quiet—anything, as long as he made her come.

When the oil dripped onto the backs of her legs, she jumped. "Easy," he murmured, spreading the oil up her legs and under the edge of her panties. "I'm taking care of you."

"Byron," she moaned, but she didn't know if she was begging or not.

His slick fingers moved in, stroking her sex until this time, she couldn't lie still. She writhed against the bed, the release she needed so close but not there yet. "Please," she moaned.

"You like that?" he asked, his voice ragged as he stroked in and out.

"Yes," she whispered. He slipped a second finger inside of her and her hips bucked from the pressure. "Oh, *Byron*."

He pulled her panties to one side and kissed the skin he'd exposed. She couldn't help the low moan that escaped her lips as he stroked and kissed her. She fisted her hands in the covers, desperate to hold herself down. "I can't— I can't," she gasped out when he hit just the right spot. A sensation of light and heat shivered through her. The pressure was so good, so intense—she couldn't take it. "Please, Byron. *Please*."

"Yeah," he said gruffly. "You tell me what you want and

let me do everything else. Let me take care of you." Then he bit down on her bottom—not hard, but more than enough to send spikes of pleasure and pain crashing through her body. She moaned as her body writhed under his touch.

"Tell me," he said in a sterner voice.

"I need you." It came out almost as a squeak.

She felt his teeth on her again, pushing those spikes of desire higher into her stomach. "Be specific."

If she hadn't been so turned on, she would have laughed. Who could be specific at a time like this? But as it was, she could barely speak enough to say, "I need you inside of me."

Even though she couldn't see him, she could feel his grin against her skin. "Wait a second—don't move."

Then he pulled away from her—his body, his fingers, his hands. She didn't want to lose his touch. But he'd told her not to move, so she didn't.

Then she heard a crinkle that she guessed went with the opening of a condom. "That's a new one, right?"

"Bought them yesterday. The massage lotion is compatible."

That made her smile. "You planned ahead."

"I can't help it if I can't stop thinking about you. Here." The pillows around her head were pulled away. Then he guided her hips up and shoved the pillows underneath. His hands lingered on her skin. "Okay?"

She couldn't speak—she could only nod. He had her so turned on that it took everything she had to lie still and wait for his next touch.

It came soon enough. He grabbed her panties and roughly yanked them down. Then he was against her. "I'm going to take good care of you, Leona," was the last thing she heard him say before he thrust into her.

She hadn't allowed herself to miss this when he'd been gone. She hadn't had the time to think back to the days when Byron would make love to her and it would take her away from everything—the stress of the late-night job, the tension at home, the fact that she was sleeping with the enemy.

But now that she had him back, she turned those memories loose. They wove themselves around her, mingling with how Byron was gripping her hips, how he was thrusting in with hard, sure strokes. "Leona," he groaned over and over again. "*My* Leona."

"Yes, *yes*," was the only sound she could make. The noise hissed out of her with every thrust as Byron took her again and again. She was his—she always had been and she saw clearly now that she always would be.

She couldn't see him, but she could feel every single thing he was doing to her. The way his fingers dug into her skin, pulling her back into him. The way he filled her over and over, pushing her to the brink of orgasm without letting her fall down the other side. The grunting noises that built in pitch until he was nearly shouting her name.

Then he relinquished his hold on her hips and fell forward onto her. His teeth scraped along her back but that feeling was quickly blotted out as he reached around and pressed against the hot little button of her sex. "Come for me," he ordered, thrusting and pressing and nibbling until the tension in her body finally, finally snapped. Her muscles tightened almost to the point of pain as she screamed her orgasm into the bed.

"Oh, God," Byron grunted, slamming his hips against her twice more before freezing. "Oh, *babe*."

The orgasm left her completely wrung out and panting. Byron collapsed onto her, his chest hot against her back.

"I want to see you," she said in a shaky voice.

The blindfold was pulled away. Even though the candlelight was dim, she still blinked. Then Byron slid off and pulled her into his arms. "Wasn't too much, was it?" he murmured into her hair.

"Just right," she replied, curling against him and tracing small circles against his chest. Now that the orgasm and anticipation and massage had all run together, she was having trouble keeping her eyes open. They lay there for a few moments, the only sounds in the room the beating of their hearts and the occasional pop of a candle burning.

He'd put her first. He'd taken care of her, just like he'd said he would. He hadn't run screaming earlier when Percy melted down.

Maybe…maybe this would work. Maybe she could marry him and they could be a family and he would love her. Maybe she should allow herself to hope that she'd get everything she ever wanted.

And then he spoke and ruined it.

"If only you'd been honest with me from the start," he said with a heavy sigh, "it could have been like this for the past year. We would have found a way to make it work."

The insult was worse than any slap in the face. "If *I'd* been honest?"

She was up and moving, off the bed and out the door before he could blink. "Leona? Hey—Leona!"

But she was already out of the room, heading down the hall. "If *you* hadn't left, Byron, maybe we could have made it work," she said, knowing he was right behind her. "But you keep making this all my fault, and I'm not going to take it anymore. You're always going to hold that over my head like a sword, aren't you? Because God forbid I try to make up for my mistakes. God forbid we try to get past it. I'll always be the Harper who lied to you, won't I?" With that, she slammed the door to her room and locked the lock.

"For God's sake, Leona," he growled from the other side of the door. The door handle jiggled. "Damn it, Leona!" No doubt he thought that, because he'd bought the house he could walk right into any room he chose.

"It's fine. I'm fine. Thank you for the massage. Good night, Byron."

"I'm not done with you yet," she heard him say on the other side of the door. "But we can talk in the morning. Get some sleep."

No, of course he wasn't done with her.

Yet.

But he would be. Sooner or later, he would be.

Fifteen

When Leona's phone rang, she was juggling an extremely fussy child, a fever-relieving liquid, some electrolyte solution, her wallet and…a pregnancy test.

She was late. Byron hadn't asked about her "schedule" since she'd moved into the house, but she was officially, seriously Late with a capital *L*.

She glanced at her phone and saw that it was Byron. For the past few days, he'd been trying to apologize to her, but she wasn't listening. She sent the call to voice mail, where it could join all the other messages he'd left her.

Percy kicked it up to eleven and began to howl. The other people in line were giving her dirty looks, as if she'd made the baby cry on purpose. Ugh. She needed to get him home.

She paid for her stuff, ignoring the clerk's smirk between her, the pregnancy test and the screaming child, and then got Percy buckled into the car. At least they were only a few minutes from home, she thought as she got stuck at a light. Percy was not a happy camper back there. "Baby, it's okay," she tried to say in a soothing voice over the screaming. "We'll go home and watch Grover and have something to drink, okay?"

Percy screamed even louder.

Leona made it home in record time. Somehow, she got the baby and her things out of the car on the first shot. "Poor baby," she soothed, setting everything down just inside the door. "Let's get you into some comfy jammies."

Percy let her change him. At some point, he quieted

down. His eyelids began to drift shut. Leona felt his head—warm, but not dangerously hot. "Poor baby," she whispered again, settling into the glider to nurse him. He wasn't feeling good and now he'd exhausted himself with all the crying. If she got lucky, he'd fall asleep for a long time. And if she wasn't lucky, well—he'd be up in an hour, screaming because his ears hurt.

From deep inside the house, she heard her phone chime again. If she'd had the damn thing on her, she would have glared at it. There was no way in heck she was going to jostle Percy just to check her messages.

After five minutes, Percy was out. All that screaming, she thought as she lowered him into the crib. She'd have to wait until he woke up again before she'd be able to dose him.

Closing his door behind her, she hurried downstairs. She knew she couldn't keep ignoring her phone—especially not if it were Mr. Lutefisk, wanting an update on the restaurant project.

But she desperately wanted to take the pregnancy test now, before Byron got home. She needed to know. The past month she'd spent forcibly not thinking about the chance that she was pregnant again? Those days were gone. Suddenly, she needed to know right now.

After all, she reasoned as she hurried to the bathroom, it was only a few more days until Saturday—the official end of the two-week trial run of living with Byron. He'd promised he'd ask her to marry him after those scant fourteen days and she still had no idea what she'd say. They were barely speaking. Percy was thriving, though, and watching Byron and the baby together made her wonder why she was fighting this so hard.

And then Byron would attempt another apology that always seemed to hit upon the fact that she hadn't told him about her father and she was mad all over again.

But if there were other factors at play, she wanted to know before she told him yes or no. If she were pregnant again, she would have to say yes. They would have to work harder to be a family, even if they couldn't love each other like they used to.

She carefully peed on the little stick and set it aside, then washed her hands. The instructions said she had to wait five minutes. After all this time, five minutes felt like way too long.

She got her phone. Sure enough, Mr. Lutefisk had called. She had to tell him that she might not be on the job tomorrow, if Percy didn't miraculously recover.

She called her boss while pacing the length of the first floor. She informed him of the situation and paused in front of the room that was now known as her office. She hung up and just stared at the space.

Her office. If she wanted to start her own design business.

Maybe after she got this job finished and things were settled with Byron, she'd strike out on her own. If she were expecting again, working from home might be just the thing. After all, she'd been completely in charge of this restaurant design. She had what it took to be her own boss now. And that prospect was thrilling.

But…that would mean she'd agreed to stay with Byron. Marry him.

Not necessarily, she thought. She could always hang out a shingle somewhere else. Sure, the rent for an office would put a strain on her finances, but she wouldn't be dependent on Byron.

She checked the time. Close enough to five minutes had passed. She hurried back to the bathroom and grabbed the stick.

Pregnant, it said in an impersonal digital font.

"Oh, God." She leaned against the sink as confused

emotions ran roughshod over her. There was the momentary panic that was familiar—the feeling that she'd messed up again.

Why couldn't she keep her hands off him? Why couldn't she stay away from the one man who seemingly could impregnate her just by looking at her? God, this complicated everything. Now Byron would push even harder for her to marry him and for them to live as a family—and if he abandoned her a second time, then where would she be?

She forced herself to breathe. She'd figured it out once before, and that had been without Byron. This time, she had no intention of letting him slip off into the night without at least paying child support. She was not the same scared girl she'd once been. She was an independent woman who could take care of her family. She could be a little freaked out by being pregnant—that was her prerogative. But she could do this. Alone, if she had to.

The doorbell rang, jolting her out of her thoughts. She mentally cursed at the bell, the phone—all the things that seemed hell-bent on waking up her sick child. Quickly, she shoved the pregnancy test into the box and the box to the bottom of the trash can. She would tell Byron, she decided, but she needed a plan for how to handle the marriage proposal she knew he'd make when she did. Until then, that little stick did not exist to the rest of the world.

"Yes?" she said, quickly throwing open the door in the hopes that whoever was out there wasn't about to ring the doorbell again.

"And hello to you, too," May said, taking a step back.

"Oh! May! You're here!"

"Clearly." She looked around again, as if she expected Byron to jump out of the bushes. "Is he home?"

"No, he's still at the restaurant, probably for another hour. Why didn't you call? Percy's fighting off another ear infection. I just got him down."

May looked guilty. "I'm sorry, Leona. I know I said I'd come out on the weekend, but I wanted to make sure you were okay." She shot Leona a weak smile. "I've been worried about you and Percy."

Leona sighed. "Come in, hon. I'm glad to see you. How have classes been?"

She showed May around the house and made tea. They discussed May's classes and what she was going to register for next semester. It was nice to talk to her sister without the entire conversation revolving around Percy's ear infections or why Byron was a bad idea.

"This is really nice," May said, looking out the kitchen windows. She looked wistful.

"There's plenty of room here for you." Maybe it wasn't the best idea to make the offer. But she couldn't deny that she still wanted to make sure that her baby sister was okay. May might not approve of her relationship with Byron but Leona couldn't turn her back on her sister—not after what they'd been through.

"I know." For once, she didn't sound pissy about it. "You've done so much for me…I think it's time for me to try and be on my own, you know?"

"I'll always be here for you," Leona said, squeezing May's hand. "This thing with Byron doesn't change that."

Then May turned to her, a tight look on her face. "Are you going to marry him?"

"I think so," Leona said. "I think he's going to stay."

She just wished she felt more confident about that—about all of it. She just wished he could look at her, touch her, without thinking about how she'd withheld her family's name from him.

May decided she wanted to be gone before Byron got home so, after using the bathroom, she hugged Leona and snuck into Percy's room to press a kiss to his little head. "I'll see you soon," she said as she walked out the door and Leona couldn't help but think there was something odd about May's voice.

The bathroom? Leona hurried to check the trash can, but the pregnancy test was still safely hidden in the bottom. She dug it back out and hid the little stick in her bedroom, where Byron wouldn't accidentally find it.

The weight of the day hit her hard and she sagged onto her bed. She was pregnant again. She had Percy to think of. She could not hide this pregnancy from Byron—she wouldn't.

They would work harder to get past what had happened a year ago, that was all. She had to do it for the children. And if they couldn't get past it...

No. They would. They had to. Otherwise, she'd be entering into a marriage that guaranteed pain and heartache and she couldn't do that, even if it might be best for the children. He was so good with Percy. She knew Byron would be a great father with the new baby, too.

Yes, he would be a wonderful father—loving, hands-on, full of laughter and stories. But what about her? He wouldn't take her children away from her, would he? He wouldn't make her love him only to use that against her time and time again—would he?

She couldn't believe that he would. She was going to have to take it on faith that he was not one of *those* Beaumonts, just like she wasn't one of *those* Harpers.

The next time he apologized, she'd listen. And she'd apologize, too. She would tell him about the pregnancy test. And she would accept his ring.

They had to find a way to make this work.

Leona still wasn't talking to him, but that wasn't anything new. What was new was how he'd look up from playing with Percy and catch her staring at him. Instead of the simmering anger he'd come to expect from her, there was something different in her eyes. It almost looked like fear.

For the life of him, he didn't know what she was afraid of. Yes, he'd said the wrong damn thing after the last time they'd had sex. Their messy past was not good pillow talk.

But where were his reassurances? Where were her promises that she wouldn't lie to him again—not even by omission? Where were his guarantees that she wasn't keeping her father up-to-date on his every move?

Nowhere, that's where. Instead, there was just silence.

That didn't matter, he told himself. So what if she rebuffed his apologies? So what if she rebuffed his advances? What really mattered was that every night he came home to his son. Every night, he made dinner and helped bathe his son and read bedtime stories and got up in the night with him. What mattered was that they'd scheduled an appointment with the doctor for getting tubes in Percy's ears.

Byron could live without Leona. He'd done so for a year. But he would not allow her to guilt him out of Percy's life. He was here to stay and the sooner she accepted that, the better it'd be for all of them.

Yeah, right.

That night, after he handed Percy off to her so she could do the nightly nursing, Leona said, "I need to talk to you," in a quiet, serious voice.

He looked at her but she didn't elaborate. "I'll be in the kitchen?"

She nodded.

His heart sank. The fear in her eyes, the serious voice— this wasn't a good thing.

He started making the cookies before he even realized he was doing it. What would she say? That she'd decided this wouldn't work? That she was leaving in the morning? Was that why she'd looked so afraid?

He almost couldn't bear it as he creamed the sugar. She'd decided this trial wouldn't work. What else could it be?

By the time she slipped into the kitchen, he was angry. "What?" he demanded, bracing himself for the worst.

"It's—" Here she paused. "It's been two weeks," she finished. He could tell how nervous she was and that fact only made him more upset.

He slammed the bowl down. "I knew you wouldn't stay. Just tell me why, okay? Because it can't have been what I said after we had sex. I've tried to apologize and you won't have any of it."

"That's not—"

"Then what is it?"

She exhaled hard, her eyes narrowing to little slits. "Why does this have to be so hard, Byron?"

"I don't know, Leona. Why don't you tell me?" When she didn't have an immediate response, he said, "You can go if you want, but I won't let you take Percy."

The words hit her like a body blow—he saw her curl forward, as if he'd physically hit her in the stomach. For a second, he thought she was going to start crying.

But then she straightened up, her eyes watery but mad. So damn mad—at him. "You promised me you weren't going to punish me by taking him away from me."

"I can't live without my son."

"I can't live without *our* son," she shot back. "You can keep trying to get rid of me so you can claim you didn't abandon me a second time, but it won't work. I'm not leaving my baby."

At least, that's what he thought she said as she turned and stomped off. But it almost sounded like she'd said something else there—babies?

No, he'd heard wrong. She hadn't said anything else about the one night the condom had broke.

Unless she was lying to him.
Again.

Byron was going to beat these damned pot racks into submission. He was also going to put together the storage racks and if things went according to plan, he'd have all of those things done before the sous chef candidate he was supposed to interview arrived at four.

The kitchen was taking shape. They'd kept the commercial-grade six-burner stove, but the rest of the appliances—the ovens, the stoves, the refrigerators and freezers—were all on order and scheduled to be delivered within the next three weeks. Once they had those and the rest of the furniture, it'd really begin to feel like a restaurant.

It was nice that something in his life was coming together. The fight with Leona from last night was still fresh in his mind. He had to go home and face her today—she'd stayed home with Percy—and he didn't know how he was going to do that.

He had been an idiot to think that he could live with her without being able to trust her. More than that, he was an idiot for thinking that, somehow, living with her without complete trust would be different for them than it'd been for his parents.

This experiment had failed. They were broken as a couple and there was no putting them back together.

But even thinking that made him hurt. Damn it all, he didn't want to give up on her, on them.

Finally, after some rather loud cussing, Byron got the pot rack screwed to the wall. He was just about to grab the second one when he heard, "Hello?" from the front of the restaurant.

"Hello!" he called back. "I'm in the kitchen!" He grabbed a rag to wipe his hands and glanced at his phone—

3:45 p.m. Either the sous chef was early or the landscapers had an issue.

The moment he crossed the threshold from the kitchen into the restaurant, he sensed something was wrong. The sous chef would have come alone. The landscapers had all been wearing matching work outfits emblazoned with their company logo.

Instead, two very large men in very tailored suits stood just inside the restaurant so they blocked out the afternoon sunlight that filtered through the open door. With their thick necks, matching buzz cuts and wraparound sunglasses, they looked like what they probably were—hired muscle.

In front of them stood a thin man in an even nicer suit. His long face and hunched shoulders made him look small, at least compared with the bruisers standing behind him.

Byron came to a quick halt. Out of the corner of his eye, he saw the landscapers' shadows moving in front of the casement windows. Hopefully, if there was trouble—and that's exactly what it looked like was about to happen—the crew would come to his aid. Otherwise, his best hope was to get back to the kitchen and grab the hammers and screwdrivers. A man could do a lot of damage with a hammer.

"Help you?" he asked warily.

"Byron Beaumont?" the smaller man said with obvious distaste.

"Who wants to know?"

One of the bruisers behind the smaller man made a snorting noise.

"Is he here?" The thin, reedy voice came from behind the muscle. The small man stepped to the side just as a gleaming silver-and-black walking stick poked between the bruisers, shoving them aside.

And there he was, Leon Harper in the flesh. He looked older than Byron remembered him, especially when he leaned on the walking stick. The lines around his eyes were deeper. But there was no mistaking him for any other elderly man in a natty suit.

Byron blinked, hoping and praying that he'd fallen off the ladder or dropped the pot rack on his head—anything that could produce a hallucination as unwanted as this.

But no. He knew this was no nightmare—especially not when Leon Harper got a good look at him and smiled viciously. It was the exact same smile he'd given Byron when he'd placed Leona into the family car and announced that Byron would never have his daughter. It was the smile of certain victory.

It was the smile of evil.

"Oh, that's him, all right. I'd recognize the Beaumont spawn anywhere," he said to the thin man. "I hear you're back—and with *my* daughter."

The way he said it—emphasizing *my* so heavily—made Byron's skin crawl. There was no love in the old man's voice. Just ownership. "And that's your business how?"

Harper clucked. "You should have stayed away from her, boy. I was content to let her have the child just so long as you didn't have it—or her."

It? Was this shell of a man seriously referring to Byron's son as an *it*? Oh, hell, *no*. The hairs on the back of Byron's neck stood at attention. Yeah, a man could do a lot of damage with a hammer.

But he knew better than to rise to the bait. Growing up in Hardwick's household had taught Byron how to not get sucked into a fight. When a blowhard old man desperately wanted you to fight back, the only way to win—and drive him nuts—was to stay silent.

So that's what Byron did. He still had the rag in his hand, so he casually wound it around his knuckles. There was no way he could take out the bruisers, but if he could get a good shot at Harper...

Well, either Harper would sue him back into the Stone

Age or Byron would be locked up for involuntary manslaughter. Possibly both.

But it might be worth it, he decided, if it kept his family free from the clutches of this vindictive old rat.

Harper waited for a moment. His eyes hardened in displeasure at Byron's lack of engagement, but then he smiled widely again. He nodded to the thin man, who moved toward Byron and held out a thick envelope.

"Since my daughter has sought to further blemish the proud Harper name by continuing her association with the likes of *you*," the old rat went on as Byron refused to take the envelope from the thin man, "I have come to the unavoidable conclusion that she must not be operating in her right mind. I'm having her declared unfit to be a mother and petitioning the state for custody."

"You're insane," Byron sputtered before he could keep his mouth shut.

The response was exactly what Harper was looking for. "Me?" He tried to look innocent, but he clearly didn't know how to do that. He probably hadn't been innocent in a good eighty years. "I'm just a concerned father worried about his daughter and the environment in which she's raising my grandchildren."

"You can't claim custody of Percy. I'm his father. And I only have one child with Leona."

Harper clucked. "Do you, now? An absentee father who shows up only long enough to impregnate her again? That doesn't give you a particularly strong leg to stand upon, you realize." He buffed his fingernails on his suit jacket and looked at them as if they were by far the most interesting things in the room.

"She's not pregnant."

"Isn't she?" Harper smiled, revealing graying teeth that matched his graying hair. Byron's gut clenched. She *had* said *babies* last night. "Or maybe she's just not telling you about it. Because she is most certainly pregnant. And I give you my word—you'll never see that child. Never." He motioned toward the lawyer. "My counsel has prepared an airtight case."

The thin man held out the envelope again and this time, Byron snatched it irritably. "You won't win."

"There's where you're wrong," Harper intoned in all seriousness. "I *always* win, boy."

He shouldn't—but he couldn't help himself. He knew there was one chink in Harper's self-righteous armor, and a huge, gaping chink at that. If the old rat was going to make Byron suffer, the least he could do was return the favor. "I'll be sure to pass that along to your first wife."

Harper stiffened, murder in his eyes. One of the bruisers took a step forward, but Harper whipped his cane up and held the man back. "Flippant, boy." Hate dripped off his every word. "Very *flippant*."

It felt good to score a hit against the old man. Leon Harper had once taken everything Byron held dear. No way Byron would let the old man win a second time. No way in hell.

"Trying to take my son away from me won't even the score, Harper. And when you lose, you'll never see the boy again."

Harper's thin lips twitched in satisfaction. "I might say the same to you. You're holding a petition to sever your paternal rights." Byron's glare bounced uselessly off the old man. "Unless you sign," Harper went on, clearly enjoying himself, "your *flippant* little tale of impregnating my daughter and then abandoning her will be front-page news. Doctors testifying to her mental state will give lengthy interviews and as for you?" His grin sharpened. "By the time I'm done with you, boy, I'll have run you, the entire Beaumont clan and this godforsaken beer company into the ground. You have a week. Good day." He turned, the bruisers parting for the old man to pass.

"I won't let you anywhere near her or my son, *old man*." Byron put as much into those words as he could because, as far as he was concerned, that's all Leon Harper was. An impotent old man with too much free time and too many lawyers kowtowing to him.

Harper paused and then slowly turned around, a smug smile distorting the features of his bitter face. "Is that so? And just who do you think called me in the first place?" He chuckled to himself and damn it all, Byron was too stunned to even come up with a stinging parting shot.

All he could do was stand there and watch as Harper and his various lackeys shuffled out.

No. He couldn't believe it—he wouldn't. Even if she'd decided that she was better off as a single parent living with her sister, she wouldn't have gone crawling back to Leon Harper. She might hate him, but she cared too much for Percy to let her father do her dirty work. Especially if she were pregnant again.

He stumbled back into the kitchen and leaned against a counter, trying to breathe. She couldn't be pregnant again, could she? No, that wasn't the right question. The condom had failed. She could be pregnant.

The question was, how could she be pregnant again and not have told him?

It didn't matter how much he apologized. It didn't matter what he did to take care of her. It didn't matter one damn bit how much he loved her—her and only her.

None of it mattered.

He was done. This was just like the last time, he realized. She would always withhold the truth and she would always hide behind her father so she didn't have to do the dirty work herself. She would always hurt him.

He had to stop letting her—them—win. He was a Beaumont, for God's sake. He would protect his son—his children—from the Harpers. Always and forever. And if that meant he had to take Leona to court, then so be it.

If the Harpers expected him to turn tail and run again, they'd soon find out—no one messed with a Beaumont.

Sixteen

Talking to Byron wasn't working, so Leona decided to take a different approach—when Percy fell asleep for a nap, she started writing him a letter.

"Dear Byron," she started, "I'm pregnant and I don't want to fight about raising our children. I want us to be a family and I want us to be as happy as we can be."

Okay, she thought, good start. She had to get that pregnant part out there first. She'd tried to tell him last night, but he'd cut her off and done everything in his power to make her feel two feet tall.

She put the pen back to the paper and wrote…nothing. What else was she supposed to say? She was tired of being made to feel like a bad person because she hadn't disclosed her father's identity on the first date? She was sorry she hadn't contacted Byron when she had Percy, and she was sorry she'd assumed he'd rejected her again—like it felt he was doing right now.

No matter what, she wasn't going to leave her children—and what she really wanted was the reassurance that he wouldn't take them from her and he wouldn't abandon her again but it was hard to see how he wasn't going to do just that when she couldn't even have a face-to-face conversation with him without it going off the rails.

Dang it. Writing it down—without having to say it to Byron's face or being interrupted—was supposed to make this easier, not harder.

The doorbell rang and she glared at the clock. If this

were May, back again without calling, Leona was going to be pissed. It was Percy's nap time—she should know that.

Leona opened the door and was stunned to see that, instead of the slight form of her sister, a weaselly-looking man in a suit was standing there. A *familiar* weaselly-looking man. "Leona Harper?"

Lights began to pop in front of Leona's eyes and for a second, she was afraid she was going to faint on the feet of her father's favorite lawyer. All of the emotions coursing through her—worry for Percy, exhilaration about the pregnancy—all of them smacked headlong into the wall that was Leon Harper.

"Mr. York?"

The lawyer stepped to the side and there her father was. His face was twisted into something that made a mockery of joy. Leona's stomach lurched again.

One thought bubbled up through the misery of the moment—she should have married Byron already. She'd told him that this was the very thing she'd lived in fear of for a year—her father deciding to make her life his business again.

She clung to the door for support. It was tempting to slam it in their faces and throw the bolt, but damn it all, she couldn't overcome years of subservience to this man.

"Father," she said, her voice a shaky whisper.

"My dear," he replied in his most acid tone. She was not now, nor had she probably ever been, *his dear* and they both knew it. "I must say, I'm disappointed in you."

What else was new? She'd always been a disappointment to him. Her name said it all. If she'd been Leon Harper, Jr., things would have been different. But no. She was Leona. A disappointment with an *a*.

"I gave you a chance," her father went on, mocking condescension in his voice. "Your mother convinced me that I should let you move out—as long as you didn't cause any more trouble than you already had."

Oh, *God*—she could not believe this. This was not happening. He was still talking *at* her—not *to* her—as if she were a messy girl of six again.

No. She couldn't stand here and take whatever he felt like dishing out. Things had changed. She was a mother, soon to be twice over. She owed it to her son, to Byron— and to herself—to be well and truly free of the blight that was Leon Harper.

"As I recall, Father, you didn't 'let' me do anything. I left without your permission."

Anger flared in the old man's eyes—dangerous anger, as she knew from too many years of experience. But she wasn't afraid of him, not anymore. Not much, anyway. So to make herself feel brave, she added, "And I'd do it all over again. What do you want?"

Any pretense of happiness at seeing her vanished off her father's face. He'd never been good at pretending he cared, anyway.

"I must admit," her father said in a calm, level voice that only amplified his rage, "that I was surprised when *he* called me."

"He who—*Byron*?"

Her father shrugged in what, on any other human on the planet, would have been an innocent gesture. "He made his intentions clear—he'd won and I had lost. He said he was going to take the child and that—and I'm quoting here— 'No Harper would ever see it again.'"

"You're lying," she gasped. So what if Byron had said almost that exact thing last night? She *couldn't* believe that he'd call her father. "You always lie."

"You can, of course, believe what you want. You always did. You're the one who convinced yourself that he could love you—that any Beaumont was capable of love—when we both know that's not really possible, is it?" He managed a pitying smile.

"No," she said again, but she didn't sound convinced, even to her own ears. Her mind flitted back to the positive test still safely hidden in her bedroom. What would her father say—what would he *do*—if he knew that she was expecting again?

Her knees began to shake and she knew that if she didn't sit down, she really would pass out. But she couldn't show him weakness. She couldn't let him think he'd won.

"He's going to take the child," Father went on. "Both of them."

Leona gasped. How did he know about that? Not even Byron knew. Then it hit her—May. May was the only other person who could possibly know. She'd been in the bathroom while the test had still been in the trash. Leona had thought May hadn't seen it—but she'd thought wrong.

"Sadly," her father continued, "I can't help you—that is, unless you help me, my dear."

If there was one thing in this world that Leon Harper did not need, it was help. "How?"

"It's easy," he said. "Turn legal guardianship of the child over to me. Come back home. Let me protect you from *them*."

Mr. York handed her a thick envelope. "Just sign these," he said in an oily voice, "and it'll all be taken care of."

She stared at the envelope that was suddenly in her hands. She'd always thought that when—not if—her father came after her, he'd do it the hard way and try to destroy her credibility, her job—destroy her.

But this? This offer of *protection*…

Was he serious?

No. Leona knew she could not trust a single word that came out of Leon Harper's mouth. He never did anything that wasn't completely self-serving.

If Byron had decided that marriage wasn't truly in the cards, he would have told her himself.

But then her father said, "I do hope you'll sign the papers before he disappears—*again*," and all of her doubt came crushing back.

Byron wouldn't take her babies and melt off into the night, only to turn up in some foreign country with byzantine custody laws, leaving her no hope of ever seeing her baby again. Would he?

No. *No.* Byron loved Percy and he would not treat her like his own mother had been treated—discarded and destroyed. They might not be able to live together, but he wanted what was best for Percy.

She'd fought too hard for her independence to crumple just because Byron didn't want her and her father lied. She was stronger than that, by God.

So she took a deep breath and stood straighter. True, she was holding on tight to the door, but it was the best she could do. "I could invite you in, but I won't. I don't know what game you're playing, but you're forgetting one simple thing. I know you too well to trust a single word that comes out of your mouth."

Her father's face hardened in rage, but she wasn't done with him. With each word she spoke, she pushed back against the terror this man had inspired in her for the past twenty-five years.

"If you ever come near me or my son again, I'll call the cops and file a restraining order against you," she promised. "If you're still on my property within five minutes, I'll make the call now. I left home for a reason, and nothing you can say or do will convince me that I have to come back for your 'protection.' I don't need it. I don't want it. The only person I need protection from is you." She tried to give him a dismissive look. "And I'll protect myself from you, thank you very much."

With that, she slammed the door in his face. Then she realized she was still holding the envelope. She threw the door back open and launched the envelope at his head before slamming the door shut again. Then she threw the bolt and sagged against the wood.

Except the sagging continued until she had to struggle to her feet and rush to the bathroom.

It was only after her system had cleared itself out and she'd brushed her teeth that she realized she didn't know if her father had been to see Byron or not.

Seventeen

The front door banged open so hard that Leona jumped and dropped her phone milliseconds after hitting Send to Byron.

The figure in the door shouted, "Leona?" at the same moment she heard the chime that Byron had picked out for her.

"Byron?" Yes, it looked like him, but at this point in her day, she wasn't sure she could trust her eyes. "Did you call my father?" she demanded angrily. "Did you tell him you were leaving me?"

Byron gaped at her. "God, no. If I never see him again, it'll be too soon." His brow furrowed. "I guess that answers the question of whether or not you've seen him. He must have come straight here." He looked like he wanted to hold her, but didn't. "Are you pregnant?"

Her eyes fluttered shut. "Yes."

"And you didn't tell me."

"I tried. Last night. And you cut me off." She walked to the kitchen island and grabbed the notebook. "So I was writing you a letter. When my father showed up—and cut me off," she said.

Byron grabbed the notebook and read the few lines she'd written down. "How do I know you didn't write this confession after he left? How do I know you didn't call him and tell him you were done with me? How do I know you're not still lying to me?"

Her mouth dropped open. "You don't, Byron. You can't

independently verify every single thing I do and say as being one hundred percent truthful at all times. You have to take it on faith when I tell you that I'm sorry for the mistakes I made in the past, that I was in the process of writing you a letter because every time we talk it turns into a fight, that I wanted you to know I was pregnant."

"So who told your father?"

She picked up her phone and dialed May—then she put it on speaker. "Hey, Leona. How's Percy?"

Leona took a deep breath and tried to project calm. "May, did you call our father?"

She could sense May's hesitancy. "Well…"

"Did you tell him I was pregnant?"

There was a long pause on May's end. Finally, she said, "The pregnancy test was right there in the trash." Her voice was accusatory, as if Leona had hidden it there just so May could find it.

The curse was right on Leona's lips. But this was still her little sister. So instead she said, "What did he give you?"

"I got an allowance." May sniffed again. "And a new car."

This time, Leona couldn't keep her anger in. "Damn it, May!"

"But Byron's going to leave you—you know he will!" May all but shouted. "He's going to abandon you again, and I can't stand to see you hurt like that—not a second time. We were happy, weren't we? We didn't need him. We could take care of the new baby like we did Percy! I thought it'd be nice to have some better things, not the junk we've had to make do with."

Byron looked at Leona in surprise, but he didn't say anything.

Leona closed her eyes and took another deep breath. "May, I am a grown woman. I know you meant well, but even if I'm going to screw up, I'll do it on my terms. I'll thank you from now on to stay out of my business."

May was crying now and it made a part of Leona hurt. She'd spent years trying to protect May from her father. She never would have guessed that May wouldn't return the favor.

"Are you mad?" May sniffed.

"You have *no* idea. I'm going to hang up now and talk with Byron. I'll call you when I'm ready to talk to you."

"But—"

Leona ended the call and stood there. "I have the pregnancy test in my room. I took it three days ago. I didn't tell you immediately because I knew you'd tell me I had to marry you and I wanted to figure out how to have that discussion. I tried last night but we both know how that went."

Byron was staring at her, openmouthed.

"So this is the deal. I'm pregnant. We already have a child together. But I won't marry you just to have you accuse me of lying to you every day. And I won't marry you and live with the fear that, as soon as you don't want me anymore, I'll be put out on the streets without a home, an income or my children. After you left and I got away from my family, I found out I could survive—even more than that, I could thrive. And I'm not going to give up that independence to exist at your whim *or* my father's."

He still hadn't come up with a response, so she went on. For once, no one was interrupting her. "I should have told you who I really was. I should have told you I was pregnant with Percy. I am sorry I didn't, but I didn't want my father to matter. *I* wanted to matter and for a long time, you made me feel like I did."

"You were the only thing in the world that mattered to me," he said in a quiet voice.

A thrill of something she only vaguely recognized as hope shot through her. She ignored it. This was not the time for hope. This was the time for the truth. "But you act as if I kept Percy a secret from you when that's not what happened. I had taken a pregnancy test that afternoon and gone to the restaurant. I was going to tell you that night, Byron, right after we got off work. And instead my father showed up—a maid had found the test and given it to my mom, who told my father. And then you were *gone*. I didn't hide Percy from you, Byron, I just never got the chance to tell you. So I'll say it again. I'm pregnant. You're the father. Now what?"

Byron looked down at the notebook he was still holding. "Is there anything else I need to know? Because if we are going to find a way to make this work, I need complete honesty from you."

She gave him a long look—so long that he lifted his gaze back to her. "I will not marry you for the children."

He nodded slowly. "And?"

Suddenly her heart was pounding faster. "And I love you. I've always loved you. I just didn't allow myself to love you when you were gone because what good would it have done me? And then you came back and I was afraid you'd become the Beaumont my father always warned me about, when all I wanted was Byron. But I will not allow you to use my feelings against me."

He took a step toward her. The air between them seemed to sharpen. "Is that why you've been fighting my apologies this week?"

"Yes. I know we can't go back to where we were before. But I just… I want something better for our family." Her eyes began to water but she blinked the tears away. "For *us*."

He took another step toward her, close enough that she could feel the warmth of his body. "Tell me what you want."

"You. I want you. I want to spend the rest of my days loving you and I want to know that you will always love me, too. I don't want to live under a cloud of suspicion or worry. And if you can't give me that, then it's better to know now. I'd rather be on my own again than live like my parents or yours."

"Is that the truth?"

"Yes, damn it." Her voice caught, but she ignored it.

Then he lifted his hand and cupped her cheek. "You want me to take it on faith that you'll be honest with me from here on out? I want the same thing from you. I will not abandon you, no matter what. I love you, too—I always have. Buying you this house—asking you to marry me—I'm just trying to show you that I won't leave you. God knows I tried and see where it got me? The moment I set foot back in Denver, I looked you up and hired you."

Her throat started to close up. "Can we do this? Can we actually make this work?"

He pulled her into him. "I won't give up on you, Leona. That was the mistake I made last time. I gave up on you— on us. I didn't fight for you. I was stupid and a coward, and I believed that rat of a man when he told me that I could never have you and I will forever regret that."

"Oh, Byron—" she started to say, but he shook his head.

"I should have waited for you. To hell with that— I should have come after you." He dropped his face and leaned his forehead against her hands. "I should have come for you because that's what a Beaumont does—we fight for what we want, to hell with what anyone else thinks. And I didn't. I hope… I hope you can forgive me for failing you."

The strain of the afternoon was too much for her. She couldn't stand in judgment of him—she wasn't doing all that great of a job at standing, period. Tears started to trickle down her face as her legs shook.

Byron sat on one of the island stools and pulled her onto his lap. He stroked her back.

"I didn't tell you I thought I was pregnant," she said, her voice trembling as the tears started to spill down her cheeks. "I was afraid—afraid that you'd find out who my father was and we'd lose everything we had. I should have called you the moment I found out—I should have told you the moment I suspected. But I was scared, too. And when he showed up—he made it seem like everything I'd ever been taught about the Beaumonts had come true."

"If I had asked you, a year ago…" He shifted, pulling his key ring out of his pocket. "If I had asked you to marry me before it all went to hell, would you have said yes? You never answered that question the other night."

She curled up into him, feeling warm and safe. "I would have. I would have said yes."

Byron hugged her fiercely. "I need you. I've always needed you. I thought— I was afraid you didn't need me."

She looked up at him, unable to stop the tears. "I need you, too. I want this to work so badly, Byron."

"I'm here for you now and I will always be here for you and Percy. No more running, no more hiding. Just you and me and our family." He unhooked the engagement ring from the key chain and held it up. "Leona, I have a very important question for you."

She grinned. "Not an order this time?"

"No. No more orders. Will you marry me? Not for Percy, not for the baby but because I love you and I want to spend the rest of my life by your side. Because it was always meant to be this way—you and me, together."

"Yes, Byron. Yes." Leona couldn't fight the tears—happy tears—as he slid the ring onto her finger.

"Oh, babe," he whispered against the spot right below her ear. "It's going to be different this time. I want to go to all your appointments and hear the heartbeat and *everything*. You and me, babe. You and me and our family."

And then Leona was laughing and crying all at the same time and Byron was kissing her and she was taking the ring from him and putting it on her finger.

"Marry me," Byron said, wiping away her happy tears with his thumb. "Not because you have to and not because it's the best way to protect Percy—marry me because you want to and I want you to."

"Oh, Byron," she said, throwing her arms around his neck and holding him tight. Finally, finally things were going how she'd always dreamed they would. She'd told her father off and defended herself and Byron was here and she'd forgiven him and he'd forgiven her and they were together. They'd always be together.

"Tell me what you want," he whispered against the sensitive skin of her neck. His voice had dropped an octave and he pressed her against his body—all of it. "Tell me you want me."

"You," she whispered back. "All I want is you."

"Then I'm yours. Forever yours."

And that was a promise she knew he'd keep.

* * * * *